"Together, the books of The Baroque Cycle form a sublime, immersive, brain-throttlingly complex marvel of a novel that will keep scholars and critics occupied for the next 100 years . . . Highly readable. It's the sort of work that quickly becomes an obsession . . . A reader's feast, featuring pirates and courtesans, palaces and prisons, Whigs and Tories, narrow escapes and gruesome executions, exotic islands and dank sewers, science and alchemy. Really, there's something for everyone."

Toronto Star

"Wonderfully inventive . . . Stephenson brings to life a cast of unforgettable characters in a time of breathtaking genius and discovery."

Contra Costa Times

"An awe-inspiring book, stuffed with heart-stopping action scenes . . . a treasure trove of forgotten historical lore."

Book

"A genre-buster, a giddy historical swashbuckler crossed with the novel of ideas, with hints of sci-fi tossed into the mix . . . Creatively anachronistic . . . brimming with a hail-fellow-well-met good cheer, at the heart of which lies a genuinely fun pirate romance."

New York Times Book Review

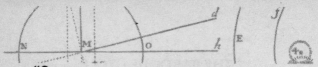

"Sprawling, irreverent, and ultimately profound."
Newsweek

"The Baroque Cycle is great fun that never seems to end."
Columbus Dispatch

"Arguably the most ambitious literary offering in this century . . . It is Dickensian potboiler and Baroque reader smashed into one hefty and masterfully paced [tale] told . . . by a maddeningly talented writer . . . Blazing action sequences . . . The Baroque Cycle . . . is an ode to Victorianism, a descendent of Dickens and Thackery. Beyond that, it is a triumph."
Virginian Pilot

"Sparkling prose, subtle humor, and a superb knowledge of the period makes this grand feast of a novel a mandatory choice . . . Highly recommended."
Library Journal

"Always entertaining . . . The [Baroque] Cycle is not for the timid. But it continues to surprise throughout."
Kansas City Star

THE BAROQUE CYCLE
by Neal Stephenson

QUICKSILVER: THE BAROQUE CYCLE #1
KING OF THE VAGABONDS: THE BAROQUE CYCLE #2

Coming Soon

ODALISQUE: THE BAROQUE CYCLE #3
THE CONFUSION, PART I: THE BAROQUE CYCLE #4
THE CONFUSION, PART II: THE BAROQUE CYCLE #5
SOLOMON'S GOLD: THE BAROQUE CYCLE #6
CURRENCY: THE BAROQUE CYCLE #7
THE SYSTEM OF THE WORLD: THE BAROQUE CYCLE #8

NEAL STEPHENSON

KING OF THE VAGABONDS

THE BAROQUE CYCLE #2

HarperTorch
An Imprint of HarperCollinsPublishers

King of the Vagabonds: The Baroque Cycle #2 was originally published by
HarperCollins in hardcover and trade paperback as part of the overall novel
Quicksilver: Volume One of the Baroque Cycle by Neal Stephenson.

Map of 1667 London reproduced with changes courtesy of Historic Urban
Plans, Inc.

HARPERTORCH
An Imprint of HarperCollins*Publishers*
10 East 53rd Street
New York, New York 10022-5299

Copyright © 2003 by Neal Stephenson
Excerpt from *Odalisque* copyright © 2003 by Neal Stephenson
Maps by Nick Springer
Family trees created by Lisa Gold; illustrated by Jane S. Kim
ISBN-13: 978-0-06-083317-6
ISBN-10: 0-06-083317-3

First HarperTorch paperback printing: March 2006
First Perennial printing: October 2004
First William Morrow hardcover printing: October 2003

HarperCollins®, HarperTorch™, and ❦™ are trademarks of HarperCollins
Publishers Inc.

Printed in the United States of America

Visit HarperTorch on the World Wide Web at www.harpercollins.com

10 9 8 7 6 5 4 3 2 1

To the woman upstairs

☙

Acknowledgments

❧

THERE ARE MANY PEOPLE to be thanked for their help in the creation of The Baroque Cycle. Accordingly, please see the acknowledgments in *Quicksilver: The Baroque Cycle #1*.

Contents

Gunfleet House
Comstock House
PICCADILLY
Waterhouse
ST. JAMES STREET
St. Giles's Fields
PALL MALL
St. James Palace
Covent Garden
ST. MARTIN'S LANE
CHARING CROSS
St. Martin-in-the-Fields
LeFebure's
THE STRAND
Holbein Gate
The New Exchange
KING STREET
King St. Gate
Whitehall Palace
Westminster

LONDON

Based on a map made after the Fire of 1666 and attributed to Robert Hooke, Royal Surveyor and Fellow of the Royal Society.

The part of London destroyed in the Fire is unshaded.

HOLBORN

FLEET STREET

Newgate Prison

St Paul's

St Lawrence Jewry

LONDON WALL

CHEAPSIDE

Navy Treasury

New Bedlam

Old Bedlam

Bishopsgate

Dutch Church Austin Friars

POULTRY THREADNEEDLE

The Change

Gresham's College

House of Ham

CORNHILL

The River Thames

South.

FISH STREET HILL

London Bridge

The Tower of London

BOOK TWO

King of the Vagabonds

There is, doubtless, as much skill in pourtraying a Dunghill, as in describing the finest Palace, since the Excellence of Things lyes in the Performance; and Art as well as Nature must have some extraordinary Shape or Quality if it come up to the pitch of Human Fancy, especially to please in this Fickle, Uncertain Age.

—*Memoirs of the Right Villanous John Hall,*
1708

The Mud Below London

1665

⚜

MOTHER SHAFTOE KEPT TRACK of her boys' ages on her fingers, of which there were six. When she ran short of fingers—that is, when Dick, the eldest and wisest, was nearing his seventh summer—she gathered the half-brothers together in her shack on the Isle of Dogs, and told them to be gone, and not to come back without bread or money.

This was a typically East London approach to child-rearing and so Dick, Bob, and Jack found themselves roaming the banks of the Thames in the company of many other boys who were also questing for bread or money with which to buy back their mothers' love.

London was a few miles away, but, to them, as remote and legendary as the Court of the Great Mogul in Shahjahanabad. The Shaftoe boys' field of operations was an infinite maze of brickworks, pig yards, and shacks crammed sometimes with Englishmen and sometimes with Irishmen living ten and twelve to a room among swine, chickens, and geese.

The Irish worked as porters and dockers and coal-haulers during the winter, and trudged off to the countryside in hay-making months. They went to their Papist churches every chance they got and frittered away their silver paying for the services of scribes, who would transform their sentiments into the magical code that could be sent across counties and seas to be read, by a priest or another scrivener, to dear old Ma in Limerick.

In Mother Shaftoe's part of town, that kind of willingness to do a day's hard work for bread and money was taken as proof that the Irish race lacked dignity and shrewdness. And this did not even take into account their religious practices and all that flowed from them, e.g., the obstinate chastity of their women, and the willingness of the males to tolerate it. The way of the mudlarks (as the men who trafficked through Mother Shaftoe's bed styled themselves) was to voyage out upon the Thames after it got dark, find their way aboard anchored ships somehow, and remove items that could be exchanged for bread, money, or carnal services on dry land.

Techniques varied. The most obvious was to have someone climb up a ship's anchor cable and then throw a rope down to his mates. This was a job for surplus boys if ever there was one. Dick, the oldest of the Shaftoes, had learnt the rudiments of the trade by shinnying up the drain-pipes of whorehouses to steal things from the pockets of vacant clothing. He and his little brothers struck up a partnership with a band of these free-lance longshoremen, who owned the means of moving swag from ship to shore: they'd accomplished the stupendous feat of stealing a longboat.

After approaching several anchored ships with this general plan in mind, they learned that the sailors aboard them—who were actually supposed to be on watch for mudlarks—expected to be paid for the service of failing to notice that young Dick Shaftoe was clambering up the anchor cable with one end of a line tied round his ankle. When the captain found goods missing, he'd be sure to flog these sailors, and they felt they should be compensated, in advance, for the loss of skin and blood. Dick needed to have a purse dangling from one wrist, so that when a sailor shone a lantern down into his face, and aimed a blunderbuss at him, he could shake it and make the coins clink together. That was a music to which sailors of all nations would smartly dance.

Of course the mudlarks lacked coins to begin with. They wanted capital. John Cole—the biggest and boldest of the fellows who'd stolen the longboat—hit upon another shrewd plan: they would steal the only parts of ships that could be reached without actually getting aboard first: namely, anchors. They'd then sell them to the captains of ships who had found their anchors missing. This scheme had the added attraction that it might lead to ships' drifting down the current and running aground on oh, say, the Isle of Dogs, at which point their contents would be legally up for grabs.

One foggy night (but all nights were foggy) the mudlarks set off in the longboat, rowing upstream. The mudlark term for a boat's oars was *a pair of wings.* Flapping them, they flew among anchored ships—all of them pointed upriver, since the anchor cables were at their bows, and they weathercocked in the river's current. Nearing the stern of a tubby Dutch *galjoot*—a single-masted trader of perhaps twice their longboat's length, and ten times its capacity—they tossed Dick overboard with the customary rope noosed around his ankle, and a knife in his teeth. His instructions were to swim upstream, alongside the *galjoot's* hull, towards the bow, until he found her port side anchor cable descending into the river. He was to lash his ankle-rope to said cable, and then saw through the cable above the lashing. This would have the effect of cutting the *galjoot* free from, while making the longboat fast to, the anchor, effecting a sudden and silent transfer of ownership. This accomplished, he was to jerk on the rope three times. The mudlarks would then pull on the rope. This would draw them upstream until they were directly over the anchor, and if they hauled hard enough, the prize would come up off the riverbed.

Dick slopped away into the mist. They watched the rope uncoil, in fits and starts, for a couple of minutes—this meant Dick was swimming. Then it stopped uncoiling for a long while—Dick had found the anchor cable and gone to work! The mudlarks dabbled with rag-swathed oars, flapping those wings against the river's flow. Jack sat holding the rope, waiting for the three sharp jerks that would be Dick's signal. But no jerks came. Instead the rope went slack. Jack, assisted by brother Bob, pulled the slack into the boat. Ten yards of it passed through their hands before it became taut again, and then they felt, not three sharp jerks, exactly, but a sort of vibration at the other end.

It was plain that something had gone wrong, but Jack Cole was not about to abandon a good rope, and so they hauled in what they could, drawing themselves upstream. Somewhere along the flank of the *galjoot,* they found a noose in the rope, with a cold pale ankle lodged in it, and out came poor Dick. The anchor cable was knotted to that same noose. While Jack and Bob tried to slap Dick back into life, the mudlarks tried to pull in the anchor. Both failed, for the anchor was as heavy as Dick was dead. Presently, choleric Dutchmen up on the *galjoot* began to fire blunderbusses into the fog. It was time to leave.

Bob and Jack, who'd been acting as journeyman and apprentice, respectively, to Dick, were left without a Master Rope-Climber to emulate, and with a tendency to have extraordinarily bad dreams. For it was clear to them—if not right away, then eventually—that they had probably caused their own brother's death by drawing the rope taut, thereby pulling Dick down below the surface of the river. They were out of the mudlark trade for good. John Cole found a replacement for Dick, and (rumor had it) gave him slightly different instructions: take your ankle out of the noose *before* you cut the anchor cable.

Scarcely a fortnight later, John Cole and his fellows were caught in the longboat in broad daylight. One of their schemes had succeeded, they'd gotten drunk on stolen grog, and slept right through sunrise. The mudlarks were packed off to Newgate.

Certain of them—newcomers to the judicial system, if not to crime—shared their ill-gotten gains with a starving parson, who came to Newgate and met with them in the Gigger. This was a chamber on the lower floor where prisoners could thrust their faces up to an iron grate and be heard, if they shouted loudly enough, by visitors a few inches away. There, the parson set up a sort of impromptu Bible study class, the purpose of which was to get the mudlarks to memorize the 51st Psalm. Or, failing that, at least the first bit:

> *Have mercie upon me, o God, according to they loving kindenes: according to the multitude of thy compassions put awaie mine iniquities.*
>
> *Wash me throughly from mine iniquities, and clense me from my sin. For I knowe mine iniquities, & my sinne is ever before me.*
>
> *Against thee, against thee onely have I sinned, & done evil in thy sight, that thou maiest be just when thou speakest, and pure when thou judgest.*
>
> *Behold, I was borne in iniquitie, and in sinne hath my mother conceived me.*

Quite a mouthful, that, for mudlarks, but these were more diligent pupils than any Clerke of Oxenford. For on the day that they were marched down the straight and narrow passage to the Old Bailey and brought below the magistrate's balcony, an open Bible was laid in front of them, and they recited these lines. Which, by the evidentiary standards then prevailing in English courts, proved that they could read. Which proved that they were clergymen. Which rendered them beyond the reach of the criminal courts; for clergymen were, by long-hallowed tradition, subject only to the justice of the ecclesiastical courts. Since these no longer existed, the mudlarks were sent free.

It was a different story for John Cole, the oldest of the group. He had been to Newgate before. He had stood in the holding-pen of the Old Bailey before. And in that yard, below that balcony, in the sight of the very same magistrate, his hand had been clamped in a vise and a red-hot iron in the shape of a T had been plunged into the brawn of his thumb, marking him forever as Thief. Which by the evidentiary standards then prevailing, *et cetera,* made it most awkward for him to claim that he was a clergyman. He was sentenced, of course, to hang by the neck until dead at Tyburn.

Bob and Jack did not actually see any of this. They heard the narration from those who had mumbled a few words of Psalm 51 and been released and made their way back to the Isle of Dogs. To this point it was nothing they had not heard a hundred times before from friends and casual acquaintances in the neighborhood. But this time there was a new twist at the end of the story: John Cole had asked for the two surviving Shaftoe boys to meet him at the Triple Tree on the morning of his execution.

They went out of curiosity more than anything. Arriving at Tyburn and burrowing their way through an immense crowd by artful shin-kicking, instep-stomping, and groin-elbowing, they found John Cole and the others on a cart beneath the Fateful Nevergreen, elbows tied behind their backs, and nooses pre-knotted around their throats, with long rope-ends trailing behind them. A preacher—the Ordinary of Newgate—was there, urgently trying to make them aware of certain very important technicalities in the Rules of Eternity. But the condemnees, who were so drunk they could barely stand up, were saying all manner of rude and funny things back to him, faster than he could talk back.

Cole, more solemn than the others, explained to Jack and Bob that when the executioner "turned him off," which was to say, body-checked him off the cart and left him to hang by his neck, Cole would very much appreciate it if Jack could grab his left leg and Bob his right, or the other way round if they preferred, and hang there, pulling him down with their combined weight, so that he'd die faster. In exchange for this service, he told them of a loose board in the floor of a certain shack on the Isle of Dogs beneath which they could find hidden treasure. He laid out the terms of this transaction with admirable coolness, as if he were hanged by the neck until dead every Friday.

They accepted the commission. Jack Ketch was now the man to watch. His office, the gallows, was of admirably simple and spare design: three tall pilings supporting a triangle of heavy beams, each beam long enough that half a dozen men could be hanged from it at once, or more if a bit of crowding could be overlooked.

Jack Ketch's work, then, consisted of maneuvering the cart below a clear space on one of the beams; selecting a loose rope-end; tossing it over the beam; making it fast with a bit of knot-work; and turning off the bloke at the opposing end of the rope. The cart, now one body lighter, could then be moved again, and the procedure repeated.

John Cole was the eighth of nine men to be hanged on that particular day, which meant that Jack and Bob had the opportunity to watch seven men be hanged before the time came for them to discharge their responsibilities. During the first two or three of these hangings, all they really noticed was the obvious. But after they grew familiar with the general outlines of the rite, they began to notice subtle differences from one hanging to the next. In other words, they started to become connoisseurs of the art, like the ten thousand or so spectators who had gathered around them to watch.

Jack noticed very early that men in good clothes died faster. Watching Jack Ketch shrewdly, he soon saw why: when Jack Ketch was getting ready to turn a well-dressed man off, he would arrange the noose-knot behind the client's left ear, and leave some slack in the rope, so that he'd fall, and gather speed, for a moment before being brought up short with an audible crack. Whereas men in ragged clothing were given a noose that was loose around the neck (at first, anyway) and very little room to fall.

Now, John Cole—who'd looked a bit of a wretch to begin with, and who'd not grown any snappier, in his appearance and toilette, during the months he'd languished in the Stone Hold of Newgate—was the shabbiest bloke on the cart, and obviously destined for the long slow kicking style of hanging. Which explained why he'd had the foresight to call in the Shaftoe boys. But it did not explain something else.

"See here," Jack said, elbowing the Ordinary out of the way. He was on the ground below the cart, neck craned to look far up at Jack Ketch, who was slinging John Cole's neck-rope over the beam with a graceful straight-armed hooking movement. "If you've got hidden treasure, why didn't you give it to him?" And he nodded at Jack Ketch, who was now peering down curiously at Jack Shaftoe through the slits in his hood.

"Er—well I din't have it *on* me, did I?" returned John Cole, who was a bit surly in his disposition on the happiest of days. But Jack thought he looked a bit dodgy.

"You could've sent someone to fetch it!"

"How's I to know they wouldn't nick it?"

"Leave off, Jack," Bob had said. Since Dick's demise, he had been, technically, the man of the family; at first he'd made little of it, but lately he was more arrogant every day. "He's s'posed to be saying his prayers."

"Let him pray while he's kicking!"

"He's not going to be doing any kicking, 'cause you and I are going to be hanging on his legs."

"But he's lying about the treasure."

"I can see that, you think I'm stupid? But as long as we're here, let's do a right job of it."

While they argued, Cole was turned off. He sprawled against the sky just above their heads. They dodged instinctively, but of course he didn't fall far. They jumped into the air, gained hand-holds on his feet, and ascended, hand-over-hand.

After a few moments of dangling from the rope, Cole began to kick vigorously. Jack was tempted to let go, but the tremors coming down Cole's legs reminded him of what he'd felt in the rope when poor Dick had been dragged down beneath the river, and he held on by imagining that this was some kind of vengeance. Bob must've had the same phant'sy, for both boys gripped their respective legs like stranglers until Cole finally went limp. When they realized he was pissing himself, they both let go at once and tumbled into the fœtid dust below the gibbet. There was applause from the crowd. Before they'd had time to dust themselves off, they were approached by the sister of the one remaining condemned man—also a slow-hanging wretch, by his looks—who offered them cash money to perform the same service. The coins were clipped, worn, and blackened, but they were coins.

John Cole's loose board turned out not to be loose, and when pried up, to cover shit instead of treasure. They were hardly surprised. It didn't matter. They were prosperous tradesmen now. On the eve of each hanging-day, Jack and Bob could be found in their new place of business: Newgate Prison.

It took them several visits just to understand the place. *Gate* in their usage meant a sort of wicket by which humans could pass through a fence around a hog-yard without having to vault over—not that vaulting was such a difficult procedure, but it was dangerous when drunk, and might lead to falling, and being eaten by the hogs. So gates they knew.

They had furthermore absorbed the knowledge that in several parts of London town were large fabricks called Gates, viz. Ludgate, Moorgate, and Bishopsgate. They had even passed through Aldgate a few times, that being their usual way of invading the city. But the connexion between gates of that type, and hog-yard-wickets, was most obscure. A gate in the hog-yard sense of the word made no sense unless built in a wall, fence, or other such formal barrier, as its purpose was to provide a means of passage through same. But none of the large London buildings called Gates appeared to have been constructed in any such context. They bestrode important roads leading into the city, but if you didn't want to pass through the actual gate, you could usually find a way round.

This went for Newgate as well. It was a pair of mighty fortress-turrets built on either side of a road that, as it wandered in from the countryside and crossed over Fleet Ditch, was named Holborn. But as it passed between those turrets, the high road was bottlenecked down to a vaulted passageway just wide enough for a four-horse team to squeeze through. Above, a castle-like building joined the turrets, and bridged the road. An iron portcullis made of bars as thick as Jack's leg was suspended within that castle so that it could be dropped down to seal the vault, and bar the road. But it was all show. For thirty seconds of scampering along side streets and alleys would take Jack, or anyone else, to the other side. Newgate was not surrounded by walls or fortifications, but rather by buildings of the conventional sort, which was to say, the half-timbered two- and three-story dwellings that in England grew up as quick and as thick as mushrooms. This Gothick fortress of Newgate, planted in the midst of such a neighborhood, was like a pelvis in a breadbasket.

If you actually did come into the city along Holborn, then when you ducked beneath that portcullis and entered the vaulted passageway beneath Newgate you'd see to the right a door leading into a porter's lodge, which was where new prisoners had their chains riveted on. A few yards farther along, you'd emerge from beneath the castle into the uncovered space of what was now called Newgate Street. To your right you would see a gloomy old building that rose to a height of three or four stories. It had only a few windows, and those were gridded over with bars. This was a separate piece of work from the turret-castle-vault building; rumor had it that it had once done service as an inn for travelers coming into the city along Holborn. But the prison had, in recent centuries, spread up Newgate Street like gangrene up a thigh, consuming several such houses. Most of the doorways that had once welcomed weary travelers were bricked up. Only one remained, at the seam between the castle and the adjoining inn-buildings. Going in there, a visitor could make a quick right turn into the Gigger, or, if he had a candle (for it grew dark immediately), he could risk a trip up or down a stairway into this or that ward, hold, or dungeon. It all depended on what sort of wretch he was coming to visit.

On Jack and Bob's first visit they'd neglected to bring a light, or money with which to buy one, and had blundered down-stairs into a room with a stone floor that made crackling noises beneath their feet as they walked. It was impossible to breathe the air there, and so after a few moments of blind panic they had found their way out and fled back into Newgate Street. There, Jack had noticed that his feet were bloody, and supposed that he must have stepped on broken glass. Bob had the same affliction. But Bob, unlike Jack, was wearing shoes, and so the blood could not have come from him. On careful inspection of the soles of those shoes, the mystery was solved: the blood was not smeared about, but spotted his soles, an array of little bursts. At the center of each burst was a small fleshy gray tube: the vacant corpse of an engorged louse that Bob had stepped on. This accounted for the mysterious crackling noise that they had heard while walking around in that room. As they soon learned, it was called the Stone Hold, and was accounted one of the lowest and worst wards of the prison, occupied only by common felons—such as the late John Cole—who had absolutely no money. Jack and Bob never returned to it.

Over the course of several later sallies into the prison they learned its several other rooms: the fascinating Jack Ketch his Kitchen; the so-called Buggering Hold (which they avoided); the Chapel (likewise); the Press-Yard, where the richest prisoners sat drinking port and claret with their periwigged visitors; and the Black Dogge Tavern, where the cellarmen—elite prisoners who did a brisk trade in candles and liquor—showed a kind of hospitality to any prisoners who had a few coins in their pockets. This looked like any other public house in England save that everyone in the place was wearing chains.

There were, in other words, plenty of lovely things to discover at the time and to reminisce about later. But they were not making these arduous trips from the Isle of Dogs to Newgate simply for purposes of sightseeing. It was a business proposition. They were looking for their market. And eventually, they found it. For in the castle proper, on the north side of the street, in the basement of the turret, was a spacious dungeon that was called the Condemned Hold.

Here, timing was everything. Hangings occurred only eight times a year. Prisoners were sentenced to hang a week or two in advance. And so most of the time there were no condemned people at all in the Condemned Hold. Rather, it was used as a temporary holding cell for new prisoners of all stripes who had been frog-marched to the Porter's Lodge across the street and traded the temporary ropes that bound their arms behind their backs, for iron fetters that they would wear until they were released. After being ironed (as this procedure was called) with so much metal that they could not even walk, they would be dragged across the vault and thrown into the Condemned Hold to lie in the dark for a few days or weeks. The purpose of this was to find out how much money they really had. If they had money, they'd soon offer it to the gaolers in exchange for lighter chains, or even a nice apartment in the Press-Yard. If they had none, they'd be taken to some place like the Stone Hold.

If one paid a visit to the Condemned Hold on a day chosen at random, it would likely be filled with heavily ironed newcomers. These were of no interest to Jack and Bob, at least not yet. Instead, the Shaftoe boys came to Newgate during the days immediately prior to Tyburn processions, when the Condemned Hold was full of men who actually had been condemned to hang. There they performed.

Around the time of their birth, the King had come back to England and allowed the theatres, which had been closed by Cromwell, to open again. The Shaftoe boys had been putting their climbing skills to good use sneaking into them, and had picked up an ear for the way actors talked, and an eye for the way they did things.

So their Newgate performances began with a little mum-show: Jack would try to pick Bob's pocket. Bob would spin round and cuff him. Jack would stab him with a wooden poniard, and Bob would die. Then (Act II) Bob would jump up and 'morphosize into the Long Arm of the Law, put Jack in a hammerlock, (Act III) don a wig (which they had stolen, at appalling risk, from a side-table in a brothel near the Temple), and sentence him to hang. Then (Act IV) Bob would exchange the white wig for a black hood and throw a noose round Jack's neck and stand behind him while Jack would motion for silence (for by this point all of the Condemned Hold would be in a state of near-riot) and clap his hands together like an Irish child going to First Communion, and (Act V) utter the following soliloquy:

John Ketch's rope doth decorate my neck.
>Though rude, and cruel, this garland chafes me not.
>For, like the Necklace of Harmonia,
>It brings the one who wears it life eternal.
>The hangman draweth nigh—he'll turn me off
>And separate my soul from weak'ning flesh.
>And, as I've made my peace with God Almighty,
>My spirit will ascend to Heaven's Door,
>Where, after brief interrogation, Christ will—
>>*Bob steps forward and shoves Jack, then yanks*
>>*the rope up above Jack's head.*

HAWKKH! God's Wounds! The noose quite strangleth me!
>What knave conceived this means of execution?
>I should have bribed John Ketch to make it quick.
>But, with so many lordly regicides
>Who've lately come to Tyburn to be penalized,
>The price of instant, painless death is quite
>Inflated—far beyond the humble means
>Of common condemnees, who hence must die
>As painf'lly as they've lived. God damn it all!
>And damn Jack Ketch; the late John Turner; and
>The judges who hath sent so many rich men to
>The gallows, thereby spurring said inflation.
>And damn my frugal self. For, at a cost
>That scarce exceeds an evening at the pub,
>Might I have hired those exc'llent Shaftoe boys,
>Young Jack, and Bob, the elder of the pair,
>To dangle from my legs, which lacking ballast,
>Do flail most ineffectu'lly in the air,
>And make a sort of entertainment for
>The *mobile.*
>>*Bob removes the noose from Jack's neck.*

But soft! The end approaches—
Earth fades—new worlds unfold before my eyes—
  Can this be heaven? It seemeth warm, as if
  A brazier had been fir'd 'neath the ground.
  Perhaps it is the warmth of God's sweet love
  That so envelops me.
Bob, dressed as a Devil, approaches with a long pointed Stick.
How now! What sort
Of angel doth sprout Horns upon his pate?
  Where is thy Harp, O dark Seraph?
  Instead of which a Pike, or Spit, doth seem
  To occupy thy gnarled claws?
DEVIL: I am
  The Devil's Turnspit. Sinner, welcome home!
JACK: I thought that I had made my peace with God.
  Indeed I had, when I did mount the scaffold.
  If I had but died then, at Heaven's Gate
  I'd stand. But in my final agony,
  I took God's name in vain, and sundry mortal
  Sins committed, and thus did damn myself
  To this!
DEVIL: Hold still!
  Devil shoves the point of his Spit up Jack's arse-hole.
JACK: The pain! The pain, and yet,
  It's just a taste of what's to come.
  If only I had hired Jack and Bob!
*Jack, by means of a conjuror's trick, causes the point of the
spit, smeared with blood, to emerge from his mouth, and is led
away by the Devil, to violent applause and foot-stomping from
the Crowd.*

After the applause had died down, Jack, then, would circulate among the condemned to negotiate terms, and Bob, who
was bigger, would watch his back, and mind the coin-purse.

❦

The Continent

LATE SUMMER 1683

❦

> When a woman is thus left desolate and void of
> counsel, she is just like a bag of money or a
> jewel dropt on the highway, which is a prey to
> the next comer.
>
> —DANIEL DEFOE, *Moll Flanders*

JACK HAD KEPT A SHREWD eye on the weather all spring and
summer. It had been perfect. He was living in unaccus-
tomed comfort in Strasbourg. This was a city on the Rhine,
formerly German and, as of quite recently, French. It lay
just to the south of a country called the Palatinate, which, as
far as Jack could make out, was a moth-eaten rag of land
straddling the Rhine. King Looie's soldiers would overrun
the Palatinate from the West, or the Emperor's armies
would rape and pillage it from the East, whenever they
couldn't think of anything else to do. The person in charge
of the Palatinate was called an Elector, which in this part of
the world meant a very noble fellow, more than a Duke but
less than a King. Until quite recently the Electors Palatinate
had been of a very fine and noble family, consisting of too
many siblings to keep track of, most quite magnificent; but
since only one (the oldest) could be Elector, all of the rest

of them had gone out of that country, and found better things to do, or gotten themselves killed in more or less fascinating ways. Eventually the Elector had died and turned matters over to his son: an impotent madman named Charles, who liked to stage mock battles around an old Rhine-castle that wasn't good for much else. The fighting was imaginary, but the trenches, siege-works, dysentery, and gangrene were real.

Now Jack had been making a sort of living, for several years, from being a fake soldier in France—a line of work that had been brought to ruin by many tiresome reforms that had recently been introduced to the French Army by one Martinet. When he'd heard about this crazy Elector he'd wasted no time in going to the Palatinate and finding gainful employment as a pretend musketeer.

Not long afterwards, King Louis XIV of France had attacked the nearby city of Strasbourg and made it his, and as frequently happened in sacked cities in those days, there had been a bit of the old Black Death. At the first appearance of buboes in the groins and armpits of the poor, the rich of Strasbourg had boarded up their houses and fled to the country. Many had simply climbed aboard boats and headed downstream on the Rhine, which had naturally taken them past that old wrack of a castle where Jack and others were playing at war for the amusement of the crazy Elector Palatine. One rich *Strasbourgeois,* there, had disembarked from his river-boat and struck up a conversation with none other than Jack Shaftoe. It was not customary for rich men to speak to the likes of Jack, and so the whole business seemed a mystery until Jack noticed that, no matter how he moved about, the rich man always found some pretext to stay well upwind of him.

This rich man had hired Jack and arranged for him to get something called a Plague Pass: a large document in that Gothickal German script with occasional excursions into something that looked like either Latin (when it was desirable to invoke the mercy and grace of God) or French (for sucking up to King Looie, only one rung below God at this point).* By flourishing this at the right times, Jack was able to carry out his mission, which was to go into Strasbourg; proceed to the rich man's dwelling; wash off the red chalk crosses that marked it as a plague-house; pry off the deals he'd nailed over the doors and windows; chase out any squatters; fend off any looters; and live in it for a while. If, after a few weeks, Jack hadn't died of the plague, he was to send word to this rich man in the country that it was safe to move back in.

Jack had accomplished the first parts of this errand in about May, but by the beginning of June had somehow forgotten about the last. In about mid-June, another Vagabond-looking fellow arrived. The rich man had hired him to go to the house and remove Jack's body so that it wouldn't draw vermin and then live in it for a while and, after a few weeks, if he hadn't died of the plague, send word. Jack, who was occupying the master bedchamber, had accommodated this new fellow in one of the children's rooms, showed him around the kitchen and wine-cellar, and invited him to make himself at home. Late in July, another Vagabond had showed up, and explained he'd been hired to cart away the bodies of the first two, *et cetera, et cetera.*

All spring and summer, the weather was ideal: rain and sun in proportions suitable for the growing of grain. Vagabonds roamed freely in and out of Strasbourg, giving wide berths to those mounds of decomposing plague-victims. Jack sought out the ones who'd come from the east, treated them to the rich man's brandy, conducted broken conversations with them in the zargon, and established two important facts: one, that the weather had been just as fine, if not finer, in Austria and Poland. Two, that Grand Vizier Khan Mustapha was still besieging the city of Vienna at the head of an army of two hundred thousand Turks.

Round September, he and his fellow-squatters found it necessary to depart from that fine house. It did not make him unhappy. Pretending to be dead was not a thing that came

---

*Jack could not read but could infer as much from the types of letters used.

naturally to Vagabonds. The population of the house had swollen to a dozen and a half, most of them were tedious people, and the wine-cellar was nearly empty. One night Jack caused the window-shutters to be thrown open and the candles to be lit, and played host and lord over a grand squatters' ball. Vagabond-musicians played raucous airs on shawms and pennywhistles, Vagabond-actors performed a comedy in zargon, stray dogs copulated in the family chapel, and Jack, presiding over all at the head of the table, dressed in the rich man's satin, almost fell asleep. But even through the commotion of the ball, his ears detected the sound of hoofbeats approaching, swords being whisked from scabbards, firelocks being cocked. He was vanishing up the stairs even as the owner and his men were smashing down the door. Sliding down an escape-rope he'd long ago fixed to a balcony's rail, he dropped neatly into the rich man's saddle, still warm from thrashing the master's chubby ass. He galloped to a potter's field on the edge of town where he had stored some provisions against this very sort of event, and took to the road well supplied with salt-cod and biscuit. He rode southwards through the night until the horse was spent, then stripped off its fine saddle and threw it into a ditch, and traded the horse itself to a delighted ferryman for passage east across the Rhine. Finding the Munich road, he struck out for the East.

The barley harvest was underway, and most of it was destined for the same place as Jack. He was able to ride along on barley-carts, and to talk his way across the Neckar and the Danube, by telling people he was off to join the legions of Christendom and beat back the Turkish menace.

This was not precisely a lie. Jack and brother Bob had come to the Netherlands more than once to soldier under John Churchill, who was in the household of the Duke of York. York spent a lot of time abroad because he was Catholic and most everyone in England hated him. But in time he had returned home anyway. John Churchill had gone with him and Bob, dutiful soldier that he was, had gone home with Churchill. Jack had stayed on the Continent, where there were more countries, more Kings, and more wars.

Great big dark mounds were visible off to his right, far away. After they continued to be there for several days in a row, he realized that they must be mountains. He'd heard of them. He had fallen in with a cart-train belonging to a barley-merchant of Augsburg, who was contemptuous of the low grain prices in Munich's great market and had decided to take his goods closer to the place where they were needed. They rode for days through rolling green country, dotted with bent peasants bringing in the barley-harvest. The churches were all Papist, of course, and in these parts they had a queer look, with domes shaped like ripe onions perched atop slender shafts.

Over days those mountains rose up to meet them, and then they came to a river named Salz that pierced the mountain-wall. Churches and castles monitored the valley from stone cliffs. Endless wagon-trains of barley came together, and clashed and merged with the Legions of the Pope of Rome who were coming up from Italy, and Bavarians and Saxons, too: mile-long parades of gentleman volunteers, decorated like knights of old with the Crusaders' red cross, bishops and archbishops with their jeweled shepherd's-hooks, cavalry-regiments that beat the earth as if it were a hollow log—each horseman accompanied by his *cheval de bataille,* a fresh *cheval de marche* or two, a *cheval de poursuite* for hunting stags or Turks, and a *cheval de parade* for ceremonial occasions, and the grooms to care for them. There were armies of musketeers, and finally a vast foaming, surging rabble of barefoot pikemen, marching with their twenty-foot-long weapons angled back over their shoulders, giving those formations the look of porcupines when they are in a mellow and complacent mood and have flattened their quills.

Here the barley-merchant of Augsburg had at last found a market, and might have sold his goods at a handsome profit.

But the sight of Christendom at war had inflamed both his avarice and his piety, and he was seized with a passion to ride farther and see what more wonders lay to the east. Like-wise Jack, sizing up those pikemen, and comparing their rags and bare feet to his stolen traveling-togs and excellent leather boots, suspected he could strike a better deal closer to Vienna. So they joined together with the general flood and proceeded, in short confused marches, to the city of Linz, where (according to the merchant) there was a very great *Messe.* Jack knew that *Messe* was the German word for a Mass, and reckoned that Herr Augsburg meant to attend church in some great cathedral there.

At Linz they grazed the south bank of the River Danube. In the plain along the river was a fine market that had been swallowed and nearly digested by a vast military camp—but no cathedral. *"Die Messe!"* Herr Augsburg exclaimed, and this was when Jack understood something about the German language: having a rather small number of words, they fre-quently used one word to mean several different things. *Messe* meant not only a Mass but a trade-fair.

Another army had marched down from the north and was laboriously crossing the Danube here, trickling across Linz's bridges and keeping Linz's watermen busy all day and all night, poling their floats across the stream laden with artillery-pieces, powder-kegs, fodder, rations, luggage, horses, and men. Jack Shaftoe spoke a few words of Ger-man. He had picked up quite a bit of French, and of course he knew English and the zargon. These men who had ridden down out of the north did not speak any of those tongues, and he could not guess whether they might be Swedes or Russians or of some other nation. But one day cheering came up from the bridges and the ferries, mingled with the thunder of thousands of war-horses, and from the woods on the north bank emerged the mightiest cavalry that Jack, in all his travels in England, Holland, and France, had ever seen. At its head rode a man who could only be a King. Now this wasn't Jack's first King, as he'd seen King Looie more than once during French military parades. But King Looie was

only play-acting, he was like a whoreson actor in a Southwark theatre, got up in a gaudy costume, acting the way he
imagined that a warrior King might act. This fellow from the
north was no play-actor, and he rode across the bridge with a
solemn look on his face that spoke of bitter days ahead for
Grand Vizier Khan Mustapha. Jack wanted to know who it
was, and finally locating someone who spoke a bit of French
he learned that what he was looking at, here, was the army
of Poland-Lithuania, and their terrible King was John Sobieski, who had made an alliance with the Holy Roman Emperor to drive the Turks all the way back to Asia, and his
mighty, gleaming cavalry were called the Winged Hussars.

Once King John Sobieski and the Winged Hussars had
crossed the Danube and made camp, and a *Messe* in the religious sense had been said, and the thrill had died down a little, both Herr Augsburg the barley-merchant and Jack
Shaftoe the vagabond-soldier made their own private calculations as to what it all meant for them. Two or (according to
rumor) three great cavalry forces were now encamped
around Linz. They were the spearheads of much larger formations of musketeers and pikemen, all of whom had to eat.
Their rations were carried on wagons and the wagons were
drawn by teams of horses. All of it was useless without the
artillery, which was, as well, drawn by teams of horses.
What it all amounted to, therefore, was the world's richest
and most competitive *Messe* for barley. Prices were thrice
what they'd been at the crossing of the Salz and ten times
what they'd been in Munich. Herr Augsburg, having chosen
the moment carefully, now struck, playing John Sobieski's
barley-buyers off against those of the Bavarian, Saxon, and
Austrian lords.

For his part, Jack understood that no force of cavalry as
lordly, as magnificent, as the Winged Hussars could possibly
exist, even for a single day, without a vast multitude of especially miserable peasants to make it all possible, and that
peasants in such large numbers could never be kept so miserable for so long unless the lords of Poland-Lithuania were
unusually cruel men. Indeed, after John Sobieski's vivid

crossing of the Danube a gray fog of wretches filtered out of the woods and congealed on the river's northern bank. Jack didn't want to be one of 'em. So he went and found Herr Augsburg, sitting on an empty barley-cart surrounded by his profits: bills of exchange drawn on trading-houses in Genoa, Venice, Lyons, Amsterdam, Seville, London, piled up high on the cart's plankage and weighed down with stones. Mounting up onto the wagon, Jack the Soldier became, for a quarter of an hour, Jack the Actor. In the bad French that Herr Augsburg more or less understood, he spoke of the impending Apocalypse before the gates of Vienna, and of his willingness, nay, eagerness, to die in the midst of same, and his prayerful hope that he might at least take a single Turk down with him, or barring that, perhaps inflict some kind of small wound on a Turk, viz. by jabbing at him with a pointed stick or whatever he might have handy, so that said Turk might be distracted or slowed down long enough for some other soldier of Christendom, armed with a real weapon, such as a musket, to actually take aim at, and slay, that selfsame Turk. This was commingled with a great deal of generally Popish-sounding God-talk and Biblical-sounding quotations that Jack claimed he'd memorized from the Book of Revelation.

In any case it had the desired effect, which was that Herr Augsburg, as his contribution to the Apocalypse, went with Jack to an armaments-market in the center of Linz and purchased him a musket and various other items.

Thus equipped, Jack marched off and offered his services to an Austrian regiment. The captain paid equal attention to Jack's musket and to his boots. Both were impressive in the highest degree. When Jack demonstrated that he actually knew how to load and fire his weapon, he was offered a position. Jack thus became a musketeer.

He spent the next two weeks staring at other men's backs through clouds of dust, and stepping on ground that had already been stepped on by thousands of other men and horses. His ears were filled with the tromping of feet, boots, and hooves; the creaking of overladen barley-carts; nonsensical teamsters' exhortations; marching-songs in unknown languages; and the blowing of trumpets and beating of drums of regimental signal-men desperately trying to keep their throngs from getting all mixed up with alien throngs.

He had a gray-brown felt hat with a gigantic round brim that needed to be pinned up on one or both sides lest it flop down and blind him. More established musketeers had fine feathered brooches for this purpose—Jack made do with a pin. Like all English musketeers, Jack called his weapon Brown Bess. It was of the latest design—the lock contained a small clamp that gripped a shard of flint, and when Jack pulled the trigger, this would be whipped around and skidded hard against a steel plate above the powder-pan, flooding the pan with sparks and igniting it in most cases. Half of the musketeer-formations were impaired by older, flintless weapons called matchlocks. Each of these matchlock-men had to go around with a long fuzzy rope twined through his fingers, one end of which was forever smouldering—as long as it didn't get wet and he remembered to blow on it frequently. Clamped into the same sort of mechanism that held Jack's flint-shard, it would ignite the powder, more often than not, by direct contact.

Jack, like all the other musketeers, had a leather belt over one shoulder whence dangled a dozen thumb-sized and -shaped wooden flasks, each sealed with its own stopper, each big enough to contain one charge of powder for the weapon. They clinked together musically when he walked. There was a powder-horn for refilling these during lulls. At the lowest point of the bandolier was a small pouch containing a dozen lead balls.

A company was a couple of hundred men like Jack walking around packed into a tight square, not because they liked crowds but because this made it harder for an opponent to ride up with an edged weapon and cut pieces off of them. The reason it was harder was because in the center of the square was a smaller square of men carrying extremely long pointed sticks called pikes. The dimensions of the squares and the length of the pikes were worked out so that when the pikes were levelled at the enemy (passing between the surrounding

musketeers) their points would project some distance beyond the edge of the formation—provided the musketeers
stood close together—discouraging enemy horsemen from
simply galloping up and having at the musketeers as they
went through their loading rituals, which, even under ideal
conditions, seemed to take as long as a Mass.*

That was the general plan. Exactly what would happen
when the Turks strung their outlandish recurved bows and
began to shower iron-tipped arrows into these formations
had not been specified. From Linz onwards, anyway, Jack
walked in the midst of such an organization. It made many,
many noises, each traceable to something like the wooden
powder-flasks. Unlike a company of matchlocks, it did not
smolder, nor make huffing and puffing noises.

They turned away from the Danube, leaving it off to their
left, and then the formations piled into one another because
they were going uphill now, assaulting the tail of that mountain range. The drums and trumpets, muffled now by trees,
echoed along river-valleys as formations split again and
again, finding passes over the hills. Jack was frequently confused, but when he wasn't, he sensed that the Poles were on
his right, the Bavarians and Saxons on his left.

Compared to the hills of England, these were high, steep,
and well-forested. But between them lay broad valleys that
made for easy marching, and even when they had to go over
hills, instead of between them, the going was easier than it
looked—the trees were tall handsome ones with bare white
trunks, and what little undergrowth there was had long since
been trampled down by others when Jack reached it.

The only way he knew that they'd reached the environs of
Vienna was that they stopped marching and began camping.

---

*The reason the pikemen didn't protectively surround the musketeers, in-
stead of being surrounded by them, was that even if the musketeers aimed
between them, or over their heads, they would get mowed down by errant
balls; because if, as frequently happened, a musket ball was a bit too small
for its barrel, it would take to bouncing from one side of the barrel to the
other as it was propelled out, and might emerge at a sharp, startling sideways angle.

They made a bivouac in a narrow steep valley where the sun rose late and set early. Some of Jack's brothers in arms were impatient to get on with it, but he appreciated that the Army of Christendom had become an immense machine for turning barley into horseshit and that the barley would fast run out. Something had to happen soon.

After they'd bivouacked for two nights, Jack slipped away one morning before dawn and clambered uphill until the ground became level under his feet. He did this partly to get away from the stink of the camp and partly because he wanted to get a look at the city from a high place. Red sunlight was weaving among white tree-trunks as he wandered to a high bluff from which he had a clear view several miles down into the city.

Vienna was a small town dwarfed by its own defenses, in turn engulfed by a larger Turkish city only a few months old. The town itself was, then, the smallest part of what he saw, but it was to the rest as a chalice was to a cathedral. Even from miles off he could see it was a miserable place—actual streets were visible nowhere, just the red tile roofs of long skinny buildings heaped up six and seven stories, wending black crevices between them indicating streets, which he could tell would be sunless trenches, thick with hurtling shit and echoing voices. He could see the foaming stain of the city spreading across the adjacent canal and, farther downstream, into the Danube itself, and from its color he could almost guess that there was a major flux epidemic underway—as indeed there was in the Turkish camp.

Just off-center in the heart of Vienna stood the tallest building Jack had ever seen—a cathedral with a dunce-cap tower topped by a curious symbol, a star wedged in the craw of a crescent moon, like a stick jammed into a shark's mouth. It seemed a prophetic map of the entire scene. Vienna was protected on the north by a canal that split away from the Danube, moated the city on that side, and later rejoined it. The bridges had been wrecked so no one could enter or leave that way. The entire remainder of the city was enveloped by the Turkish camp, narrowest at the two points

where it touched the river, and, in the middle, as fat as Vienna itself—therefore, a crescent with the city trapped between its horns. It was a fluttering world of heathenishly
colored tents and flags and streamers, with the ruins of Vienna's burnt suburbs poking out here and there like ribs of
wrecked ships from a foaming sea.

Between Turkish camp and Christian city was a belt of
what a naïve person would identify as empty (albeit curiously sculpted and chiseled) terrain. Jack, a trained professional, by squinting and tilting his head this way and that,
could imagine that it was as densely crisscrossed with sight-
lines and cannonball-arcs and other geometrickal phant'sies
of engineers as the space above a ship's deck was with ropes
and rigging. For this corridor between camp and fort had
been claimed by the engineers—as anyone who stepped into
it would learn in as little time as it took a musket-ball to
cover the distance. The Engineer-Empire, Jack'd been noticing, waxed as older ones waned. Just as Turks and Franks
had their own styles of building, so did Engineers rehearse,
again and again, the same shapes: sloping walls, backed up
by earth (to deflect and absorb cannonballs) laid out in
nested zig-zags, a bastion at each corner from which to
shoot at anyone who tried to climb the neighboring stretches
of wall. Oh, Vienna had a traditional pre-Engineer wall: a
thin curtain of masonry, crenellated on top. But that was
nothing but an antiquarian curiosity now, enveloped and
shamed by the new works.

Besides that cathedral, there was only one building in Vienna worth a second look, and that was a great big cream-
colored, many-windowed building, five stories high and a
crossbow-shot in length, constructed right on the edge of the
city and rising high above the wall, with wings behind it enclosing courtyards he'd never see. It was obviously the
Palace of the Holy Roman Emperor. It had a steep high
roof—plenty of attic space—with a row of tiny dormers sur-
mounted by funny copper domes like spiked helmets. Each
dormer had a little window, and through one of them (though

the distance was very great) Jack convinced himself he could see a figure dressed in white peering out. He wanted to arrange something involving a trapped princess, a dashing rescue, and a reward; however, in between him and whomever was peering out that window were certain complications, viz. directly below the Palace, a huge bastion was thrust out into the glacis, like a giant's plowshare parting an empty field, and against this very stronghold the Grand Vizier had chosen to mount his attack.

Apparently the Turks had been in too much of a hurry to trundle siege artillery all the way across Hungary and so they were undoing the work of the Engineers one shovel-load at a time. Vienna's walls and bastions had been smooth regular shapes, so the Turks' handiwork was as obvious as a mole-hill in a Duke's bowling-green. They had dug a metropolis of trenches in what had been a perfectly flat glacis. Each trench was surrounded by the dirt that had been flung out of it, giving it the swollen look of an infected wound. A few of these trenches led straight from the heart of the Turkish camp toward the Emperor's Palace, but these were just the great avenue-trenches from which countless street-trenches branched off left and right, running generally parallel to the city's walls, and spaced as closely together as they could be without collapsing. These trenches were as rungs in a horizontal ladder by which the Turks had advanced until they'd reached the foot of the first ravelins: outlying, arrowhead-shaped earthworks between bastions. Here they had gone underground and undermined the ravelins, packed the mines with black powder, and blown them up, creating avalanches where walls had stood—as when molten wax spills from the top of a candle and mars its regular shape with a lumpy cataract. Fresh trenches, then, had been cut across those irregular debris-piles, bringing the Turks into a position whence they could bring musketry to bear on the city walls, to protect their sappers and miners as they advanced, ditch by ditch, across the dry moat. Now they were attacking the great bastion directly before the Palace in the same way. But it was a gradual sort of war, like watching a tree absorb a stone fence, and nothing was happening at the moment.

All well and good; but the question on Jack's mind was: where was the best looting to be found? He chose some likely targets, both in the Turk's camp and in the city of Vienna itself, and committed to memory a few landmarks, so that he could find what he desired when things were smoky and confused.

When he turned to go back to the camp, he discovered that there was another man up on this hill, a stone's throw away: some kind of monk or holy man, perhaps, as he was dressed in a rough sackcloth robe, with no finery. But then the bloke whipped out a sword. It was not one of your needle-thin rapiers, such as fops pushed at each other in the streets of London and Paris, but some kind of relic of the Crusades, a two-handed production with a single crossbar instead of a proper guard—the sort of thing Richard the Lionhearted might've used to slay camels in the streets of Jerusalem. This man went down on one knee in the dirt, and he did it with verve and enthusiasm. You see your rich man kneeling in church and it takes him two or three minutes, you can hear his knees popping and sinews creaking, he totters this way and that, creating small alarums amongst the servants who are gripping his elbows. But this brute knelt easily, even *lustily* if such a thing were possible, and facing toward the city of Vienna, he planted his sword in the ground so that it became a steel cross. The morning light was shining directly into his grizzled face and glinting from the steel of the blade and glowing in some indifferent colored jewels set into the weapon's hilt and crossbar. The man bowed his head and took to mumbling in Latin. The hand that wasn't holding the sword was thumbing through a rosary—Jack's cue to exit stage right. But as he was leaving he recognized the man with the broadsword as King John Sobieski.

LATER IN THE MORNING, a ration of brandy was issued to each man—it being a military axiom that a drunk soldier was an effective soldier. The brandy gave the men, at last, something to gamble with, and so dice and cards came out of pockets. This led to Jack having half a dozen brandy-rations in his belly, and his comrades-in-arms glaring at him suspiciously and muttering foul accusations in barbarous tongues. But then there was more trumpet-blowing and drum-beating and they were up on their feet (Jack barely so), and now another few hours of tromping around staring at the backs of the men in front of them, the horizon in all directions a fur of bayonets and pikes.

Like a storm that has fallen upon the mountains, the companies and regiments drained through trees into ravines and down ravines into valleys, coming together into black thundering floods that foamed out across the plain, finally, and rushed toward Vienna.

The artillery began to fire, first on one side, then the other. But if men were being cut down in swathes by Turkish grape-shot, it was not happening anywhere near Jack. They were moving double-time. They marched from hot, clear air into dust-clouds, then from dust-clouds into permanent banks of gunpowder-smoke.

Then the earth seemed to quail beneath their feet and their entire formation shied back, men piling into one another's backs, and the smoke roiled and parted. Glints of gold and polished brass bobbed through it, and Jack understood that right along their flank, King John Sobieski was charging into the Turks at the head of the Winged Hussars.

Divots of earth continued to rain down for long moments after they had passed. In the Poles' wake, an empty corridor was left across the battlefield, and suddenly there was no man in front of Jack. A yard of open space was more inviting than a pitcher of beer. He couldn't not bolt forward. The other men did likewise. The formation was broken and men of various regiments were simply boiling into the beaten path of the Polish cavalry. Jack followed along, as much out of a desire not to be trampled by the men behind him as to reach the looting. He was listening carefully for the sounds of Turkish cannonades from the front, or the rumble of retreating hussars, coming back toward them in panic, but he heard no such thing. There was plenty of musket-fire, but not in the sputtering waves of organized combat.

He nearly tripped over a severed arm, and saw that it was clad in a curious Oriental fabric. After limbs came bodies— mostly Turkish ones, some clad in vests of fine mail studded with jeweled badges and gold stars. The men around him saw the same thing, and a cheer went up. They were all running now, and they kept getting farther and farther apart, dispersing into some place that, in the dust and smoke, Jack knew as a city, maybe not so great as London, but much bigger, say, than Strasbourg or Munich. It was a city of tents: huge cones supported by central poles and guyed off to the sides with many radiating lines, and curtains hanging down from the rims of the cones to form the walls. The tents were not of rude canvas but of embroidered stuff, all decorated with crescents and stars and spidery words.

Jack ran into a tent and found thick carpet under his feet, a pattern like twining flowers woven into the pile, and then discovered a cat the size of a wolf, with spotted golden fur, chained to a post, a jewelled collar round its neck. He had never seen a cat large enough to eat him before and so he backed out of that tent and continued to wander. At an intersection of great ways, he discovered a tiled fountain with huge golden fish swimming in it. The overflow spilled into a ditch that led to a garden planted with sweet white flowers.

A tree grew in a pot on wheels, its branches burdened with strange fruit and inhabited by emerald-green and ruby-red birds with hooked beaks, which screamed sophisticated curses at him in some tongue he had never heard. A dead Turk with an enormous waxed mustache and a turban of apricot silk lay in a marble bath full of blood. Other pikemen and musketeers wandered about, too flabbergasted to loot.

Jack tripped and landed face-first on red cloth, then stood up to find that he had stepped on a scarlet flag twenty feet on a side, embroidered with swords and heathen letters in gold thread. This was too big to carry away and so he let it lie, and wandered down tent-streets and tent-avenues scattered with collapsible lanterns; wrought-silver incense burners; muskets with stocks inlaid with mother-of-pearl, lapis, and gold; grapefruit-sized hand grenades; turbans clasped with jeweled badges; hand-drums; and vatlike siege mortars, their bombs nearby, half-covered by spiderwebs of fuse. Standards with long horsehair tassels topped by copper crescent moons gaping like dead men at the sky. Embroidered quivers and discarded ramrods, both wooden and iron. Stray Bavarian matchlock men ran to and fro, smouldering ropes still tangled in their fingers, glowing red from the wind of their movement so that they appeared as bobbing red sparks in the smoke and dust, trailing long wavy tendrils of finer smoke behind them.

Then there was the sound of hooves nearby, coming closer, and Jack spun around and stared into the face of a horse, in glowing armor. Above it an armed man in a winged helmet, shouting at him in what he now recognized as Polish, holding up some reins. The reins belonged to a second horse, a *cheval de bataille,* also richly armored and saddled, but in a wholly different style, adorned with crescents rather than crosses, and boxlike metal stirrups. It must be the warhorse of some Turkish lord. The Winged Hussar was thrusting its reins toward Jack and bellowing orders in his thick, sneering language. Jack reached out and accepted a fistful of reins.

Now what? Did this Polish lord want Jack to mount the other horse and ride with him through the camp? Not likely! He was pointing at the ground, repeating the same words over and over until Jack nodded, pretending to understand. Finally he drew his sword and pointed it at Jack's chest and said something very impolite and galloped away.

Jack now understood: this Winged Hussar had very grand ambitions for the day's looting. He had found this horse early in the day. It was a prize worth keeping, but it would only hinder him if he tried to lead it around. If he tied it to a tree it would be looted by someone else. So he had looked for an armed peasant (to him, anyone on foot would be a peasant) and enlisted him as a sort of flesh-and-blood hitching-post. Jack's job was to stand still holding these reins until the Winged Hussar came back—all day if need be.

Jack had scarcely had time to reflect on the fundamental unsoundness of this plan when a beast darted out of the smoke, headed right for him, then changed direction and ran past. It was the strangest thing Jack had ever seen, certainly one for the Book of Revelation: two-legged, feathered, therefore, arguably, a bird. But taller than a man, and apparently not capable of flight. It ran in the gait of a chicken, pecking the air with each stride to keep its balance. Its neck was as long and bare as Jack's arm and as wrinkled as his Jolly Roger.

A small mob of infantrymen came running after it.

Now, Jack did not have the faintest idea what the giant trotting bird (supposing it was a bird) was. It hadn't occurred to him to chase it, except perhaps out of curiosity. And yet the sight of other men chasing it, working so hard, with such desperate looks on their faces, gave him a powerful urge to do the same. They must be chasing it for a reason. It must be worth something, or else good to eat.

The bird had gone by very fast, easily out-loping the scrambling, miserably shod pursuers. They'd never catch it. On the other hand, Jack was holding the reins of a horse, and (he began to notice) a magnificent horse it was, with a saddle the likes he'd never seen, decorated in golden thread.

It probably had not even occurred to that Winged Hussar that Jack would know how to ride. In his part of the world, a serf could no more ride on horseback than he could speak Latin or dance a minuet. And disobeying the command of an armed lord was even less likely than riding around on a horse.

But Jack was not Polish scum of the earth, barefoot and chained to the land, or even French scum of the earth, in wooden clogs and in thrall to the priest and the tax-farmer, but English scum of the earth in good boots, equipped with certain God-given rights that were (as rumor had it) written down in a Charter somewhere, and armed with a loaded gun.

He mounted the horse like a lord, spun it round smartly, reached back and slapped it on the ass, and he was off. In a few moments he had ridden through the middle of that knot of men who were hoping to catch the giant bird. Their only hope had been that their prey would forget that it was being chased, and stop running. Jack had no intention of letting that happen and so he jabbed his boot-heels into his mount's sides and lit out after the bird in a way that was calculated to make it run like hell. Which it did, and Jack galloped after it, far outdistancing his competition. But the bird was astoundingly swift. As it ran, its wings splayed this way and that like an acrobat's balancing-pole. Seeing into those wings from behind, Jack was reminded of decorations he'd seen in the hats of fine French gentlemen, and their mistresses, during military parades: those were the plumes of the, what's it called the, the . . . the ostrich.

The reason for this merry chase was plain now: the ostrich, if caught, could be plucked, and its plumes taken to markets where fine things from exotic lands were sold, and exchanged for silver.

Now, Jack calculated. If he scoured the entire Turkish camp, he might find finer things to loot—but the legions of Christendom were all running wild through this place and others were likely to have found them first. The finest things of all would be taken by lords on horseback, and the musketeers and pikemen would be left to brawl over trifles. The plumes of this ostrich were not the finest prize to be had in this camp, but a bird in the hand was worth two in the bush, and this one was almost in his hand. Ostrich-plumes were small and light, easy to conceal from the prying fingers and eyes of customs men, no burden to carry all the way across Europe if need be. And as the chase continued, his odds only improved, because this ostrich was speeding away from all noise and commotion, tending toward parts of the Grand Turk's camp where nothing was going on. If only it would hold still long enough for him to bring it down with a musket-shot.

The ostrich flailed, squawked, and vanished. Jack reined

in his mount and proceeded carefully, and arrived at the lip of a trench. He hadn't the faintest idea where he was, but this trench looked like a big one. He nudged the horse forward, expecting it to balk, but it cheerfully set to work, planting its hooves carefully in the loose earth of the trench's sloping wall and picking its way down. Jack saw fresh ostrich prints in the muck on the bottom, and set the horse to trotting that direction.

Every few yards a smaller trench intersected this one at right-angles. None of these trenches had the palisades of sharpened outward-pointing sticks that the Turks would've installed if they'd been expecting an attack, and so Jack reckoned that these trenches did not belong to the camp's *outer* works, which had been put up to defend it from encircling armies of Christians. These trenches must, instead, be part of the assault against Vienna. The smoke and dust were such that Jack could not see whether the city was ahead of, or behind, him and the ostrich. But by looking at the way that the earth had been piled up to one side of those trenches, to protect the inhabitants from musketballs, any fool could make out in which direction the city lay. The ostrich was going towards Vienna, and so was Jack.

The walls of the big trench steadily became higher and steeper, to the point where they'd had to be shored up with pilings and retaining walls of split logs. Then all of a sudden the walls curved together above him, forming an arch. Jack reined the horse in and stared forward into a dark tunnel, large enough for two or three horsemen to ride abreast. It was cut into the foundation of a steep hill that rose abruptly from generally flat land. Through a momentary parting in the drifting clouds of smoke, Jack looked up and saw the mutilated face of the great bastion looming up above him, and glimpsed the high roof of the Emperor's Palace beyond and above that.

This must be a mine, an enormous one, that the Turks had dug beneath the bastion in the hopes of blowing it to kingdom come. The tunnel floor had been paved with logs that had been mostly driven down into the mud by the weight of

oxen and wagons as they hauled dirt out, and gunpowder in.
In the mud, Jack could see ostrich-prints. Why should that
bird settle for merely burying its head in the sand when it
could go wholly underground, and not even have to bend
over? Jack did not love the idea of following it, but the die
was cast; loot-wise, it was the ostrich or nothing.

As one would expect in any well-organized mining opera-
tion, torches were available near the entrance, soaking head-
down in a pot of oil. Jack grabbed one, shoved it into the
coals of a dying fire until flames emerged, then rode his
horse forward into the tunnel.

It had been carefully timbered to keep it from collapsing.
The tunnel descended gently for some distance, until it
pierced the water table and became a sort of unpleasant
mire, and then it began to climb again. Jack saw lights burning ahead of him. He noticed that the floor of the tunnel was
striped with a bright line of steaming blood. This triggered
what little Jack had in the way of prudent instincts: he threw
the torch into a puddle and nudged the horse along at a slow
walk.

The lights ahead of him illuminated a space larger than
the tunnel: a room that had been excavated, deep underneath—where? Thinking back on the last few minutes' ride,
Jack understood that he had covered a considerable distance—he must have passed all the way beneath the bastion—at least as far as the city's inner wall. And as he drew
closer to the lights (several large torchières), he could see
that the Turks' tunnel-work, and its supporting timbers, were
all involved with things that had been planted in the earth
hundreds of years ago: tarred pilings, driven in one alongside the next, and footings of mortared stone and of brick.
The Turks had burrowed straight through the foundations of
something enormous.

Following the rivulet of blood into the illuminated space,
Jack saw a few small, bright, billowing tents that had been
pitched, for some unfathomable Turkish reason, in the middle of this chamber. Some were standing, others had collapsed into the dirt. A pair of men were striking those gay

tents with curt sword-blows. The ostrich stood to one side, cocking its head curiously. The tents tumbled to the floor with blood flying out of them.

There were people in those tents! They were being executed, one by one.

It would be easy to kill the ostrich here with a musket-shot, but this would certainly draw the attention of those Turkish executioners. They were formidable-looking fellows with handsome sabers, the only Turks Jack had laid eyes on today who were actually alive, and the only ones who were in any condition to conduct violence against Christians. He preferred to leave them be.

A saber struck at the top of one of those colorful tents, and a woman screamed. A second blow silenced her.

So, they were all women. Probably one of those famous harems. Jack wondered, idly, whether the mudlarks of East London would ever believe him if he went home and claimed he had seen a live ostrich, and a Turk's harem.

But thoughts of this sort were chased away by others. One of those moments had arrived: Jack had been presented with the opportunity to be stupid in some way that was much more interesting than being shrewd would've been. These moments seemed to come to Jack every few days. They almost never came to Bob, and Bob marveled that two brothers, leading similar lives, could be so different that one of them had the opportunity to be reckless and foolish all the time while the other almost never did. Jack had been expecting such a moment to arrive today. He'd supposed, until moments ago, that it had already come: namely, when he decided to mount the horse and ride after the ostrich. But here was a rare opportunity for stupidity even more flagrant and glorious.

Now, Bob, who'd been observing Jack carefully for many years, had observed that when these moments arrived, Jack was almost invariably possessed by something that Bob had heard about in Church called the Imp of the Perverse. Bob was convinced that the Imp of the Perverse rode invisibly on

Jack's shoulder whispering bad ideas into his ear, and that the only counterbalance was Bob himself, standing alongside, counseling good sense, prudence, caution, and other Puritan virtues.*

But Bob was in England.

"Might as well get this over with, then," Jack muttered, and gave his Turkish steed some vigorous heel-digs, and galloped forward. One of the Turks was just raising his saber to strike down the last of the tent-wearing women. And he would've done just that, except that this woman suddenly darted away (as much as a person in such a garment could dart), forcing a postponement of the attack. He shuffled forward—directly into the path of Jack and Jack's horse. They simply rode the Turk down. It was clear that the horse was well-trained in this maneuver—Jack made a mental note to treat the animal kindly.

Then with one hand Jack gave a stiff tug on a rein while unslinging his musket from the opposite shoulder. The horse wheeled around, giving Jack a view of the ground he'd just ridden over. One of the Turks was flattened into the ground, crushed in two or three places under the horse's hooves, and the other was actually striding towards Jack and sort of wiggling his saber in the way of a man limbering up his wrist for a display of swordsmanship. Not wanting to see any such thing, Jack aimed his musket carefully at this Turk and pulled the trigger. The Turk stared calmly into Jack's eyes, up the barrel of the weapon. He had brown hair and green eyes and a bushy mustache flecked with gold, all of which vanished in a smoky flash when the powder in the pan ignited. But the musket did not kick. He heard the *foosh* of the flash in the pan, but not the *boom* of the barrel.

This was known as a hang fire. The fire in the pan had not traveled into the barrel—perhaps the touch-hole had become blocked by a bit of dirt. Nonetheless, Jack kept the weapon

---

*Not that Bob was a Puritan—far from it—but he was known to talk that way, to demonstrate his superiority over Jack.

aimed in the general direction of the Turk (which involved some guesswork because the Turk was hidden behind the cloud of smoke from the pan). There might still be a slow fire working its way through the touch-hole—the musket was likely to fire, without warning, at any point during the next couple of minutes.

By the time Jack could see again, the Turk had grabbed the horse's bridle with one hand and raised the other to strike. Jack, peering out sidelong through burning eyes, wheeled his musket about to make some kind of barrier between him and the bloody saber and felt a mighty shock when the two weapons connected, instantly followed by a hot blast that knocked his hands apart and spat metal into his face. The horse reared up. Under other circumstances, Jack might've been ready for this. As it was, blind, shocked, and burnt, he performed a reverse-somersault down the animal's muscular ass, plunged to the ground, and then rolled away blindly, terrified that the hind hooves might come down on top of him.

At no time during these acrobatics did Jack stop holding the stock of the musket very firmly with his right hand. He staggered up, realized his eyes were clenched shut, buried his face in the crook of his left arm, and tried to wipe away the heat and pain. The raw feel of his sleeve against his eyelids told him that he had been burnt, but not badly. He took the arm away and opened his eyes, then spun around like a drunk, trying to bring the enemy in view. He raised his musket again, to defend himself from any more sword-blows. But it moved far too easily. The weapon had been broken in half only a few inches past the flintlock—a yard of barrel was simply gone.

The female in the tent had already stepped forward and seized the horse's reins and was now speaking to it in soothing tones. Jack couldn't see the second Turk at all, which panicked him for a moment, until he finally saw him on the ground, arms wrapped around his face, rolling from side to side and making muffled cries. That much was good, but the situation was, in general, not satisfactory: Jack had lost his weapon to some sort of accident, and his mount to some Saracen female, and had not acquired any loot yet.

He ran forward to seize the horse's reins, but a glitter on the ground caught his eye: the Turk's sword. Jack snatched it up, then shouldered the woman out of the way, mounted the horse again, and got it turned around to where he could keep a good eye on matters. Where was the damned ostrich? Over there—cornered. Jack rode over to it, cutting the air a few times to learn the balance of the saber. Striking heads off, from the back of a moving horse, was normally a job for highly trained specialists, but only because the neck of a man was a small target. Decapitating an ostrich, which consisted almost entirely of neck, was almost too easy to be satisfying. Jack did the deed with one swift backhand slash. The head fell into the dirt and lay there, eyes open, making swallowing motions. The rest of the ostrich fell down, then climbed up and began to stalk around the chamber with blood spraying out of its severed neck. It fell down frequently. Jack did not especially want to get blood sprayed on him and so he guided the horse away from the bird—but the bird changed direction and came after him! Jack rode the other way and the ostrich once again changed tack and plotted an intercept course.

The woman was laughing at him. Jack glared at her. She stifled herself. Then a voice came out of that tent, saying something in a barbarian tongue. Jack circumvented another blind ostrich-charge, moving the horse around smartly.

"Sir knight, I know none of the tongues of Christendom, save French, English, Qwghlmian, and a dash of Hungarian."

It was the first time that Jack Shaftoe had been called "sir" or mistaken for a knight. He glared meanly at the ostrich, which was staggering around in circles and losing the strength to stand. The woman had meanwhile switched into yet another strange language. Jack interrupted her: "My Qwghlmian is rusty," he announced. "Wandered up to Gttr Mnhrbgh once when I was a boy, as we'd heard a rumor that a Spanish Treasure-Galleon had been wrecked, and pieces of eight scattered up and down the shore, as thick as mussels. But all we found was a few drunken Frenchmen, stealing the chickens and burning the houses."

He was prepared to relate many more dramatic details, but at this point he faltered because there'd been a violent shifting-around of the contents of the tent, exposing, up towards its summit, a complex arrangement of silk handkerchiefs: one tied over the bridge of the nose, hiding everything below, and another tied round the forehead, hiding everything above. Between them, a slit through which a pair of eyes was looking up at him. They were blue eyes. "You are an Englishman!" she exclaimed.

Jack noted that this one was not preceded by a "Sir knight." To begin with, Englishmen were not accorded the respect given naturally to the men of great countries, such as France or Poland-Lithuania. Among Englishmen, Jack's way of speaking, of course, marked him out as No Gentleman. But even if he spoke like an Archbishop, from the nature of the yarn he'd just been relating to her, concerning his scavenging-trip to Qwghlm, it was now obvious that he *had been* at some point an actual Vagabond. Damn it! Not for the first time, Jack imagined cutting his own tongue out. His tongue was admired by that small fraction of mankind who, owing to some want of dignity or wit, were willing to let it be known that they admired any part of Jack Shaftoe. And yet if he had merely held it back, reined it in, this blue-eyed woman might still be addressing him as Sir Knight.

That part of Jack Shaftoe that, up until this point in his life, had kept him alive, counseled him to pull sharply on one rein or the other, wheel the horse around, and gallop away from Trouble here. He looked down at his hands, holding those reins, and noted that they failed to move—evidently, the part of Jack that sought a merry and short life was once again holding sway.

Puritans came frequently to Vagabond-camps bearing the information that at the time of the creation of the Universe—thousands of years ago!—certain of those present had been predestined by God to experience salvation. The rest of them were doomed to spend eternity burning in hell-fire. This intelligence was called, by the Puritans, the Good News. For days, after the Puritans had been chased away, any Vagabond boy who farted would claim that the event had been foreordained by the Almighty, and enrolled in a cœlestial Book, at the dawn of time. All in good fun. But now here Jack Shaftoe sat astride a Turkish charger, willing his hands to pull one rein or the other, willing his boot-heels to dig into the sides of the beast, so that it would carry him away from this woman, but nothing happened. It must have been the Good News at work.

The blue eyes were downcast. "I thought you were a Knight at first," she said.

"What, in these rags?"

"But the horse is magnificent, and it blocks my view somewhat," Trouble said. "The way you fought those Janissaries—like a Galahad."

"Galahad—he's the one who never got laid?" Again with the tongue. Again the sense that his movements were predestined, that his body was a locked carriage running out of control down a hill, directly towards the front entrance of Hell.

"That is one of the few things that *I* have in common with that legendary Knight."

"No!"

"I was *gozde,* which means that the Sultan had taken note of me; but before I was made *ikbal* which means bedded, he gave me to the Grand Vizier."

"Now I am not a learned fellow," said Jack Shaftoe, "but from what little I know of the habits of Turkish Viziers, it is not usual for them to keep beautiful, saucy young blonde slaves about their camps—*as virgins.*"

"Not forever. But there is something to be said for saving a few virgins up to celebrate a special occasion—such as the sacking of Vienna."

"But wouldn't there be plenty of virgins to be rustled in Vienna?"

"From the tales told by the secret agents that the Wazir

sent into the city, he feared that there would be none at all."

Jack was inclined to be suspicious. But it was no less plausible for the Vizier, or the Wazir as Blue Eyes called him, to have English virgins than it was for him to have ostriches, giant bejeweled cats, and potted fruit-trees. "These soldiers haven't gotten to you?" asked Jack. He waved the saber around at the dead Turks, inadvertently flicking bullets of blood from the tip.

"They are Janissaries."

"I've heard of 'em," Jack said. "At one point I considered going to Constantinople, or whatever they're calling it now, and joining 'em."

"But what about their Oath of Celibacy?"

"Oh, that makes no difference to me, Blue Eyes—look." He was struggling with his codpiece.

"A Turk would already be finished," the woman said, patiently observing. "They have, in the front of their trousers, a sort of sally-port, to expedite pissing and raping."

"I'm no Turk," he said, finally rising up in the stirrups to afford her a clear view.

"Is it supposed to look like that?"

"Oh, you're a sly one."

"What happened?"

"A certain barber-surgeon in Dunkirk put out the word that he had learnt a cure for the French Pox from a traveling alchemist. My mates and I—we had just got back from Jamaica—went there one night—"

"You had the French Pox?"

"I only wanted a beard trim," Jack said. "My mate Tom Flinch had a bad finger that needed removal. It had bent the wrong way during a naval engagement with French privateers, and begun to smell so badly that no one would sit near him, and he had to take his meals abovedecks. That was why we went, and that was why we were drunk."

"I beg your pardon?"

"We had to get Tom drunk so he'd make less of a fuss when the finger went flying across the barber-shop. The rules of etiquette stated that we must therefore be as drunk as he."

"Pray continue."

"But when we learned that this Barber could also cure the French Pox, why, codpieces were flying around the place like cannonballs."

"So you did have the said Pox."

"So this barber, whose eyes had gotten as big as doubloons, stoked up his brazier and began to heat the irons. While he was performing the amputation of Tom Flinch's digit, the irons were waxing red- and then yellow-hot. Meantimes his young apprentice was mixing up a poultice of herbs, as dictated by the alchemist. Well, to make a long story short, I was the last of the group to have the afflicted member cauterized. My mates were all lying in a heap on the floor, holding poultices over their cocks and screaming, having completed the treatment. The barber and his apprentice tied me into the chair with a large number of stout lines and straps, and jammed a rag into my mouth—"

"They robbed you!?"

"No, no, missy, this was all part of the treatment. Now, the afflicted part of my member—the spot that needed cauterizing, you understand—was on the top, about halfway along. But my Trouser-Snake was all shrunk into m'self by this point, from fear. So the apprentice grasped the tip of my Johnson with a pair of tongs and stretched old One-Eyed Willie out with one hand—holding a candle with the other so that the site of the disease was plainly visible. Then the barber rummaged in his brazier and chose just the right sort of iron—methinks they were all the same, but he wanted to put on a great show of discretion, to justify his price. Just as the barber was lowering the glowing iron into position, what should happen but the tax-man and his deputies smashed down both front and back door at the same instant. 'Twas a raid. Barber dropped the iron."

"'Tis very sad—a strapping fellow such as you—strong and shapely—buttocks like the shell-halves of an English

walnut—a fine set of calves—handsome, after a fashion—
never to have children."

"Oh, the barber was too late—I already have two little
boys—that's why I'm chasing ostriches and killing Janissaries—got a family to support. And as I still have the
French Pox, there's only a few years left before I go crazy
and die. So now's the time for building up a handsome
legacy."

"Your wife is lucky."

"My wife is dead."

"Too bad."

"Nah, I didn't love her," Jack said bravely, "and after the
Barber dropped the iron I'd no practical use for her. Just as I
have no practical use for you, Trouble."

"How do you suppose?"

"Well, just take a look. I can't do it."

"Maybe not as the English do. But certain arts have been
taught to me from Books of India."

Silence.

"I've never had high regard for book-learning," Jack said,
his voice sounding a bit as though a noose were drawing
tight around his neck. "Give me practical experience any
day."

"I have that, too."

"Aha, but you said you were a virgin?"

"I did my practicing on women."

"What!?"

"You don't think the entire harem just sits around waiting
for the master to stiffen up?"

"But what's the point—what is the very *meaning*—of doing it when there is no penis available?"

"It is a question you might even have asked yourself," said
Blue Eyes.

Jack had the feeling now—hardly for the first time—that a
Change of Subject was urgently called for. He said, "I know
that you were lying when you said that I was handsome,
when really I'm quite bashed, gouged, pox-marked, rope-
burned, weather-tanned, and so on."

"Some women like it," Blue Eyes said, and actually batted her eyelashes. Her eyes, and a few patches of skin in their vicinity, were the only parts of her that Jack could actually see, and this magnified the effect.

It was important that he put up some kind of defense. "You look very young," he said, "and you talk like a girl who is in need of a spanking."

"Books of India," she said coolly, "have entire chapters about that."

Jack began riding the horse around the chamber, inspecting its walls. Scraping away packed earth with one hand, he observed the staves of a barrel, branded with Turkish letters, and with more digging and scraping he found more barrels stacked around it—a whole cache of them, jammed into a niche in the chamber wall and mortared together with dirt.

In the center of the chamber was a pile of timbers and planks where the Turkish carpenters had built the reinforcements to prevent the chamber from caving in. Diverse tools were strewn around, wherever the Turks had dropped them when they'd decided to flee. "Here, make yourself useful, lass, and bring me that axe," Jack said.

Blue Eyes brought him the axe, staring him coolly in the eyes as she handed it over. Jack rose in the stirrups and swung it round so it bit into one of those Turkish kegs. A stave crumpled. Another blow, and the wood gave way entirely, and black powder poured out and hissed onto the ground.

"We're in the cellar of that Palace," Jack said. "Directly above us is the Court of the Holy Roman Emperor, and all around us are his vaults, full of treasure. Do you know what we could get, if we touched this off?"

"Premature deafness?"

"I intend to plug my ears."

"Tons of rock and earth collapsing atop us?"

"We can lay a powder-trail up the tunnel, put fire to it, and watch from a safe distance."

"You don't think that the sudden explosion and collapse of the Holy Roman Emperor's Palace will draw some attention?"

" 'Twas just an idea."

"If you do that, you're going to lose me, brother . . . besides, that is not how you become ennobled. Blowing a hole in the palace floor and slinking in like a rat, with smoke coming out of your clothes . . ."

"I'm supposed to take advice on ennoblement from a *slave*?"

"A slave who has lived in palaces."

"How would you propose to do it, then? If you're so clever—let's hear your plan."

The blue eyes rolled. "Who is noble?"

Jack shrugged. "Noblemen."

"How do most of them get that way?"

"By having noble parents."

"Oh. Really."

"Of course. Is it different in Turkish courts?"

"No different. But from the way you were talking, I thought that, in the courts of Christendom, it had something to do with being clever."

"I don't believe it has any connection at all to cleverness," Jack said, and prepared to relate a story about Charles the Elector Palatine. But before he could do this, Blue Eyes asked:

"Then we don't need a clever plan *at all*, do we?"

"This is an idle conversation, lass, but I am an idle man, and so I don't mind it. You say we do not need any clever plan to become ennobled. But we lack noble birth—so how do you propose to become noble?"

"It's easy. You buy your way in."

"That requires money."

"Let's get out of this hole and get us some money, then."

"How do you propose to do that?"

"I'll need an escort," the slave-girl said. "You have a horse and a sword."

"Blue Eyes, this is a battlefield. Many do. Find a knight."

"I'm a slave," she said. "A knight will take what he wants and then leave me."

"So it's matrimony you're after?"

"Some kind of partnership. Needn't be matrimonial."

"I'm to ride in front, slaying Janissaries, dragons, knights, and you'll tag behind and do—what, exactly? And don't speak to me about Books of India any more."

"I'll handle the money."

"But we have no money."

"That is why you need someone to handle it."

Jack didn't follow, but it sounded clever, and so he nodded sagely, as if he'd taken her meaning very clearly. "What's your name?"

"Eliza."

Rising in his stirrups, doffing his hat, and bowing slightly at the waist. "And I am Half-Cocked Jack at the lady's service."

"Find me a Christian man's clothes. The bloodier the better. I'll pluck the bird."

Erstwhile Camp of Grand Vizier Khan Mustapha

❧

"AND ANOTHER THING——" JACK SAID.

"What, yet *another*!?" said Eliza, in an officer's bloody coat, her head swaddled in ripped shirts, slumped over in the saddle so that her head wasn't far from that of Jack, who was directing the horse.

"If we make it as far as Paris—and that's by no means easily done—and if you've given me so much as a blink of trouble—one cross look, one wifely crossing of the arms—cutting thespian-like asides, delivered to an imaginary audience—"

"Have you had many women, Jack?"

"—pretending to be shocked by what's perfectly normal—calculated moods—slowness to get underway—murky complaints about female trouble—"

"Now that you mention it, Jack, this *is* my time of the month and I need you to stop right here in the middle of the battlefield for, oh, half an hour should suffice—"

"Not funny at all. Do I look amused?"

"You look like the inside of a handkerchief."

"Then I'll inform you that I don't look amused. We are skirting what's left of Khan Mustapha's camp. Over to the right, captive Turks stand in file in a trench, crossing themselves—that's odd—"

"I can hear them, uttering Christian prayers in a Slavic

tongue—those are Janissaries, most likely Serbs. Like the ones you saved me from."

"Can you hear the cavalry-sabers whipping into their necks?"

"Is *that* what that is?"

"Why d'you think they're praying? Those Janissaries are being put to the sword by Polish hussars."

"But why?"

"Ever stumble into a very old family dispute? It wears that face. Some kind of ancient grievance. Some Janissaries must've done something upsetting to some Poles a hundred years ago."

Echelons of cavalry traversed the ruins of the Grand Vizier's camp like ripples snapped across a bedsheet. Though 'twere best not to begin thinking of bedsheets. "What was I just saying?"

"Oh, you were adding another codicil to our partnership agreement. Just like some Vagabond-lawyer."

"That's another thing—"

"*Yet still* another?"

"Don't call me a Vagabond. I may call *myself* one, from time to time, as a little joke—to break the ice, charm the ladies, or whatnot. All in good fun. But you must never direct that notorious epithet my way." Jack noticed that with one hand he was rubbing the base of the other hand's thumb, where a red-hot iron, shaped like a letter V, had once been pressed against his flesh, and held down for a while, leaving a mark that itched sometimes. "But to return to what I was trying to say, before all of your uncouth interruptions—the slightest trouble from you, lass, and I'll abandon you in Paris."

"Oh, horror! Anything but that, cruel man!"

"You're as naïve as a rich girl. Don't you know that in Paris, any woman found on her own will be arrested, cropped, whipped, *et cetera,* by that Lieutenant of Police— King Looie's puissant man, who has an exorbitant scope of powers—a most cruel oppressor of beggars and Vagabonds."

"But you'd know nothing of Vagabonds, O lordly gentleman."

"Better, but still not good."

"Where do you get this stuff like 'notorious epithet' and 'exorbitant scope' and 'puissant'?"

"The thyuhtuh, my dyuh."

"You're an actor?"

"An actor? An *actor*!?" A promise to spank her later was balanced on the tip of his tongue like a ball on a seal's nose, but he swallowed it for fear she'd come back at him with some flummoxing utterance. "Learn manners, child. Sometimes Vagabonds *might*, if in a generous Christian humour, allow actors to follow them around at a respectful distance."

"Forgive me."

"Are you rolling your eyes, under those bandages? I can tell, you know—but soft! An officer is nearby. Judging from heraldry, a Neapolitan count with at least three instances of bastardy in his ancestral line."

Following the cue, Eliza, who fortunately had a deep, unsettlingly hoarse alto, commenced moaning.

"Monsieur, monsieur," Jack said to her, in attempted French, "I know the saddle must pain those enormous black swellings that have suddenly appeared in your groin the last day or two, since you bedded that pair of rather ill-seeming Gypsy girls against my advice—but we must get you to a Surgeon-Barber, or, failing that, a Barber-Surgeon, so that the Turkish ball can be dug out of your brains before there are any more of those shuddering and twitching fits . . ." and so on until the Neapolitan count had retreated.

This led to a long pause during which Jack's mind wandered—though, in retrospect, Eliza's apparently *didn't*.

"Jack, is it safe to talk?"

"For a man, talking to a woman is never precisely safe. But we are out of the camp now, I no longer have to step over occasional strewn body-parts, the Danube is off to the right, Vienna rises beyond that. Men are spreading out to set up camp, queuing before heavily guarded wagons to receive their pay for the day's work—yes, safe as it'll ever be."

"Wait! When will *you* get paid, Jack?"

"Before the battle we were issued rations of brandy, and

worthless little scraps of paper with what I take to've been letters inscribed on them, to be redeemed (or so the Captain claimed) in silver at the end of the day. They did not fool Jack Shaftoe. I sold mine to an industrious Jew."

"How much did you get for it?"

"I drove an excellent bargain. A bird in the hand is worth two in the—"

"You got only *fifty percent*!?"

"Not so bad, is it? Think, I'm only getting half of the proceeds from those ostrich plumes—*because of you*."

"Oh, Jack. How do you suppose it makes me feel when you say such things?"

"What, am I speaking too loudly? Hurting your ears?"

"No . . ."

"Need to adjust your position?"

"No, no, Jack, I'm not speaking of my *body's* feelings."

"Then what the hell are you on about?"

"And, when you say 'one funny look and I'll drop you off among the Poles who brand runaway serfs on the forehead' or 'just wait until King Looie's Lieutenant of Police gets his hands on you . . .'"

"You're only cherry-picking the worst ones," Jack complained. "Mostly I've just threatened to drop you off at nunneries and the like."

"So you *do* admit that threatening to brand me is more cruel than threatening to make me into a nun."

"That's obvious. But—"

"But why be cruel to *any* degree, Jack?"

"Oh, excellent trick. I'll have to remember it. Now who is playing the Vagabond-lawyer?"

"Is it that you feel worried that, perhaps, you erred in salvaging me from the Janissaries?"

"What kind of conversation is this? What place do you come from, where people actually care about how everyone feels about things? What possible bearing could anyone's feelings have on anything that makes a bloody difference?"

"Among harem-slaves, what is there to pass the long hours of the day, except to practice womanly arts, such as sewing, embroidery, and the knotting of fine silk threads into elaborate lace undergarments—"

"Avast!"

"—to converse and banter in diverse languages (which does not go unless close attention is paid to the other's feelings). To partake of schemes and intrigues, to haggle in souks and bazaars—"

"You've already boasted of your prowess there."

"—"

"Was there something else you were going to mention, girl?"

"Well—"

"Out with it!"

"Only what I alluded to before: using all the most ancient and sophisticated practices of the Oriental world to slowly drive one another into frenzied, sweaty, screaming transports of concupiscent—"

"That's quite enough!"

"You asked."

"You led me to ask—schemes and intrigues, indeed!"

"Second nature to me now, I'm afraid."

"What of your first nature, then? No one could look more English."

"It is fortunate my dear mother did not hear that. She took extravagant pride in our heritage—pure Qwghlmian."

"Unadulterated mongrel, then."

"Not a drop of English blood—nor of Celtic, Norse, or what-have-you."

"A hundred percent what-have-you is more likely. At what age were you abducted, then?"

"Five."

"You know your age very clearly," Jack said, impressed. "Of a noble family, are you?"

"Mother maintains that all Qwghlmians—"

"Stay. I already know your ma better than I knew mine. What do you *remember* of Qwghlm?"

"The door of our dwelling, glowing warmly by the light of a merry guano-fire, and all hung about with curious picks and hatchets so that Daddy could chip us out of the place after one of those late June ice-storms, so vigorous and bracing. A clifftop village of simple honest folk who'd light bonfires on moonless nights to guide mariners to safety—Jack, why the noises? Phlegmatical trouble of some kind?"

"They light those fires to *lure* the mariners."

"Why, to trade with them?"

"So that they'll run aground and spill their cargoes on Caesar's Reef, or Viking's Grief, or Saracen's Doom, or Frenchie's Bones, or the Galleon-Gutter, or Dutch-Hammer, or any of the other Hazards to Navigation for which your home is ill-famed."

"Aah—" Eliza said, in melodious tones that nearly struck Jack dead on his feet, "puts a new light on some of their other practices."

"Such as?"

"Going out in the night with great big long knives to 'put stranded sailors out of their suffering . . .'"

"At their own request, I'm sure?"

"Aye, and coming back with chests and bales of goods offered as payment for the service. Yes, Jack, your explanation's much more reasonable—how lovely of my sainted Mummy to shield my tender ears from this awkward truth."

"Now, then, d'you understand why the Kings of England have long suffered—nay, encouraged, and possibly even bribed—the Barbary Corsairs to raid Qwghlm?"

"It was the second week of August. Mother and I were walking on the beach—"

"Wait, you've *beaches* there?"

"In memory, all is golden—perhaps it was a mud-flat. Yes, it was on the way to Snowy Rock, which gleamed a radiant white—"

"Ha! Even in summer?"

"Not with snow. 'Twas the gifts of seagulls, by which Qwghlm is ever nourished. Mother and I had our slx and sktl—"

"Again?"

"The former is a combined hammering, chopping, scraping, and poking tool consisting of an oyster shell lashed to a thigh-bone."

"Why not use a stick?"

"Englishmen came and took all of the trees. The sktl is a hopper or bucket. We were halfway out to the Rock when we became conscious of a rhythm. Not the accustomed pounding of mountainous waves on jagged rocks—this was faster, sharper, deeper—a beating of savage African drums! North-, not Sub-Saharan, but African anyway, and not typical of the area. Qwghlmian music makes very little use of percussion—"

"It being difficult to make drum-heads of rat-hides."

"We turned towards the sun. Out on the cove—a wrinkled sheet of hammered gold—a shadow like a centipede, its legs swinging fore and aft to the beating of the drum—"

"Wait, a giant bug was walking on water?"

"'Twas a many-oared coastal raiding-galley of the Barbary Corsairs. We tried to run back towards the shore, but the mud sucked at our bare feet so avidly that we had skwsh for a week thereafter—"

"Skwsh?"

"Heel-hickeys. The pirates launched a long-boat and ran it up on the mud-flat before us, cutting off our escape. Several men—turbaned silhouettes so strange and barbarous to my young eyes—vaulted out and made for us. One of them went straight into quicksand—"

"Haw! Stop! Now, that, as we say in Wapping, is Entertainment!"

"Only a Qwghlmian born and bred could have found her way across that flat without perishing. In a trice, he'd sunk down to his neck and was thrashing about in exactly the wrong way, hollering certain key verses of the Holy Qur'an."

"And your mother said, 'We could escape now, but we have a Christian duty to this poor sailor; we must sacrifice our freedom to save his life' and you stayed there to help him out."

"No, Mummy said something more like, 'We could try to

struggle away through all of this mud, but those darkies have muskets—so I'll pretend to stay behind to help that stupid wog—maybe we can rack up some brown-nosing points.'"

"What a woman!"

"She commandeered an oar and extended it to the trapped sailor. Seeing she'd found solid footing, others made bold to leave the boat and haul this fellow in. Mummy and I were then subjected to a curious sniffing procedure administered by an officer who did not speak English, but who made it plain, by his posture and expressions, that he was embarrassed and apologetic. We were taken aboard the long-boat and then to the galley, and then rowed out to a rendezvous with a forty-gun pirate-galleon cruising offshore. Not some ramshackle barge but a proper ship of the line, captured or perhaps bought, leased, or borrowed from a European navy."

"Where your mother was cruelly used by horny Mahometans."

"Oh, no. These men seemed to be of that sort who only desire women for that which they have in common with men."

"What—eyebrows?"

"No, no!"

"Toenails then? Because—"

"Stop it!"

"But the mercy that your Mum showed to the poor sailor was richly repaid later on, right? When, in a moment of crisis, unlooked-for, he appeared and showed her some favor, and thus saved the day—right?"

"He died a couple of days later, from bad fish, and was tossed overboard."

"Bad fish? On a *ship*? In the *ocean*? I thought those Mussulmen were ever so particular about their victuals."

"He didn't eat it—just touched it while preparing a meal."

"Why would anyone—"

"Don't ask me," Eliza said, "ask the mysterious Personage who subjected my Mummy to his unnatural vice."

"I thought you said—"

"You asked me if she'd been used *by Mahometans*. The

Personage was not a Mahometan. Or a Jew. Or any other sort that practices circumcision."

"Er—"

"Would you like to stop, so that I can draw you a picture?"

"No. What sort of man was he, then?"

"Unknown. He never left his cabin in that high-windowed castle at the stern of the ship. It seemed he had a fear of sunlight, or at least of tanning. When Mummy was taken into that place, that curved expanse of glass was carefully shuttered, and the curtains drawn—heavy curtains they were, in a dark green shade like the skin of the *aguacate,* which is a fruit of New Spain. But with thread of gold woven through, here and there, to produce a sparkling effect. Before my mother could react, she was thrown back against the carpet—"

"You mean, *down onto* the carpet."

"Oh, no. For the walls, and even the ceiling, of the cabin were lined, every inch of them, in carpet. Hand-knotted wool, with a most deep and luxurious pile (or so it seemed to Mummy, who'd never seen or touched a carpet before), all in a hue that recalled the gold of fields ripe for harvest—"

"I thought you said it was dark."

"She came back from these trysts with the fibers all over her. And even in the dark she could feel, with the skin of her back, that cunning artisans had sculpted the golden carpet into curious patterns."

"Doesn't sound that bad, so far—that is, by the standards of white women abducted and enslaved by Barbary Corsairs."

"I haven't gotten to the part about the smell yet."

"The world smells bad, lass. Best to hold your nose and get on with it."

"You are a child in the world of bad smells, until—"

"Excuse me. Have you ever been to Newgate Prison? Paris in August? Strasbourg after the Black Death?"

"Think about fish for a moment."

"Now you're on about fish again."

"The only food that the Personage would eat was fish that had gone bad—quite some time ago."

"That's it. No more. I'll not be made a fool of." Jack put his fingers in his ears and sang a few merry madrigal tunes with a great deal of "fa la la" material in them.

A FEW DAYS might have passed here—the road West was long. But in time she inevitably resumed. "The Barbary Corsairs were no less incredulous than you, Jack. But it was evident that the Personage was a man of tremendous power, whose wishes must be obeyed. Every day, some sailor who'd committed an infraction would be sentenced to dress the rotten fish for this man's private table. He'd drop to his knees and beg to be flogged, or keel-hauled, rather than carry out that duty. But always one would be chosen, and sent over the side, and down the ladder—"

"How's that?"

"The fish was ripened in an open long-boat towed far, far behind the ship. Once a day, it would be pulled up alongside, and the luckless sailor would be forced, at pistols drawn, to descend a rope-ladder, clutching a scrap of paper in his teeth on which was inscribed whatever receipt the Personage had selected. Then the tow-rope was hastily paid out again by a gagging team of sailors, and the chef would go to work, preparing the meal on a little iron stove in the long-boat. When he was finished, he'd wave a skull and crossbones in the air and be pulled in until he was just astern. A rope would be thrown out the windows of that gaudy castle—below, the chef would tie it to a basket containing the finished meal. The basket would be drawn up and in through the window. Later, the Personage would ring a bell and a cabin-boy would be heartily bastinadoed until he agreed to go aft to recover the china, and toss it overboard."

"Fine. The cabin smelled bad."

"Oh, this Personage tried to mask it with all the spices and aromatic gums of the East. The place was all a-dangle with small charms, cleverly made in the shape of trees, impregnated with rare perfumes. Incense glowered through the wrought-gold screens of exotic braziers, and crystalline vials of perfumed spirits, dyed the colors of tropical blossoms, sloshed about with great sodden wicks hanging out of 'em to disperse the scent into the air. All for naught, of course, for—"

"The cabin smelled bad."

"Yes. Now, to be sure, Mummy and I had noticed an off odor about the ship from about a mile out, as we were being rowed to it, and had chalked it up to the corsairs' barbarous ways and overall masculinity. We had watched the spectacle of the dinner preparation twice without understanding it. The second time, the chef—who, that day, was the very man Mummy had saved—never waved the Jolly Roger, but seemed to fall asleep in the long-boat. Efforts were made to rouse him by blowing horns and firing cannon-salvos, to no avail. Finally they pulled him in, and the ship's physician descended the rope-ladder, breathing through a compress soaked in a compound of citrus oil, myrrh, spearmint, bergamot, opium, rose-water, camphor, and anise-seed, and pronounced the poor man dead. He had nicked his hand while chopping some week-old squid-meat, and some unspeakable residue had infected his blood and slain him, like a crossbow bolt 'tween the eyes."

"Your description of the Personage's cabin was suspiciously complete and particular," Jack observed.

"Oh, I was taken there, too—after Mummy failed the sniff-test, he flew into a rage, and in desperation they offered me up as a sacrifice. He got no satisfaction from me, as I'd not, at that age, begun to exude the womanly humours that—"

"Stop. Only stop. My life, since I approached Vienna, is become some kind of Bartholomew-Fair geek-baiting."

HOURS, OR A DAY or two, might've passed.

"So, then, I suppose I'm meant to believe that you and dear Mummy were originally taken from the mud-flats simply in hopes that Mummy would pass the sniff-test."

"'Twas thought she *had* passed it—but the officer who administered that olfactory examination was deceived—his sensorium overwhelmed—by—"

"By the miasma of those Qwghlmian mud-flats and guano-mountains. My God, it is the worst thing I have ever heard—to think I feared that *you* would be appalled by *my* story." Jack waved his arms in the air, gaining the attention of an approaching friar, and shouted: "Which way is Massachusetts? I'm become a Puritan."

"Later in the voyage, finally, the Personage had his way with poor Mummy on one or two occasions, but only because no other choices were available to him, and we did not pass near any more remote settlements where women could be easily abducted."

"Well, c'mon, let's have it—what'd he do in that carpeted castle?"

Eliza then became uncharacteristically shy. Now, by this time they were several days out of Vienna. She had taken off the wounded-officer disguise and was sitting in the saddle with a blanket wrapped around her, covering the tent she'd been wearing the first time Jack had seen her. From time to time she'd offer to dismount and walk, but she was barefoot, and Jack didn't want to be slowed down. Her head, anyway, projected from a vast whorl of fabric, and Jack could therefore turn round and look at it anytime he chose. Generally he didn't, because he knew that only trouble could come of paying undue attention to that visage—its smooth symmetry, its fine set of teeth, and all of those ever-so-important Feelings flickering across it, supple and quick and mesmerizing as fire-light. But at this particular moment he did turn round to look, because her silence was so sudden that he supposed she'd been punched out of the saddle by a stray cannon-ball. She was there, gazing at some other travelers just ahead of them: four nuns.

They overtook the nuns shortly and left them behind. "Now you can say it," Jack said. But Eliza just set her jaw and gazed into the distance.

A quarter of an hour later they passed the actual nunnery. And a quarter of an hour after *that* suddenly she was back to normal, relating the details of what had gone on behind those aguacate-colored curtains on the carpet of harvest gold. Several odd practices were described—Books of India stuff, Jack suspected.

The high points of Eliza's story were, in sum, curiously synchronized with the appearance of nunneries and towns along their route. At a certain point Jack had heard all he wanted to—a bawdy tale, when told in so much detail, became monotonous, and then started to seem calculated to inspire Feelings of profound guilt and self-loathing in any male listeners who happened to be nearby.

Reviewing his memories of the last few days' journey from Vienna, Jack observed that, when they'd been in open country or forest, Eliza had kept to herself. But whenever they'd neared any kind of settlement, and especially nunneries (which were thick as fleas in this Popish land), the tongue would go into action and reach some highly interesting moment in the tale just as they were passing by the town's gate or the nunnery's door. The story would never resume until they'd passed some distance onwards.

"Next stop: the Barbary Coast. As we'd proven unsatisfactory to the Personage, we were added to the general pool of European slaves there—some tens of thousands of 'em."

"Damn, I'd no idea!"

"Their plight is ignored by all Europe!" Eliza said, and Jack realized too late he'd set her off. A torrential rant ensued. If only her head was still wrapped in those fake bandages—some tightening and knotting and his troubles would be over. Instead, by paying out the reins Jack was able to lead the noble horse, which he'd named, or re-named, Turk, from a distance, much as the Corsair-ship in Eliza's ridiculous fable had towed the unspeakable fish-boat. Snatches and fragments of the Rant occasionally drifted his way. He learned that Mummy had been sold into the harem of an Ottoman military official at the Qasbah of Algiers, and in her copious spare time had founded the Society of Britannic Abductees, which now had branches in Morocco, Tripoli, Bizerta, and Fez; which met on a fortnightly rotation except during Ramadan; which had bylaws running to several hundred pages, which Eliza had to copy out by hand on filched Ottoman stationery whenever a new chapter was founded . . .

They were close to Linz. Monasteries, nunneries, rich men's houses, and outlying towns came frequently. In the middle of Eliza's sermon about the plight of white slaves in North Africa, Jack (just to see what would happen) slowed, then stopped before the gates of an especially gloomy and dreadful Gothickal convent. Eerie Papist chanting came out of it. Suddenly Eliza was off on a new topic.

"Now, when you started that sentence," Jack observed, "you were telling me about the procedure for amending the bylaws of the Society of Britannic Abductees, but by the time you got to the end of it, you had begun telling me about what happened when the ship packed to the gunwales with Hindoostani dancing-girls ran aground near a castle of the Knights of Malta—you're not *worried* that I'm going to drop you off, or sell you to some farmer, are you?"

"Why should you care about my *feelings*?"

"Now has it never occurred to you that you might be *better off* in a nunnery?"

Clearly it *hadn't*, but now it *did*. A most lovely consternation flooded into her face, and she turned her head, slightly, toward the nunnery.

"Oh, I'll hold up my end of the partnership. Years of dangling from hanged men's feet taught me the value of honest dealings." Jack stopped talking for a moment to stifle his mirth. Then, "Yes, the advantages of being on the road with Half-Cocked Jack are many: no man is my master. I have boots. A sword, axe, and horse, too. I cannot be but chaste. Secret smugglers' roads are all known to me. I know the zargon and the code-signs of Vagabonds, who, taken together, constitute a sort of (if I may speak poetically) network of information, spreading all over the world, functioning smoothly even when damaged, by which I may know which *pays* offer safe haven and passage, and which oppress wandering persons. You could do worse."

"Why then did you say I might be better off there?" Eliza said, nodding toward the great nunnery with its wings curling around toward the road like a beetle's tongs.

"Well, some would say I should've mentioned this to you earlier, but: you've taken up with a man who can be hanged on arrival in most jurisdictions."

"Ooh, you're an infamous criminal?"

"Only some places—but that's not why."

"Why then?"

"I'm *of a particular type*. The Devil's Poor."

"Oh."

"Shames me to say it—but when I was drunk and battle-flushed I showed you my other secret and so now I've no way, I'm sure, to fall any lower in your esteem."

"What is the Devil's Poor? Are you a Satan-worshipper?"

"Only when I fall in among Satan-worshippers. Haw! No, it is an English expression. There are two kinds of poor—God's and the Devil's. God's poor, such as widows, orphans, and recently escaped white slave-girls with pert arses, can and should be helped. Devil's poor are beyond help—charity's wasted on 'em. The distinction 'tween the two categories is recognized in all civilized countries."

"Do you expect to be hanged down there?"

They'd stopped on a hill-top above the Danube's flood-plain. Linz was below. The departure of the armies had shrunk it to a tenth of its recent size, leaving a scar on the earth like the pale skin after a big scab has fallen away. "Things will be loose there just now—many discharged soldiers will be passing through. They can't all be hanged—not enough rope in Austria for that. I count half a dozen corpses hanging from trees outside the city gate, half a dozen more heads on pikes along the walls—low normal, for a town of that size."

"Let's to market, then," Eliza said, peering down into Linz's square with eyes practically shooting sparks.

"Just ride in, find the Street of Ostrich-Plume Merchants, and go from one to the next, playing 'em off against each other?"

Eliza deflated.

"That's the problem with specialty goods," Jack said.

"What's your plan then, Jack?"

"Oh, anything can be sold. In every town is a street where buyers can be found for *anything*. I make it my business to know where those streets are."

"Jack, what sort of price do you suppose we'll fetch at a thieves' market? We could not conceivably do *worse*."

"But we'll have silver in our pockets, lass."

"Perhaps the reason you're the Devil's Poor is that, having gotten something, you slip into town like a man who *expects* ill-treatment—possibly including capital punishment—and go straight to the thieves' market and sell it to a middleman's middleman's middleman."

"Please note that I am alive, free, that I have boots, most of my bodily parts—"

"And a pox that'll make you demented and kill you in a few years."

"Longer than I'd live if I went into a town like that one pretending to be a merchant."

"But my point is—as you yourself said—you need to build up a legacy for your boys *now*."

"Precisely what I just proposed," Jack said. "Unless you've a better idea?"

"We need to find a fair where we can sell the ostrich plumes directly to a merchant of fine clothes—someone who'll take them home to, say, Paris, and sell them to rich ladies and gentlemen."

"Oh, yes. Such merchants are always eager to deal with Vagabonds and slave-girls."

"Oh, Jack—that's simply a matter of dressing *up* instead of *down*."

"There are sensitive men—touchy blokes—who'd find something disparaging in that remark. But I—"

"Haven't you wondered why, whenever I move, I make all of these rustling and swishing noises?" She demonstrated.

"I'm too much the gentleman to make inquiries about the construction of your undergarments—but since you mentioned it—"

"Silk. I've about a mile of silk wrapped around me, under this black thing. Stole it from the Vizier's camp."

"Silk! I've heard of it."

"A needle, some thread, and I'll be every inch a lady."

"And what will I be? The imbecile fop?"

"My manservant and bodyguard."

"Oh, no—"

"It's just play-acting! Only while we're in the fair! The rest of the time, I'm as ever your obedient slave, Jack."

"Since I know you like to tell fables, I'll play-act with you briefly. Now begging your pardon, but doesn't it take time to sew fine costumes out of Turkish silk?"

"Jack, *many* things take time. This will only take a few weeks."

"A few weeks. And you're aware that you are now in a place that has winters? And that this is October?"

"Jack?"

"Eliza?"

"What does your zargon-network tell you of fairs?"

"Mostly they are in spring or autumn. We want the Leipzig one."

"We do?" Eliza seemed impressed. Jack was gratified by this—a bad sign. No man was more comprehensively doomed than him whose chief source of gratification was making favorable impressions on some particular woman.

"Yes, because it is where goods of the East, coming out of Russia and Turkey, are exchanged for goods of the West."

"For silver, more likely—no one wants Western stuff."

"That's correct, actually. Your elder Vagabonds will tell you that the Parisian merchants are best robbed on the road *to* Leipzig, as that's when they carry silver, whereas on the way *back* they have goods that must be tediously hauled around and fenced. Though your young fellows will take issue with that, and say that no one carries silver anymore— all business is done with bills of exchange."

"At any rate, Leipzig is perfect."

"Except for the small matter that the autumn fair's already over, and we'll have a winter to survive before the next one."

"Keep me alive through that winter, Jack, and come spring, in Leipzig, I'll fetch you ten times what you'd get down *there*."

This was not a proper Vagabond method—making a plan six months in advance. The error was compounded a thousandfold by the prospect of spending so much time with one particular woman. But Jack had already trapped himself by mentioning his sons.

"Still thinking about it?" Eliza asked, some time later.

"Stopped thinking about it long ago," Jack said. "Now I'm trying to remember what I know of the country between here and Leipzig."

"And what have you remembered thus far?"

"Only that we'll see nothing alive that is more than fifty years old." Jack began walking toward a Danube ferry. Turk followed and Eliza rode in silence.

Bohemia
AUTUMN 1683

THREE DAYS NORTH of the Danube, the road focused to a rut in a crowd of scrawny trees that were striving to rise clear from a haze of grasping weeds. The weeds seethed with bugs and stirred with small unseen beasts. Paving-blocks skewed out of pounded ground, forming a sort of shoal that unsettled Turk, who straightened, blinked suspiciously, and slowed. Jack drew the Janissary's sword out of the rolled blanket where it had been hid since Vienna and washed the dried blood off in a creek-bend. When it was clean, he stood in a buttress of sunlight, thigh-deep in brown water, nervously wiping it and swinging it in the air.

"Something troubling you, Jack?"

"Since the Papists slew all the decent folk, this is a country of bandits, haiduks, and Vagabonds—"

"I guessed that. I meant, something about the sword?"

"Can't seem to get it dry—that is, it's dry to the touch, but it ripples like a brook in the sun."

Eliza answered with a scrap of verse:

Watered steel-blade, the world perfection calls,
Drunk with the viper poison foes appals.
Cuts lively, burns the blood whene'er it falls;
And picks up gems from pave of marble halls.

". . . or so says the Poet."

"What manner of poet speaketh such barbarities?" Jack scoffed.

"One who knew more of swords than you. For that is Damascus steel, more than likely. It might be more valuable than Turk and the ostrich plumes summed."

"Save for this defect," Jack said, fitting the ball of his thumb into a notch in the edge, not far from the point. Around it the steel was blackened. "I wouldn't've thought it could happen."

"That's where it cut into your musket's soft belly?"

"Soft? You saw only the wooden stock. But concealed within was an iron ramrod, running the whole length of the weapon through a skinny hole augered into the wood, alongside the musket-barrel itself. This sword cut through the wood—no great feat—but then it must've sliced clean through the ramrod, and then well into the barrel—deep enough to make it weak there. When the powder finally caught, it shoved the ball up only as far as the weak place, and then the barrel burst—that was the end of the Janissary, for he had his face up practically—"

"I saw it. You're rehearsing the story, aren't you, to entertain your friends?"

"I have no friends. It's to cow mine enemies." Jack thought this sounded formidable, but Eliza stared at the horizon and heaved a sigh.

"Or," she said, "it could entice a buyer who was in the market for a legendary blade . . ."

"I know it's difficult, but put all thoughts of markets out of your mind. As the Grand Vizier recently learned, all the riches in the world are of no use if you can't defend 'em. This is wealth, and the means to defend it, combined into one—perfection."

"Do you suppose that a man with a sword and a horse will be defense *enough,* in a place like this?"

"No highwayman of standing would situate himself in a waste."

"Are all the forests of Christendom like this? From

Mummy's færy-tales I was expecting great majestic trees."

"Two or three generations ago, 'twas a wheat-field," Jack said, using the sword to harvest a sheaf of overripe stalks growing wild in a sunny break on the bank of the stream. He sheathed the sword and smelled the grain. "The good peasants would come here during the harvest with their dulled whistles slung over their tired shoulders." Before Jack had waded in he had kicked off his boots. He waded around the swirling pool, groping at the bottom with his bare toes, and after a minute bent down, reached in, and brought up a long curved scythe-blade, notched from striking rocks—just a solid crescent of rust now, a few fingers of slimy black wood projecting from the handle-socket. "They would whet their whistles using rocks that had been worn smooth by the river." He brought up one such rock in his other hand and scrubbed it against the blade for a moment, then tossed it up on the bank. "And while they were doing so they might not be above taking a bit of refreshment." Still probing with his feet, he bent down again and produced an earthenware drinking-jug, turned it over, and poured out a green-brown tube of stagnated water. The jug he tossed also onto the bank. Still holding the long rusty arc of the whistle in one hand, he turned round and waded back in search of an exhibit he had detected earlier. He found it again, and nearly fell over, the stream's current dividing round his thigh as he stood flamingo-style and passed the other foot over something down there. "And so went their simple, happy lives— until something intervened—" Jack now swung the whistle-blade slowly and (he liked to suppose) dramatically across the surface of the pool, a pantomime Grim Reaper.

"Plague? Famine?"

"Religious controversy!" Jack said, and produced from the pool a browned human skull, jaw-bone absent, an obvious sword-dent caving in one of the temples. Eliza (he thought) seemed quite struck by his presentation—not by the skull (she'd seen worse) so much as by the cleverness of the performance. He posed with whistle and skull, extending the moment. "Ever seen a morality play?"

"Mummy told me about 'em."

"The intended audience: Vagabonds. The purpose: to impress on their feeble and degenerate minds some idiotic moral."

"What is the moral of your play, Jack?"

"Oh, it could be a number of things: stay the hell out of Europe, for example. Or: when the men with swords come, run away! Especially if they've got Bibles, too."

"Sound advice."

"Even if it means giving up things."

Eliza laughed like a wench. "Ah, now we *are* coming to a moral, I can sense it."

"Laugh all you like at this poor fellow," Jack said, hefting the skull. "If he'd left his wheat-harvest behind, and taken to the road, instead of clinging to his land and his hut like a miser, why he might be alive today."

"Are there such things as fourscore-year-old Vagabonds?"

"Probably not," Jack admitted, "they just *look* twice as old as they are."

THEY WENT NORTH into the dead country of Bohemia, following spoors and traces of old roads, and the trails of the game that had flourished here in the absence of hunters. Jack lamented the loss of Brown Bess, which would have brought down all the deer they might have wanted, or at least scared the hell out of them.

Sometimes they would come down out of the wooded hills to cross over plains—probably old pastures that had grown up into vast thickets. Jack would put Eliza up into the saddle so that thorns, nettles, and bugs wouldn't make a mess of her—not that he cared—but her chief reason for existence was to give him something pleasant to look at. Sometimes he'd put the Damascus blade to the ignoble purpose of hacking through brush. "What do you and Turk see?" he'd say, because all he could see was useless vegetation, gone all brown in preparation for winter.

"To the right, the ground rises to a sort of shelf, high dark hills behind it—on the shelf the walls of a castle, thick and

ill-made compared to Moorish ones, which are so elegant—
but not thick enough to resist whatever destroying force
knocked it down—"

"Artillery, lass—the doom of all ancient forts."

"The Pope's artillery, then, breached the walls in several
places—creating spills of rock across the dry-moat. White
mortar clings to the dark stones like shards of bleached
bone. Then fire burnt out the insides, and took all but a few
blackened rafters from the roof—all the windows and gun-
ports have spreading smoke-stains above them, as if flames
jetted from those openings for hours—it is like an Alchemist's furnace in which a whole town was purified of
heresy."

"You have alchemists in Barbary?"

"You have them in Christendom?"

"It is very poetickal—as were the previous half-dozen
ruined-castle-descriptions—but I was more interested in
practical matters: do you see the smoke of cook-fires anywhere?"

"I'd have mentioned it. Trails in the brush, trampled down
by men or horses, I'd have mentioned, too."

"Anything else?"

"To the left a pond—rather shallow-looking."

"Let's go there."

"Turk's been taking us thither—he's thirsty."

They found several such ponds, and after the third or
fourth (all of them near ruins) Jack understood that these
ponds had been excavated, or at least enlarged and rounded
out, by (safe to say) thousands of wretches with picks and
shovels. It recalled to his mind some bit of zargon-lore he'd
picked up from a gypsy in Paris, who'd ranted to him about
lakes, far to the East, but not so far as Romania, where big
fish were raised just as herdsman raised beef-cattle in pastures. From the fish skeletons scattered along the shores of
these ponds, Jack could see others had been here, harvesting
the vestiges of those dead Protestants' clammy flocks. It
made his mouth water.

"Why'd the Papists hate this country so much?" Eliza inquired. "Mummy told me there are many Protestant lands."

"It is not the sort of thing I would bother to know about, as a rule," Jack said, "but, as it happens, I've just come from an almost equally ruined land where every peasant knows the tale, and won't leave off telling it. That country is called the Palatinate and its lords, for a few generations anyway, were Protestant heroes. One of those lords married an English girl, name of Elizabeth—the sister of Chuck the First."

"Charles the First—isn't he the one who ran afoul of Cromwell, and got his head chopped off in Charing Cross?"

"The same—and his sister fared little better, as you'll soon see. Because right here in Bohemia, some Protestants got weary of being ruled by Papists, and threw several of 'em out a castle window into a dung-heap, and declared this country free of Popery. But unlike the Dutchmen, who have little use for royalty, these Bohemians couldn't imagine having a country without monarchs. As Protestant monarchs were in short supply hereabouts, they invited Elizabeth and this Palatine fellow to come here and rule them. Which they did—for a single winter. Then the Pope's legions came up here and made it what it is today."

"What of Elizabeth and her husband?"

"The Winter Queen and the Winter King, as they were called after that, ran away. They couldn't go to the Palatinate because that had likewise been invaded (which is why the people who live there won't shut up about it, even today), so they roamed about like Vagabonds for a while and finally ended up at The Hague, where they sat out the war that had been started by all this."

"Did she have children?"

"She wouldn't *stop* having 'em. My god. To hear people talk, she must've been punching them out, nine and a half months apart, all through the war . . . I cannot remember how many."

"You cannot remember? How long *was* this war?"

"Thirty years."

"Oh."

"She had at least a dozen. The eldest became Elector Palatinate after the war, and the others scattered to the four winds, as far as I know."

"You speak very callously of them," Eliza sniffed, "but I am certain that each bears in his or her heart the memory of what was done to the parents."

"Forgive me, lass, but now I'm confused: are you talking about those Palatine whelps, or yourself?"

"Both," Eliza admitted.

He and Eliza had hit on a new way of subsisting, mostly on wheat. As Jack liked to remind Eliza several times a day, he was not the sort who accumulated possessions. But he had a sharp eye for what might be useful in a pinch, and so had filched a hand-mill from a military baggage-train when the cooks had gone off to loot. Wheat poured into the top would become flour if one only turned the crank a few thousand times. All they needed, then, was an oven. Or so Jack had supposed until one evening between Vienna and Linz when Eliza had thrust a couple of sticks into the ashes of their fire and pulled out a flat blackened disk. Brushed off, it proved to be brown and tan underneath—torn apart, it steamed and smelled more or less like bread. It was, Eliza said, a Mohametan style of bread, requiring no oven, and reasonably good to eat if you didn't mind grinding a few cinders between your teeth. They'd now been eating it for upwards of a month. Compared to real viands it was miserable, compared to starvation it was extremely palatable. "Bread and water, bread and water—it's like being in the brig again. I'm for some fish!" Jack said.

"When were you in a brig?"

"It's just like you to ask. Er, I believe it was after we sailed from Jamaica, but before the pirate attack."

"What were you doing in Jamaica?" Eliza asked suspiciously.

"Worked my extensive military connections to stow away on a ship bringing balls and powder to His Majesty's fortifications there."

"Why?"

"Port Royal. I wanted to see Port Royal, which is to pirates as Amsterdam is to Jews."

"You wanted to become a pirate?"

"I wanted freedom. As a Vagabond, I have it—so long as I keep my wits about me. But a pirate is (or so I thought) like a Vagabond of the seas. They say that all of the seas, put together, are larger than all of the dry land, put together, and I supposed that pirates must be that much freer than Vagabonds. Not to mention a good deal richer—everyone knows that the streets of Port Royal are paved with Spanish silver."

"Are they?"

"Very near, lass. All of the world's silver comes from Peru and Mexico—"

"I know it. We used pieces of eight in Constantinople."

"—and all of it must pass by Jamaica in order to reach Spain. Those Port Royal pirates siphoned off a goodly fraction of it. I reached the place in seventy-six—only a few years since Captain Morgan had personally sacked Portobelo and Panama, and brought all the proceeds back to Port Royal. It was a rich place."

"I'm pleased that you wanted to be a buccaneer . . . I was afraid you had ambitions of being a sugar planter."

"Then, lass, you are the only person in the world who esteems pirates above planters."

"I know that in the Cape Verde Islands and Madeira, all sugar is cultivated by slaves—the same is true in Jamaica?"

"Of course! The Indians all died, or ran away."

"Then better to be a pirate."

"Never mind. A month aboard ship taught me that there's no freedom at all to be had on the high seas. Oh, the ship might be moving. But all water looks the same, and while you wait for land to crawl over the horizon, you're locked up in a box with a lot of insufferable fools. And pirate-ships are no different. There is no end of rules as to how booty and swag are to be collected, valued, and divided among the numerous different classes and ranks of pirates. So after a bad month in Port Royal, trying to keep my arsehole away from randy buccaneers, I sailed for home on a sugar-ship."

Eliza smiled. She did not do this frequently. Jack did not like the effect it had on him when she did. "You have seen much," she said.

"I'm more than twenty years old, lass. An old gaffer like me, in the twilight of his years, has had plenty of time to live a full life, and to see Port Royal and other wonders—you're only a child, you've a good ten or, God willing, twenty years left."

"It was on the sugar-ship that you were thrown into the brig?"

"Yes, for some imagined offense. Then pirates attacked. We were holed by a cannonball. The ship's master saw his profits dissolving. All hands were called on deck, all sins pardoned."

ELIZA WENT ON WITH FURTHER interrogations. Jack heard not a word of it, as he was making observations of this pond, and of the mostly abandoned village that crowded along one shore of it. He paid particular attention to a gossamer-thread of smoke that rose and piled up against some invisible barrier in the atmosphere above. It was coming from a lean-to thrown up against the wall of an old collapsed house. A dog whined somewhere. The scrub between the pond and a nearby forest was scored with various trails cutting purposefully toward water's edge, and the forest itself trapped in a miasma of smoke and vapors.

Jack followed the pond-shore, fish-bones crackling beneath the soles of his boots, until he'd come to the village. A man was dragging a faggot as big as himself down a road toward the lean-to. "No axes—they therefore must burn twigs, instead of cordwood, all winter," Jack said to Eliza, significantly patting the axe that they'd taken from the chamber beneath Vienna.

The man was wearing wooden shoes, and was dressed in rags that had gone the color of ash, and he shimmered in an oily cloud of flies. He was staring lustfully at Jack's boots, with an occasional, sad glance at the sword and the horse, which told him he would never get the boots.

"J'ai besoin d'une cruche," Jack offered.

Eliza was amused. "Jack, we're in Bohemia! Why are you speaking French?"

"Il y a quelques dans la cave de ça—là-bas, monsieur," said the peasant.

"Merci."

"De rien, monsieur."

"You have to look at the shoes," Jack explained airily, after allowing a minute for Eliza's embarrassment to ripen. "No one but a Frenchman wears those sabots."

"But how . . . ?"

"France is a worse than normal place to be a peasant. Some *pays* especially. They know perfectly well there's empty land to the east. As do our dinner guests."

"Guests?"

Jack found a great earthenware jug in a cellar and set Eliza to work dropping pebbles into its open neck until it was so weighed down as to sink. Meanwhile he was working with the contents of his powder-horn, which had been useless weight to him since the destruction of Brown Bess. He tore a long thin strip of linen from a shirt and rolled it in powder until it was nearly black, then sparked one end of it with flint and steel and observed a steady and satisfactory progress of sputtering and smoky flame. The Frenchman's children had come over to watch. They were so infested with fleas that they rustled. Jack made them stay well back. The fuse demonstration was the most wondrous event of their lives.

Eliza was finished with the pebble work. The rest was simple enough. All the remaining supply of gunpowder, plus a piece of new fuse, went into the jug. Jack lit the fuse, dropped it in, jammed a warm candle-stub into the neck to keep water out, and hurled the apparatus as far as he could into the pond, which swallowed it. A few moments later it belched—the water swelled, foamed, and produced a cloud of dry smoke, like a miracle. A minute later the water became lumpy and thick with dead or unconscious fish.

"Dinner is served!" Jack hollered. But the murky forest had already come alive—queues of people were moving down the paths like flame down the fuse. "Up on the horse, lass," Jack suggested.

"Are they dangerous?"

"Depends on what's catching. I have the good fortune to've been born immune and impervious to plague, leprosy, impetigo . . ." but Eliza was up on the horse already, in a performance of a scampering nature that no man alive (excepting sodomites) would not have enjoyed watching. Jack, for lack of other occupations, had taught her what he knew of riding, and she backed Turk off expertly and rode him up onto a little mossy hummock, gaining as much altitude as possible.

"'Twas the Year of our Lord sixteen hundred and sixty-five," Jack said. "I was coming up in the world—having established a thriving business of sorts with brother Bob, providing specialized services to the condemned. My first clew was the scent of brimstone—then heavy yellow smoke of it hanging in the streets, thicker and fouler than the normal fogs of London. People burnt it to purify the air."

"Of what?"

"Then it was wains trundling down streets piled with corpses of rats, then cats, then dogs, then people. Red chalk crosses would appear on certain houses—armed watchmen stood before them to prevent any of the miserable residents from breaking out of those nailed-shut doors. Now, I couldn't've been more than seven. The sight of all those blokes planted in the brimstone-fog, like hero-statues, with pikes and muskets at the ready—churches' bells sounding death-knells all round—why, Bob and I had voyaged to another world without leaving London! Public entertainments were outlawed. Irish even stopped having their Popish feasts, and many absconded. The great hangings at Tyburn stopped. Theatres: shut down for the first time since Cromwell. Bob and I had lost both income and the entertainment to spend it on. We left London. We went to the forest. Everyone did. They were infested. The highwaymen had to pack up and

move away. Before we—the Londoners fleeing the Plague—
even came into those woods, there had been towns of lean-
tos and tree-houses there: widows, orphans, cripples, idiots,
madmen, journeymen who'd thought better of their contracts, fugitives, homeless reverends, victims of fire and
flood, deserters, discharged soldiers, actors, girls who'd gotten pregnant out of wedlock, tinkers, pedlars, gypsies, runaway slaves, musicians, sailors between sailings, smugglers,
confused Irishmen, Ranters, Diggers, Levellers, Quakers,
feminists, midwives. The normal Vagabond population, in
other words. To this was added, now, any Londoner fleet
enough to outrun the Black Death. Now, a year later London
burnt to the ground—there was yet another exodus. Same
year, the Naval Pay Office went into default—thousands of
unpaid sailors joined us. We moved around the South of England like Christmas Carolers from Hell. More'n half of us
expected the Apocalypse within a few weeks, so we didn't
trouble with planning. We broke down walls and fences, undoing Enclosure, poached game in forests of some extremely worshipful lords and bishops. They weren't happy."

By this time, the Vagabonds had mostly come out into the
open. Jack didn't look at them—he knew what they'd be—
but rather at Eliza, who'd become anxious. Turk the Horse
sensed this and looked askance at Jack, showing a white Mohametan crescent-moon in the eye. Jack knew, then, that, as
it was with Turk, so it'd be with every person and beast they
met along their way: they'd gladly suffer Eliza to climb on
their backs and ride them, they'd feel her feelings as if she
were an actress on a Southwark stage, and they'd shoot dirty
looks at Jack. He'd only have to find a way to use it.

Eliza breathed easier when she saw that the Vagabonds
were just people. If anything they were cleaner and less
brutish than those peasants who'd settled in the village, especially after they swam out into the pond to retrieve fish. A
couple of Gypsy boys drew a crowd as they struggled to
wrestle a prodigious carp, the size of a blacksmith, up onto
the shore. "Some of these fish must remember the war," Jack
mused.

Several people came near, but not too near, to pay their respects to Jack and (more so) Eliza. One was a stringy fellow with pale green eyes staring out of an anatomical complex that looked like anything but a face—his nose was gone, leaving twin vertical air-holes, and his upper lip was missing, and his ears were perforated baby's fists stuck to the sides of this head, and angry words were burnt into his forehead. He came toward them, stopped, and bowed deeply. He had an entourage of more complete persons who obviously loved him, and they all grinned at Eliza, encouraging her not to throw up or gallop away screaming.

She was politely aghast. "A leper?" she asked. "But then he wouldn't be so popular."

"A recidivist," Jack said. "When Polish serfs run away, their lords hunt 'em down and brand 'em, or cut off this or that piece—saving the pieces that can do useful work, needless to say—so if they're seen out on the roads again they'll be known as runners. That, lass, is what I mean by the Devil's Poor—one who keeps at it regardless—who won't be mastered by any man, nor reformed by any church. As you can see, his perseverance has won him a whole Court of admirers."

Jack's gaze had drifted to the lakeshore, where Vagabonds were now scooping guts out of carp-bellies by the double handful, exerting a hypnotic power over various mangy dogs. He looked up at Eliza and caught her in the act of examining him. "Trying to picture me without a nose?"

Eliza looked down. He'd never seen her eyes downcast before. It affected him, and made him angry to be affected. "Don't look at me—I'll not be the subject of such investigation. The last person who peered at me that way, from the back of a fine horse, was Sir Winston Churchill."

"Who's that? Some Englishman?"

"A gentleman of Dorsetshire. Royalist. Cromwell's men burnt down his ancestral estate and he squatted in the cinders for ten or fifteen years, siring children and fighting off Vagabonds and waiting for the King to come back—that accomplished, he became a man about town in London."

"Then whyever was he peering at you from horseback?"

"In those days of Plague and Fire, Sir Winston Churchill had the good sense to get himself posted to Dublin on the King's business. He'd come back from time to time, suck up to the Royals, and inspect what was left of his country estates. On one of those occasions, he and his son came back to Dorset for a visit and rallied the local militia."

"And you happened to be there?"

"I did."

"No coincidence, I presume."

"Bob and I and certain others had come to partake of a charming local custom."

"Clog-dancing?"

"Clubmen—armies of peasants who'd once roamed that part of the country with cudgels. Cromwell had massacred them, but they were still about—we hoped for a revival of the tradition, as Vagabondage of the meek school had become overly competitive in those dark years."

"What did Sir Winston Churchill think of your idea?"

"Didn't want his home burnt again—he'd just gotten a roof on it, finally, after twenty years. He was Lord Lieutenant thereabouts—that's a job that the King gives to the gents with the brownest noses of all—entitled him to command the local militia. Most Lord Lieutenants sit in London all the time, but after the Plague and the Fire, the countryside was in an uproar because of people like me, as I've been explaining, and so they were given the power to search for arms, imprison disorderly persons, and so on."

"Were you imprisoned, then?"

"What? No, we were mere boys, and we looked younger than we were because of not eating enough. Sir Winston decided to carry out a few exemplary hangings, which was the normal means of persuading Vagabonds to move to the next county. He picked out three men and hanged them from a tree-limb, and as a last favor to them, Bob and I hung from their legs to make 'em perish faster. And in so doing we caught Sir Winston's eye. Bob and I looked similar, though for all we know we've different fathers. The sight of these two matched urchins plying their trade, with coolness born of experience, was amusing to Sir Winston. He called us over and that was when he (and his son John, only ten years older than meself) gave us that look you were giving me just now."

"And what conclusion did *he* arrive at?"

"I didn't wait for him to arrive at conclusions. I said something like, 'Are you the responsible official here?' Bob'd already made himself scarce. Sir Winston laughed a little too heartily and allowed as how he was. 'Well, I'd like to register a complaint,' I said. 'You said you were going to carry out one or two exemplary hangings. But is this your notion of exemplary? The rope is too thin, the noose is ill-made, the tree-limb is barely adequate to support the burden, and the proceedings were, if I may say so, carried out with a want of pomp and showmanship that'd have the crowd at Ty-burn baying for Jack Ketch's blood if he ever staged one so shabbily.'"

"But Jack, didn't you understand that 'exemplary' meant that Sir Winston Churchill was *making an example* of them?"

"Naturally. And just as naturally, Sir Winston began to give me the same tedious explanation I've just now had from you, albeit I interrupted with many more foolish jests—and in the middle of it, young John Churchill happened to glance away and said, 'I say, look, Father, the other chap's going through our baggage.'"

"What—Bob?"

"My performance was a diversion, girl, to keep them looking at me whilst Bob pilfered their baggage-train. Only John Churchill had a lively enough mind to understand what we were doing."

"So . . . what did Sir Winston think of you, then?"

"He had his horsewhip out. But John spoke with him *sotto voce,* and, as I believe, changed his mind—Sir Winston claimed, then, that he'd seen qualities in us Shaftoe boys that would make us useful in a regimental setting. From that moment on we were boot-polishers, musket-cleaners, beerfetchers, and general errand-boys for Sir Winston Churchill's local regiment. We'd been given the opportunity to prove we were God's, and not the Devil's, Poor."

"So that's where you got your knowledge of matters military."

"Where I *began* to get it. This was a good sixteen years ago."

"And also, I suppose, it's how you became so sympathetic to the likes of these," Eliza said, flicking her blue eyes once toward the Vagabonds.

"Oh. You suppose I arranged this carp-feast out of charity?"

"Come to think of it—"

"I—*we*—need information."

"From *these* people?"

"I have heard that in some cities they have buildings called libraries, and the libraries are full of books, and each book contains a story. Well, I can tell you that there never was a library that had as many stories as a Vagabond-camp. Just as a Doctor of Letters might go to a library to read one of those stories, I need to get a certain tale from one of these people—I'm not sure which one, yet—so I drew 'em all out."

"What sort of tale?"

"It's about a wooded, hilly country, not far north of here, where hot water spills out of the ground year-round and keeps homeless wanderers from freezing to death. You see, lass, if we wanted to survive a northern winter, we should've begun laying in firewood months ago."

Jack then went among the Vagabonds and, speaking in a none too euphonious stew of zargon, French, and sign language, soon got the information he needed. There were many haiduks—runaway serfs who'd made a living preying on the Turks farther east. They understood the tale told by Jack's horse and sword, and wanted Jack to join them. Jack thought it wise to slip away before their friendly invitations hardened into demands. Besides which, the entire scene of motley Vagabonds gutting and mutilating these immense fifty-year-old carp had become almost as strange and apocalyptic as anything they'd seen in the Turk's camp, and they just wanted to put it behind them. Before dark, Jack and Eliza were northbound. That night, for the first time, it got so chilly that they were obliged to sleep curled up next to the fire under the same blanket, which meant Eliza slept soundly and Jack hardly at all.

Bohemia

WINTER OF 1683–1684

✣

FOR THE TWO WEEKS that followed Jack's Christ-like miracle of feeding a thousand Vagabonds from a small bag of gunpowder, he and Eliza talked very little, except about immediate concerns of staying alive. They passed from the rolling country of burnt castles and carp-ponds, with its broad flat valleys, into a mountainous zone farther north, which either had not suffered so badly during the war, or else had recovered faster. From hill-tops and mountain-passes they looked down upon brown fields where haystacks scattered like bubbles on placid ponds, and tidy prosperous towns whose chimneys bristled like so many pikes and muskets brandished against the cold. Jack tried to compare these vistas against the tales the Vagabonds had told him. Certain nights, they were all but certain they were going to perish, but then they'd find a hut, or cave, or even a cleft in the face of some bluff where they could build a nest of fallen leaves and a fire.

Finally one day they came, sudden as an ambush, into a vale where the tree-branches were grizzled with mist, and steam rose from a smelly rill that trickled down a strangely colored and sculpted river-bed. "We're here," Jack said, and left Eliza hidden back in the woods while he rode out into the open to talk to a pair of miners who were working with picks and shovels in the stream, digging up brittle rock that smelled like London in the Plague Years. Brimstone! Jack spoke little German and they spoke no English, but they were thoroughly impressed by his sword, his horse, and his boots, and through grunts and shrugs and signs they made it known they'd make no trouble if he camped for the winter at the headwaters of the hot spring, half a league up the valley.

So they did. The spring emerged from a small cave that was always warm. They could not stay there for very long because of the bad air, but it served as a refuge into which they could retreat, and so kept them alive long enough to reconstitute a tumbledown hut they found on the bank of the steaming creek. Jack cut wood and dragged it back to Eliza, who arranged it. The roof would never keep rain out, but it shrugged off the snow. Jack still had a bit of silver. He used it to buy venison and rabbit from the miners, who set clever snares for game in the woods.

Their first month at the hot springs, then, consisted of small struggles won and forgotten the next day, and nothing passed between them except for the simple plans and affairs of peasants. But eventually things settled to the point where they did not have to spend every moment in toil. Jack did not care one way or the other. But Eliza let it be known that certain matters had been on her mind the entire time.

"Do you *mind*?" Jack was forced to blurt, one day in what was probably December.

"Pay no attention," Eliza snuffled. "Weather's a bit gloomy."

"If the *weather's* gloomy, what're *you*?"

"Just thinking of . . . things."

"Stop thinking then! This hovel's scarcely big enough to lie down in—have some consideration—there's a rivulet of tears running across the floor. Didn't we have a talk, months ago, about female moods?"

"Your concern is ever so touching. How can I thank you?"

"Stop weeping!"

She drew a few deep quivering breaths that made the hut shudder, and then crucified Jack with a counterfeit smile. "The regiment, then—"

"What's this?" Jack asked. "Keeping you alive isn't enough? I'm to provide entertainment as well?"

"You seem reluctant to talk about this. Perhaps you're a bit melancholy, too?"

"You have this clever little mind that never stops working. You're going to put my stories to ill-considered purposes. There are certain details, not really important, in which you'll take an unwholesome interest."

"Jack, we're living like brutes in the middle of the wilderness—what could I possibly do with a story as old as I am? And for God's sake, what else is there to do, when I lack thread and needles?"

"There you go again with the thread and the needles. Where do you suppose a brute in the wilderness would obtain such things?"

"Ask those miners to pick some up when next they go to town. They fetch oats for Turk all the time—why not a needle and thread?"

"If I do that, they'll know I've a woman here."

"You won't for long, if you don't tell me a story, or get me thread and needles."

"All right, then. The part of the story to which you're almost certain to over-react is that, although Sir Winston Churchill was not really an important man, his son John was *briefly* important. He's not any more. Probably never will be again, except in the world of courtiers."

"But you made his father out to be one notch above a Vagabond."

"Yes—and so John never would've reached the high position he did had he not been clever, handsome, brave, dashing, and good in the sack."

"When can you introduce me to him?"

"I know you're just trying to provoke me with that."

"Into what 'high position' exactly did he get?"

"The bed of the favorite mistress of King Charles the Second of England."

A brief pause for pressure to build, and then volcanic laughter from Eliza. Suddenly it was April. "You mean for me to believe that *you*—Half-Cocked 'don't call me a

Vagabond' Jack—are personally acquainted with the lover of a mistress of a King?"

"Calm yourself—there are no chirurgeons here, if you should rupture something. And if you knew anything of the world outside of Asiatick Harems, you wouldn't be surprised—the King's *other* favorite mistress is Nell Gwyn— an *actress*."

"I sensed all along that you were a Person of Quality, Jack. But pray tell—now that I've finally set your tongue in motion—how'd John Churchill get from his papa's regiment in Dorset to the royal sack?"

"Oh, mind you, John was never *attached* to that regiment—just visiting with his Dad. The family lived in London. Jack went to some foppish School there. Sir Winston pulled what few strings were available to him—probably whined about his great loyalty during the Interregnum—and got John appointed as a page to James, the Duke of York— the King's Papist brother—who, last I heard, was up in Edinburgh, going out of his mind and torturing Scotsmen. But back then, of course, round about 1670, the Duke of York was in London, and so John Churchill—being a member of his household—was there, too. Years passed. Bob and I fattened and grew like cattle for the Fair on soldiers' tablescraps."

"And so you did!"

"Don't pretend to admire me—you know my secrets. We plugged away at duties Regimental. John Churchill went to Tangiers for a few years to fight Barbary Pirates."

"Ooh, why couldn't he've rescued *me*?"

"Maybe he will, some day. What I'm getting to, though, is the Siege of Maestricht—a city in Holland."

"That's nowhere near Tangiers."

"Try to follow me here: he came back from Tangiers, all covered in glory. Meantimes Charles II had made a pact with, of all people, that King Looie of France, the arch-Papist, so rich that not only did he bribe the English opposition, but the *other* party, too, just to keep things interesting. So England and France, conjoined, made war, on land and at sea, with Holland. King Looie, accompanied by a mobile city of courtiers, mistresses, generals, bishops, official historians, poets, portrait-painters, chefs, musicians, and the retinues of *those* people, and the retinues' retinues, came up to Maestricht and threw a siege the way common kings throw parties. His camp was not quite as handsomely furnished as the Grand Vizier's before Vienna, but the folk were of higher quality. All the fashionable people of Europe had to be there. And John Churchill was quite fashionable. He came. Bob and I came with him."

"Now, that's where I have trouble following. Why invite two naughty lads?"

"First: we hadn't been naughty *recently*. Second: even the noblest gathering requires someone to empty piss-pots and (if it's a battle) stop musket-balls before they reach the better folk."

"Third?"

"There is no third."

"You lie. I can tell there was a third. Your lips parted, your finger came halfway up, and then you reconsidered."

"Very well then. The third was that John Churchill—courtier, sometime gigolo, fashionable blade-about-town—is the best military commander I have ever seen."

"Oh."

"Though that John Sobieski was not half bad. Anyway—pains me to admit it."

"Obviously."

"But it's true. And being an excellent commander, about to go into a real battle, he had the wit to bring along a few people who could actually get things done for him. It may seem hard for you to believe, but mark my word—whenever serious and competent people need to get things done in the real world, all considerations of tradition and protocol fly out the window."

"What did he suppose you and Bob could get done in the real world?"

"Carry messages across battlefields."

"Was he right?"

"Half right."

"*One* of you succeeded, and the other—"

"I didn't *fail*. I just found more intelligent ways to use my time."

"John Churchill gave you an order, and you refused?"

"No, no, no! It came about as follows. Now—did you pay any attention to the Siege of Vienna?"

"I watched with a keen eye, remember my virginity hung in the balance."

"Tell me how the Grand Vizier did it."

"Dug one trench after another before the walls, each trench a few yards closer than the last. From the foremost, dug tunnels beneath a sort of arrowhead-shaped fortress that lay outside the city—"

"A ravelin, it's called. All modern forts have them, including Maestricht."

"Blew it up. Advanced. And so on."

"That's how all sieges are conducted. Including Maestricht."

"So, then—?"

"All the pick-and-shovel work had been done by the time the swells arrived. The trenches and mines had been dug. Time was ripe to storm a particular outlying work, which an engineer would properly call a demilune, but similar to the ravelins you saw in Vienna."

"A separate fortress just outside of the main one."

"Yes. King Louie wanted that the English gentleman-warriors should, at the conclusion of this battle, either be in his debt, or in their graves, and so he gave to them the honor of storming the demilune. John Churchill and the Duke of Monmouth—King Charles's bastard—led the charge and carried the day. Churchill himself planted the French flag (disgusting to relate) on the parapet of the conquered fort."

"How splendid!"

"I told you he was important *once*. Back they came over the trench-scarred glacis, to our ditch-camp, for a night of celebration."

"So you were never asked to carry messages at all?"

"Next day, I felt the earth turn over, and looked toward that demilune to see fifty French troopers flying into the air. Maestricht's defenders had exploded a vast countermine beneath the demilune. Dutchmen charged into the gap and engaged the survivors in sword- and bayonet-play. They looked sure to retake the demilune and undo Churchill's and Monmouth's glorious deeds. I was not ten feet from John Churchill when it happened. Without a moment's hesitation he was off and running, sword in hand—it was obvious muskets would be useless. To save time, he ran across the surface—ignoring the trenches—exposing himself to musket-fire from the city's defenders, in full view of all those historians and poets watching through jeweled opera glasses from the windows of their coaches, just outside of artillery range. I stood there in amazement at his stupidity, until I realized that brother Bob was right behind him, matching him step-for-step."

"Then?"

"Then I was amazed at Bob's stupidity, too. Placing me, as I need hardly tell you, in an awkward spot."

"Always thinking of yourself."

"Fortunately the Duke of Monmouth appeared before me, that very moment, with a message that he wanted me to take to a nearby company of French musketeers. So I ran down the trench and located Monsieur D'Artagnan, the officer in ch—"

"Oh, stop!"

"What?"

"Even I've heard of D'Artagnan! You don't expect me to believe you—?"

"Is it all right with you if I get on with the story?"

Sigh. "Yes."

"Monsieur D'Artagnan, whom you don't appear to realize was a real human being and not just a figure in romantic legends, ordered his Musketeers forward. *All of us* advanced upon the demilune with conspicuous gallantry."

"I'm enthralled!" said Eliza, only a little sarcastic. At first she would not believe that Jack had actually met the celebrated D'Artagnan, but now that she did she was caught up in the tale.

"Because we did not bother to use the trenches, as *cowards* would've done, we reached the site of the fighting from a direction where the Dutch hadn't bothered to post proper defenses. All of us—French Musketeers, English bastards and gigolos, and Vagabond-messengers—got there at the same instant. But we could only advance through an opening just wide enough to admit one man at a time. D'Artagnan got there first and stood in the path of the Duke of Monmouth himself and begged him in the most gallant and polite French way not to go through that dangerous pass. Monmouth insisted. D'Artagnan consented—but only on the condition that he, D'Artagnan, should go through first. He did just that, and got shot in the head. The others advanced over him and went on to win ridiculous glory, while I stayed behind to look after D'Artagnan."

"He still lived!?"

"Hell no, his brains were all over me."

"But you stayed behind to guard his body—?"

"Actually, I had my eye on some heavy jewelled rings he was wearing."

For half a minute or so, Eliza adopted the pose of someone who'd just herself taken a musket-ball to the head and suffered an injury of unknown severity. Jack decided to move on to more glamorous parts of the tale, but Eliza dug in her heels. "While your brother risked all, you were *looting D'Artagnan's corpse*? I've never heard worse."

"Why?"

"It's so . . . so craven."

"You don't need to make it sound *cowardly*—I was in more danger than Bob was. The musket-balls were going through my *hat*."

"Still . . ."

"The fighting was *over*. Those rings were the size of *doorknockers*. They would have buried that famed Musketeer with those rings on his fingers—if someone else hadn't looted them first."

"Did you take them, Jack?"

"He'd put them on when he was a younger and thinner man. They were impossible to move. So there I was with my foot planted in his fucking armpit—not the worst place my foot's ever been, but close—bending my fingernails back trying to get this ring up past the rolls of fat that'd grown up around it during his days of wine and women—asking myself whether I shouldn't just cut the damn finger off." Eliza now looked like someone who'd eaten a bad oyster. Jack decided to move on hastily. "When who should show up but brother Bob, with a look of self-righteous horror on his face, like a vicar who's just surprised an altar boy masturbating in the sacristy—or like *you*, for that matter—all dressed up in his little drummer boy outfit—carrying a message—frightfully urgent of course—from Churchill to one of King Looie's generals. He stops to favor me with a lecture about military honor. 'Ach, you don't really *believe* that stuff, do you?' I ask. 'Until today I didn't, Jack, but if you could see what I've seen just now—the feats that those brothers in arms, John Churchill and the Duke of Monmouth and Louis Hector de Villars, have performed—you'd believe.'"

"And then he sped onwards to deliver the message," Eliza said, getting a faraway look in her eye that was somewhat annoying to Jack, who wanted her to remain there in the hut with him. "And John Churchill never forgot Bob's loyalty and bravery."

"Yes—why, just a few months later Bob went to Westphalia with him and campaigned under French generals, as a mercenary, against hapless Protestants, sacking the Palatinate for the hundredth time. Can't remember what that had to do with military honor, exactly."

"*You*, on the other hand—"

"I took a few belts of cognac from D'Artagnan's flask and slunk back to the ditch."

This, at least, brought her back to the here (hut in Bohemia) and now (end of A.D. 1683). She directed the full power of her blue-eyed gaze against him. "You're always making yourself out to be such a ne'er-do-well, Jack—saying you'd have cut D'Artagnan's fingers off—proposing to blow up the Holy Roman Emperor's palace—but I don't think you're as bad as you say you are."

"My deformity gives me fewer chances to be bad than I should prefer to have."

"It is funny you should mention that, Jack. If you could find me a length of sound, unbroken deer or sheep intestine—"

"Why?"

"A Turkish practice—easier to show than explain. And if you could devote a few minutes in the hot spring to making yourself quite a bit cleaner than you are at the moment—the chance to be bad might present itself."

"ALL RIGHT, LET'S REHEARSE IT again. 'Jack, show the gentleman that bolt of the yellow watered silk.' Go on—that's your cue."

"Yes, milady."

"Jack, carry me across yonder mud-puddle."

"With pleasure, milady."

"Don't say 'with pleasure'—sounds naughty."

"As you wish, milady."

"Jack, that is very good—there's been a marked improvement."

"Don't suppose it has anything to do with that you've got your fist lodged in my arse-hole."

Eliza laughed gaily. "Fist? Jack, this is but two fingers. A fist would be more like—this!"

Jack felt his body being turned outside in—there was some thrashing and screaming that was cut short when his head accidentally submerged in the sulfurous water. Eliza got a grip on his hair and hauled his head back up into the cold air with her other hand.

"You're *sure* this is how they do it in India?"

"Would you like to register . . . a *complaint*?"

"Aaugh! Never."

"Remember, Jack: whenever serious and competent people need to get things done in the real world, all considerations of tradition and protocol fly out the window."

There followed a long, long, mysterious procedure—tedious and yet somehow not.

"What're you groping about for?" Jack muttered faintly. "My gall-bladder is just to the left."

"I'm trying to locate a certain *chakra*—should be somewhere around here—"

"What's a *chakra*?"

"You'll know when I find it."

Some time later, she did, and then the procedure took on greater intensity, to say the least. Suspended between Eliza's two hands, like a scale in a market-place, Jack could feel his balance-point shifting as quantities of fluids were pumped between internal reservoirs, all in preparation for some Event. Finally, the crisis—Jack's legs thrashed in the hot water as if his body were trying to flee, but he was staked, impaled. A bubble of numenous light, as if the sun were mistakenly attempting to rise inside his head. Some kind of Hindoo apocalypse played out. He died, went to Hell, ascended into Heaven, was reincarnated as various braying, screeching, and howling beasts, and repeated this cycle many times over. In the end he was reincarnated, just barely, as a Man. Not a very alert one.

"Did you get what you wanted?" she inquired. Very close to him.

Jack laughed or wept soundlessly for a while.

"In some of these strange Gothickal German towns," he at last said, "they have ancient clocks that are as big as houses, all sealed up most of the time, with a little door where a cuckoo pops out upon the hour to sing. But once a day, it does something special, involving more doors, and once a week, something even specialer, and, for all I know, at the year, decade, and century marks, rows of great doors, all sealed shut by dust and age, creak open, driven by sudden descent of ancient weights on rusted chains, and the whole inner workings of the thing unfold through those openings. Hitherto unseen machines grind into action, strange and surprising things fly out—flags wave, mechanical birds sing—

old pigeon-shit and cobwebs raining down on spectators' heads—Death comes out and does a fandango—Angels blow trumpets—Jesus writhes on the cross and expires—a mock naval battle plays out with repeated discharge of cannons—and would you please take your arm out of my asshole now?"

"I did a long time ago—you nearly broke it!" Peeling off the knotted length of sheep-gut like an elegant lady removing a silken glove.

"So this is a permanent condition?"

"Stop whining. A few moments ago, Jack, unless my eyes deceived me, I observed a startlingly large amount of yellow bile departing your body, and floating away downstream."

"What are you talking about? I didn't barf."

"Think harder, Jack."

"Oh—*that* kind. I should not call it *yellow* but a pearly off-white. Though it has been years since I saw any. Perhaps it has yellowed over time, like cheese. Very well! Let's say 'twas yellow."

"Do you know what yellow bile is the humour of, Jack?"

"What am I, a physician?"

"It is the humour of anger and ill-temper. You were carrying a lot of it around."

"Was I? Good thing I didn't let it affect my behavior."

"Actually I was hoping you might have a change of heart concerning needle and thread."

"Oh, that? I was never opposed to it. Consider it done Eliza."

Leipzig
APRIL 1684

✣

From all I hear of Leibniz he must be very intelligent, and pleasant company in consequence.
It is rare to find learned men who are clean, do
not stink, and have a sense of humour.
— LISELOTTE IN A LETTER TO SOPHIE,
30 JULY 1705

"JACQUES, SHOW THE GENTLEMAN THAT bolt of the yellow watered silk . . . Jacques? *Jacques!*" Eliza moved on smoothly
to some cruel jest about how difficult it was to find reliable
and hard-working varlets nowadays, speaking in a French
that was too good for Jack to understand. The gentleman in
question—evidently a Parisian in the rag trade—took his
nose out of Eliza's cleavage long enough to glance up into
her eyes and chuckle uncertainly—he sensed a *bon mot* had
been issued but he hadn't heard it.

"Cor, he's surprised your tits come wi' a head attached,"
Jack observed.

"Shut up . . . one of these days, we're going to meet someone who speaks English," Eliza returned, and nodded at the
bolt. "Would you please stay awake?"

"Haven't been so awake in half a year—that's the difficulty," Jack said, stooping down to unroll an arm's length of

silk, and drawing it through the air like a flag, trying to make it waft. A shaft of sunlight would've been useful. But the only radiant heavenly body shedding light into this court-yard was Eliza's—turned out in one of a few dresses she'd been working on for months. Jack had watched them come together out of what looked to him like scraps, and so the effect on him was not as powerful. But when Eliza walked through the market, she drew such looks that Jack practically had to bind his right arm to his side, lest it fly across his body and whip out the Damascus blade and teach the merchants of Leipzig some manners.

She got into a long difference of opinion with this Parisian, which ended when he handed her an old limp piece of paper that had been written on many times, in different hands, and then collected the bolt of yellow silk from Jack and walked away with it. Jack once again had to restrain his sword-hand. "This kills me."

"Yes. You say that every time."

"You're certain that those scraps are worth something."

"Yes! Says so right here," Eliza said. "Would you like me to read it to you?" A dwarf came by selling chocolates.

"Won't help. Nothing will, but silver in my pocket."

"Are you worried I'm going to cheat you—being that you can't read the numbers on these bills of exchange?"

"I'm worried something'll happen to 'em before we can turn 'em into real money."

"What is 'real' money, Jack? Answer me that."

"You know, pieces of eight, or, how d'you say it, dol-lars—"

"Th—it starts with a T but it's got a breathy sound behind it—'thalers.'"

"D-d-d-dollars."

"That's a silly name for money, Jack—no one'll ever take you seriously, talking that way."

"Well, they shortened 'Joachimsthaler' to 'thaler,' so why not reform the word even further?"

* * *

A KIND OF STEADILY WAXING madness had beset them after a month or so at their hot-springs encampment—Jack had assumed it was the slow-burning fuse of the French Pox finally reaching significant parts of his mind, until Eliza had pointed out they'd been on bread and water and the occasional rasher of carp jerky for months. A soldier's pay was not generous, but put together with what Jack had previously looted from the rich man's house in Strasbourg, it would supply not only Turk with oats but also them with cabbages, potatoes, turnips, salt pork, and the occasional egg—*as long as Jack didn't mind spending all of it.* As his commission-agents, he employed those two brimstone-miners, Hans and Hans. They were not free agents, but employees of one Herr Geidel of Joachimsthal, a nearby town where silver was dug out of the ground. Herr Geidel hired men like Hans and Hans to dig up the ore and refine it into irregular bars, which they took to a mint in the town to be coined into Joachims-thalers.

Herr Geidel, having learned that a strange armed man was lurking in the woods near his brimstone mine, had ridden out with a few musketeers to investigate, and discovered Eliza all alone, at her sewing. By the time Jack returned, hours later, Eliza and Herr Geidel had, if not exactly become friends, then at least recognized each other as being of the same type, and therefore as possible business partners, though it was by no means clear what *kind* of business. Herr Geidel had the highest opinion of Eliza and voiced confidence that she would make out handsomely at the Leipzig Fair. His immediate opinion of Jack was much lower—the only thing Jack seemed to have going for him was that Eliza was willing to partner up with him. Jack, for his part, put up with Herr Geidel because of the flabbergasting nature of what he did for a living: *literally making money.* The first several times this was explained to Jack, he put it down to a translation error. It couldn't be real. "That's all there is? Dig up some dirt, run it through a furnace, stamp a face and some words on it?"

"That's what he seems to be saying," Eliza had answered, puzzled for once. "In Barbary, all the coins were pieces of eight from Spain—I've never been anywhere near a mint. I was about to say 'wouldn't know a mint from a hole in the ground,' but apparently that's just what it *is*."

When it had gotten warm enough to move, they'd gone down into Joachimsthal and confirmed that it was little more than that. In essence the mint was a brute with a great big hammer and a punch. He was supplied with blank disks of silver—these were not money—put the punch on each one and bashed it with the hammer, mashing the portrait of some important hag, and some incantations in Latin, into it—at which point it *was* money. Officials, supervisors, assayers, clerks, guards, and, in general, the usual crowd of parasitical gentlefolk clustered around the brute with the hammer, but like lice on an ox they could not conceal the simple nature of the beast. The simplicity of money-making had fascinated Jack into a stupor. "Why should we ever leave this place? After all my wanderings I've found Heaven."

"It can't be that easy. Herr Geidel seems depressed—he's branching out into brimstone and other ores—says he can't make any money making money."

"Obvious nonsense. Just trying to scare away competition."

"Did you see all those abandoned mines, though?"

"Ran out of ore," Jack had attempted.

"Then why were the great mining-engines still bestriding the pit-mouths? You'd think they'd've moved them to shafts that were still fruitful."

Jack had had no answer. When next they'd seen Herr Geidel, Eliza had subjected him to a round of brutal questioning that would've gotten Jack into a duel had he done it, but coming from Eliza had only given Herr Geidel a heightened opinion of her. Geidel's French was as miserable as Jack's and so the discussion had gone slowly enough for Jack to follow: for reasons that no one around here fathomed, the Spanish could mine and refine silver in Mexico, and ship it halfway round the world (in spite of the most strenuous efforts by English, Dutch, French, Maltese, and Barbary pirates) cheaper than Herr Geidel and his drinking buddies could produce it in Joachimsthal and ship it a few days' journey to Leipzig. Consequently, only the very richest mines in Europe were still operating. Herr Geidel's strategy was to put idle miners to work digging up brimstone (before the European silver mines had crashed, this never would've worked because they had a strong guild, but now miners were cheap), then ship the brimstone to Leipzig and sell it cheap to gunpowder-makers, in hopes of bringing the cost of gunpowder, and hence of war, down.* Anyway, if war got cheap enough, all hell would break loose, some Spanish galleons might even get sunk, and the cost of silver would climb back to a more wholesome level.

"But won't that also make it cheaper for highwaymen to attack you on the way to Leipzig?" Jack had asked, always working the violent crime angle.

Eliza had given him a look that promised grim penalties the next time she got her hand on the *chakra.* " 'What if war breaks out between here and Leipzig?' is what Jack meant to say."

But Herr Geidel had been completely unfazed. Wars broke out all the time, all over the place, with no effect on the Leipzig Fair. If all of this came to pass, he'd be a rich merchant again. And for five hundred years the Leipzig fairs had operated under a decree from the Holy Roman Emperor stating that as long as the merchants stuck to certain roads and paid a nominal fee to local princes whose lands they traversed, they could pass freely to and from Leipzig, and must

---

*It turned out that if you did the mathematicks on a typical war, the cost of powder was more important than just about anything else—Herr Geidel insisted that the gunpowder in the arsenal of Venice, for example, was worth more than the annual revenue of the entire city. This explained a lot of oddness Jack had witnessed in various campaigns and forced him to reconsider (briefly) his opinion that all officers were mad.

not be molested even if they were traipsing across an active battlefield. They were *above wars.*

"But what if you were carrying gunpowder to sell to the enemy?" Eliza had tried, but for once Herr Geidel had looked impatient and waved her off, as if to say that wars were mere diversions for bored princes, but trade fairs were *serious.*

It turned out to be perfectly all right that Jack had mentioned highwaymen, because Herr Geidel had been doing a lot of thinking on that very subject. His wagon-train had been forming up in the open places of Joachimsthal. Harnessed pairs of draft-horses were being walked down streets by teamsters leaning back to put tension on the traces, talking the animals into place before wagons. Mule-drivers were pretending to be flabbergasted when their animals balked after testing the weight of their loads: the first act of a timeless play that would eventually lead to profanity and violence. Herr Geidel was *not* a rich merchant now, and for the first part of the journey, he would not be taking any of those roads where armed escorts were for hire *anyway,* and so the trip to the Easter fair in Leipzig might be exciting. Herr Geidel had a few men who could go through the motions needed to charge and discharge a musket, but he wouldn't mind adding Jack to his escort, and of course Eliza was welcome to ride along in one of the wagons.

Jack, wotting that Eliza and his boys' inheritance were at stake, had taken this soldiering job more seriously than most. From time to time he had sallied ahead of the cart-train to look for ambushes. Twice he'd found rabbles of unemployed miners loitering sheepishly in narrow parts of the way, armed with pikes and cudgels, and gotten them to disperse by explaining Herr Geidel's plan to restore vigor to the silver mining business. In truth it wasn't his oratory that moved them out of the way so much as that he and his comrades were carrying flintlocks and pistols. Jack, who knew his wretches, could tell at a glance that these men weren't hungry enough, or persuasively led enough, to buy loot with their lives—particularly when the loot was brimstone, which, he reminded them, would be difficult to turn into silver—they'd have to lug it to a fair and sell it, unless there was an Alchemist among them. He did not mention that buried under the rubble of brimstone in one of Herr Geidel's wagons was a chest full of freshly minted Joachimsthalers. He did *think* about mentioning it, and then leading an ambush *himself,* but he knew that in that event he'd ride away without Eliza, the one woman in the world, or at least the only one he personally knew, capable of providing him with carnal satisfaction. He understood then why Herr Geidel had observed his conversations with Eliza so intently—trying to see whether Jack could be trusted. Apparently he'd concluded Eliza had Jack well in hand. This did not sit well with Jack—but he'd be rid of Herr Geidel soon enough, though not of Eliza.

Anyway, they had ridden north out of those mountains, which Herr Geidel had referred to in his tongue simply as the Ore Range, and into Saxony, about which there was nothing to say except that it was flat. They joined up with a very great and old road that according to Herr Geidel ran from Verona all the way north to Hamburg. Jack was impressed by the mileposts: ten-foot-high stone spikes, each ornately carved with the arms of some dead King, each giving the number of miles to Leipzig. This road was congested with many other merchants' wagon-trains.

In a moist flat basin scribbled all over with the courses of aimless rivers, it intersected another great road that was said to run from Frankfurt to the Orient, and Leipzig *was* that intersection. Jack had most of a day to ramble around and view it from its outskirts, which he did on the general principle of wanting to know where the exits were before entering any confined place. The wagon-trains were backed up for half a mile waiting to get in at the south gate. Leipzig, he found, was smaller and lower-slung than Vienna—a city of several modest spires, not one sky-raking cathedral, which Jack guessed was a sign of its being a Lutheran burg. Of course it was surrounded by the obligatory ramparts and bastions. Outside these were estates and gardens, several of 'em larger than the entire city, all of them belonging not to nobles but to merchants.* Between these estates lay the usual embarrassing swine-crowded suburbs cowering in makeshift barricades that were more like baskets than walls. A few lazily turning mill-wheels took advantage of the nearly imperceptible stirring of the rivers, but millers scarcely ranked above peasants in a town so topheavy with merchants.

JACK AND ELIZA HAD PAID ten pfennigs each at the town gate, then had their silks weighed, and paid duty on them (Eliza had sewn the ostrich-plumes between layers of petticoats, and they were not detected). From the gate a broad street ran north to the center of the town, no more than a musket-shot away. Climbing down from the saddle, Jack was startled by the feel of cobblestones under his feet for the first time in half a year. He was treading on ground that pushed back now, and he knew that his boots needed re-soling. The street was lined with vaulted orifices spewing noise; he felt continually under ambush from left and right, and kept patting his sword-pommel, then hating himself for behaving like a stupid peasant on his first trip to Paris. But Eliza was no less amazed, and kept backing into him, liking to feel his pressure against her back. Queer signs and effigies, frequently in gold leaf, loomed on the fronts of the buildings: a golden snake, a Turk's head, a red lion, a golden bear. So they were a bit like English taverns, which had effigies instead of names, so that people like Jack, who could not read, could know them. But they were not taverns. They were like large town-houses, with many windows, and each had this large vaulted opening giving way to a courtyard full of Bedlam.

Jack and Eliza had kept moving out of an unvoiced fear that if they stopped they'd appear just as lost and stupid as

---

*Which Jack could tell by interpreting the coats of arms carved on the gateposts and embroidered on the flags.

they in fact were. Within a few minutes they'd entered into the town square, and drawn up near a scaffold with the usual selection of dead men hanging from it: a place of comforting familiarity to Jack, even if Eliza did make shrewish comments about the thrumming clouds of flies. Notwithstanding the odd dangling corpse, Leipzig didn't even smell that bad: there was the sewage and smoke of any big town, but it was amazing what a few tons of saffron, cardamom, star anise, and black pepper, distributed round in sacks and bales, would do to freshen a place up.

The town hall ran along one side of the square, and sported Dutch-looking gables above and an arcade of vaulted brown stone at ground level, where well-dressed men were working quietly and intensely. Narrow ditches were incised across the square to channel sewage, and planks had been thrown over them so carts could roll across, or ladies, and fat or lame men, pass over without having to make spectacles of themselves. Jack turned around a couple of times. It was plain that buildings were limited by law to four stories because none (save church towers) had more than that. But clearly the law said nothing about *roofs* and so these were all extremely high and steep—frequently as high as the four-story buildings that supported them—so seen from the street each roof looked like a mountain ridge seen from the valley: a vast terrain densely settled and built up with dormers, towers, gables, cupolas, balconies, and even miniature castles; vegetation (in window-boxes) and statues—not of Jesus or some saint but of Mercury in his winged slippers and hat. Sometimes he was paired against Minerva with her snaky shield, but most of the time Mercury appeared alone and it didn't take a Doctor of Letters to understand that he, and not some dolorous martyr, had been chosen as Patron of Leipzig.

Looking up at vast rooves had been Jack's way to relieve his eyes and mind from the strain of following the action on the ground. There were Eastern men in felt hats with giant rims of rich gleaming fur, talking to long-bearded Jews about racks of animal pelts—the faces of small nasty critters gaping blankly at the sky. Chinese carrying crates of what he had to assume was China, coopers repairing busted casks, bakers hawking loaves, blonde maidens with piles of oranges, musicians everywhere, grinding hurdy-gurdys or plucking at mutant lutes with huge cantilevers projecting asymmetrically from their necks to support thumping bass halyards. Armenian coffee-sellers carrying bright steaming copper and brass tanks on their persons, bored guards with pikes or halberds, turbaned Turks attempting to buy back strange goods that (Jack realized with a shock) had *also* been looted from the Vienna siege-camp—he was amused but, actually, embarrassed and irritated that others had had the same idea. A hookah-smoking area where Turkish boys in pointy-toed slippers scurried from one small table to the next carrying smouldering braziers of ornately wrought silver from which they selected individual coals with silver tongs and placed them carefully atop the hookahs' tobacco-bowls to keep them burning. Everywhere, goods: but here in the square they were in casks, or wrapped up in square bales held together by rope-nets, all marked with curious initials and monograms: trade-marks of diverse merchants.

They'd found a place to stable Turk, then gone down a street, worked up their courage, and entered into one of those broad vaulted portals—wide and high enough for three or four horsemen to ride abreast—and entered the courtyard of one of those buildings. This yard was only some ten by twenty paces, and hemmed in on all sides by the four-story-high walls of the building, which were painted a merry yellow so that what sun did enter the yard cast a symbolic golden radiance on all. The court itself was stuffed with people displaying spices, metal goods, jewels, books, fabric, wine, wax, dried fish, hats, boots, gloves, weapons, and porcelain, frequently standing cheek-to-cheek and talking directly into each other's ears. One whole side of the courtyard, then, gave way to a line of open-sided vaults: an arcade a couple of steps above courtyard level, separated from the courtyard only by a row of stout pillars, and tucked in underneath the actual house. In each vault a grave man in good clothes sat at a mighty desk, or *banca,* with several immense Books, strapped, buckled, and padlocked shut when not in use; an inkwell; quills; and on the floor next to him, a black chest all wrapped about with bronze or iron straps, hinges, chains, and locks of a weight and quality normally seen on arsenal-gates. Sometimes bales and casks of goods were mounded up next to him. More often, the stuff was piled out in the courtyard. Sixty or eighty feet above, stout beams projected from the tops of dormers, thrusting pulleys out over the yard, and by means of ropes through those pulleys, laborers hoisted the goods up for storage in the cavernous attics.

"They are betting prices will rise," Eliza said, observing this, and this was the first inkling Jack received that this was more than a country swap-meet, and that there were layers of cleverness at work here that went far beyond simply knowing how many thalers should buy a tub of butter.

Jack saw so much that was strange in Leipzig, and saw it so fast, that he had to put most of it out of his mind immediately to make room for new material, and didn't remember it until later, when taking a piss or trying to go to sleep, and when he *did* remember it, it seemed so strange to him that he couldn't be sure whether it was a dream, or something that had really happened, or proof that the mines that the French Pox had (he suspected) been patiently excavating under his brain for the last several years, had finally begun to detonate.

There had been, for example, a trip inside one of the factories* to exchange some odd coins that Jack had picked up along his travels and been unable to spend, as no one recognized them. In this room, men sat behind desks with books in whose pages were circular cut-outs made to hold coins— two of each coin, so both heads and tails could be viewed in the same glance, and each coin labeled with various cryptic numbers and symbols in different colors of ink. The money-

---

*As the trading-houses were called, because important men called factors inhabited and ran them.

changer paged steadily through this book until he found a page holding coins just like Jack's, though crisper and shinier. He took out a færy-sized scale made out of gold, whose pans, no larger than dollars, were suspended from its fragile cross-bar by blue silken cords. He put Jack's coins on one pan and then, using tweezers, piled featherweight scraps of marked gold foil on the other pan until they balanced. Then he put the scale back into its wooden carrying-case, which was smaller than Eliza's hand; did some calculations; and offered Jack a couple of Leipziger Ratsmarken (Leipzig minted its own coins). Eliza insisted they visit a couple of other money-changers and repeat the ceremony, but the results were always the same. So finally they accepted the Leipziger coins and then watched the money-changer fling Jack's old coins into a box in the corner, half full of assorted coins and fragments of jewelry, mostly black from tarnish. "We'll melt it down," he explained when he saw the look on Jack's face. Eliza, meanwhile, was staring at a wall-chart of exchange rates, reading the names of the coins that had been chalked up there: "Louis d'or, Maximilian d'or, souverain d'or, rand, ducat, Louis franc, Breslau ducat, Schildgroschen, Hohlheller, Schwertgroschen, Oberwehr groschen, Hellengroschen, pfennig, Goldgulden, halberspitzgroschen, Engelsgroschen, Real, Ratswertmark, ⅔ thaler, English shilling, ruble, abassid, rupiah . . ."

   "Just goes to prove we have to get into the money-making business," Jack said when they left.

   "To me it proves that the business is crowded and hard-fought," Eliza said. "Better to get into silver-mining. All the coiners must buy from miners."

   "But Herr Geidel would rather have burning splints under his nails than own another silver mine," Jack reminded her.

   "It would seem to me *better* to buy into something when it is cheap, and wait for it to become dear," Eliza said. "Think of those trading-houses with their attics."

   "We don't have an attic."

   "I meant it as a figure of speech."

"So did I. We have no way to purchase a silver mine and sew it into your skirts and carry it round until the price goes up." This sounded to Jack like a sure-fire conversation ender but only produced a thoughtful expression on Eliza's face.

Consequently they found themselves at the Bourse, a small tidy rectangular building of white stone packed with well-dressed men screaming at each other in all the languages of Christendom but bound together by some Pentecostal faith in the Holy Spirit of the Messe that made all tongues one. There were no goods in evidence, only bits of paper, which was so odd that Jack would've stayed up all night wondering over it if he hadn't forgotten immediately in light of later developments. After a brief conversation with a trader who was taking a breather on the edge of the floor, smoking a clay-pipe and quaffing some of that fine golden beer from Pilsen, Eliza returned to Jack with a triumphant and determined look about her that boded ill. "The word is *Kuxen*," she said, "we wish to buy *Kuxen* in a silver mine."

"We *do*?"

"Isn't that what we just decided?" She was joking, perhaps.

"First tell me what *Kuxen* are."

"Shares. The mine is divided in half. Each half into quarters. Each quarter into eighths, and so on—until the number of shares is something like sixty-four or one twenty-eight—that number of shares is then sold. Each share is called a *kux*."

"And by share, I suppose you mean—?"

"Same as when thieves divvy up their swag."

"I was going to liken it to how sailors partake of a voyage's proceeds, but you stooped lower, faster."

"That man nearly shot beer from his nostrils when I said I wished to invest in a silver mine," Eliza said proudly.

"Always a positive omen."

"He said only one man's even trying to sell them at this fair—the Doctor. We need to talk to the Doctor."

Through involved and tedious investigations that little improved the balance of Jack's humours, they tracked the Doctor down in the general quarter of the *Jahrmarkt,* which (never mind what the German words literally meant) was a fun fair—a sideshow to the *Messe.* "Eeeyuh, I hate these things—loathsome people exhibiting all manner of freakish behaviors—like a morality play depicting my own life."

"The Doctor is in there," Eliza said grimly.

"Why not let's wait until we actually have money to buy Kuxen *with?*" Jack pleaded.

"Jack, it is all the same—if we want kuxen, why pass through the intermediate step of exchanging silk or ostrich-plumes for coin, and then coin for kuxen, when we could simply exchange silk or plumes for kuxen?"

"Ow, that one was like a stave to the bridge of the nose. You're saying—"

"I'm saying that at Leipzig all goods—silk, coins, shares in mines—lose their hard dull gross forms and liquefy, and give up their true nature, as ores in an alchemist's furnace sweat mercury—and all mercury is mercury and can be freely swapped for mercury of like weight—indeed cannot be distinguished from it."

"That's lovely, but DO WE REALLY WANT TO OWN SHARES IN A MINE?"

"Oh, who knows?" Eliza said with an airy tossing movement of the hand. "I just like to shop for things."

"And I'm doomed to follow you, carrying your purse," Jack muttered, shifting the burden of silk-bolts from one shoulder to the other.

So to the Fun Fair—indistinguishable (to Jack) from a hospital for the possessed and deformed and profoundly lost: contortionists, rope-walkers, fire-eaters, foreigners, and mystical personalities, a few of whom Jack recognized from Vagabond-camps here and there. They knew the Doctor from his clothing and his wig, about which they'd been warned. He was trying to initiate a philosophickal dispute with a Chinese fortune-teller, the subject of the debate being a diagram on a book-page consisting of a stack of six short horizontal lines, some of which were continuous (—) and others interrupted (- -). The Doctor was trying various languages out on the Chinese man, who only looked more aggrieved and dignified by the moment. Dignity was a clever weapon to use against the Doctor, who did not have very much of it at the moment. On his head was the largest wig Jack had ever seen, a thunderhead of black curls enveloping and dwarfing his head and making him look, from behind, as if a yearling bear-cub had dropped from a tree onto his shoulders and was trying to wrench his head off. His attire was no less formidable. Now, during the long winter, Jack had learned that a dress had more parts, technical zargon, and operating procedures associated with it than a flintlock. The Doctor's outfit mocked any dress: between Leipzig and his skin there had to be two dozen layers of fabric belonging to Christ knew how many separate garments: shirts, waistcoats, vests, and things of which Jack did not know the names. Rank upon rank of heavy, close-spaced buttons, containing, in the aggregate, enough brass to cast a swivel-gun. Straps and draw-strings, lace gushing from the openings around throat and wrists. But the lace needed washing, the wig needed professional maintenance, and the Doctor himself was not, at root, a good-looking man. And despite the attire, Jack ended up suspecting he was not a vain one; he was dressed that way to a purpose. In particular, perhaps, to make himself seem older—when he turned around at the sound of Eliza's voice, it was evident he was no more than about forty years old.

He was up on his three-inch platform heels right away, favoring Eliza with a deep, courtly bow and shortly moving on to hand-kissing. For a minute all was in French that Jack couldn't quite follow, and so he went by appearances: Eliza looked uncharacteristically nervous (though she was trying to be plucky), and the Doctor, a lively and quick sort, was observing with polite curiosity. But there was no drooling or leering. Jack reckoned him for a eunuch or sodomite.

Suddenly the Doctor broke into English—making him the first person, other than Eliza, whom Jack had heard speaking in the tongue of that remote Isle in a couple of years. "I assumed, from your attire, that you were a fashionable Parisian lady. But I judged too hastily, for I perceive, on closer enjoyment, that you have something that such women typically lack: genuine taste."

Eliza was speechless—flattered by the words, but flustered by the choice of language. The Doctor splayed a hand across his breast and looked apologetic. "Have I made the wrong guess? I thought I detected that the lady's superb French was enlivened and invigorated by the firm sure tread of an Anglo-Saxon cadence."

"Bullseye," Jack said, drawing a raised eyebrow from the Doctor and a glare from Eliza. Now that he knew the Doctor spoke English, it was all Jack could do to limit himself to that one word—he wanted to talk, talk, talk—to make jests* and to voice his opinions on diverse subjects, relate certain anecdotes, *et cetera.* He said "Bullseye" because he was afraid Eliza might try to brazen it out by claiming to be from some odd corner of France, and Jack, who had much experience in brazening, and attempting to sustain elaborate lies, sensed that this would be a losing bet with the annoyingly perceptive Doctor.

"When you have resolved your differences with the Oriental gentleman, I should like to take you up on the subject of *Kuxen,*" said Eliza.

A double eye-brow raise greeted this news, causing the topheavy wig to pitch alarmingly. "Oh, I'm free *immediately,*" he said, "this Mandarin seems to have no desire to refine his philosophickal position—to disentangle the worthy *science* of number *theory* from the base *superstition* of *numerology*—most unfortunate for him and the rest of his race."

"I am not well versed in any of those subjects," Eliza began, obviously (to Jack) making an heroic bid to change the subject, and obviously (to the Doctor) begging to be given an advanced course of instruction.

---

*E.g., "Hey, Doc, how many goats were shaved to make that wig?"

"Fortune-tellers frequently make use of a random element, such as cards or tea-leaves," the Doctor began. "This fellow tosses sticks on the ground and reads them, never mind exactly how—all I'm interested in is the end result—a set of half a dozen lines, each of which is either solid or broken. We could do the same thing by flipping six coins—*videlicet . . .*" and here he went into a performance of slapping himself all over, like a man who has a mouse in his clothing, and whenever he detected a coin in one of the manifold pockets of his many garments, he scooped it out and flipped it into the air, letting it clang like a Chinese gong (for the coins tended to be big ones—many of them gold) on the paving-stones. "He's rich," Jack muttered to Eliza, "or connected with rich persons."

"Yes—the clothes, the coins . . ."

"All fakeable."

"How do you know him to be rich, then?"

"In the wilderness, only the most terrible beasts of prey cavort and gambol. Deer and rabbits play no games."

"Very well, then," said the Doctor, bending to peer at the fallen coins. "We have heads, tails, tails, tails, heads, and tails." He straightened up. "To the Chinese mystic this pattern has some great significance which he will, for a small fee, look up in a book, jammed with heathen claptrap, and read to you." The Doctor had forgotten about the coins, and about the circle of fun-fair habitués closing in on it like a noose, each making his best guess (as they lacked scales and books) as to which of them was most valuable. Jack stepped in, using his thumb to nudge his sword a hand's breadth out of its scabbard. Their reaction made it plain they were all keeping one eye on him. He picked up the coins, which he would return to the Doctor in a tremendously impressive display of honesty and sound moral character whenever he snapped out of his rant. "To me, on the other hand, this pattern means: seventeen."

"Seventeen?" Jack and Eliza said in unison—both of them had to step lively, now, to keep pace with the Doctor as he stomped out of the *Jahrmarkt* making good time on those high heels. He wasn't a big man but he had a fine set of calves on him, which his stockings showed off nicely.

"Dyadic, or binary numbers—old news," the Doctor said, waving a hand in the air so that the lace cuff flopped around. "My late friend and colleague Mr. John Wilkins published a cryptographic system based on this more than forty years ago in his great *Cryptonomicon*—unauthorized Dutch editions of it are still available over yonder in the Booksellers' Quarter should you desire. But what I take away from the Chinese method of fortune-telling is the notion of producing *random* numbers by the dyadic technique, and by this Wilkins's system could be incomparably strengthened." All of which was like the baying of hounds to Jack.

"Crypto, graphy . . . writing of secrets?" Eliza guessed.

"Yes—an unfortunate necessity in these times," the Doctor said.

About now, they escaped the closeness of the Fun Fair and stopped in an open square near a church. "Nicolaikirche—I was baptized there," the Doctor said. "*Kuxen!* A topic strangely related to dyadic numbers in that the number of *Kuxen* in a particular mine is always a power of two, *videlicet:* one, two, four, eight, sixteen . . . But that is a mathematical curiosity in which you'll have little interest. I am selling them. Should you buy them? Formerly a prosperous industry, upon which the fortunes of great families such as the Fuggers and Hacklhebers were founded, silver mining was laid low by the Thirty Years' War and the discovery, by the Spaniards, of very rich deposits at Potosí in Peru and Guanajuato in Mexico. Buying *Kuxen* in a European mine that is run along *traditional* lines, as is done in the Ore Range, would be a waste of the lady's money. But my mines or I should say the mines of the House of Brunswick-Lüneburg, which I have been given the responsibility to manage, will be, I think, a better investment."

"Why?" Eliza asked.

"It is *extremely* difficult to explain."

"Oh, but you're so good at explaining things . . ."

"You really must leave the flattery to me, milady, as you are more deserving of it. No, it has to do with certain new sorts of engines, of my own design, and new techniques for extracting metal from ore, devised by a very wise and, as alchemists go, non-fraudulent alchemist of my acquaintance. But a woman of your conspicuous acumen would never exchange her coins—"

"Silk, actually," Jack inserted, turning half round to flash the goods.

"Er . . . lovely silks, then, for *Kuxen* in my mine, just because I *said* these things in a market."

"Probably true," Eliza admitted.

"You would have to inspect the works first. Which I invite you to do . . . we leave tomorrow . . . but if you could exchange your goods for *coin* first it would be—"

"Wait!" Jack said, it being his personal duty to play the role of coarse, armed bumpkin. Giving Eliza the opportunity to say: "Good Doctor, my interest in the subject was just a womanish velleity—forgive me for wasting your time—"

"But why bother talking to me at all then? You must've had some reason. Come on, it'll be fun."

"Where is it?" Jack asked.

"The *lovely* Harz Mountains—a few days' journey west of here."

"That'd be in the general direction of Amsterdam, then?"

"Young sir, when I spied your Turkish sword, I took you for some sort of Janissary, but your knowledge of the lands to the West proves otherwise—even if your East London accent hadn't already given you away."

"Uh, okay, so that's a yes, then," Jack mumbled, leading Eliza a few paces away. "A free ride in the Doctor's train—can't be too much wrong with that."

"He's up to something," Eliza protested.

"So are *we,* lass—it's not a crime."

Eventually she wafted back over to the Doctor and allowed as how she'd be willing to "leave my entourage behind" for a few days, with the exception of "my faithful manservant and bodyguard," and "detour to the Harz Mountains" to inspect the works. They talked, for a while, in French.

"He says a lot in a hurry sometimes," Eliza told Jack as they followed the Doctor, at a distance, down a street of great trading-houses. "I tried to find out approximately what a *kux* would cost—he said not to worry."

"Funny, from a man who claims he's trying to raise money . . ."

"He said that the reason he first took me for Parisian was that ostrich plumes, like the sample in my hat, are in high fashion there just now."

"More flattery."

"No—his way of telling me that we should ask a high price."

"Where's he taking us?"

"The House of the Golden Mercury, which is the factory of the von Hacklheber family."

"We've already been kicked out of there."

"He's going to get us in."

AND THAT HE DID, by means of a mysterious conversation that took place inside the factory, out of their view. This was the biggest courtyard they'd seen in Leipzig: narrow but long, lined with vaulted arcades on both sides, a dozen cranes active at once elevating goods that the von Hacklhebers expected to rise in price, and letting down ones they thought had reached their peak. At the end nearest the street, mounted to the wall above the entry arch, was a skinny three-story-high structure cantilevered outwards over the yard, like balconies on three consecutive floors all merged into one tower. It was enclosed with windows all round except on the top floor, where a golden roof sheltered an open platform and supported a pair of obscenely long-necked gargoyles poised to vomit rain (should it rain) out onto the traders below. "Reminds me of the castle on the butt-end of a galleon," was Eliza's comment, and it wasn't for a few minutes that Jack understood that this was a reminder of the naughty business off Qwghlm years ago, and (therefore) her oblique female way of saying she didn't like it. This despite the gold-plated Mercury, the size of a man, bracketed to it, which seemed to be springing into flight above their heads, holding out a golden stick twined about with snakes and sur- mounted by a pair of wings. "No, it's a Cathedral of Mer- cury," Jack decided, trying to get her mind off the galleon. "Your Cathedral of Jesus is cross-shaped. This one takes its plan from that stick in his hand—long and slender—the vaults on the sides like the snakes' loops. The wings of the factory spreading out from the head of it, where is mounted the bishop's pulpit, and all of us believers crowded in below to celebrate the *Messe*."

Eliza sold the stuff. Jack assumed she sold it well. He knew they were soon to leave Leipzig and so amused himself by looking around. Watching the bales and casks ascend and descend on their ropes, his eye was drawn to a detail: from many of the countless windows that lined the courtyard, short rods projected horizontally into the air, and mounted to their ends, on ball-joints like the one where the thigh-bone meets the pelvis, were mirrors about a foot square, canted at diverse angles. When he first noticed them Jack supposed that they were a clever trick for reflecting sunlight into those many dim offices. But looking again he saw that they shifted frequently, and that their silvered faces were always aimed *down* toward the courtyard. There were scores of them. Jack never glimpsed the watchers who lurked in the dark rooms.

Later he chanced to look up at the highest balcony, and discovered a new gargoyle looking back at him: this was made of flesh and blood, a stout man who hadn't bothered to cover his partly bald, partly grizzled head. He had battled smallpox and won at the cost of whatever good or even bad looks he might ever have had. Quite a few decades of good living had put a lot of weight into his face and drawn the pocked flesh downwards into jowls and wattles and chins, lumpy as cargo nets. He was giving Eliza a look that Jack did not find suitable. Up there on that balcony he was such an arresting presence that Jack did not notice, for a few min- utes, that another man, much more finely turned out, was up there, too: the Doctor, talking in the relentless way of one who's requesting a favor, and gesturing so that those white lace cuffs seemed to flit around him like a pair of doves.

Like a couple of peasants huddled together in the Cathedral of Notre Dame, Jack and Eliza performed their role in the Mass and then departed, leaving no sign that they'd ever been there, save perhaps for a evanescent ripple in the coursing tide of quicksilver.

Saxony

LATE APRIL 1684

LEAVING LEIPZIG WITH THE DOCTOR did not happen at any one particular moment—it was a ceremonial procession that extended over a day. Even after Jack and Eliza and Turk the Horse had located the Doctor's entourage, several hours of wandering around the town still awaited them: there was a mysterious call at the von Hacklheber factory, and a stop at the Nicolaikirche so that the Doctor could make devotions and take communion, and then it was over to the University (which like all else in Leipzig was small and serious as a pocket-pistol), where the Doctor simply sat in his carriage for half an hour, chatting with Eliza in French, which was the language he preferred for anything of a high-flown nature. Jack, restlessly circling the carriage—which was chocolate-brown, and painted all over with flowers—put his ear to the window once and heard them talking about some noble lady named Sophie, a second time, a few minutes later, it was dressmaking, then Catholic vs. Lutheran views on transubstantiation . . . Finally Jack pulled the door open. "Pardon the interruption, but I had a notion to go on a pilgrimage to Jerusalem, crawling there and back on my hands and knees, and wanted to make sure that it wouldn't delay our departure . . ."

"Ssh! The Doctor's trying to make a very difficult decision," Eliza said.

"Just *make* it—that's what I say—doesn't get easier if you

think about it," Jack advised. The Doctor had a manuscript on his lap, and a quill poised above it, a trembling drop of ink ready to break loose, but his hand would not move. His head teetered and tottered through a ponderous arc (or maybe it was the wig that magnified all movements) as he read the same extract over and over, under his breath, each time adopting a different sequence of facial expressions and emphasizing different words, like an actor trying to make sense of some ambiguous verse: should this be read as a jaded pedant? A dim schoolmaster? A skeptical Jesuit? But since the words had been written by the Doctor himself, that couldn't be it—he was trying to imagine how the words would be received by different sorts of readers.

"Would you like to read it out loud, or—"

"It is in Latin," Eliza said.

More waiting. Then: "Well, what *is* the decision that wants making?"

"Whether or not to heave it over the transom of yonder doorway," Eliza said, pointing to the front of one of those Leipziger houses-that-weren't-houses.

"What's it say on that door?"

"*Acta Eruditorum*—it is a journal that the Doctor founded two years ago."

"I don't know what a journal is."

"Like a gazette for savants."

"Oh, so that stack of papers is something he wants to have printed?"

"Yes."

"Well, if *he* founded it, it's *his* journal, so why's he got leeches in his breeches?"

"Ssh! All the savants of Europe will read the words on that page—they must be perfect."

"Then why doesn't he take it with him and work on it some more? This is no place to make anything perfect."

"It has been finished for years," the Doctor said, sounding unusually sad. "The decision: should I publish it *at all?*"

"Is it a good yarn?"

"It is not a narrative. It is a mathematical technique so advanced that only two people in the world understand it," the Doctor said. "When published, it will bring about enormous changes in not only mathematics, but all forms of natural philosophy and engineering. People will use it to build machines that fly through the air like birds, and that travel to other planets, and its very power and brilliance will sweep old, tottering, worn-out systems of thought into the dustbin."

"And you invented it, Doctor?" Eliza asked, as Jack was occupied making finger-twirling movements in the vicinity of his ear.

"Yes—seven or eight years ago."

"And still no one knows about it, besides—"

"Me, and the other fellow."

"Why haven't you told the world about it?"

"Because it seems the other fellow invented it ten years before I did, and didn't tell anyone."

"Oh."

"I've been waiting for him to say something. But it's been almost twenty years since he did it, and he doesn't show the slightest inclination to let anyone else in on it."

"You've waited eight years—why today? It's well after midday," Jack said. "Take it with you—give it another two or three years' thought."

"Why *today*? Because I do not believe God put me on this earth, and gave me either the best or second-best mind currently in existence, so that I could spend my days trying to beg money from the likes of Lothar von Hacklheber, so that I could dig a large hole in the ground," the Doctor said. "I don't want my epitaph to be, 'He brought the price of silver down one-tenth of one percent.'"

"Right! Sounds like a decision to me," Jack said. Reaching into the carriage he gathered up the manuscript, carried it up the walk to the door in question, and heaved it through the transom. "And now, off to the mountains!"

"One more small errand in the Booksellers' Quarter," the Doctor said, "as long as I'm getting myself into trouble."

* * *

THE BOOKSELLERS' QUARTER LOOKED AND worked like the rest
of Leipzig except all the goods were books: they tumbled
out of casks, rose in unsteady stacks, or were arranged into
blocks that were wrapped and tied and then stacked into
larger blocks. Bent porters carried them around in hods and
back-baskets. The Doctor, never one to accomplish anything
in a hurry, devoted several minutes to arranging his carriage
and escort-train before the widest and clearest of the Book-
Fair's exits. In particular he wondered if Jack wouldn't mind
mounting Turk and (for lack of a better word) *posing* between the booksellers and the carriage. Jack did so, and was
reasonably merry about it, having given up any hope that
they'd escape the city before nightfall.

The Doctor squared his shoulders, adjusted numerous
subsystems of clothing (today he wore a coat embroidered
with flowers, just like the ones painted on his carriage), and
walked into the Book-Fair. Jack couldn't see him any more,
but he could *hear* him. Not his voice, actually, but rather the
effect that the Doctor's appearance had on the overall sound
of the fair. As when a handful of salt is thrown into a pot
that's about to boil: a hush, then a deep steady building.

The Doctor came running. He moved well for a man on
high heels. He was pursued by the booksellers of* Königs-
berg, Basel, Rostock, Kiel, Florence, Strasbourg, Edinburgh, Düsseldorf, Copenhagen, Antwerp, Seville, Paris,
and Danzig, with a second echelon not far behind. The
Doctor made it past Jack well before any of them. The
sight of a mounted man with a heathen saber brought them
to a jagged halt. They contented themselves after that with
flinging books: any book that was handy. They gang-
tackled porters, molested promotional displays, kicked
over casks to get ammunition, and the air above and
around Jack grew rather dark with books, as when a flock
passes overhead. They fell open on cobblestones and

---

*Just guessing, here.

spilled out their illustrative woodcuts: portraits of great men, depictions of the Siege of Vienna, diagrams of mining-engines, a map of some Italian city, a dissection of the large bowel, vast tables of numbers, musketeer drills, geometers' proofs, human skeletons in insouciant poses, the constellations of the Zodiac, rigging of foreign barkentines, design of alchemical furnaces, glaring Hottentots with bones in their noses, thirty flavors of Baroque window-frames. This entire scene was carried out with very little bellowing, as if ejection of the Doctor was a routine matter for the booksellers. At the crack of the coachman's whip, they made a few desultory final heaves and then turned back to resume whatever conversations the Doctor had interrupted. Jack for his part adopted a ceremonial rear-guard position behind the Doctor's baggage-cart (inadvertently laden, now, with a few random books). The brittle sparking impacts of horse-shoes and wheel-rims against cobblestones were like heavenly chimes to his Vagabond-ears.

He could not get an explanation until hours later, when they had put Leipzig's north gate a few miles behind them, and stopped at an inn on the road to Halle. By this time Eliza had been thoroughly saturated with the Doctor's view of events as well as his gloomy and resentful mood. She stayed in the Ladies' Bedchamber, he stayed in the Men's, they met in the Common-Room. "He was born in Leipzig—educated himself in Leipzig—went to school in Leipzig—"

"Why'd he go to school if he educated himself? Which is it?"

"Both. His father was a professor who died when he was very young—so he taught himself Latin at the same age when you were hanging from dead men's legs."

"That's funny—you know, I tried to teach myself Latin, but what with the Black Death, the Fire, *et cetera* . . ."

"In lieu of having a father, he read his father's library—*then* went to school. And you saw for yourself how they treated him."

"Perhaps they had an excellent reason," Jack said—he was bored, and getting Eliza steamed up would be as good an entertainment as any.

"There is no reason for you to be gnawing at the Doctor's ankles," Eliza said. "He is one of that sort of man who forms very profound *friendships* with members of the gentler sex."

"I saw what sort of friendship he had with you when he was pointing out your gentle bosom to Lothar von Hacklheber," Jack returned.

"There was probably a reason—the Doctor is a tapestry of many threads."

"Which thread brought him to the Book-Fair?"

"For some years he and Sophie have been trying to persuade the Emperor in Vienna to establish a grand library and academy for the entire Empire."

"Who is Sophie?"

"Another one of the Doctor's woman friends."

"What fair did he pick *her* up at?"

Eliza arched her eyebrows, leaned forward, and spoke in a whisper that could etch glass: "Don't speak of her that way—Sophie is none other than the daughter of the Winter Queen herself. She is the Duchess of Hanover!"

"Jeezus. How'd a man like the Doctor end up in such company?"

"Sophie inherited the Doctor when her brother-in-law died."

"What do you mean by that? Is he a slave?"

"He is a librarian. Sophie's brother-in-law hired him in that capacity, and when he died, Sophie inherited the library, and the Doctor along with it."

"But that's not good enough—the Doctor has ambitions— he wants to be the Emperor's librarian?"

"As it is now, a savant in Leipzig may never become aware of a book that's been published in Mainz, and so the world of letters is fragmented and incoherent—not like in England, where all the savants know each other and belong to the same Society."

"What!? A Doctor *here* wants to make things *more like England*?"

"The Doctor proposed to the Emperor that a new decree be drawn up, ordering that all booksellers at the Leipzig and Frankfurt fairs must write up a description of every book they publish, and send these, along with copies of each book, to—"

"Let me guess—to the Doctor?"

"Yes. And then he would make them all part of some vast, hard-to-understand thing he wants to build—he couldn't re-strain himself from breaking into Latin here, so I don't know exactly—part library, part academy, part machine."

"Machine?" Jack was imagining a mill-wheel assembled from books.

But they were interrupted by ribald, helpless, snorting laughter from the corner of the Common-Room, where the Doctor himself was sitting on a stool, reading (as they saw when they came over and joined him) one of the hurled books that had lodged in the baggage-cart. As usual their progress across the room, or to be specific *Eliza's,* was carefully tracked by lonely merchants whose eyeballs were practically growing out of their heads on stalks. Jack had at first been sur-prised, and was now growingly annoyed, that other men were capable of noticing Eliza's beauty—he suspected that they did so in some base way altogether different from how *he* did it.

"I love reading novels," the Doctor exclaimed. "You can understand them without thinking too much."

"But I thought you were a philosopher," Eliza said, appar-ently having waxed close enough to him now that she could get away with teasing and pouting maneuvers.

"But when philosophizing, one's mind follows its natural inclination—gaining profit along with pleasure—whereas following *another* philosopher's meditations is like stum-bling through a mine dug by others—hard work in a cold dark place, and painful if you want to zig where they decided to zag. But this—" holding up the book "—you can read without stopping."

"What's the story about?"

"Oh, all these novels are the same—they are about pica-roons—that means a sort of rogue or scoundrel—could be male or female—they move about from city to city like Vagabonds (than whom, however, they are much more clever and resourceful)—getting into hilarious scrapes and making fools—or trying to—out of Dukes, Bishops, Generals, and

". . . *Doctors*."

Lengthy silence, then, followed by Jack saying, "Errr . . . is this the chapter where I'm supposed to draw my weapon?"

"Oh, stop!" the Doctor said. "I didn't bring you all this way to have an *imbroglio*."

"Why, then?" Jack asked—quickly, as Eliza was still so red-faced he didn't think it would be clever *or* resourceful to give her a chance to speak.

"For the same reason that Eliza sacrificed some of your silk to make some dresses, and thereby fetched a higher price. I need to draw some attention to the mine project—make it seem exciting—fashionable even—so that people will at least think about investing."

"I'm guessing, then," Jack said, "that my role will be to hide behind a large piece of furniture and not emerge until all rich fashionable persons have departed?"

"I gratefully accept your proposal," the Doctor said. "Meanwhile, Eliza—well—have you ever seen how mounte-banks ply their trade in Paris? No matter what they are sell-ing, they always have an accomplice in the crowd, attired like the intended victims—"

"That means, like an ignorant peasant," Jack informed Eliza. "And at first this accomplice seems to be the most skeptical person in the whole crowd—asking difficult ques-tions and mocking the entire proceedings—but as it contin-ues he is conspicuously won over, and gladly makes the first purchase of whatever the mountebank is selling—"

"Kuxen, in this case?" Eliza said.

The Doctor: "Yes—and in this case the audience will be made up of Hacklhebers, wealthy merchants of Mainz,

Lyons bankers, Amsterdam money-market speculators—in sum, wealthy and fashionable persons from all over Christendom."

Jack made a mental note to find out what a money-market speculator was. Looking at Eliza, he found her looking right back at him, and reckoned that she was thinking the same thing. Then the Doctor distracted her with: "In order to blend in with that crowd, Eliza, we shall only have to find some way to make you seem half as intelligent as you really are, and to dim your natural radiance so that they'll not be blinded by awe or jealousy."

"Oh, Doctor," Eliza said, "why is it that men who desire *women* can never speak such words?"

"You've only been in the presence of men who are in the presence of *you*, Eliza," Jack said, "and how can they pronounce fine words when the heads of their yards are lodged in their mouths?"

The Doctor laughed, much as he'd been doing earlier.

"What's your excuse, Jack?" Eliza responded, eliciting some sort of violent thoracic Incident in the Doctor.

Tears of joy came to Jack's eyes. "Thank God women have no way to rid themselves of the yellow bile," he said.

At this same inn they joined up with a train of small but masty ore-wagons carrying goods that the Doctor had acquired at Leipzig and sent on ahead to wait for them. Some of these were laden with saltpeter from India, others with brimstone from the Ore Range.* The others—though laden only with a few small crates—sagged and screeched like infidels on the Rack. Peering between the boards of same, Jack could see that they contained small earthenware flasks packed in straw. He asked a teamster what was in them: "*Quecksilber*" was the answer.

> *Mammon* led them on,
> *Mammon*, the least erected Spirit that fell

---

*Which they knew because it bore the trademark of none other than Herr Geidel.

From heav'n, for ev'n in heav'n his looks and
      thoughts
Were always downward bent, admiring more
The riches of Heav'ns pavement, trod'n Gold,
Then aught divine or holy else enjoy'd
In vision beatific; by him first
Men also, and by his suggestion taught,
Ransack'd the Center, and with impious hands
Rifl'd the bowels of thir mother Earth
For Treasures better hid.
                    —MILTON, *Paradise Lost*

THE ENTIRE TRAIN, amounting to some two dozen wagons, proceeded west through Halle and other cities in the Saxon plain. Giant stone towers with dunce-cap rooves had been raised over city gates so that the burghers could see armies or Vagabond-hordes approaching in time to do something about it. A few days past Halle, the ground finally started to rise up out of that plain and (like one of the Doctor's philosophical books) to channel them this way and that, making them go ways they were not especially inclined to. It was a slow change, but one morning they woke up and it was no longer disputable that they were in a valley, the most beautiful golden valley Jack had ever seen, all pale green with April's first shoots, thickly dotted with haystacks even after cattle had been reducing them all winter long. Broad fells rose gently but steadily from this valley and developed, at length, into shapes colder and more mountainous—ramps built by giants, leading upwards to mysterious culminations. The highest ridge-lines were indented with black shapes, mostly trees; but the Saxons had not been slow to construct watch-towers on those heights that commanded the most sweeping views. Jack couldn't help speculating as to what they were all waiting for. Or perhaps they sparked fires in them at night to speed strange information over the heads of sleeping farmers. They passed a placid lake with what had been a brown stone castle avalanching into it; wind came up and raised goose-bumps on the water, destroying the reflection.

Eliza and the Doctor mostly shared the coach, she amending her dresses according to what he claimed was now in fashion, and he writing letters or reading picaroon-novels. It seemed that Sophie's daughter, Sophie Charlotte, was fixing to marry the Elector of Brandenburg later this year, and the trousseau was being imported direct from Paris, and this gave occasion for them to talk about clothing for *days*. Sometimes Eliza would ride in the seat atop the carriage if the weather was fine, giving the teamsters reason to live another day. Sometimes Jack would give Turk a rest by walking alongside, or riding on, or in, the coach.

The Doctor was always doing *something*—sketching fantastic machines, writing letters, scratching out pyramids of ones and zeroes and rearranging them according to some set of contrived rules.

"What're you doing there, Doc?" Jack asked one time, just trying to be sociable.

"Making some improvements to my Theory of Matter," the Doctor said distantly, and then said no more for three hours, at which time he announced to the driver that he had to piss.

Jack tried to talk to Eliza instead. She'd been rather sulky since the conversation at the Inn. "Why is it you'll perform intimate procedures on one end of me, but you won't kiss the other end?" he asked one evening when she returned his affections with eye-rolling.

"I'm losing blood—the humour of passion— what do you expect?"

"Do you mean that in the normal monthly sense, or—"

"More than usual this month—besides I only kiss people who care about me."

"Aw, whatever made you think otherwise?"

"You know almost nothing about me. So any fond emotions you might have, proceed from lust alone."

"Well, whose fault is that, then? I asked you, months ago, to tell me how you got from Barbary to Vienna."

"You did? I remember no such thing."

"Well, p'r'aps it's just the French Pox going to my brain, lass, but I clearly remember—you gave it a few days' profound thought, hardly speaking, and then said, 'I don't wish to reveal that.'"

"You haven't asked me *recently*."

"Eliza, how'd you get from Barbary to Vienna?"

"Some parts of the story are too sad for me to tell, others too tedious to hear—suffice it to say, that when I reached an age that a horny Moor construes as adulthood, I came, in their minds, to bear the same relationship to my mother as a dividend does to a joint stock corporation—viz. a new piece of wealth created out of the normal functioning of the old. I was liquidated."

"What?"

"Tendered to a Vizier in Constantinople as part of a trade, no different from the trades that sustain the City of Leipzig—you see, a person can also be rendered into a few drops of mercury, and combine with the mysterious international flow of that substance."

"What'd that Vizier have to pay for you? Just curious."

"As of two years ago the price of one me, in the Mediterranean market, was a single horse, a bit slimmer and faster than the one you've been riding around on."

"Seems, er . . . well, *any* price would seem too low, of course—but even so—for Christ's sake . . ."

"But you're forgetting that Turk's an uncommon steed—a bit past his prime, to be sure, and worn round the edges—but, what matters, capable of fathering others."

"Ah . . . so the horse that paid for you was a thoroughbred stallion."

"A strange-looking Arab. I saw it on the docks. It was perfectly white, except for the hooves of course, and its eyes were pink."

"The Berbers are breeders of racehorses?"

"Through the network of the Society of Britannic Abductees, I learned that this stallion was bound, eventually, for *la France*. Someone there is connected to the Barbary pirates—I assume it is the same person who caused me and my mother to be made slaves. Because of that man I shall never see Mum again, for she had a cancer when I left her in Barbary. I will find that man and kill him someday."

Jack counted silently to ten, then said: "Oh, hell, I'll do it. I'm going to die of the French Pox anyway."

"First you have to explain to him *why* you're doing it."

"Fine, I'll try to plan in an extra few hours—"

"It shouldn't take that long."

"No?"

"Why would you kill him, Jack?"

"Well, there was your abduction from Qwghlm—perverse goings-on in the ship—years of slavery—forcible separation from an ailing—"

"No, no! That's why *I* want to kill him. Why do *you*?"

"Same reason."

"But *many* are involved in the slave trade—will you kill all of them?"

"No, just—oh, I get it—I want to kill this evil man, whoever he is, because of my fierce eternal pure love for you, my own Eliza."

She did not swoon, but she did get a look on her face that said *This conversation is over*, which Jack took as a sign he was going in the right direction.

Finally, after a couple of days of skirting and dodging, the Doctor gave the word and they turned north and began straightforwardly ascending into what had plainly become a mountain range. At first this was a grassy rampart. Then strange dark hummocks began to pock the fields. At the same time, they began frequently to see pairs of men turning windlasses, like the ones mounted above wells, but this equipment was stouter and grimier, and it brought up not buckets of water but iron baskets filled with black rock. Jack and Eliza had seen it before at Joachimsthal and knew that the dark mounds were the fœces left behind when the metal (copper here) had been smelted out of the ore. Germans called it *schlock.* When they were wet with rain (which was frequently, now), the schlock-heaps glistened and gave back light tinged blue or purple. Men collected the ore from the hand-haspels (as the winches were called) into wheelbar-rows and staggered behind them, among schlock-piles, to smoking furnaces tended and stirred by coal-smeared men.

Several times they entered into wooded valleys full of smoke, and followed the traces of dragged logs across the ground until they came to gunpowder-mills. Here, tall whip-thin trees, the trunks hairy with miserable scrawny branches,* were cut and burnt endlessly until they became charcoal. This was taken to a water-powered mill to be ground to dust and mixed with the other ingredients. Men came out of these mills looking all drawn and nervous from never really knowing when they'd be blown up, and the Doc-tor supplied them with brimstone and saltpeter from the wagons. Teaching Jack that wars, like great rivers, had their wellsprings in numerous high remote valleys.

Eliza was beginning to see some of the enormous trees of Mum's færy-tales, though many had blown down and could be viewed only as fists of roots thrust into the air still clutch-ing final handfuls of dirt. The air up here was not still for a moment—it was never rainy, cloudy, or sunny for more than a quarter of an hour at a time—but when they were out of those smoky valleys, it was cold and clear. Their progress was slow, but one time the sky cleared as they came through an open place in the woods (it was clear that Harz was a rock and the forest no more substantial than the film of hop-vines that sometimes grew on an ancient schlock-heap), and then it was obvious that they'd risen to a great height above the plains and valleys. Those schlock-heaps like cowls of robed men in a procession. Patrols of black vultures chased and swirled about one another like ashes ascending a flue. Here and there a tower braced itself on a mountain-top or a con-spiracy of trees huddled. Crows raided distant fields for the

---

Faulbaum, the Germans said, meaning "lazy and rotten tree." They were alders.

farmers' seed-corn, and flocks of silver birds wheeled and drilled for some unvoiced purpose on invisible breezes.

So the Doctor decided to cheer them up by taking them down into an old abandoned copper mine.

"Sophie was the first woman to enter a mine," he said helpfully. "You, Eliza, might be the second."

This mine's vein (or the vein-shaped cavity where the vein had once been) was close to the surface and so there was no need to descend numerous ladders in some deep shaft: they pulled up before an old semi-collapsed building, rummaged in a skewed cabinet for lights, sledded down a ramp where once a short staircase had been, and there they were in a tunnel as high as Jack's head and an arm's length wide. Their lights were called kienspans: splits of dry resinous wood about the dimensions of a rapier blade, dipped in some kind of wax or pitch, which burnt enthusiastically, and looked like the flame-swords wielded by Biblical standouts. By this means, they could see that the mine-tunnel was lined with logs and timbers: a hefty post-and-beam lintel every couple of yards, and many horizontal logs, as thick as a person's thigh, laid parallel down the tunnel so as to join each post-and-lintel with the ones before and after it. In this way a long tubular wooden cage was formed, not to keep them in (though it did) but to protect them from a stalled avalanche of loose rubble pressing in from all sides.

The Doctor led them down this tunnel—the entrance quickly lost from view. Frequently, side-tunnels took off to one side or another, but these came up only to mid-thigh on Jack and there was no question of entering them.

Or so he thought until the Doctor stopped before one. The floor all around was strewn with curiously wrought planks, half-moon-shaped pieces of ox-hide, and tabular chunks of black rock. "There is a wonder at the end of this tunnel—no more than half a dozen fathoms back—which you must see."

Jack took it for a joke until Eliza agreed to scurry down the tunnel without hesitation—which meant that according to Rules that applied even to Vagabonds, Jack had to do it first, in order to scout for danger. The Doctor told him that the pieces of ox-hide were called arsch-leders, which was self-explanatory, so Jack put one on. The Doctor then demonstrated the use of the planks, which miners used to protect elbows and forearms from the stony floor when creeping along on their sides. All of this settled, Jack lay down on the floor and crept into it, wielding the plank with one arm and the kienspan with the other. He found it reasonably easy going as long as he didn't think about . . . well, about *anything*.

The kienspan, lunging ahead of him, shed sparks against the end of the tunnel and dazzled him. When his vision settled he found that he was sharing a confined space with a giant black bird—or something—like the ostrich—but with no wings—pawing at the ore, or maybe at Jack's face, with talons bigger than fingers—its long bony neck twisted round almost into a knot, an arrowhead of a skull at the end, jaws open with such . . . big . . . teeth . . .

He only screamed once. Twice, actually, but number two didn't count because it came from smashing his head on the ceiling in a poorly thought-out bid to stand up. He scurried back a couple of fathoms, working on blind fear and pain, stopped, listened, heard nothing but his heart.

Of course it was dead—it was all bones. And the Doctor might be a human oddity in several respects, but he wouldn't send Jack into a monster's lair. Jack retreated slowly, trying not to make his head ache any worse. He could hear the Doctor talking to Eliza: "There are shells scattered upon the mountains! See, this rock has a grain like wood—you can split it into layers—and look at what's between the *strata*! This creature must've been buried in mud—probably the fine dirt that rivers carry—smashed flat, as you can see—its body decomposed leaving a void, later filled in by some other sort of rock—as sculptors cast bronze statues in plaster molds."

"Where do you *get* this stuff? Who told you *that* one?" Jack demanded, a bloody head popping out between their feet, looking up at them.

"I reasoned it out myself," said the Doctor. "*Someone* has to come up with *new* ideas."

Jack rolled over on his belly to find the floor loosely paved with rock-slabs bearing imprints of sundry other Book-of-Revelation fauna. "What river carried this supposed dirt? We're in the middle of a *mountain* of *rock*. There is no *river*," Jack informed the Doctor, after they had gotten Eliza on her way down the tunnel. Jack waited with her traveling-dress slung over his arm while she inched down the tunnel in her knickers and an arsch-leder.

"But there *used* to be," the Doctor said, "Just as there used to be such creatures—" playing his light over impressions of fish with fins too many and jaws too big, swimming creatures shaped like grappling-hooks, dragonflies the size of crossbow-bolts.

"A river in a mountain? I don't think so."

"Then where did the shells come from?"

FINALLY THEY TRAVELED to the rounded top of a mountain where an old stone tower stood, flanked by schlock-heaps instead of bastions. A half-wit could see that the Doctor had been at work here. Rising from the top of the tower was a curious windmill, spinning round sideways like a top instead of rolling like a wheel, so that it didn't have to turn its face into the wind. The base of the tower was protected by an old-fashioned stone curtain-wall that had been repaired recently (they were afraid of being attacked by people who, however, did not have modern artillery). Likewise the gate was new, and it was bolted. A musket-toting engineer opened it for them as soon as the Doctor announced himself, and wasted no time bolting it behind them.

The tower itself was not a fit place for people to lodge. The Doctor gave Eliza a room in an adjoining house. Jack put the fear of God into all the rats he could find in her room, then climbed the stone stair that spiraled* up the inside of the tower. The tower did its part by moaning in wind-gusts like an empty jug when an idler blows over the top. From the

---

*The Doctor: "Actually, it is a helix, not a spiral."

windmill at the top a shaft, consisting of tree-trunks linked one to the next with collars and fittings hammered out of iron, dropped through the center of the tower to an engineering works on the dirt floor. The floor, then, was pierced by a large hole that was obviously the mouth of a mine-shaft. An endless chain of buckets had been rigged so that the windmill's power raised them up from the shaft laden with water. As they went round a giant pulley they emptied into a long wooden tray: a mill-race that carried the water out through a small arched portal in the tower wall. Then the empty buckets dove back into the shaft for another go-round. In this way water was drained away from some deep part of the mines that would normally be flooded. But up here, the water was a good thing to have. After gathering a bit of head in a system of trenches outside, it powered small mill-wheels that ran bellows and trip-hammers for the smiths, and finally collected in cisterns.

Up top, Jack, who'd wisely spent some of their profits on warm clothes, had a view over a few days' journey in every direction. The mountains (excepting one big one to the north) were not of the craggy sort, but swelling round-topped things separated by bottomless cleavages. The woods were dappled—partly leaf-trees with pale spring growth and partly needle-trees that were almost black. Here and there, pools of pasture-land lay on south-facing slopes, and of snow on north-facing ones. Villages, with their red tile rooves, were strewn about unevenly, like blood-spatters. There was a big one just below, in the gorge that divided this mountain from an even higher one to the north: a bald crag whose summit was crowned with a curious arrangement of long stones. Clouds whipped overhead, as fast and furious as the Winged Hussars, and this made Jack feel as if the tower were eternally toppling. The strangely curved blades of the Doctor's windmill hummed over his head like poorly aimed scimitar-cuts.

"JUST A MINUTE, DOCTOR—with all due respect—you've replaced miners-on-treadwheels with a windmill to pump out the water—but what happens when the wind stops blowing?

The water floods back in? Miners are drowned?"

"No, they simply follow the old underground drainage channel, using small ore-boats."

"And how do these miners feel about being replaced by machines, Doctor?"

"The increase in productivity should more than—"

"How easy would it be to slip a *sabot* off one's foot and 'accidentally' let it fall into the gears—"

"Err . . . maybe I'll post guards to prevent any such *sabotage*."

"*Maybe?* What will these guards cost? Where will they be housed?"

"Eliza—please—if I may just interrupt the rehearsal," the Doctor said, "don't do this job *too* well, I beg of you—avoid saying anything that will make a lasting impression on the, er, audience . . ."

"But I thought the whole idea was to—"

"Yes, yes—but remember drinks will be served—suppose some possible investor feels the need to step out and relieve himself at the climax of the performance, when the scales fall from your eyes and you see that this is, after all, a brilliant opportunity—"

Thus the rehearsal. Eliza performed semi-reclining on a couch, looking pale. Crawling down that cold tunnel probably had not been a good idea for one in her delicate state. It occurred to Jack that, since they had a bit of money now, there was no reason not to go down into the town he'd noticed below, find an apothecary, and buy some kind of potion or philtre that would undo the effects of the bleeding and bring pink back to her cheeks and, in general, the humour of passion back to her veins.

Of this town, which was called Bockboden, the Doctor had had little to say, save for a few mild comments such as "I wouldn't go there," "Don't go there," "It's not a very good place to be in," and "Avoid it." But none of these had been reinforced by the lurid fabrications that a Vagabond would've used to drive the point home. It seemed an orderly town from above, but not dangerously so.

Jack set out on foot, as Turk had been favoring one leg the last day or so, and followed an overgrown path that wound among old schlock-heaps and abandoned furnaces down towards Bockboden. As he went, the idea came to him that if he kept a sharp eye out, he might learn a few more things about the money-making trade, perhaps to include: how to profit therefrom without going through the tedious steps of investing one's own money and waiting decades for the payoff. But the only novel thing he saw on his way into Bockboden was some kind of improvised works, situated well away from dwellings, where foul-smelling steam was gushing from the mouths of iron tubs with Faulbaum-bonfires raging beneath them. It smelled like urine, and so Jack assumed it was a cloth-fulling mill. Indeed, he spied a couple of disgusted workmen pouring something yellow from a cask into one of the boiling-tubs. But there was no cloth in sight. It seemed they were boiling all of this perfectly good urine away to no purpose.

As Jack entered the town, shrewdness came to him belatedly, and he perceived it had not been a good idea—not because anything in particular happened but because of the old terror of arrest, torture, and execution that frequently came upon him in settled places. He reminded himself that he was wearing new clothes. As long as he kept a glove on his hand, where a letter V had been branded years ago, in the Old Bailey, he bore no visible marks of being a Vagabond. Moreover, he was a guest of the Doctor, who must be an important personage hereabouts. So he kept walking. The town gradually embraced and ensnared him. It was all built half-timbered, like most German towns and many English ones—meaning that they began by raising a frame of heavy struts, and then filled in the open spaces between them with whatever they could get. Around here, it looked like they'd woven mats of sticks into the gaps and then slathered them with mud that stiffened as it dried. Each new building borrowed strength, at first, from an older one, i.e., there was hardly an isolated freestanding house in the whole town; Bockboden was a single building of many bodies and tentacles. The frames of the houses—nay, the single frame of the entire town—had probably been level, plumb, and regular at one point, but over centuries it had sagged, warped, and tottered in different ways. The earthen walls had been patched to follow these evolutions. The town no longer looked like something men had built. It looked like the root-ball of a tree, with dirt-colored stuff packed between the roots, and hollowed out to provide a living-place.

Even here there were little schlock-heaps, and dribbles of ore up and down the streets. Jack heard the unsteady ticking of a hand-haspel behind a door. Suddenly the door was rammed open by a wheelbarrow full of rocks, pushed by a man. The man was astonished to find a stranger there staring at him. Jack however did not even have time to become edgy and to adopt an expression of false nonchalance before the miner got an aghast look and made a pitifully abject bowing maneuver, as best he could without letting go the wheelbarrow and precipitating a merry sequence of downhill mishaps. "Apothecary?" Jack said. The man answered in a strangely familiar-sounding kind of German, using his head to point. Behind the door, the hand-haspel stopped ticking for about six heartbeats, then started again.

Jack followed the wheelbarrow-man to the next cross-street, the latter trying to scurry away from him but impeded by his own weight in rocks. Jack wondered whether all of the mines beneath this country might be interconnected so that they all benefited from the Doctor's project of pumping away the ground-water without having to share in the costs. Perhaps that explained why strangers, coming from the direction of the tower, made them so nervous. Not that one really *needed* a reason.

The apothecary shop, at least, stood alone, on the edge of a grassy, schlock-mottled yard, cater-corner from a blackened church. The roof was high and steep as a hatchet-blade, the walls armored in overlapping plates of charcoal-colored slate. Each of its stories was somewhat larger than the one below, and sheltered 'neath the overhangs were rows of carved wooden faces: some faithful depictions of nuns, kings, helmeted knights, hairy wild-men, and beady-eyed Turks, but also angels, demons, lycanthropes, and a goatlike Devil.

Jack entered the place and found no one minding the dispensary window. He began to whistle, but it sounded plaintive and feeble, so he stopped. The ceiling was covered with huge grotesque forms molded in plaster—mostly persons changing into other beings. Some of them he recognized, dimly, from hearing the tales referred to in plays—there was for example the poor sap of a hunter who chanced upon the naked hunt-goddess while she was bathing, and was turned to a stag and torn apart by his own hounds. *That* wretch, caught in mid-metamorphosis, was attached to the ceiling of the dispensary room in life-size.

Perhaps the apothecary was hard of hearing. Jack began to wander about in a loud, obvious, banging way. He entered a big room filled with things he knew it would be a bad idea to touch: glowing tabletop furnaces, murky fluids bubbling in retorts above the flames of spirit-burners, flames as blue as Eliza's eyes. He tried another door and found the apothecary's office—jumping a little when he caught sight of a dangling skeleton. He looked up at the ceiling and found more heavy plaster-works, all of female goddesses: the goddess of dawn, the spring-goddess riding a flowery chariot up out of Hell, the one Europe was named after, the goddess of Love preening in a hand-mirror, and in the center, helmeted Minerva (he knew *some* names at least) with a cold and steady look about her, one arm holding her shield, decorated with the head of a monster whose snaky hair descended almost into the middle of the room.

A big dead fish, all sucked into itself and desiccated, was suspended from a string. The walls were lined with shelves and cabinets dense with professional clutter: diverse tongs, in disturbingly specific shapes; a large collection of mortars and pestles with words on them; various animal skulls; capped cylinders made of glass or stone, again with words on them; a huge Gothickal clock out of whose doors grotesque creatures sallied when Jack least expected it, then retreated before he could turn and really see them; green glass retorts in beautifully rounded shapes that reminded him of female body parts; scales with vast arrays of weights, from cannonballs down to scraps of foil that could be propelled into the next country by a sigh; gleaming silver rods, which on closer inspection turned out to be glass tubes filled, for some reason, with mercury; some kind of tall, heavy, columnar object, shrouded in heavy fabric and producing internal warmth, and expanding and contracting slowly like a bellows—

"*Guten Tag,* or should I say, good afternoon," it said.

Jack fell back on his ass and looked up at a man, wrapped in a sort of traveling-cloak or monk's robe, standing next to the skeleton. Jack was too surprised to cry out—not least because the man had spoken English.

"How'd you know . . . ?" was all Jack could get out. The man in the robe had a silver robe and a look of restrained amusement nestled in his red beard, which suggested that Jack should wait a minute before leaping up, drawing his sword, and running him through.

". . . that you were an Englishman?"

"Yes."

"You may not know this, but you have a way of talking to yourself as you go about—telling yourself a story about what's happening, or what you suppose is happening—for this reason I already know you are Jack. I'm Enoch. Also, there is something peculiarly English in the way you go about investigating, and amusing yourself with, things that a German or Frenchman would know to be none of his business."

"There's much to think about in that speech," Jack said, "but I don't suppose it's too offensive."

"It's not meant to be offensive at all," Enoch said. "How may I help you?"

"I am here on behalf of a Lady who has gone pale and unsteady from too much feminine, er . . ."

"Menstruation?"

"Yes. Is there anything here for that?"

Enoch gazed out a window at a dim gray sky. "Well— never mind what the apothecary would tell you—"

"You are *not* the apothecary?"

"No."

"Where is he?"

"Down at the town square, where all decent folk should be."

"Well, what does that make you and me then, brother?"

Enoch shrugged. "A man who wants to help his woman, and a man who knows how."

"How, then?"

"She wants iron."

"Iron?"

"It would help if she ate a lot of red meat."

"But you said *iron*. Why not have her eat a horseshoe?"

"They are so unpalatable. Red meat contains iron."

"Thank you . . . did you say the apothecary was in the town square?"

"Just that way, a short distance," Enoch said. "There's a butcher there, too, if you want to get her some red meat . . ."

"Auf wiedersehen, Enoch."

"Until we meet again, Jack."

And thus did Jack extricate himself from the conversation with the madman (who, as he reflected while walking down the street, had a thing or two in common with the Doctor) and go off in search of someone sane. He could see many people in the square—how would he know which one was the apothecary? Should've asked old Enoch for a description.

Bockboden had convened in a large open ring around a vertical post fixed in the ground and half buried in a pile of faggots. Jack did not recognize the apparatus at first because he was used to England, where the gallows was customary. By the time he'd figured out what was going on, he had pushed his way into the middle of the crowd, and he could hardly turn around and leave without giving everyone the impression that he was soft on witches. Most of them, he knew, had only showed up for the sake of maintaining their reputations, but those sorts would be the *most* likely to accuse a stranger of witchcraft. The *real* witch-haters were up at the front, hollering in the local variant of German, which sometimes sounded maddeningly like English. Jack could not make out what they were saying. It sounded like threats. That was nonsensical, because the witch was about to be killed anyway. But Jack heard snatches like *"Walpurgis"* and *"heute Nacht,"* which he knew meant "tonight" and then he knew that they were threatening not the woman who was about to die, but others in the town they suspected of being witches.

The head of the woman had been shaved, but not recently. Jack could guess, from the length of her stubble, that her ordeal had been going on for about a week. They had been going at her feet and legs with the old wedges-and-sledgehammers trick, and so she would have to be burnt in the seated position. When they set her down on the pile of faggots she winced from the pain of being moved, then leaned back against the stake, seeming glad that she was about to leave Bockboden for good. A plank was nailed into place above her, with a piece of paper on it, on which had been written some sort of helpful information. Meanwhile, a man tied her hands behind the stake—then passed the loose end of the rope around her neck a couple of times, and flung the slack away from the stake: a detail that infuriated the front-row crowd. Someone else stepped up with a big earthenware jug and sloshed oil all around.

Jack, as former execution facilitator, watched with professional interest. The man with the rope pulled hard on it while the fire was started, strangling the woman probably within seconds, and ruining the entire execution in the opinion of some. Most of them watched but didn't see. Jack had found that people watching executions, even if they kept open eyes turned to the entire performance, did not really see the death, and could not remember it later, because what they were really doing was thinking about their own deaths.

But this one affected Jack as if it were Eliza who'd been burnt (the witch was a young woman), and he walked away

with shoulders drawn tightly together and watery snot trickling out of his nose. Blurry vision did him no favors vis-à-
vis navigation. He walked so fast that by the time he realized
he was on the wrong street, the town square—his only star to
steer by—was concealed around the bends of Bockboden.
And he did not think that aimless wandering, or anything
that could be considered suspicious by anyone, was a good
idea here. The only thing that was a good idea was to get out
of town.

So he did, and got lost in the woods.

The Harz Mountains

Me miserable! which way shall I flie
Infinite wrauth, and infinite despaire?
Which way I flie is Hell; my self am Hell;
And in the lowest deep a lower deep
Still threatning to devour me opens wide,
To which the Hell I suffer seems a Heav'n.

—MILTON, *Paradise Lost*

JACK SAT ON A DEAD tree in the woods for a time, feeling hungry, and, what was worse, feeling stupid. There was little daylight left and he thought he should use it wisely (he was not above being wise as long as there was no preacher or gentleman *demanding* that he do so). He walked through the trees over a little rise and down into a shallow basin between hills where he was fairly certain he could light a fire without announcing himself to the citizenry of Bockboden. He spent the remainder of the daylight gathering fallen branches and, just as the sun was setting, lit a fire—having learned that the tedious and exacting work of flint, steel, and tinder could be expedited if you simply used a bit of gunpowder in lieu of the tinder. With some pyrotechnics and a cloud of smoke, he had a fire. Now he need only throw sticks on it from time to time and sit there like the lost fool he was until sleep finally caught him unawares. He did not want to think about the witch he'd seen burnt, but it was hard not to. Instead he tried to make himself think about brother Bob, and his two boys, the twins Jimmy and Danny, and his long- and oft-delayed plan to find them a legacy.

He was startled to find three women and a man, their faces all lit up by firelight, standing nearby. They looked as if they had ventured into the woods in the middle of the night expecting to find some *other* vagrant sitting by a fire sleeping.* Jack's first thought might've been *Witch-hunters!* if not for that they'd had longer to react to *him* than he to *them*, and *they* looked worried (they'd noticed the sword)—besides, they were mostly females and they were unarmed, unless the fresh-cut tree-branches that they used as leafy walking-sticks were meant as weapons. At any rate, they turned and hustled off, their sticks giving them the look of a group of stout chamber-maids going off to sweep the forest with makeshift brooms.

After that Jack could not sleep. Another group much like the first came by a few minutes later. This forest was damnably *crowded*. Jack picked up his few belongings and withdrew into the shadows to observe what other moths were attracted to the flame. Within a few minutes, a squadron of mostly women, ranging from girls to hags, had taken over the fire, and stoked it up to a blaze. They'd brought along a black iron kettle that they filled with buckets of water from a nearby creek and set up on the fire to boil. As steam began to rise from the pot—illuminated by firelight down below, vanishing into the cold sky as it ascended—they began to throw in the ingredients of some kind of stew: sacks of some type of fat dark-blue cherries, red mushrooms with white speckles, sprigs of herbs. No meat, or recognizable vegetables, to the disappointment of Jack. But he was hungry enough to eat German food now. The question was: how to secure an invitation to the feast?

In the end, he just went down and got some, which was

---

*Various pieces of evidence suggested to Jack that he'd been sleeping.

what everyone else seemed to be doing. Traffic through this part of the woods had become so heavy that he could not rely on going unnoticed anyway. First he used his sword to cut a leafy branch like everyone else's. None of these persons was armed, and so he stuck the sword and scabbard down his trouser-leg and then, to conceal it better, fashioned a false splint of sticks, and rags torn from his shirt, around the leg so that he would look like a man with a frozen knee, hobbling round with the aid of the staff. Thus disguised, he limped into the firelight and was politely, not to say warmly, greeted by the stew-cookers. One of them offered him a ladle full of the stuff and he swallowed it down fast enough to burn his insides all the way down to his stomach. Probably just as well—it was foul-tasting. On the principle that you never know when you'll find food again, he gestured for more, and they somewhat reluctantly handed him a second ladle, and uneasily watched him drink it. It was as bad as the first, though it had chunks of mushrooms or something on the bottom that might give some nourishment.

He must have *looked* lost, then, because after he'd stood near the fire for a few minutes warming himself the stew-makers began helpfully pointing in the direction that all the other people were migrating. This happened to be generally uphill, which was the way Jack planned to travel anyhow (either it would take him to the Doctor's tower, or to a height-of-land whence he could *see* the tower come morning) and so off he hobbled.

The next time he was really aware of anything (he seemed to be walking and sleeping *at the same time,* though everything had a dreamlike quality now, so the *whole thing* might be a dream) he had evidently covered a couple of miles uphill, judging from that it was much colder and the wind was blowing so hard that he could hear trees being struck down all over, like reports of guns in a battle. Clouds stampeded across the face of a full moon. Occasionally something would rip through the branches overhead and shower him with twigs and brush. Looking up, he saw it was broken-off tree branches, or maybe even small uprooted trees, propelled through the air by the hurricanoe. He was working his way uphill, though not sure why anymore. Others were all around him. The forest was very tall skinny black trees closely packed together like the massed pikes of a military formation, the eruptions of moonlight between fleeing clouds like the bursting of bombs, and Jack heard, or dreamed, the tramping of feet and blowing of trumpets. Forgetting why his leg was splinted, he supposed he must have been wounded in action (possibly in the head as well as the leg) and the wound dressed by a barber. For a while he was almost certain he was still fighting Turks in Vienna and all of the Eliza stuff just a long, elaborate, cruel dream.

But then he was back in the woods above Bockboden. Branches and heavier things were still ripping through space above his head like cannonballs. He looked up at the moon trying to see them, and with the torn clouds streaming by, it was difficult to make out their shapes, but he was fairly certain now that *people* were riding on those branches, as Winged Hussars rode on chargers. They were charging the hilltop! Jack finally stumbled out onto a path that wound up the mountain, and was nearly run over by the *infantry* part of the charge: a river of people with cut branches, and other ornaments, such as the forks farmers used to shovel manure. Forgetting about the splinted leg, Jack wheeled and tried to run with them, but fell, and took a while getting up.

He reached the collection of outcroppings that was the mountain-top somewhat after the main group, but in time to see them chasing away half a dozen musketeers who had apparently been posted there, and who were not welcome. None of them fired his weapon, as they had no desire to kill a few people only to be surrounded by hundreds of their stick-brandishing friends. As this occurred, people farther from the action were shouting threats and offering sour comments in much the same vein as the spectators at the witch-burning had earlier, except that they were using the word

Wächer, which (Jack's murderously overtaxed mind guessing wildly here) perhaps meant "Watchers."

Battle won, the Hexen (no point in denying it any more) quickly lit up the whole mountain-top with fires (many people had carried faggots on their backs), which burnt with white heat in the continuing wind-blast. Jack hobbled around and looked. He could see that many ages ago a tall stone column had risen from the top of the mountain, bifurcated at the top into what might have been shaped like a pair of goat's horns. It might've looked something like a crossbow standing up on end. But it had been toppled so long ago that it was now covered in moss and dirt. A couple of dozen standing-stones had ringed it; most of them had been toppled as well. The Hexen had led a black goat up onto the ruin of the high column and leashed him there to look out over the whole fiery prospect.

People, frequently naked, danced around those bonfires. Many spring flowers had been brought up and used to decorate rocks, or people. A certain amount of fucking went on, as one would expect, but at least some of it seemed to be *ceremonial* fucking—the participants, actors in a sort of immorality play—the woman always bedecked with garlands of spring wildflowers and the man always donning an eyepatch. Certain small animals might have died unnatural deaths. There was chanting and singing in a language that wasn't exactly German.

Of course, presiding over the entire thing was Satan the Prince of Darkness, or so Jack assumed—as what else would you call a jet-black figure, horned and bearded, maybe a hundred feet high, dancing in the boiling, smoky, cloudy sky just above the summit, sometimes visible and sometimes not, occasionally seen in profile as he lifted his bearded chin to howl, or laugh, at the moon. Jack fully believed this, and knew beyond doubt that every word the preachers had ever said about Lucifer was true. He decided that running away wasn't a bad idea. Choosing the direction he happened to be pointed in at the moment he panicked, he ran. The moon

came out a few moments later and showed him he had one
or two strides left on rock before he would find himself running in midair—a fantastical gorge plunged straight down
for farther than could be seen by moonlight. Jack stopped
and turned around, having no other choices, and with a
forced and none too sincere calmness, looked at the entire
panorama of fire and shadow hoping to find a route that
wouldn't take him too near Satan—or actually any of the
several Satans of different sizes who seemed to be huddling
in council around the mountain-top.

His eye was caught by a tiny black silhouette outlined in a
brilliant hairy fringe, elevated above the whole scene: the
black goat, tilting its head back to bray. One of the vast Satans duplicated the move precisely. Jack understood that he
had been running from shadows of the goat cast against
clouds and smoke by the light of the fire.

He sat down at the point where he'd almost hurled himself
into the gorge, laughed, and tried to clear his head, and to
get his bearings. The cliff, and the somewhat lower bluff
across from it, were craggy, with great big shards and flakes
of rock angling crazily into the air—and (by the way) ex-
ploding the Doctor's idea of how these rocks had been
formed, because the grain of these rocks ran straight up and
down. Obviously it was the remains of a giant, killed in
some antediluvian rock fight, who'd died on his back with
his bony fingers thrust up into the air.

Jack drew nearer to a fire, partly because he was cold and
partly because he wanted a closer look at one particular
naked girl who was dancing around it—somewhat on the
fleshy side and clearly destined to become another broom-
wielding hag in the long run, but the least columnar German
female Jack had recently seen. By the time he got close
enough to have a good look at her, the fire was uncomfort-
ably hot, which should have warned him that the light was
very bright, on his face. But he did not consider this important fact at all until he heard the fatal word *Wache!* Turning
towards the voice he saw, almost close enough to touch, one
of those women who had woken him up earlier in the eve-

ning, down below, when he'd been sleeping by his little fire
with his sword in view. His sword was exactly what she was
looking for, now that she'd gained everyone's attention by
uttering their least favorite word. Concealing the weapon in
a leg-splint had worked when it was dark, and people were
not specifically *looking* for a sword, but here and now it did
not work at all—the woman hardly needed do more than
glance at Jack before screaming, in a voice that could probably be heard in Leipzig, *"Er ist eine Wache! Er hat ein
Schwert!"*

So the party was over for *everyone* and most of all *Jack.*
Anyone could've given him a smart shove and sent him into
the fire and that would've been the end, or at least an interesting *beginning,* but instead they all ran away from him—
but, he had to assume, not for long. The only one who stayed
behind was the one who'd fingered him. She hovered out of
sword-range giving him a piece of her mind, so furious she
was sobbing. Jack had no desire to draw his sword and get
these people more angry than they were, but (a) they
couldn't possibly get much *more* angry no matter what he
did, and (b) he had to get the damn splint off his leg if he
were going to do any serious fleeing. And fleeing was the order of the night. So. Out came his dagger. The woman
gasped and jumped back. Jack controlled the urge to tell her
to shut up and calm down, and slashed through all the rag
bands around his leg so that the splint-sticks fell away from
him. Then he freed his leg by pulling out the scabbard and
sword. The woman now *screamed.* People were running *towards* Jack now, and cries of *"Wächter!"* were making it difficult to hear anything else—Jack had absorbed enough
German by now to understand that this meant not "the
Watcher" but "the Watchers." They'd made up their minds
that Jack must be only one of a whole platoon of armed in-
filtrators, which of course would be the only way his presence there would make any sense. Because to be here alone
was suicide.

Jack ran.

He hadn't been running for long before he understood that

the Hexen were generally trying to drive him in the direction of the cliff—an excellent idea. But, as yet, they were not very organized and so there were gaps between them. Jack sallied through one of these and began to lose altitude the slow, safe, and sane way. The commotion had dropped a couple of octaves in pitch. At first it had mostly been shocked females spreading the alarm (which had worked pretty well), and now it was angry males organizing the hunt. Jack had to assume it wasn't the first time they had hunted for large animals in these woods.

Even so, the hunt lasted for perhaps an hour, making its way generally downhill. Jack's only hope was to get out in front of them and flee through the darkness. But they had torches and they knew their way around, and had spread the alarm down the mountain and so no matter what Jack achieved in the way of running, he found himself always surrounded. There were any number of near-escapes that ended in failure. The million poky branches of the alder trees clawed his face and threatened to blind him and caused him to make more noise than he wanted to as he moved about.

Toward the end, he got into situations where he could have escaped, or at least added a few minutes to his life, by killing one or two people. But he didn't—an act of forbearance he wished could have been observed and noted down by some other sort of Watcher, a lurking mystery with a mirror on a stick, so that news of his noble decisions could be provided to Eliza and everyone else who'd ever looked at him the wrong way. Far from earning him universal admiration, this only led to his being surrounded by some half a dozen men with torches, standing just out of sword-range and darting in to sweep flames past his face when they thought they saw an opening. Jack risked a look back over his shoulder and saw no one behind him, which seemed a poor way to surround someone. He wheeled, ran a couple of steps, and hit a wall. A *wall*. Turning back around, he saw a torch-flame headed right for his face and reflexively parried the blow. Another came in from another direction and he parried that, and when

the third came in from yet another direction he parried it
with the *edge* instead of the *flat* of his blade, and cut the handle of the torch in two. The burning half spun in the air and
he snatched it while slashing blindly in the other direction
and hurting someone. Now that he'd drawn blood, the other
hunters stepped back, knowing that reinforcements were on
their way.* Jack, keeping his back to the building, crept sideways, sword in one hand and torch in the other, occasionally
taking advantage of the latter's light to glance over his shoulder and gain some knowledge of what he'd run into.

It was an old wooden building. The door was closed by a
padlock the size of a ham. Wooden shutters had been pulled
shut over the windows and bolted from the inside. A gentleman would've been stymied, but Jack knew that the weakest
part of any building was usually the roof—so as soon as he
found a wood-pile stacked against the wall, he climbed up it
and got up on top, and found clay tiles under his boots.
These were thick and heavy, made to withstand hail-storms

---

*It being one of the many peculiar features of Jack's upbringing that (1) he
had a perpetual sparring partner (Bob)—perpetual in the sense that they
slept in the same bed at night and, as brothers do, fought all day—against
whom he was evenly matched, and (2) at the age when every boy engages in
mock sword-fight, he and Bob happened to suddenly find themselves living
in a military barracks, where their duels served as free entertainment for
large numbers of men who actually *did* know a few things about fighting
with swords, and who found the entertainment lacking if it was not well
played, both in a *technical* sense (blows had to be delivered and parried in
some way that was realistic to their discerning eyes) and in a *dramatic* sense
(extra points scored, and extra food thrown in their direction, for enhance-
ments such as hanging by the knees from joists and fighting upside-down,
swinging like apes from ropes, etc.). The result being that from a young age
the Shaftoe boys had sword-fighting abilities considerably above their sta-
tion in life (most people like them never came into contact with a sword at
all, unless it was with the edge of the blade in the last instant of their life),
but limited to the type of sword called the spadroon—a cut-and-thrust
weapon—which, they'd been warned, might not be very effective against
Gentlemen armed with long slender poky rapiers and trained to insert them
deftly through narrow gaps in one's defenses. The Janissary-blade was a
rough Mahometan equivalent of a spadroon, therefore, ideally matched to
Jack's style, or Bob's for that matter. He waved it around dramatically.

and tree-branches, but Jack with the strength of panic stomped until a few of them cracked. Fist-sized rocks were pelting down around him now. He stopped one that was trying to roll off, and used it as a hammer. Finally he created a hole through the tiles, threw in the torch, squeezed through feet-first between the wooden laths on which the tiles were mounted, and dropped through, landing on a table. He snatched up the torch lest it set fire to the place, and found himself looking at a portrait of Martin Luther.

His hunters—several dozen by now, he guessed—had surrounded the building and begun pounding, in an exploratory way, on its doors and shutters. The booms in the dark gave Jack a general idea of the building's size and shape. It had several rooms, and was therefore probably not a church, but not a mere cottage either. No one had tried to pursue him through the hole in the roof and he was certain no one would—they'd burn it. It was inevitable. He could even hear axes thudding into trees out in the forest—more fuel.

This particular room was a rude chapel; the thing he'd landed on, the altar. Next to the Luther portrait was an old and not very good rendition of a woman proffering a chalice with a communion wafer levitating above it, suspended by some ongoing miraculous intervention. It made Jack (who'd had enough, for one night, of accepting mystery drinks from eerie females) shudder. But from having spent too much time lately around miners, he recognized the woman as St. Barbara, patron of men who dug holes in the ground, albeit with all of her Catholic insignia filed off. The rest of the room was striped by plank benches. Jack hopped from one to the next to the back, then went sideways and found a kind of sitting-room with a couple of chairs and one of the towering black iron stoves favored by Germans. Turning on his heel and going the *other* way, he found a very heavy scale dangling from the ceiling; weights for it, the size of cheese-wheels; a cabinet; and, what he most wanted to see, a stairway going *down*.

It was getting smoky in there, and not just from his torch. Jack mauled the cabinet open and grabbed a handful of kienspans. He'd lost his hat while running through the woods and so he stole one of the miners': a conical thing of extremely thick felt that would soften impacts of head against stone. Then he was down the stairs, and none too soon as the old wooden building was burning like gunpowder. They'd make a big fire of it, throwing on whole trees: a fire that could be seen by the burghers of Bockboden, sending those Hexen-hunters a powerful message by which they'd be completely baffled.

The stairway went down for perhaps two dozen steps and then levelled off into a tunnel that went at least as far as Jack's torch (which had consumed most of its fuel) could throw light. He lit a kienspan, which burnt a little brighter, but he still could not see the end of the tunnel, which was good, and to be expected. He began running along in a kind of crouch, not wanting to smash his head on the ceiling timbers, and after a minute, passed by a hand-haspel crammed into a niche in the tunnel wall, its ropes descending into a shaft. A minute later he passed by another, then another, and finally he stopped and decided he should just go down one of those shafts. He'd been down here long enough to stop being so proud of his own cleverness, and he'd begun to worry. The Hexen knew the territory better than he. They couldn't *not* know that the building was a mine entrance, and they must have anticipated that he'd find the tunnel. Perhaps the mine had other entrances, and they'd soon be coming down with torches and dogs and God knows what, as when they hunted burrowing vermin with their sausage-shaped dogs.

One of the hand-haspel's buckets was at the top, the other down below. Jack climbed into the one that was up, and hugged the opposite rope, and by letting it slide through his arms was able to descend smoothly for a short distance: until he relaxed, and the rope slid too fast, and he hugged it tight out of panic, so it burnt him and made him let go, causing the same cycle to repeat, except worse. The only thing that interrupted this round was when, at the halfway mark, the lower bucket came up and caught him under the chin and caused him to let go entirely—which was fine, as he would have been stuck at that point anyway. He dropped, then, with only the empty, ascending bucket as counterweight, and what saved him was that the impact of his chin against same had set it swinging briskly back and forth, its rim biting into the rough wall of the shaft faster and faster as it rose higher and higher, throwing sparks and dislodging fusillades of jagged rock in Jack's direction with every impact, but also slowing his fall with a corresponding series of violent jerks. Jack kept his head down and his kienspan up in case this shaft terminated in water, a possibility he should have considered earlier.

Actually it terminated in rock—the bucket landed unevenly and ejected Jack. Loose bits of stone continued to clatter down from above for a little while and hurt his legs, which was welcome as proof he hadn't been paralyzed. The kienspan still burnt; Jack held it in a death-grip and watched the blue flame pour out of it and turn yellow as it moved sideways along the shaft, contrary to the normal habit of flames, which was to tend *upwards*. Jack kicked the bucket out of the way and did some moving about, and found that there was a rapidly building draft, approaching a breeze, moving toward him along the tunnel. But when he backed up to the other side of the shaft opening in the ceiling, the air was moving the opposite direction. Two flows of air converged at this point and moved up the shaft, starting now to make a certain wailing noise that Jack could not fail to liken to damned souls or whatever. *Now* he understood why the Hexen had gone to work felling trees up above: they knew that with a sufficiently enormous fire they could suck all of the air out of the mine.

He had to find a way out, which did not seem all that likely now, as he'd made the (in retrospect) mistake of going *down* to a lower level. But he chose the direction from which there came the strongest flow of air, and began to move as quickly as he could. The faster he ran into the wind, the more brightly his kienspan burnt. But it burnt less brightly as time went on. He tried lighting a fresh one, but it, too, burnt feebly unless he waved it in the air, and then the light flared

up and shone between the heavy bars of the wooden cage
that kept the rocks from crushing him on all sides, and cast
rapidly moving shadows, sometimes looking like angry
faces of mangled giants, or huge ostrich-skeleton-monsters
with scimitar teeth: all of which went together neatly with
the deafening chorus of moans and wails made by all of the
passageways as the breath was sucked out of them.

Around this time Jack also noted that he was on his hands
and knees skidding the dully glowing kienspan along the
floor. From time to time he'd see the low portal of one of
those side-tunnels go by him to the left or right. Going by
one of these he felt a strong cool breeze, and the kienspan
flared up; but when he went past it, the air became dead and
the kienspan went out entirely. He was breathing very fast,
but it did him no good. With what strength he still had, he
backtracked through absolute darkness until he felt the wind
from that side-tunnel on his face. Then he lay down flat on
the rock for a while and simply breathed.

Some time later his head was working more clearly and
he understood that the flow of air implied an exit somewhere. He groped around on the floor until he found one of
those elbow-planks, and then crawled sideways, headed upwind. He followed the air for an amount of time impossible
to guess at. The low side-tunnel opened out into a smooth-
floored space that seemed to be a natural cave. Here the river
of air had been broken up into many trickles curving around
rocks and stalagmites (tricky to follow), but (nose to floor,
tongue out) he followed them for what seemed like a mile,
sometimes standing up and walking through spaces that
echoed like cathedrals, sometimes squirming on his belly
through spaces so close that his head got wedged between
the floor and ceiling. He sloshed through a pond of dead water that froze his legs, climbed up the other shore, and entered a mine-tunnel, then passed through tunnels of low and
high ceilings, and up-and-down vertical shafts, so many
times that he lost track of how many times he had lost track.
He wanted badly to sleep, but he knew that if the fire went
out while he slumbered, the air-current would stop and he'd

lose the thread that, as with that bloke in the myth, was showing him the way out. His eyes, not satisfied with total darkness, fabricated demon-images from all of the bad things he'd seen or thought he'd seen in the last days.

He heard a bubbling, hissing sound, such as a dragon or Worm might make, but followed it, and the air-current, along a slowly descending tunnel until he came to water's edge. Knocking off a few sparks from his flint and steel he saw that the air he'd been following this whole time was boiling up out of a subterranean lake that filled the tunnel before him and completely blocked his way out. Having nothing else to do, he sat down to die, and fell asleep instead, and had nightmares that were an improvement on reality.

NOISE AND LIGHT, BOTH FAINT, woke him. He refused to take the light seriously: a green glow emanating from the pool (which had stopped bubbling). It was so unearthly that it could only be another of the mind tricks that the broth of the Hexen had been wreaking on him. But the noise, though distant, sounded interesting. Before, it had been drowned out by the seething of the water, but now he could hear a rhythmic hissing and booming sound.

The green light grew brighter. He could see the silhouettes of his hands in front of it.

He'd been dreaming, before he woke up, about the giant water-pipes, the hubbly-bubblies that the Turks smoked in Leipzig. They'd suck on the tube, and smoke from the tobacco bowl would pass *down* through the water and come back upwards into the tube, cooled and purified. The dream had, he guessed, been inspired by the last sound he'd heard before falling asleep, because the cave had made a similar seething and gurgling noise. As he considered it (having no other way to spend the time), he wondered whether the mine might not have acted like a giant water-pipe, and the fire like a giant Turk sucking on its tube, drawing air downwards, through a water-filled sump, from the outside, so that it bubbled up into this tunnel.

Might it be possible, then, that by swimming for some

short distance through this water he would come up into the air? Could the green light be the light of sunrise, filtered through greenish pond-scum? Jack began to work up his courage, a procedure he expected would take several hours. He could think only of poor brother Dick who had drowned in the Thames: how he'd swum off all active and pink, and been pulled up limp and white.

He concluded he'd best do the deed *now,* while the witch-brew was still impairing his judgment. So he took off most of his clothes. He could come back for them later if this worked. He took only his sword (in case trouble awaited), flint, and steel, and his miner's hat, which would be good to have if he smashed his head against any underwater ceilings. Then he backed up the tunnel several paces, got a running start downhill, and dove in. The water was murderously cold and he almost screamed out his one lungful of air. He grazed the ceiling once—the light grew brighter—the ceiling wasn't there any more, and so he kicked against the sump's floor and burst up into fresh air! The distance had been only three or four yards.

But the light, though brighter, was not the light of the sun. Jack could tell, by the echoes of the trickling waters and of the murmur of voices, that he was still underground. The strange green light shone from around a nearby bend in the cavern, and glinted curiously off parts of the walls.

Before doing anything else, Jack slipped back into the water, swam back through the sump, retrieved his boots and clothes, and then returned to the glowing cavern. He got dressed and then crept toward the light on hands and knees, trying but failing to control a violent shiver. The glint he'd noticed earlier turned out to come from a patch of clear crystals, the size of fingers, growing out of a wall—diamonds! He had entered into some place of fabulous riches. The walls were fuzzy with gems. Perhaps the light was green because it was shining through a giant emerald?

Then he came round a bend and was nearly struck blind by a smooth disk of brilliant green light, flat on the floor of a roundish chamber. As his eyes adjusted he could see that a circle of persons—or of *something*—stood around the edge, dressed in outlandish and bizarre costumes.

In the center stood a figure in a long robe, a hood drawn over his head, enclosing his face in shadow, though the light shone upwards against chin and cheek-bones to give him a death's-head appearance, and it glinted in his eyes.

A voice spoke out in French—Eliza's voice! She was angry, distressed—the others turned towards her. This was Hell, or Hell's side entrance, and the demons had captured Eliza—or perhaps she was *dead*—dead because of Jack's failure to return with medicine—and she was at this moment being inducted—

Jack plunged forth, drawing his sword, but when he set foot on the green disk it gave way beneath him and he burst *through* it—suddenly he was *swimming* in green light. But there was solid rock underneath. He jumped back up, knee-deep in the stuff, and hollered, "Let her go, ye demons! Take me instead!"

They all screamed and ran away, including Eliza.

Jack looked down to find his clothes saturated with green light.

The hooded figure was the only one left. He sloshed calmly up out of the pool, opened a dark-lantern, took out a burning match, and went round igniting some torchières stuck into the ground all around. Their light was infinitely brighter, and made the green light vanish. Jack was standing in a brown puddle and his clothes were all wet.

Enoch pulled the hood back from his head and said, "What was really magnificent about that entrance, Jack, was that, until the moment you rose up out of the pool all covered in phosphorus, you were invisible—you just seemed to materialize, weapon in hand, with that Dwarf-cap, shouting in a language no one understands. Have you considered a career in the theatre?"

Jack was still too puzzled to take umbrage at this. "Who, or what, were those—?"

"Wealthy gentlefolk who, until just moments ago, were thinking of buying *Kuxen* from Doctor Leibniz."

"But—their freakish attire, their bizarre appearance—?"

"The latest fashions from Paris."

"Eliza sounded distressed."

"She was interrogating the Doctor—demanding to know just what this conjuror's trick, as she called it, had to do with the viability of the mine."

"But why even bother with mining silver, when the walls of this cavern are encrusted with diamonds?"

"Quartz."

"What is the glowing stuff anyway, and while I'm on that subject, what *does* it have to do with the mine?"

"Phosphorus, and nothing. Come, Jack, let's get you out of those wet clothes before you burst into flame." Enoch began leading Jack down a side-passage. Along the way they passed a large item of machinery that was making loud booming and sucking noises as it pumped water out of the mine. Here Enoch prevailed on Jack to strip and bathe.

Enoch said, "I don't suppose that this story shall ever be told in the same admiring way as the Strasbourg Plague House Takeover and the Bohemian Carp Feast."

"What!? How did you know about those?"

"I travel. I talk to Vagabonds. Word gets around. You might be interested to know that your achievements have been compiled into a picaresque novel entitled *L'Emmerdeur,* which has already been burnt in Paris and bootlegged in Amsterdam."

"Stab me!" Jack for the first time began to think that Enoch's friendly behavior toward him might be well-meaning, and not just an extremely subtle form of mockery. Enoch shouldered a six-inch-thick door open and led Jack into a windowless crypt, a vaulted room with a large table in the middle, candles, and a stove, which happened to look exactly like the sort of place Dwarves would inhabit. They sat down and started smoking and drinking. Presently the Doctor came in and joined them. Far from being outraged, he seemed relieved, as if he'd never wanted to be in the mining business anyway. Enoch gave the Doctor a significant look, which Jack was fairly sure meant *I warned you not to involve Vagabonds,* and the Doctor nodded.

"What are the, er, investors doing?" Jack asked.

"Standing up above in the sunlight—the females trying to outdo each other in swooning, the males engaging in a learned dispute as to whether you were an enraged Dwarf come to chase us away from his hoard, or a demon from Hell come to seize us."

"And Eliza? Not swooning I assume."

"She is too busy receiving the compliments, and credentials, of the others, who are all dumbfounded by her acumen."

"Ah, then it's possible she *won't* kill me."

"Far from it, Jack, the girl is blushing, she is radiant, and not in a dipped-in-phosphorus sense."

"Why?"

"Because, Jack, you volunteered to be taken down into eternal torment in place of her. This is the absolute *minimum* (unless I'm mistaken) that any female requires from her man."

"So *that's* what they're all after," Jack mused.

Eliza backed through the door, unable to use her arms, which were hugging a bundle of letters of introduction, visiting-cards, bills of exchange, scraps with scrawled addresses, and small purses a-clink with miscellaneous coinage. "We've missed you, Jack," she said, "where've you been?"

"Running an errand—meeting some locals—partaking of their rich traditions," Jack said. "Can we get out of Germany now, please?"

The Place

SUMMER 1684

⚜

> Trade, like Religion, is what every Body talks of, but few understand: The very Term is dubious, and in its ordinary Acceptation, not sufficiently explain'd.
> —DANIEL DEFOE, *A Plan of the English Commerce*

"IF NOTHING HAPPENS IN AMSTERDAM, save that everything going *into* it, turns round and comes straight back *out—*"

"Then there must be nothing else *there,*" Eliza finished.

Neither one of them had ever been to Amsterdam—yet. But the amount of stuff moving toward that city, and away from it, on the roads and canals of the Netherlands, was so vast that it made Leipzig seem like a smattering of poor actors in the background of a play, moving back and forth with a few paltry bundles to create the *impression* of commerce. Jack had not seen such bunching-together of people and goods since the onslaught on Vienna. But that had only happened once, and this was continuous. And he knew by reputation that what came in and out of Amsterdam over land, compared to what was carried on ships, was a runny nose compared to a river.

Eliza was dressed in a severe black ensemble with a high stiff white collar: a prosperous Dutch farmer's wife to all appearances, except that she spoke no Dutch. During their weeks of almost mortally tedious westing across the Duchy

of Braunschweig-Wolfenbüttel, the Duchy of Braunschweig-
Lüneburg, the Bishopric of Hildesheim, Duchy of Kalen-
berg, Landgraviate of something-or-other, County of Lippe,
County of Ravensburg, Bishopric of Osnabrück, County of
Lingen, Bishopric of Münster, and County of Bentheim, she
had mostly gone in man's attire, booted, sworded, and
spurred. Not that anyone really believed she was a man: she
was pretending to be an Italian courtesan on her way to a
tryst with a Genoese banker in Amsterdam. This made hardly
any sense at all, but, as Jack had learned, border guards
mostly just wanted something to relieve the tedium. It was
easier to flaunt Eliza than to hide her. Trying to predict when
they'd reach the next frontier, and whether the people on the
far side of it would be Protestant or Catholic, and how *serious*
about being Prot. or Cath. they'd be, was simply too difficult.
Much simpler to be saucily irreligious *everywhere* and, if
people got offended, run away. It worked most places. The
locals had other concerns: if half the rumors were true, then
King Looie—not satisfied with bombarding Genoa, laying
siege to Luxembourg, challenging Pope Innocent XI to a
staredown, expelling Jewry from Bordeaux, and massing his
armies on the Spanish border—had just announced that he
owned northwestern Germany. As they happened to *be* in
northwestern Germany, this made matters tense, yet fluid, in
a way that was not entirely bad for them.

Great herds of scrawny young cattle were being driven
across the plain out of the East to be fattened in the man-
made pastures of the Netherlands. Commingled with them
were hordes of unemployed men going to look for work in
Dutch cities—Hollandgänger, they were called. So the bor-
ders were easy, except along the frontier of the Dutch Republic, where all the lines of circumvallation ran across their
path: not only the natural rivers but walls, ditches, ramparts,
palisades, moats, and pickets: some new and crisp and popu-
lated by soldiers, others the abandoned soft-edged memories of battles that must have happened before Jack had been
born. But after being chased off a time or two, in ways that
would probably seem funny when remembered later, they

penetrated into Gelderland: the eastern marches of that Republic. Jack had patiently inculcated Eliza in the science of examining the corpses, heads, and limbs of executed criminals that decorated all city gates and border-posts, as a way of guessing what sorts of behavior were most offensive to the locals. What it came down to, here, was that Eliza was in black and Jack was on his crutch, with no weapons, and as little flesh as possible, in sight.

There were tolls everywhere, but no center of power. The cattle-herds spread out away from the high road and into pastures flat as ponds, leaving them and the strewn parades of Hollandgänger to traipse along for a day or two, until they began joining up with other, much greater roads from the south and east: nearly unbroken queues of carts laden with goods, fighting upstream against as heavy traffic coming from the north. "Why not just stop and trade in the middle of the road?" Jack asked, partly because he knew it would provoke Eliza. But she wasn't provoked at all—she seemed to think it was a good question, such as the philosophical Doctor might've asked. "Why indeed? There must be a reason. In commerce there is a reason for *everything*. That's why I like it."

The landscape was long skinny slabs of flat land divided one from the next by straight ditches full of standing water, and what happened on that land was always something queer: tulip-raising, for example. Individual vegetables being cultivated and raised by hand, like Christmas geese, and pigs and calves coddled like rich men's children. Odd-looking fields growing flax, hemp, rape, hops, tobacco, woad, and madder. But queerest of all was that these ambitious farmers were doing things that had nothing to do with farming: in many places he saw women bleaching bolts of English cloth in buttermilk, spreading it out in the fields to dry in the sun. People raised and harvested thistles, then bundled their prickly heads together to make tools for carding cloth. Whole villages sat out making lace as fast as their fingers could work, just a few children running from one person to the next with a cup of water for them to sip, or a bread-crust to snap at. Farmers whose stables were filled, not with *horses,* but with *painters*—young men from France, Savoy, or Italy who sat before easels making copy after copy of land- and sea-scapes and enormous renditions of the Siege of Vienna. These, stacked and bundled and wrapped into cargo-bales, joined the parade bound for Amsterdam.

The flow took them sometimes into smaller cities, where little trade-fairs were forever teeming. Since none of the farmers in this upside-down country grew food, they had to buy it in markets like city people. Jack and Eliza would jostle against rude boers and haggle against farmers' wives with silver rings on their fingers trying to buy cheese and eggs and bread to eat along their way. Eliza saw storks for the first time, building their nests on chimneys and swooping down into streets to snatch scraps before the dogs could get them. Pelicans she liked, too. But the things Jack marveled at— four-legged chickens and two-headed sheep, displayed in the streets by boers—were of no interest to her. She'd seen better in Constantinople.

In one of those towns they saw a woman walking about imprisoned in a barrel with neck- and arm-holes, having been guilty of adultery, and after this, Eliza would not rest, nor let Jack have peace or satisfaction, until they'd reached the city. So they drove themselves onwards across lands that had been ruined a dozen years before, when William of Orange had opened the sluices and flooded the land to make a vast moat across the Republic and save Amsterdam from the armies of King Looie. They squatted in remains of buildings that had been wrecked in that artificial Deluge, and followed canals north, skirting the small camps where canal-pirates, the watery equivalent of highwaymen, squatted round wheezing peat-fires. Too, they avoided the clusters of huts fastened to the canal-banks, where lepers lived, begging for alms by flinging ballasted boxes out at passing boats, then reeling them in speckled with coins.

One day, riding along a canal's edge, they came to a confluence of waters, and turned a perfect right angle and stared down a river that ran straight as a bow-string until it ducked beneath the curvature of the earth. It was so infested with shipping that there seemed to be not enough water left to float a nutshell. Obviously it led straight to Amsterdam.

Their escape from Germany (as that mess of Duchies, Electorates, Landgraviates, Margraviates, Counties, Bishoprics, Archbishoprics, and Principalities was called) had taken much longer than Jack had really wanted. The Doctor had offered to take them as far as Hanover, where he looked after the library of the Duchess Sophia* when he wasn't building windmills atop their Harz silver-mines. Eliza had accepted gratefully, without asking whether Jack might have an opinion on the matter. Jack's opinion would have been *no,* simply because Jack was in the habit of going wherever he wished whenever the mood took him. And accompanying the Doctor to Hanover meant that they could not leave Bockboden until the Doctor had settled all of his business in that district.

"WHAT'S HE WASTING *TODAY* ON?" Jack demanded of Enoch Root one morning. They were riding along a mountain road, followed by a couple of heavy ox-carts. Enoch went on errands like this one every morning. Jack, lacking any other kind of stimulation, had decided to take up the practice.

"Same as yesterday."

"And that is? Forgive an ignorant Vagabond, but I am used to men of *action*—so when the Doctor spends all day, every day, *talking* to people, it seems to me as if he's doing *nothing.*"

"He's *accomplishing* nothing—that's very different from *doing* nothing," Enoch said gravely.

"What's he trying to *accomplish*?"

"He'd persuade the masters of the Duke's mines not to abandon all of his innovations, now that his latest attempt to sell *Kuxen* has gone the way of all the others."

"Well, why should they listen to him?"

"We are going where the Doctor went yesterday," Enoch

---

*And of her husband, Duke Ernst August.

said, "and heard what he wanted to from the master of a mine."

"Beggin' yer pardon, guv'nor, but that striketh me not as an answer to my question."

"This entire day will be your answer," Enoch said, and then looked back, significantly, at a heavy cart following behind them, which was laden with quicksilver flasks packed in wooden crates.

They came to a mine like all the others: schlock-heaps, hand-haspels, furnaces, wheelbarrows. Jack had seen it in the Ore Range and he'd seen it in the Harz, but today (perhaps because Enoch had suggested that there was something to be learned) he saw a new thing.

The shards of ore harvested from the veins growing in the earth, were brought together and dumped out in a pile on the ground, then raked out and beaten up with hammers. The fragments were inspected in the light of day by miners too old, young, or damaged to go down into the tunnels, and sorted into three piles. The first was stone with no silver in it, which was discarded. The second was ore rich in silver, which went straight to the furnaces to be (if what Jack had seen in the Ore Range was any guide) crushed between millstones, mixed with burning-lead, shoveled into a chimney-like furnace blown by great mule-powered bellows, and melted down into pigs of crude silver. The third, which Jack had not seen at Herr Geidel's mine, was ore that contained silver, but was not as rich as the other. Geidel would have discarded this as not worth the trouble to refine it.

Jack followed a wagon-load of this down the hill to a flat meadow decorated by curious mounds hidden under oiled canvas tarps. Here, men and women were pounding this low-grade ore in big iron mortars and turning the proceeds out into clattering sieves. Boys shook these to sift out powdered ore, then mixed it with water, salt, and the dross from copper-making to produce a sticky clay. This they emptied into large wooden tubs. Then along came an elder, trailed by a couple of stout boys sweating under heavy backloads that looked familiar: they were the quicksilver-flasks that the

Doctor had bought in Leipzig, and that Enoch had delivered to them this very morning. The elder stirred through the mud with his hand, checking its quality and consistency, and, if it was right, he'd hug a flask and draw out the wooden bung and tip it, making a bolt of quicksilver strike into the mud like argent lightning. Barefoot boys went to work stomping the mercury into the mud.

Several such vats were being worked at any one time. Enoch explained to Jack that the amalgam had to be mixed for twenty-four hours. Then the vat was upended to make a heap of the stuff on the ground. At this particular mine, there were dozens of such heaps arrayed across the meadow, each one protected from the rain by a canopy of rugged cloth, and each stuck with a little sign scrawled with information about how long it had been sitting there. "This one was last worked ten days ago—it is due," Enoch told him, reading one of the signs. Indeed, later some of the workers rolled an empty tub up to that pile, shoveled the amalgam into it, added water, and began to work it with their feet again.

Enoch continued to wander about, peeling back canvas to inspect the heaps, and offering suggestions to the elders. Locals had begun filtering out of the woods as soon as visitors had arrived, and were now following him around—greed for knowledge drawing them closer, and fear pushing them back. "This one's got too much quicksilver," he said of one, "that's why it's black." But another was the color of bran. More quicksilver was wanted. Most of them were shades of gray, which was apparently desirable—but Enoch thrust his hand into these to check their warmth. Cold ones needed to have more copper dross added, and overly hot ones needed water. Enoch was carrying a basin, which he used to wash samples of the heaps in water until little pools of silver formed in the bottom. One of the heaps, all of a uniform ash color, was deemed ready. Workers shoveled it into wheelbarrows and took it down to a creek, where a cascade had been set up to wash it. The water carried the ashy stuff away as swirling clouds, and left silvery residue. This they packed into conical bags, like the ones used to make sugar-loaves, and hung them up over pots, rows of them dangling like the tits on a sow, except that instead of producing milk they dripped quicksilver, leaving a gleaming semi-solid mass inside the bags. This they formed into balls, like boys making snowballs, and put them, a few at a time, into crucibles. Over the top of each crucible they put an iron screen, then flipped the whole thing upside-down and placed it over a like crucible, half-buried in the ground, with water in the bottom, so that the two were fitted rim-to-rim, making a capsule divided in half by the iron screen. Then they buried the whole thing in coal and burned it until it was all red-hot. After it cooled, they raked off the ash and took it all apart to reveal that the quicksilver had been liberated from the balls of amalgam and escaped through the screen, to puddle below, leaving above a cluster of porous balls of pure silver metal all stuck together, and ready to be minted into thalers.

Jack spent most of the ride home pondering what he'd seen. He noticed after a while that Enoch Root had been humming in a satisfied way, evidently pleased with himself for having been able to so thoroughly shut Jack up.

"So Alchemy has its uses," Enoch said, noting that Jack was coming out of his reverie.

"You invented this?"

"I improved it. In the old days they used only quicksilver and salt. The piles were cold, and they had to sit for a year. But when dross of copper is added, they become warm, and complete the change in three or four weeks."

"The cost of quicksilver is—?"

Enoch chuckled. "You sound like your lady friend."

"That's the first question she's going to ask."

"It varies. A good price for a hundredweight would be eighty."

"Eighty of *what*?"

"Pieces of eight," Enoch said.

"It's important to specify."

"Christendom's but a corner of the world, Jack," Enoch said. "Outside of it, pieces of eight are the universal currency."

"All right—with a hundredweight of quicksilver, you can make how much silver?"

"Depending on the quality of the ore, about a hundred Spanish marks—and in answer to your next question, a Spanish mark of silver, at the standard level of fineness, is worth eight pieces of eight and six Royals . . ."

"A PIECE OF EIGHT HAS eight *reals*—" Eliza said, later, having spent the last two hours sitting perfectly motionless while Jack paced, leaped, and cavorted about her bedchamber relating all of these events with only modest improvements.

"I know that—that's why it's called a piece of eight," Jack said testily, standing barefoot on the sack of straw that was Eliza's bed, where he had been demonstrating the way the workers mixed the amalgam with their feet.

"Eight pieces of eight plus six royals, makes seventy royals. A hundred marks of silver, then, is worth seven *thousand* royals . . . or . . . eight hundred seventy-five pieces of eight. And the price of the quicksilver needed is—again?"

"Eighty pieces of eight, or thereabouts, would be a *good* price."

"So—those who'd make money need silver, and those who'd make silver need quicksilver—and a piece of eight's worth of quicksilver, put to the right uses, produces enough silver to mint ten pieces of eight."

"And you can re-use it, as they are careful to do," Jack said. "You have forgotten a few other necessaries, by the way—such as a silver mine. Mountains of coal and salt. Armies of workers."

"All gettable," Eliza said flatly. "Didn't you understand what Enoch was telling you?"

"Don't say it!—don't tell me—just wait!" Jack said, and went over to the arrow-slit to peer up at the Doctor's windmill, and down at his ox-carts parked along the edge of the stable-yard. Up and down being the only two possibilities when peering through an arrow-slit. "The Doctor provides quicksilver to the mines whose masters do what the Doctor wants."

"So," Eliza said, "the Doctor has—what?"

"Power," Jack finally said after a few wrong guesses.

"Because he has—what?"

"Quicksilver."

"So that's the answer—we go to Amsterdam and buy quicksilver."

"A splendid plan—if only we had money to buy it *with*."

"Poh! We'll just use someone else's money," Eliza said, flicking something off the backs of her fingernails.

Now, STARING DOWN THIS CROWDED canal towards the city, Jack saw, in his mind, a map he'd viewed in Hanover. Sophie and Ernst August had inherited their library, not to mention librarian (i.e., the Doctor), when Ernst August's Papist brother—evidently, something of a black sheep—had had the good grace to die young without heirs. This fellow must have been more interested in books than wenches, because his library had (according to the Doctor) been one of the largest in Germany at the time of his demise five years ago, and had only gotten bigger since then. There was no place to put it all, and so it only kept getting shifted from one stable to another. Ernst August apparently spent all of his time either fending off King Louis along the Rhine, or else popping down to Venice to pick up fresh mistresses, and never got round to constructing a permanent building for the collection.

In any event, Jack and Eliza had paused in Hanover for a few days on their journey west, and the Doctor had allowed them to sleep in one of the numerous out-buildings where parts of the library were stored. There had been many books, useless to Jack, but also quite a few extraordinary maps. He had made it his business to memorize these, or at least the parts that were finished. Remote islands and continents splayed on the parchment like stomped brains, the interiors blank, the coastlines trailing off into nowhere and simply ending in mid-ocean because no one had ever sailed farther than that, and the boasts and phant'sies of seafarers disagreed.

One of those maps had been of trade-routes: straight lines joining city to city. Jack could not read the labels. He could

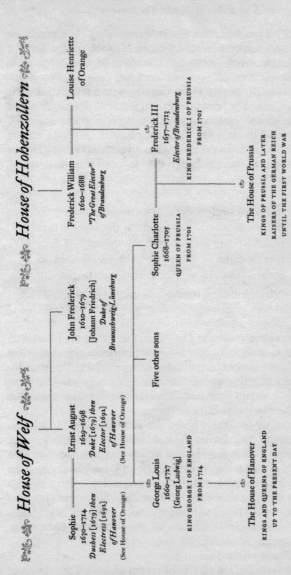

House of Welf · House of Hohenzollern

Sophie
1630–1714
Duchess [1679] *then*
Electress [1692]
of Hanover
(See House of Orange)

Ernst August
1629–1698
Duke [1679] *then*
Elector [1692]
of Hanover
(See House of Orange)

John Frederick
1620–1679
[Johann Friedrich]
Duke of
Braunschweig-Lüneburg

Frederick William
1620–1688
"The Great Elector"
of Brandenburg

Louise Henriette
of Orange

Frederick III
1657–1713
Elector of Brandenburg
KING FREDERICK I OF PRUSSIA
FROM 1701

George Louis
1660–1727
[Georg Ludwig]
KING GEORGE I OF ENGLAND
FROM 1714

Five other sons

Sophie Charlotte
1668–1705
QUEEN OF PRUSSIA
FROM 1701

The House of Hanover
KINGS AND QUEENS OF ENGLAND
UP TO THE PRESENT DAY

The House of Prussia
KINGS OF PRUSSIA AND LATER
KAISERS OF THE GERMAN REICH
UNTIL THE FIRST WORLD WAR

identify London and a few other cities by their positions, and Eliza helped him read the names of the others. But one city had no label, and its position along the Dutch coast was impossible to read: so many lines had converged on it that the city itself, and its whole vicinity, were a prickly ink-lake, a black sun. The next time they'd seen the Doctor, Jack had triumphantly pointed out to him that his map was defective. The arch-Librarian had merely shrugged.

"The Jews don't even bother to give it a name," the Doctor had said. "In their language they just call it *mokum*, which means 'the place.'"

> From desire, ariseth the thought of some means we have seen produce the like of that which we aim at; and from the thought of that, the thought of means to that mean; and so continually, till we come to some beginning within our own power.
>
> —HOBBES, *Leviathan*

AS THEY CAME CLOSER to The Place, there were many peculiar things to look at: barges full of water (fresh drinking-water for the city), other barges laden with peat, large flat areas infested with salt-diggers. But Jack could only gawk at these things a certain number of hours of the day. The rest of the time he gawked at Eliza.

Eliza, up on Turk's back, was staring at her left hand so fixedly that Jack feared she had found a patch of leprosy, or something, on it. But she was moving her lips, too. She held up her right hand to make Jack be still. Finally she held up the left. It was pink and perfect, but contorted into a strange habit, the long finger folded down, the thumb and pinky restraining each other so that only Index and Ring stood out.

"You look like a Priestess of some new sect, blessing or cursing me."

"D" was all she said.

"Ah, yes, Dr. John Dee, the famed alchemist and mountebank? I was thinking that with some of Enoch's parlor tricks, we could fleece a few bored merchants' wives . . ."

"The letter D," she said firmly. "Number four in the alphabet. Four is this," holding up that versatile left again, with only the long finger folded down.

"Yes, I can see you're holding up four fingers . . ."

"No—these digits are *binary*. The pinky tells ones, the ring finger twos, the long finger fours, the index eights, the thumb sixteens. So when the long finger *only* is folded down, it means four, which means D."

"But you had the thumb and pinky folded down also, just now . . ."

"The Doctor also taught me to encipher these by adding *another* number—seventeen in this case," Eliza said, displaying her right with the thumb and pinky tip-to-tip. Putting her hand back as it had been, she announced, "Twenty-one, which means, in the English alphabet, U."

"But what is the point?"

"The Doctor has taught me to hide messages in letters."

"It's your intention to be *writing letters* to this man?"

"If I do not," she said innocently, "how can I expect to *receive* any?"

"Why would you *want* to?" Jack asked.

"To continue my education."

"Owff!" blurted Jack, and he doubled over as if Turk had kicked him in the belly.

"A guessing-game?" Eliza said coolly. "It's got to be either: you think I'm *already* too educated, or: you hoped it would be something else."

"Both," Jack said. "You've put *hours* into improving your mind—with *nothing* to show for it. I'd hoped you had gotten *financial backing* out of the Doctor, or that Sophie."

Eliza laughed. "I've told you, over and over, that I never came within half a mile of Sophie. The Doctor let me climb a church-steeple that looks down over Herrenhausen, her great garden, so that I could watch while she went out for one of her walks. That's as close as someone like me could ever come to someone like her."

"Why bother, then?"

"It was enough for me simply to lay eyes on her: the daughter of the Winter Queen, and great-granddaughter of Mary Queen of Scots. You would never understand."

"It's just that you are always on about money, and I cannot see how staring at some bitch in a French dress, from a mile away, relates to that."

"Hanover is a poor country anyway—it's not as if they have much money to gamble on our endeavours."

"Haw! If that's poverty, give me some!"

"Why do you think the Doctor is going through such exertions to find investors for the silver mine?"

"Thank you—you've brought me back to my question: what does the Doctor want?"

"To translate all human knowledge into a new philosophical language, consisting of numbers. To write it down in a vast Encyclopedia that will be a sort of machine, not only for finding old knowledge but for making new, by carrying out certain logical operations on those numbers—and to employ all of this in a great project of bringing religious conflict to an end, and raising Vagabonds up out of squalor and liberating their potential energy—whatever *that* means."

"Speaking for myself, I'd like a pot of beer and, later, to have my face trapped between your inner thighs."

"It's a big world—perhaps you and the Doctor can both realize your ambitions," she said after giving the matter some thought. "I'm finding horseback-riding *enjoyable* but ultimately *frustrating.*"

"Don't look to *me* for sympathy."

The canal came together with others, and at some point they were on the river Amstel, which took them into the place, just short of its collision with the river Ij, where it had long ago been dammed up by the beaver-like Dutchmen. Then (as Jack the veteran reader of fortifications could see), as stealable objects, lootable churches, and rapable women had accumulated around this Amstel-Dam, those who had the most to lose had created Lines of Circumvallation. To the north, the broad Ij—more an arm of the sea than a proper river—served as a kind of moat. But on the landward side they'd thrown up walls, surrounding Amstel-Dam in a U, the prongs of the U touching the Ij to either side of where the Amstel joined it, and the bend at the bottom of the U crossing the Amstel upstream of the Dam. The dirt for the walls had to come from somewhere. Lacking hills, they'd taken it from excavations, which conveniently filled with groundwater to become moats. But to the avid Dutch there was no moat that could not be put to work as a canal. As the land inside each U had filled up with buildings, newly arrived strivers had put up buildings *outside* the walls, making it necessary to create new, larger Us encompassing the old. The city was like a tree, as long as it lived surrounding its core with new growth. Outer layers were big, the canals widely spaced, but in the middle of town they were only a stone's throw apart, so that Jack and Eliza were always crossing over cleverly counter-weighted drawbridges. As they did so they stared up and down the canals, carpeted with low boats that could skim underneath the bridges, and (on the Amstel, and some larger canals) creaking sloops with collapsible masts. Even the small boats could carry enormous loads below the water-line. The canals and the boats explained, then, why it was possible to move about in Amsterdam at all: the torrent of cargo that clogged roads in the countryside was here transferred to boats, and the streets, for the most part, opened to people.

Long rows of five-story houses fronted on canals. A few ancient timber structures still stood in the middle of town, but almost all of the buildings were brick, trimmed with white and painted over with tar. Jack marvelled like a yokel at the sight of barn doors on the fifth story of a building, opening out onto a sheer drop to a canal. A single timber projected into space above to serve as a cargo hoist. Unlike those Leipziger houses, with storage only in the attic, these were for nothing *but*.

The richest of those warehouse-streets was Warmoesstraat, and when they'd crossed over it they were in a long plaza called Damplatz, which as far as Jack could tell was just the original Dam, paved over. It had men in turbans and outlandish furry hats, and satin-clad cavaliers sweeping their plumed chapeaus off to bow to each other, and mighty buildings, and other features that might have given Jack an afternoon's gawking. But before he could even begin, some kind of phenomenon on the scale of a War, Fire, or Biblical Deluge demanded his attention off to the north. He turned his face into a clammy breeze and stared down the length of a short, fat canal to discover a low brown cloud obscuring the horizon. Perhaps it was the pall of smoke from a fire as big as the one that had destroyed London. No, it was a brushy forest, a leafless thicket several miles broad. Or perhaps a besieging army, a hundred times the size of the Turk's, all armed with pikes as big as pine-trees and aflutter with ensigns and pennants.

In the end, it took Jack several minutes' looking to allow himself to believe that he was viewing all of the world's ships at one time—their individual masts, ropes, and spars merging into a horizon through which a few churches and windmills on the other side of it could be made out as dark blurs. Ships entering from, or departing toward, the Ijsselmeer beyond, fired rippling gun-salutes and were answered by Dutch shore-batteries, spawning oozy smoke-clouds that clung about the rigging of all those ships and seemingly glued them all into a continuous fabric, like mud daubed into a wattle of dry sticks. The waves of the sea could be seen as slow-spreading news.

Once Jack had a few hours to adjust to the peculiarity of Amsterdam's buildings, its water-streets, the people's aggressive cleanliness, their barking language, and their inability to settle on this or that Church, he understood the place. All of its quarters and neighborhoods were the same as in any other city. The knife-grinders might dress like Deacons, but they still ground knives the same way as the ones in Paris. Even the waterfront was just a stupendously larger rendition of the Thames.

But then they wandered into a neighborhood the likes of which Jack had never seen *anywhere*—or rather the neighborhood wandered into *them,* for this was a rambling Mobb.

Whereas most of Amsterdam was divided among richer and poorer in the usual way, this roving neighborhood was indiscriminately mixed-up: just as shocking to Vagabond Jack as it would be to a French nobleman. Even from a distance, as the neighborhood came up the street towards Jack and Eliza, he could see that it was soaked with tension. They were like a rabble gathered before palace gates, awaiting news of the death of a King. But as Jack could plainly see when the neighborhood had flowed round them and swept them up, there *were* no palace gates here, nor anything of that sort.

It would have been nothing more than a passing freak of Creation, like a comet, except that Eliza grabbed Jack's hand and pulled him along, so that they became part of that neighborhood for half an hour, as it rolled and nudged its way among the buildings of Amsterdam like a blob of mercury feeling its way through a wooden maze. Jack saw that they were anticipating news, not from some external source, but *from within*—information, or rumors of it, surged from one end of this crowd to the other like waves in a shaken rug, with just as much noise, movement, and eruption of debris as that would imply. Like smallpox, it was passed from one person to the next with great rapidity, usually as a brief furious exchange of words and numbers. Each of these conversations was terminated by a gesture that looked as if it might have been a handshake, many generations in the past, but over time had degenerated into a brisk slapping-together of the hands. When it was done properly it made a sharp popping noise and left the palm glowing red. So the propagation of news, rumors, fads, trends, &c. through this mob could be followed by listening for waves of hand-slaps. If the wave broke over you and continued onwards, and your palm was not red, and your ears were not ringing, it meant that you had missed out on something important. And Jack was more than content to do so. But Eliza could not abide it. Before long, she had begun to ride on those waves of noise, and to gravitate towards places where they were most intense. Even worse, she seemed to understand what was going on. She knew some Spanish, which was the language spoken by many of these persons, especially the numerous Jews among them.

Eliza found lodgings a short distance south and west of the Damplatz. There was an alley just narrow enough for Jack to touch both sides of it at one time, and someone had tried the experiment of throwing a few beams across this gap, between the second, third, and fourth stories of the adjoining buildings, and then using these as the framework of a sort of house. The buildings to either side were being slurped down into the underlying bog at differing rates, and so the house above the alley was skewed, cracked, and leaky. But Eliza rented the fourth story after an apocalyptic haggling session with the landlady (Jack, who had been off stabling Turk, only witnessed the final half-hour of this). The landlady was a hound-faced Calvinist who had immediately recognized Eliza as one who was predestined for Hell, and so Jack's arrival and subsequent loitering scarcely made any impression. Still, she imposed a strict rule against visitors—shaking a finger at Jack so that her silver rings clanked together like links in a chain. Jack considered dropping his trousers as proof of chastity. But this trip to Amsterdam was Eliza's plan, not Jack's, and so he did not consider it meet to do any such thing. They had a place, or rather Eliza did, and Jack could come and go via rooftops and drainpipes.

They lived in Amsterdam for a time.

Jack expected that Eliza would begin to *do* something, but she seemed content to while away time in a coffee-house alongside the Damplatz, occasionally writing letters to the Doctor and occasionally receiving them. The moving neighborhood of anxious people brushed against this particular coffee-house, The Maiden, twice a day—for its movements were regular. They gathered on the Dam until the stroke of noon, when they flocked down the street to a large courtyard called the Exchange, where they remained until two o'clock. Then they spilled out and took their trading back up to the Dam, dividing up into various cliques and cabals that frequented different coffee-houses. Eliza's apartment actually straddled an important migration-route, so that between it and her coffee-house she was never out of earshot.

Jack reckoned that Eliza was content to live off what they had, like a Gentleman's daughter, and that was fine with Jack, who enjoyed spending more than getting. He in the meantime went back to his usual habit, which was to spend many days roaming about any new place he came into, to learn how it worked. Unable to read, unfit to converse with, he learned by watching—and here there was plenty of excellent watching. At first he made the mistake of leaving his crutch behind in Eliza's garret, and going out as an able-bodied man. This was how he learned that despite all of those Hollandgänger coming in from the East, Amsterdam was still ravenous for labor. He hadn't been out on the street for an hour before he'd been arrested for idleness and put to work dredging canals—and seeing all the muck that came off the bottom, he began to think that the Doctor's story of how small creatures got buried in river-bottoms made more sense than he'd thought at first.

When the foreman finally released him and the others from the dredge at day's end, he could hardly climb up onto the wharf for all the men crowded around jingling purses of heavy-sounding coins: agents trying to recruit sailors to man those ships on the Ij. Jack got away from them fast, because where there was such a demand for sailors, there'd be press-ganging: one blunder into a dark alley, or one free drink in a tavern, and he'd wake up with a headache on a ship in the North Sea, bound for the Cape of Good Hope, and points far beyond.

The next time he went out, he bound his left foot up against his butt-cheek, and took his crutch. In this guise he was able to wander up and down the banks of the Ij and do all the looking he wanted. Even here, though, he had to move along smartly, lest he be taken for a vagrant, and thrown into a workhouse to be reformed.

He knew a few things from talking to Vagabonds and from examining the Doctor's expansive maps: that the Ij broadened into an inland sea called Ijsselmeer, which was protected from the ocean by the island called Texel. That there was a good deep-water anchorage at Texel, but between that island and Ijsselmeer lay broad sand-banks that, like the ones at the mouth of the Thames, had mired many ships. Hence his astonishment at the size of the merchant fleet in the Ij: he knew that the *great* ships could not even *reach* this point.

They had driven lines of piles into the bottom of the Ij to seal off the prongs of the U and prevent French or English warships from coming right up to the Damplatz. These piles supported a boardwalk that swung across the harbor in a flattened arc, with drawbridges here and there to let small boats—ferry kaags, Flemish pleyts, beetle-like water-ships, keg-shaped smakschips—into the inner harbor; the canals; and the Damrak, which was the short inlet that was all that remained of the original river Amstel. Larger ships were moored to the outside of this barrier. At the eastern end of the Inner Harbor, they'd made a new island called Oostenburg and put a shipyard there: over it flew a flag with small letters O and C impaled on the horns of a large V, which meant the Dutch East India Company. This was a wonder all by itself, with its ropewalks—skinny buildings a third of a mile long—windmills grinding lead and boring gun-barrels, a steam-house, perpetually obnubilated, for bending wood, dozens of smoking and clanging smithys including two mighty ones where anchors were made, and a small tidy one for making nails, a tar factory on its own wee island so that when it burnt down it wouldn't take the rest of the yard with it. A whole warehouse district of its own. Lofts big enough to make sails larger than any Jack had ever seen. And, of course, skeletons of several big ships on the slanted ways, braced with diagonal sticks to keep 'em from toppling over, and all aswarm with workers like ants on a whale's bones.

Somewhere there must've been master wood-carvers and gilders, too, because the stems and sterns of the V.O.C. ships riding in the Ij were decorated like Parisian whorehouses, with carved statues covered in gold-leaf: for example, a maiden reclining on a couch with one shapely arm draped over a globe, and Mercury swooping down from on high to crown her with the laurel. And yet just outside the picket of windmills and watch-towers that outlined the city, the landscape of pastures and ditches resumed. Mere yards from India ships offloading spices and calico into small boats that slipped through the drawbridges to the Damrak, cattle grazed.

The Damrak came up hard against the side of the city's new weigh-house, which was a pleasant enough building almost completely obscured by a perpetual swarm of boats. On the ground floor, all of its sides were open—it was made on stilts like a Vagabond-shack in the woods—and looking in, Jack could see its whole volume filled with scales of differing sizes, and racks and stacks of copper and brass cylinders engraved with wild snarls of cursive writing: weights for all the measures employed in different Dutch Provinces and the countries of the world. It was, he could see, the third weigh-house to be put up here and still not big enough to weigh and mark all of the goods coming in on those boats. Sloops coming in duelled for narrow water-lanes with canal-barges taking the weighed and stamped goods off to the city's warehouses, and every few minutes a small heavy cart clattered away across the Damplatz, laden with coins the ships' captains had used to pay duty, and made a sprint for the Exchange Bank, scattering wigged, ribboned, and turbaned deal-makers out of its path. The Exchange Bank was the same thing as the Town Hall, and a stone's throw from there was the Stock Exchange—a rectangular courtyard environed by colonnades, like the ones in Leipzig but bigger and brighter.

One afternoon Jack came by the Maiden to pick Eliza up at the end of her hard day's drinking coffee and spending the Shaftoes' inheritance. The place was busy, and Jack reckoned he could slip in the door without attracting any bailiffs. It was a rich airy high-ceilinged place, not at all tavernlike, hot and close, with clever people yammering in half a dozen languages. In a corner table by a window, where northern light off the Ij could set her face aglow, Eliza sat, flanked by two other women, and holding court (or so it seemed) for a parade of Italians, Spaniards, and other swarthy rapier-carrying men in big wigs and bright clothes. Occasionally she'd reach for a big round coffee-pot, and at those moments she'd look just like the Maid of Amsterdam on the stern of a ship—or for that matter, as painted on the ceiling of this very room: loosely draped in yards of golden satin, one hand on a globe, one nipple poking out, Mercury always behind and to the right, and below her, the ever-present Blokes with Turbans, and feather-bedecked Negroes, presenting tributes in the form of ropes of pearls and giant silver platters.

She was flirting with those Genoese and Florentine merchants' sons, and Jack could cope with that, to a point. But they were rich. And this was all she did, every day. He lost the power of sight for a few minutes. But in time his rage cleared away, like the clouds of ash washing away from the amalgam, clearing steadily to reveal a pretty gleam of silver under clear running water. Eliza was staring at him—seeing everything. She glanced at something next to him, telling him to look at it, and then she locked her blue eyes on someone across the table and laughed at a witticism.

Jack followed her look and discovered a kind of shrine against the wall. It was a glass-fronted display case, but all gold-leafed and decked out with trumpet-tooting seraphs, as if its niches had been carved to house pieces of the True Cross and fingernail-parings of Archangels. But in fact the niches contained little heaps of dull everyday things like ingots of lead, scraps of wool, mounds of saltpeter and sugar and coffee-beans and pepper-corns, rods and slabs of iron, copper and tin, and twists of silk and cotton cloth. And, in a tiny crystal flask, like a perfume bottle, there was a sample of quicksilver.

"So, I'm meant to believe that you're transacting business in there?" he asked, once she had extricated herself, and they were out on the Damplatz together.

"You believed that I was doing *what,* then?"

"It's just that I saw no goods or money changing hands."

"They call it *Windhandel*."

"The wind business? An apt name for it."

"Do you have any idea, Jack, how much quicksilver is stored up in these warehouses all around us?"

"No."

"I do."

She stopped at a place where they could peer into a portal of the Stock Exchange. "Just as a whole workshop can be powered by a mill-wheel, driven by a trickle of water in a race, or by a breath of air on the blades of a windmill, so the movement of goods through yonder Weigh-House is driven by a trickle of paper passing from hand to hand in *there*" (pointing to the Stock Exchange) "and the warm wind that you feel on your face when you step into the Maiden."

Movement caught Jack's eye. He imagined for a moment that it was a watch-tower being knocked down by a sudden burst of French artillery. But when he looked, he saw he'd been fooled for the hundredth time. It was a windmill spinning. Then more movement out on the Ij: a tidal swell coming through and jostling the ships. A dredger full of hapless Hollandgänger moved up a canal, clawing up muck—muck that according to the Doctor would swallow and freeze things that had once been quick, and turn them to stone. No wonder they were so fastidious about dredging. Such an idea must be anathema to the Dutch, who worshipped motion above all. For whom the physical element of Earth was too resistant and inert, an annoyance to traders, an impediment to the fluid exchange of goods. In a place where all things were suffused with quicksilver, it was necessary to blur the transition from earth to water, making out of the whole Republic a gradual shading from one to the other as they neared the banks of the Ij, not entirely complete until they got past the sandbanks and reached the ocean at Texel.

"I must go to Paris."

"Why?"

"Partly to sell Turk and those ostrich plumes."

"Clever," she said. "Paris is retail, Amsterdam wholesale—you'll fetch twice the price there."

"But really it is that I am accustomed to being the one fluid thing in a universe dumb and inert. I want to stand on the stone banks of the Seine, where *here* is solid and *there* is running water and the frontier between 'em is sharp as a knife."

"As you wish," Eliza said, "but I belong in Amsterdam."

"I know it," Jack said, "I keep seeing your picture."

The Dutch Republic
1684

JACK RODE WEST OUT OF Amsterdam, through Haarlem, and then found himself suddenly alone, and perilously close to being under water: autumn rains had submerged the pastures, leaving the walled towns as islands. Soon he reached the line of dunes that fenced the country off from the North Sea. Not even Dutchmen could find a use for this much sand. Turk was unsettled by the change in the ground, but then he seemed to remember how to go on it—perhaps his Turkish master had used to take him for gallops in some Mohametan desert. With a plodding and swimming kind of gait he took Jack up to the crest of a dune. Below them, a mile away, Alp-sized green waves were hurling themselves up onto the sand with monstrous roaring and hissing. Jack sat there and stared until Turk grew annoyed. To the horse it was cold and foreign, to Jack it was just this side of cozy. He was trying to count the years since he'd seen open salt water.

There had been the voyage to Jamaica—but after that, his life (he began to think) had been impossibly confusing. Either that, or else the French Pox had amazed and riddled his memories. He had to count on his fingers. Nay, he had to dismount and use his crutch-tip to draw family trees and maps on the sand.

His return from Jamaica was a good place to start: 1678. He had bedded the fair Mary Dolores, six feet of Irish vigor, and then fled to Dunkirk to avoid a warrant, and then there'd been the penis incident. While he'd been recovering from that, Bob had showed up with news: Mary Dolores was pregnant. Also, that John Churchill fellow, improbably, was *married,* and had been made a Colonel—no, wait, a Brigadier—and had any number of regiments under him now. He was avidly recruiting, and still remembered the Shaftoes—did Jack want a steady job, perhaps, so that he could wed Mary Dolores and raise his offspring?

"Just the sort of tidy plan that Bob would come up with," Jack shouted at the waves, still annoyed, six or seven years later. Turk was becoming edgy. Jack decided to talk to him, as long as he was speaking out loud anyway. Did horses understand what was going on, when you spoke to people who weren't there? "So far, simple enough—but here it becomes very deep," he began. "John Churchill was in the Hague—then he was in Brussels—why? Even a horse can see the contradiction in *that*—but I forget you're an Ottoman horse. All right, then: all of this land—" (stomping the dune for emphasis) "was part of Spain—you heard me—Spain! Then these fucking Dutchmen turned Calvinist and revolted, and drove the Spanish away, down south of the Maas and a bunch of other rivers with hard-to-remember names—past Zeeland, anyway—we'll be seeing more than we want to of those rivers soon. Leaving only a wedge of Papist Spain trapped between the Dutch Republic on its north, and France on its south. This Spain-wedge contains Brussels and Antwerp and a large number of battlefields, basically—it is like the jousting-ground where Europe goes to have its wars. Sometimes the Dutch and the English ally against France, and they have battles in the Spanish Netherlands. Sometimes England and France ally against the Dutch, and they have battles in the Spanish Netherlands. Anyway—at this particular time, I believe, it was England and the Dutch against France, for the reason that all England was up in arms against Popery. Importation of French goods had been outlawed—that's why I was in Dunkirk—obvious opportunities for smuggling. And that's also why John Churchill was raising new armies. He went to Holland to parley with William of Orange, who was thought to know more'n anyone about staving off the Catholic hordes, as he'd stopped King Looie at the cost of turning half his country into a moat.

"So far it makes sense, then. But why—an intelligent horse might ask—why was John Churchill *also* in Brussels—part of *Spain's,* and therefore the *Pope's,* dominions? Why, it's because—thanks to the maneuverings of his daddy Winston—ever since John had been just a lad, he'd been in the household of James, King Chuck's brother, the Duke of York. And York—then, and now, first in line for the throne— was, and is today—you'll like this—a fanatical Papist! *Now* do you understand why London was, and probably still is, nervous? The King decided it'd be better if his brother took a long vacation out of the country, and naturally James chose the Catholic city that was closest at hand: Brussels! And John Churchill, being in his household, was obliged to follow him, at least part of the time.

"Anyway—Bob took the King's shilling and I did not. From Dunkirk, he and I rode together through the no-man's-land—which, not to repeat myself, you'll soon be seeing plenty of—by Ypres, Oudenaarde, Brussels, and as far as Waterloo, where we parted ways. I went down to Paris, he went back to Brussels, and probably spent a lot of his time, thereafter, scurrying to and fro carrying messages, as when he was a boy."

During this recital, Jack had been unwinding his crutch: a curved stick with a padded crossbar at the top to go under his armpit, all lashed together with a mile of crude twine. When he'd undone the windings, he was left with two pieces of wood and some rags he'd used for padding. But protruding from the top of the long crutch-pole was the pommel of a Janissary-sword.

He had searched half of the Harz Mountains to find a stick whose curve matched that of the sword. Having found it, he'd split it in half, and hollowed out a space in the middle big enough to contain the scabbard. The pommel and guard still stuck out the top, but when he added the crutch's crossbar, then swaddled it in rags, and bound all in twine, he had a crutch that seemed innocuous enough—and if a border-guard threatened to unmake it, Jack could always cup a hand under his armpit and complain about the painful black swellings that had recently flared up there.

The crutch was a convenience in settled places where only Gentlemen had the right to bear arms—but between here and northern France, he hoped to see as little of that sort of country as possible. He belted on the sword and strapped the crutch-pole alongside Turk's saddle, and then Jack the crip-pled vagrant was suddenly Jack the armed rider, galloping down the sea-coast on the back of a Turkish war-horse.

DOWN PAST THE HAGUE, around the Hook of Holland, Jack paid a visit on certain boat-owning fellows of his acquain-tance, and learned, from them, that the French had banned the inexpensive cloth coming out of Calicoe in India. Natu-rally the Dutch were now smuggling it down the coast, and there was a steady traffic of the small cargo-vessels called flutes. Jack's friends ferried him, Turk, and a ton of Calicoe across Zeeland, which was the name the Dutch gave to the huge sandy morass where such rivers as the Maas and the Schelde emptied into the North Sea. But an autumn storm was blowing up in the Channel, and they had to take shelter in a little privateers' cove in Flanders. From there, Jack took advantage of a fortuitous low tide to make a night gallop down the coast to Dunkirk, and the hospitality of the dear old Bomb & Grapnel.

But from Mr. Foot, the proprietor of the *Bomb,* Jack got an earful about how, ever since King Looie had bought Dunkirk from King Chuck, things weren't the same: the French had enlarged the harbor so that it could harbor the big warships of that arch-privateer Jean Bart, and these changes had driven away the small Channel pirates and smugglers who had once made Dunkirk such a prosperous and merry town.

Disgusted and dismayed, Jack left immediately, striking inland into Artois, where he could still go armed. It was hard up against the frontier of the Spanish Netherlands, and the soldiers who'd been sent up to prosecute King Looie's wars

there had not been slow to grasp that there was more to be
made by robbing travelers on the London-Paris route—who
were still so grateful to've survived the Channel crossing
that they practically gave it away—than from dutiful soldiering.

Jack made himself look like one of these highwaymen—
no great feat, since he *had been* one for a year or two—and
that brought him swift and more or less safe passage down
into Picardy: the home of a famous Regiment, which, since
they were not there when Jack arrived, he reckoned that they
must be up laying waste to the Spanish Netherlands. A few
changes in attire (his old floppy musketeer-hat, e.g.) gave
him the look of a deserter, or scout, from same.

In one of those Picard villages the church-bell was clanging without letup. Sensing some kind of disorder, Jack rode
toward it, across fields crowded with peasants bringing in
the harvest. They rotated their crops so that one-third of the
fields had wheat, one-third oats, and the remaining third
were fallow, and Jack tended to ride across the ones that
were fallow. These wretches looked at him with fear that was
abject even by the standard of French peasants. Most of
them scanned the northern sky, perhaps looking for clouds
of smoke or dust, and some dropped to the ground and put
their ears against it, listening for hoofbeats, and Jack concluded that it wasn't him *personally* they feared, so much as
what might be behind him.

He assessed this village as one where he could get away
with being armed, and rode into it, because he needed to buy
oats for Turk. The only person he saw was a barefoot boy in
coarse dirty linen, visible from the waist down through a low
doorway in the base of the bell-tower, his raggedy ass thrusting out rudely with each jerk on the bell-rope.

But then Jack encountered a rider in good but plain clothing who had apparently come up from the direction of Paris.
They drew up, a safe distance apart, in the town's deserted
market-square, circled round each other once or twice, and
then began shouting at each other over the din of the bell,
and settled on a mixture of English and French.

Jack: "Why are they ringing the bell?"

"These Catholics think it wards off thunderstorms," said the Frenchman. "Why are they so—?" he then asked and, not trusting his English or Jack's French, pantomimed a furtive cringing peasant.

"They're afraid that I'm a forerunner of the Picardy Regiment, coming home from the wars," Jack guessed. He intended this as a wry jest about the tendency of regiments to "live off the land," as the euphemism went. But it was quite significant to this Huguenot.

"Is it true? Is the regiment coming?"

"How much would it be worth to you?" Jack asked.

Everything about this Huguenot reminded him of the Independent traders of England, who'd ride out to remote districts in harvest-time to buy up goods at better than market price. And both Jack and this trader—who introduced himself as Monsieur Arlanc—understood that the price would drop still further if the sellers believed, rightly or wrongly, that the Picardy Regiment was coming to eat it out from under them.

So there was, inadvertently, a sort of business proposition on the table. Vagabond and Huguenot rode around each other a few more times. All around them, the peasants labored at the harvest. But they were keeping an eye on the two strangers, and soon a village elder came hustling in from the fields on a donkey.

But in the end, Monsieur Arlanc could not bring himself to do it. "We are already hated enough," he said, apparently meaning the Huguenots, "without spreading false panics. These peasants have enough to be afraid of already—that is why my sons and I ride out to such dangerous marches."

"Fine. But incidentally, I don't intend to rob you," Jack said irritably, "you needn't make up phant'sies about your supposed pack of heavily armed sons, just over the rise."

"Tales don't offer sufficient protection in these times, I'm afraid," said Monsieur Arlanc, tucking his cloak back to divulge no fewer than four separate firearms: two conventional pistols, and two more cleverly worked into the handle of a tomahawk and the barrel of a walking-stick respectively.

"Well played, Monsieur—Protestant practicality and French *savoir-faire* united."

"I say, are you sure you'll be all right riding to the Inn at Amiens armed with nothing but a sword? The highways—"

"I do not stay at Inns of the French sort, nor do I generally ride on highways," Jack said. "But if that is *your* habit, and if you are going that way . . ."

So they rode to Amiens together, after purchasing oats from the head man of the village. Jack bought enough to fill Turk's belly, and Monsieur Arlanc bought the rest of the year's harvest (he would send wagons later to take delivery). Jack told no lies—just lounged on the rim of the town well, looking like a Volunteer, as the local deserters and highwaymen were called. After that it was a good stiff ride to Amiens, where there was a large establishment throttling a crossroads: livery stables nearly buried in hay, and paddocks crowded with oxen; queues of empty wagons lining the road (some soon to be hired by M. Arlanc); several smithys, some geared for shoeing horses, others for putting rims on wagon-wheels. As well, harness-shops, and various carpenters specializing in wheels, ox-yokes, cart-frames, and barrel-making. Trains of harvest-laden carts filling the roadway, waiting to be inspected, and to pay tolls. Somewhere, a lodging for traders and travelers that accounted for its being called an Inn. From a distance, it was a great dark smoking knot, clearly recognizable as not Jack's sort of place—he unbelted his sword, slid it back into its concealment in the crutch-pole, and began winding it up again.

"You must come to the Inn, and see that I do in fact have sons," said Monsieur Arlanc. "They are still only boys, but . . ."

"I have never seen my own—I cannot see yours," Jack said. "Besides, I cannot tolerate these French Inns—"

Monsieur Arlanc nodded understandingly. "In your country, goods are free to move on the roads—?"

"—and an Inn is a hospitable place for travelers, not a choke-point."

So he bade good-bye to Monsieur Arlanc, from whom he had learned a thing or two about where in Paris he should sell his ostrich-plumes and his war-horse. In return, the Huguenot had learned some things about phosphorus, silver mines, and Calicoe-smuggling from Jack. Both men had been safer together than they would've been apart.

JACK THE ONE-LEGGED TINKER, leading his plow-horse, smelled Paris half a day before he saw it. The fields of grain gave way to market-gardens crowded with vegetables, and pastures for dairy cattle, and dark, heavy carts came endlessly up the road from the city laden with barrels and tubs of human shit collected from the gutters and stoops, which were worked into the vegetable-fields by peasants using rakes and forks. Parisians seemed to shit more than other humans, or perhaps the garlic in their food made it seem that way—in any case Jack was glad when he got clear of those rank vegetable-fields and entered into the suburbs: endless warrens of straw-roofed huts crowded with misplaced country folk, burning whatever sticks and debris they could rake together to cook their food and ward off the autumn chill, and publicly suffering from various picturesque ailments. Jack didn't stop moving until he reached the perpetual pilgrim-camp around St.-Denis, where almost anyone could get away with loitering for a few hours. He bought some cheese for himself and some hay for Turk from some farmers who were on their way down to the city. Then he relaxed among the lepers, epileptics, and madmen who were hanging around the Basilica, and dozed until a couple of hours before dawn.

When it got light enough to move about, he joined in with the thousands of farmers who came into the city, as they did every morning, bringing vegetables, milk, eggs, meat, fish, and hay into the markets. This crowd was larger than he remembered, and it took longer for them to get into the city. The gate of St.-Denis was impossibly congested, so he tried his luck at the gate of St. Martin, a musket-shot away. By the time he passed under it, dawn-light was glancing prettily off its new stone-work: King Looie as a primordial naked Hercules leaning insouciantly on a tree-sized club, naked except for a periwig the size of a cloud, and a lion skin slung over one arm so that a flapping corner just covered the royal Penis. Victory was swooping down from Heaven, one arm laden with palm-branches and the other reaching out to slap a laurel-wreath atop that wig. The King's foot rested on the mangled form of someone he'd just apparently beaten the crap out of, and, in the background, a great Tower burnt.

"God damn you, King Looie," Jack muttered, passing under the gate; because he could feel himself cringing. He'd tried to ride across France as fast as he could, specifically to prevent this: but still, it had taken several days. The sheer vastness of it compared to those tiny German principalities, and the component states of the Dutch Republic, was such that by the time you reached Paris, you'd been traveling across this King's dominions for so long that as you passed through the gate you couldn't not cringe beneath his power.

Never mind; he was in Paris. Off to his left the sun was rising over the towers and bastions of the Temple, where those Knights of Malta had their own city within the city—though the old curtain-walls that once enclosed it had lately been torn down. But for the most part his views in all directions were sealed off by vertical walls of white stone: Paris's six- and seven-story buildings rising on either side of the street, funneling the farmers and the fishwives, and the vendors with their loads of flowers, oranges, and oysters into narrow race-ways wherein they jostled sharply for position, all trying to avoid falling into the central gutter. Not far into the city, much of this traffic angled off to the right, toward the great market-place of Les Halles, leaving a (for Paris) clear vista straight down to the Seine and the Île de la Cité.

Jack had developed a suspicion that he was being tailed by an agent of King Looie's Lieutenant of Police, who had unfortunately caught his eye for a moment as he'd gone through the gate. Jack knew not to turn around and look. But by watching the faces of oncoming pedestrians—particularly, scum—he could see that they were surprised by, and then scared of, someone. Jack could hardly slip off into the crowd when he was leading a great big horse, but he could try to make himself not worth following. Les Halles would be a good place for that, so he followed the crowd to the right. The dramatickal option—mounting Turk, producing a weapon—would lead to the galleys. In fact, there were very few roads out of Paris that would *not* end with Jack chained to an oar in Marseille.

Someone behind him came in for brutal tongue-lashings from the fishwives at Les Halles. Jack overheard comparisons between his pursuer's moustache, and the armpit hair of various infidel races. The hypothesis was floated, and generally agreed upon, that this policeman spent rather too much of his time performing oral sex on certain large farm animals infamous for poor hygiene. Beyond that, Jack's French simply was not quick or vile enough. He trolled several times through Les Halles, hoping that the crowd, the smell of yesterday's fish-guts, the fishwives, and sheer boredom would shake this man off his tail, but it didn't work. Jack bought a loaf, so that he could explain why he'd come here, if someone bothered to ask, and to demonstrate that he was not a penniless vagrant, and also because he was hungry.

He put the sun to his back and began to dodge and maneuver through various streets, headed for the Rue Vivienne. The police wanted to arrest him for being in Paris with no business, which normally would have been the case for him. So much so, that he'd forgotten that this time he actually *did* have business.

The streets had begun to congest with strolling retailers: a cheese-seller pushing a large wheel of blue-veined stuff on a sort of wheelbarrow, a mustard-seller carrying a small capped pail and a scoop, numerous *porteurs d'eau,* their stout bodies harnessed into frames all a-dangle with wooden buckets, a butter-seller with baskets of butter-pats strapped to his back. This kind of thing would only get worse, to the point that it would immobilize him. He had to get rid of Turk. No trouble: the horse business was every-where, he'd already passed by several livery stables, and hay-wains filled narrow streets with their thatched bulk and narcotic fragrance. Jack followed one to a stable and made arrangements to have Turk put up there for a few days.

Then out the other side, and into a large open space: a plaza with (surprisingly enough) a monumental statue of King Looie in the center. On one side of its pedestal, a relief of Looie personally spearheading a cavalry charge across a canal, or perhaps that was the Rhine, into a horizontal forest of muskets. On the other, Looie on the throne with a queue of Kings and Emperors of Europe waiting, crowns in hand, to kneel down and kiss his high-heeled booties.

He must be on the right course, because he was beginning to see a higher class of vendor: sellers of books strolling along holding advertisements over their heads on sign-boards, a candy-man carrying small scales, a seller of *eau-de-vie* carrying a basket of tiny bottles, and a goblet; a seller of pâtés carrying a sort of painter's palette with smudges of different varieties, and many orange-girls: all of them crying the particular cries that belonged to that sort of vendor, like birds with their own distinct calls. Jack was on Rue Vivi-enne. It was starting to look like Amsterdam: finely-dressed men of many lands, strolling along having serious conversa-tions: making money by exchanging words. But it also looked a bit like the Booksellers' Quarter in Leipzig: whole cart-loads of books, printed but not bound, disappearing into one especially fine House: the King's Library.

Jack crutched his way up one side of the street and down the other until he found the House of the Golden Frigate, adorned with a sculpture of a warship. This had obviously been made by an artisan who'd never come near the ocean, as it was queerly distorted and had an unlikely profusion of gun-decks. But it looked good. An Italian gentleman was there on the front stoop, worrying a hand-wrought iron key of many curious protuberances into a matching keyhole.

"Signor Cozzi?" Jack inquired.

"*Si,*" replied he, looking only a little surprised to be accosted by a one-legged wanderer.

"A message from Amsterdam," Jack said in French, "from your cousin." But this last was unnecessary, as Signor Cozzi had already recognized the seal. Leaving the key jutting from the lock, he broke it open right there and scanned a few lines of beautiful whirling script. A woman with a cask of ink on her back, noting his interest in written documents, shouted a business proposal to him, and before he could deflect it, there was a second woman with a cask of vastly superior and yet far cheaper ink on her back; the two of them got into an argument, and Signor Cozzi took advantage of it to slip inside, beckoning Jack in with a trick of his large brown eyes. Jack could not resist turning around, now, to look behind him for the first time since he had entered the city. He caught sight of a sworded man in a somber sort of cape, just in the act of turning around to slink away: this policeman had spent half the morning tailing a perfectly legitimate banker's messenger. "You are being followed?" Signor Cozzi inquired, as if asking Jack whether he was breathing in and out.

"Not now," Jack answered.

It was another one of those places consisting of *bancas* with large padlocked books, and heavy chests on the floor. "How do you know my cousin?" Cozzi asked, making it clear he wasn't going to invite Jack to take a seat. Cozzi himself sat down behind a desk and began to pull quills out of a little jar and examine their points.

"A lady friend of mine has, uh, made his acquaintance. When he learned, through her, that I was about to journey to Paris, he pressed that letter on me."

Cozzi wrote something down, then unlocked a desk-drawer and began to rummage through it, picking out coins. "It says that if the seal has been tampered with I should send you to the galleys."

"I assumed as much."

"If the seal is intact, and you get it to me within fourteen days of the date it was written, I'm to give you a louis d'or. Ten days gets you two. Fewer than ten, an additional louis d'or for each day you shaved off the trip." Cozzi dropped five gold coins into Jack's hand. "How the hell did you do it? *No one* travels from Amsterdam to Paris in seven days."

"Think of it as a trade secret," Jack said.

"You are dead on your feet—go somewhere and sleep," Cozzi said. "And when you are ready to return to Amsterdam, come to me, and maybe I'll have a message for you to take to my cousin."

"What makes you think I'm going back?"

Cozzi smiled for the first time. "The look in your eye when you spoke of your lady friend. You are mad with love, no?"

"Mad with syphilis, actually," Jack said, "but still mad enough to go back."

WITH THE MONEY HE'D BROUGHT with him, and the money he'd earned, Jack could have stayed somewhere decent—but he didn't know how to find such a place, or how to behave once he found one. The last year had been an education in how little having money really mattered. A rich Vagabond was a Vagabond still, and 'twas common knowledge that King Charles, during the Interregnum, had lived without money in Holland. So Jack wandered across town to the district called the Marais. Movement was now a matter of forcing his body into narrow, ephemeral gaps between other pedestrians—primarily vendors, as of (in some districts) *peaux de lapins* (bundles of rabbit-pelts), baskets (these people carried enormous baskets filled with smaller baskets), hats (small uprooted trees with hats dangling from branch-ends), *linge* (a woman all adrape with lace and scarves), and (as he came into the Marais) *chaudronniers* with pots and pans impaled by their handles on a stick. Vinegar-sellers with casks on wheels, musicians with bagpipes and hurdy-gurdies, cake-sellers with broad flat baskets of steaming confections that made Jack light in the head.

Jack got into the heart of the Marais, found a pissing-corner where he could stand still, and scanned the air above the people's heads for half an hour or so, and listened, until he heard a particular cry. *Everyone* in the street was shouting *something,* usually the name of whatever they were selling, and for the first couple of hours it had just been Bedlam to Jack. But after a while Jack's ear learned to pick out individual voices—something like hearing drum-beats or bugle-calls in battle. Parisians, he knew, had developed the skill to a high degree, just as the Lieutenant of Police could scan a torrent of people coming in through a gate at dawn and pick out the Vagabond. Jack was just able to hear a high-pitched voice crying "*Mort-aux-rats! Mort-aux-rats!*" and then it was easy enough to turn his head and see a long pole, like a pike, being carried at an angle over someone's shoulder, the corpses of a couple of dozen rats dangling from it by their tails, their freshness an unforgeable guarantee that this man had been working *recently.*

Jack shoved his way into the throng, using the crutch now like a burglar's jimmy to widen small openings, and after a few minutes' rattling pursuit caught up with St.-George and clapped him on the shoulder, like a policeman. Many would drop everything and sprint away when so handled, but one did not become a legend in the rat-killer's trade if one was easily startled. St.-George turned around, making the rats on his pole swing wide, like perfectly synchronized pole-dancers at a fun-fair, and recognized him. Calmly, but not coldly. "Jacques—so you *did* escape from those German witches."

"'Twas nothing," Jack said, trying to cover his astonishment, then his pride, that word of this had spread as far as Paris. "They were fools. Helpless. Now, if *you* had been chasing me—"

"Now you have returned to civilization—why?" Steely curiosity being another good rat-killer trait. St.-George had curly hair the color of sand, and hazel eyes, and had probably looked angelic as a boy. Maturity had elongated his cheekbones and (according to legend) other parts of his body in a way that was not so divine—his head was funnel-shaped, tapering to a pair of pursed lips, staring eyes that looked as if they were painted on. "You know that the *passe-volante* trade has been quashed—why are you here?"

"To renew my friendship with you, St.-George."

"You have been riding on horseback—I can smell it."

Jack decided to let this pass. "How can you smell *anything* except man-shit here?"

St.-George sniffed the air. "Shit? Where? Who has been shitting?" This, being a sort of joke, was a signal that Jack could now offer to buy St.-George something, as a token of friendship. After some negotiations, St.-George agreed to be the recipient of Jack's generosity—but not because he *needed* it—only because it was inherent in human nature that one must from time to time give things away, and at such times, one needed someone to give things away *to,* and part of being a good friend was to be that someone, as needed. Then there were negotiations about what Jack was going to buy. St.-George's objective was to figure out how much money Jack was carrying—Jack's was to keep St.-George wanting to know more. In the end, for tactical reasons, St.-George agreed to allow Jack to buy him some coffee—but it had to be from a particular vendor named Christopher.

They were half an hour tracking him down. "He is not a tall man—"

"Hard to find, then."

"But he wears a red fez with a brave golden tassel—"

"He's a Turk?"

"Of course! I told you he sold coffee, didn't I?"

"A Turk named—Christopher?"

"Don't play the clown, Jacques—remember that I know you."

"But—?"

St.-George rolled his eyes, and snapped, "All of the Turks who sell coffee in the streets are actually Armenians dressed up as Turks!"

"I'm sorry, St.-George, I didn't know."

"I should not be so harsh," St.-George admitted. "When you left Paris, coffee was not fashionable yet—not until the Turks fled from Vienna, and left mountains of it behind."

"It's been fashionable in England since I was a boy."

"If it is in England, it is not *fashionable*, but a *curiosity*," St.-George said through clenched teeth.

Onwards they searched, St.-George wending like a ferret through the crowd, passing round, e.g., furniture-sellers carrying fantastic complexes of stools and chairs all roped together on their backs, milk-men with pots on their heads, *d'oublies* carrying unlit lanterns, and bent under enormous dripping barrels of shit; knife-grinders trundling their wheels. Jack had to put the crutch to much rude use, and considered taking out the sword. Eliza had been right—Paris *was* retail—funny she'd known this without ever having set foot in the city, while Jack, who'd lived here, on and off, for years . . .

Best to keep his mind on St.-George. Only the rat-pole prevented Jack from losing him. Though it helped that people were always running out of shops, or shouting from windows, trying to engage his services. The only people who could afford to keep fixed shops were members of a few princely trades, viz. makers of dresses, hats, and wigs. But St.-George treated all men alike, asking them a series of penetrating questions and then firmly sending them home. "Even noblemen and savants are as peasants in their understanding of rats," St.-George said incredulously. "How can I be of service to them when their thinking is so pre-theoretical?"

"Well, as a start, you could get rid of their rats . . ."

"One does not *get rid of* rats! You are no better than these people!"

"Sorry, St.-George. I—"

"Does anyone ever *get rid of* Vagabonds?"

"Individual ones, certainly. But—"

"Individual to *you*—but to a Gentleman, all the same, like rats, *n'est-ce pas*? One must live with rats."

"Except for the ones dangling from your pole—?"

"It is like the exemplary hanging. The heads on the spikes before the city-gates."

"To scare *les autres*?"

"Just so, Jacques. These were, to rats, as you, my friend, are to Vagabonds."

"You are too kind—really, you flatter me, St.-George."

"These were the cleverest—the ones who would find the smallest of holes, who would explore the drain-pipes, who would say to the common rats: 'gnaw through this grate, *mes amis*—it will shorten your teeth to be sure—but once through, such things you will feast on!' These were the savants, the Magellans—"

"And they're dead."

"They displeased me too many times, these did. Many others, I allow to live—to breed, even!"

"No!"

"In certain cellars—unbeknownst to the apothecaries and parfumiers who live above—I have rat seraglios where my favorites are allowed to procreate. Some lines I have bred for a hundred generations. As a breeder of canines creates dogs fierce against strangers, but obedient to the master—"

"You create rats that obey St.-George."

"Pourquoi non?"

"But how can you be so certain that the rats are not breeding *you*?"

"I beg your pardon?"

"Your father was *mort-aux-rats,* no?"

"And his father before him. Killed in plagues, may God have mercy on their souls."

"So you believe. But perhaps the rats killed them."

"You anger me. But your theory is not without promise—"

"Perhaps you, St.-George, are the result of a breeding program—you have been allowed to live, and flourish, and have children of your own, because you have a theory that is congenial to the rats."

"Still, I kill very many."

"But those are the stupid ones—without introspection."

"I understand, Jacques. For you, I would serve as *mort-aux-rats* and would do it for free. But these—" he made a flicking gesture at a man in an excellent wig who was trying to call him over to a shop. The man looked crestfallen—temporarily. But then St.-George softened, and moved in the direction of a narrow doorway—more hatch than door—set into the wall of this wig-maker's shop, next to his open shop-window. This suddenly burst open, and a round-bodied five-foot-tall man with a vigorous moustache and curly-toed slippers emerged from a stairway no wider than he was, preceded by a smoking and steaming apparatus of hammered copper that was strapped to his body.

When Christopher (for it was none other) stood in the sun, which he always tried to do, the golden light gleamed off the copper and hung in the steam and glittered off his golden fez-tassel and shone in his embroidered slippers and brass buttons and made him very magnificent, a walking mosque. He switched among French, Spanish, and English in mid-sentence, and he claimed to know all about Jack Shaftoe (whom he addressed as *l'Emmerdeur*), and tried to give him coffee for free. He had just refilled his tanks upstairs, he explained, and was heavy burdened. St.-George had warned that Christopher would make this offer "because he will want to calculate how much money you are carrying," and together they had rehearsed a few scenarios of how the coffee-price negotiation might play out. The plan was that Jack would run their side of the dealings, and that St.-George would hover and, at just the right moment, divulge that Jack was looking for a place to stay. Jack had never said as much to St.-George, but then it was not necessary; this was why one approached St.-George upon one's arrival in the Marais. His work took him into every building—especially to the parts of buildings where people like Jack were apt to stay.

To accept coffee for free was to demean oneself; to overpay was to publicly shame Christopher, by implying that he was the sort of man who cared about something as low and dirty as money; to merely agree on a fair price was to proclaim oneself a simpleton, and accuse Christopher of the same. Arduous haggling, however, laid bare the soul and made the participants blood-brothers. In any event the matter was settled—to the relief of the wig-maker, who stood wringing his hands as this one-legged Vagabond, fat pseudo-Turk, and rat-catcher shouted at each other directly in front of his shop, scaring away business. Meanwhile St.-George was striking a deal of his own with the wig-maker. Jack was too busy to eavesdrop, but he gathered that St.-George was using his influence to get Jack a room, or at least a corner, upstairs.

Just so: after a ceremonial cup of coffee in the street, Jack bid adieu to St.-George (who had immediate responsibilities in the cellar) and to Christopher (who had coffee to vend), stepped through the tiny door, and began to ascend stairs—past the wig-maker's shop on the ground level, and then, on the first story, his dwelling—the fine parts of it anyway, such as parlour and dining-room. Then a story for the family bedchambers. Then a story where his servants had their quarters. Then one he had rented out to a tradesman of lesser rank. As the storys mounted, the quality plunged. In the bottom levels the walls and steps alike were solid stone, but this gave way to wooden steps and plaster walls. As Jack continued to climb, the plaster developed cracks, then began to bulge and flake off the lath. At the same time, the stair-steps became creaky, and began to flex beneath his weight. In the top story there was no plaster on the walls at all, just birds' nests of straw and wattle spanning gaps among timbers. Here, in one large room interrupted by a few struts to shore up the roof, lived Christopher's family: countless Armenians sleeping and sitting on squarish bales of coffee-beans. A ladder in the corner gave access to the roof, whereupon a sort of lean-to shack, called by the grand name of *entresol*, had been improvised. A sailor-hammock hung corner-to-corner. Several bricks were shoved together to form a pad where a fire could be lit. On the tile roof downhill of the entresol, a tissue of brown streakage gave a hint as to where previous occupants had done their shitting and pissing.

Jack vaulted into the hammock and discovered that previous tenants had thoughtfully punched various peep-holes through the adjoining walls. It would be a drafty hovel in winter, but Jack liked it: he had clear views, and open escape-routes, across roof-tops in several directions. The building across the street had a garret, no farther away from Jack's entresol than one room in a house was from another, but separated from him by a crevasse sixty or seventy feet deep. This was more typical of the sort of place Jack would expect to dwell (though he could almost hear St.-George telling him that, now that he was a man of wealth, he must set his sights higher). So he could hear the conversations, and smell the food and the bodies, of the people across the way. But, lying there in his hammock, he got to watch them as if their life were a play, and he in the audience. It appeared to be the usual sort of high-altitude bolt-hole for prostitutes on the run from pimps, runaway servants, women pregnant out of wedlock, and youthful peasants who'd walked to Paris expecting to find something.

Jack tried to nap, but it was the middle of the afternoon and he could not sleep with Paris happening all around him. So he set out across the roof-tops, memorizing the turns he'd take, the leaps he'd make, the crevices he'd hide in, the places he'd stand and fight, if the Lieutenant of Police ever came for him. This led to his tromping over numerous roof-tops, setting off great commotions and panics among many garret-dwellers who lived in fear of raids. Mostly he had the roof-tops to himself. There were a few Vagabondish-looking children moving in packs, and a large number of roof-rats. On almost every block there were tattered ropes, or frail tree-branches, bridging gaps over streets, not strong enough for humans, but enthusiastically used by rats. In other places the ropes lay coiled neatly on roofs, the sticks rested in rain-gutters. Jack reckoned that they must have been put up by St.-George, who used them to channel and control the migrations of rats, as a general might tear down bridges in one part of a disputed territory while improvising new ones elsewhere.

Eventually Jack descended to street-level, and found that he'd arrived in a better part of town, near the river. He headed, without thinking about it, toward his old playground, the Pont-Neuf. The street was a wiser place for him to be—persons who clambered about on roof-tops were not well thought of—but it was dark, and confined between the stone walls of the buildings. Even the view down the street was closed off by balconies jutting out more than halfway across it from either side. The houses all had great arched portals closed off by ironbound fortress-doors. Sometimes a servant would have one open just at the moment Jack happened by. He'd slow down and look through and get a glimpse down a cool shaded passageway into a courtyard lit with sun, half filled in by landslides of flowers, watered by gurgling fountains. Then the door would be shut. Paris to Jack and most others, then, was a network of deep trenches with vertical walls, and a few drafty battlements atop those walls—otherwise, the world's largest collection of closed and locked doors.

He walked by a statue of King Looie as Roman general in stylish Classical armor with exposed navel. On one side of the pedestal, Winged Victory was handing out loaves to the poor, and on the other, an angel with a flaming sword, and a shield decorated with a trinity of fleur-de-lis, backed up by a cross-swinging, chalice-and-wafer-brandishing Holy Virgin, was assaulting and crushing diverse semi-reptilian demons who were toppling backwards onto a mess of books labelled (though Jack could not read, he knew this) with such names as M. Luther, J. Wycliffe, John Hus, John Calvin.

The sky was opening. Sensing he was near the Seine, Jack lunged forward and finally reached the Pont-Neuf. "Pont" was French for an artificial isthmus of stone, spanning a river, with arches beneath to let the water flow through—pylons standing in the flow, dividing it with their sharp blades; atop, a paved street lined with buildings like any other in Paris, so that you wouldn't know you were crossing

over a river unless a Parisian told you so. But in this one respect the Pont-Neuf was different: it had no buildings, just
hundreds of carved heads of pagan gods and goddesses, and
so you could *see* from there. Jack went and did some seeing.
Many others had the same idea. Upstream, late-afternoon
sunlight set the backs of the buildings on the Pont au Change
to glowing; a steady rain of shit flew out of the windows, and
was swallowed by the Seine. The river's crisp stone banks
were occluded by a permanent jam of small boats and
barges. Newly arriving ones attracted surging riots of men
hoping to be hired as porters. Some boats carried blocks of
stone that had been cut to shape by freemasons working out
in the open, somewhere upstream; these boats pulled up
along special quays equipped with cranes powered by pairs
of large stepped wheels in which men climbed forever without ascending, turning a gear-train that reeled in a cable that
passed over a pulley at the end of a tree-sized arm, hoisting
the blocks up out of the boats. The entire crane—wheels,
men, and all—could be rotated around and the block
dropped into a heavy cart.

Elsewhere, the same amount of labor might've made a
keg of butter or a week's worth of firewood; here it was
spent on raising a block several inches, so that it could be
carted into the city and raised by other workers, higher and
higher, so that Parisians could have rooms higher than they
were wide, and windows taller than the trees they looked out
at. Paris was a city of stone, the color of bone, beautiful and
hard—you could dash yourself against it and never leave a
mark. It was built, so far as Jack could tell, on the principle
that there was nothing you couldn't accomplish if you
crowded a few tens of millions of peasants together on the
best land in the world and then never stopped raping their
brains out for a thousand years. Off to the right, as he looked
upstream, was the Île de la Cité, crowded and looming with
important stuff: the twin, square towers of Notre Dame, and
the twin, round towers of the Conciergerie, holding out
prospects of salvation and damnation like a mountebank
telling him to pick a card, any card. The Palais de Justice

was there, too, a white stone monster decorated with eagles, ready to pounce.

A dog ran down the bridge trying to escape from a length of chain that had been tied to its tail. Jack strolled to the other side of the river, shrugging off innumerable mountebanks, beggars, and prostitutes. Turning around, he was able to look downstream and across the river toward the Louvre, where the King had lived until Versailles had gotten finished. In the garden of Tuileries, which was now falling into the long shadow of the city's western wall, trees, planted in neat rows, were being tortured and racked by the King's gardeners for any deviation from correct form.

Jack was leaning back against a stone wall that had been warmed by the sun, when he heard a faint rustling just behind his head. Turning around, he saw the impression of a small creature, crushed flat, and suspended in the rock—a common enough sight in this type of stone, and known to be a trick of Nature, as when animals were born joined at the hip, or with limbs growing out of the wrong places. The Doctor had another theory: that these had been living beings, trapped and immobilized, imprisoned forever. Now with the weight of all the stone in Paris seeming to press down on him, Jack believed it. He heard that faint rustle again, and scanning the wall carefully, finally saw movement there: between a couple of old scallop-shells and fishbones, he saw a small human figure, half trapped in the stone, and struggling to get out of it. Peering carefully at this creature, no larger than his little finger, he saw that it was Eliza.

Jack turned away and walked back across the Pont-Neuf toward his entresol in the Marais. He tried to stare only at the stone paving-blocks below his feet, but sometimes there were moving creatures trapped in them, too. So he would look up and see peddlers selling human heads—then avert his gaze into the bright sky and see an angel with a flaming sword, like a kienspan, bearing down on the city—then he'd try to concentrate instead on the carved gods' heads that adorned the Pont-Neuf, and they would come alive, and cry out to him for release from this gibbet of stone.

Jack was finally going mad, and it was a small comfort to know that he'd picked the right city for it.

Paris

WINTER OF 1684–1685

☙

THE ARMENIANS LIVING ABOVE THE wig-maker and below Jack did not appear to have any intermediate settings between killing strangers and adopting them into the family. As Jack had come recommended by St.-George, and had further established his *bona fides* by bargaining shrewdly with Christopher over coffee, they could not very well kill him— so: Jack became the thirteenth of thirteen brothers. Albeit something of an estranged, idiot half-brother, who lived in the entresol, came and went at odd times and in odd ways, and did not speak the language. But this did not trouble the matriarch, Madame Esphahnian. *Nothing* troubled her, except for suggestions that anything was troubling her, or *could theoretically* trouble her—if you suggested that anything was troubling her, she would look taken aback, and remind you that she had borne and raised twelve sons—so what, again, was the difficulty? Christopher and the others had learned simply not to bother her. Jack, likewise, quickly got into the habit of entering and leaving his shack via rooftops so that he would not have to say good-bye to Madame Esphahnian when he left, and hello when he returned. She spoke no English, of course, and just enough French to enable Jack to impregnate her mind with colorful, grotesque misunderstandings whenever he tried to say *anything*.

His stay in Paris was typical of his wanderings: the first day was a great event, but next thing he knew it was a month later, then two months. By the time he thought seriously about leaving, it was not a good time of year to travel northwards. The streets had become even more crowded, now with an influx of hairy firewood-sellers, from parts of France where being torn apart by wild beasts was still a major cause of mortality. The wood-sellers knocked people down like bowling-pins, and were a danger to everyone, especially when they were fighting with each other. The garret-dwellers across the street from Jack began selling themselves as galley-slaves, just to get warm.

The strange visions that had made Jack's first day in Paris so memorable, went away after he had gotten a night's sleep, and usually did not come back unless he got very tired, or drunk. Lying in his hammock and peering across at the garret, he had reason, every day, to thank St.-George for having put him up in a place that did not have so many outbreaks of typhus, sudden raids by the Lieutenant of Police, stillborn babies, and other annoyances: he saw young women—runaway servants—showing up one day only to be dragged out the next, and (he assumed) taken to the city gates to be cropped, whipped, and spat out into the countryside. Either that, or else some private arrangement would be made, and then Jack would be subjected to the sounds and (depending on wind) aromas of some police inspector satisfying himself carnally, in a way no longer attainable to Jack.

He put the ostrich plumes up for sale, and went about it in his favorite way: getting someone else to do it. After he'd been hanging around for a fortnight, and showed no signs of getting ready to leave, Artan (oldest of the Esphahnian brothers who was actually resident there at the time) inquired as to what Jack intended to *do*, actually, in Paris—making it clear that if the answer was "cat-burglary" or "serial rape" the Esphahnians would not think any the less of him—they just needed to *know*. To demonstrate this open-mindedness, Artan brought Jack up to date on the family saga.

It seemed that Jack, here, had blundered into the fourth or

fifth act of a drama—neither a comedy nor a tragedy, but a history—that had begun when Monsieur Esphahnian *père* had sailed the first ship of coffee, *ever,* into Marseille in 1644. It was worth a lot of money. The larger Esphahnian family, which was headquartered in Persia, had plowed a lot of their India trading profits into buying this boat-load of beans in Mocha and getting it up the Red Sea and the Nile to Alexandria and thence to France. Anyway—Pa Esphahnian sold the beans, realized a handsome profit, but *realized* it in *reals*—Spanish money—pieces of eight. Why? Because there was an extreme currency shortage in France and he couldn't have taken payment in French money if he'd wanted to—there *was* none. And why was that? Because (and here it was necessary to imagine an Armenian pounding himself on the head with both hands—*imbécile!*) the Spanish mines in Mexico were producing ludicrous amounts of silver—

"Yeah, I know about this," Jack said, but Artan could not be stopped: there were *piles* of silver lying on the ground in Porto Belo, he insisted—consequently its value, compared to that of gold, was plunging—so in Spain (where they used silver money) there was inflation, because it was not worth as much as it *had* been, whereas in France all gold coins were being hoarded, because gold was expected to be worth more in the future. So now Monsieur Esphahnian had lots of rapidly depreciating silver. He should have sailed to the Levant where silver was always in demand, but he didn't. Instead he sailed for Amsterdam expecting to make some kind of unspecified, brilliant commodities deal that would more than recoup his exchange-rate losses. But (as luck would have it) his ship ran aground, and he got his nuts caught in the mangle of the Thirty Years' War. Sweden happened to be just in the act of conquering Holland when Monsieur Esphahnian's ship eased up onto the sandbank and stopped moving; and, to make a long story short, the Esphahnian dynastic fortune was last seen northbound, strapped to the ass of a Swedish pack-horse.

This, by the way, was all first-act material—*before* the first act, really—if it were a play, it would *open* with the

young Monsieur Esphahnian, huddled in the beached wreckage of a ship, spewing expository pentameter, gazing miserably off into the audience as he pretended to watch the
Swedish column dwindle into the distance.

The upshot, anyway, was that Monsieur Esphahnian, at
that point, fell from the graces of his own family. He somehow made his way back to Marseille, collected Madame Esphahnian and her (already!) three sons, and perhaps a
daughter or two (daughters tended to be shipped east at pu-
berty), and, in time, drifted as far as Paris (end of Act I),
where, ever since, they'd all been trying to work their way
off the shit list of the rest of the family in Isfahan. Primarily
they did this by retailing coffee, but they would move just
about anything—

"Ostrich plumes?" Jack blurted, not really trusting himself to be devious and crafty around such as the Esphahnians. And so at that point the selling of those ostrich plumes,
which Jack could've accomplished in a trice a year and a
half ago in a thieves' market in Linz, became a global con-
spiracy, yoking together Esphahnians as far away as London, Alexandria, Mocha, and Isfahan, as letters were sent to
all of those places and more inquiring as to what ostrich-
plumes were selling for, whether the trend was up or down,
what distinguished a Grade A ostrich-plume from a B, how a
B could be made to look like an A, *et cetera*. While they
waited for the intelligence to come back, Jack had very little
to do on the plume front.

His addled brain forgot about Turk for a while. When he
finally went back to the livery stable, the owner was just
about to sell him off to pay for all the hay he'd been eating.
Jack paid the debt, and began to think seriously about how to
turn the war-horse into cash.

Now in the old days it was like this: he would go and loiter
around the Place Dauphine, which was the sharp downstream tip of the Île de la Cité, spang in the center of the
Pont-Neuf. It was the royal execution grounds and so there
was always something to see there. Even when there were no

executions underway, there were mountebanks, jugglers, puppeteers, fire-eaters; failing that, you could at least gawk at the dangling remains of people who'd been executed *last* week. But on days of big military parades, the aristocrats who were supposedly in command—at least, who were being paid by King Looie to be in command—of various regiments would issue from their *pieds-à-terre* and *hôtels particuliers* on the Right Bank and come across the Pont-Neuf, recruiting vagrants along the way to bring their regiments up to strength. The Place Dauphine would become a vigorous body-market for a few hours. Rusty firelocks would be passed out, money would change hands, and the new-made regiments would march south over to the Left Bank, to the cheers of the patriotic onlookers. They'd follow those aristocrats' high-stepping chargers out through the city gates, there at the carrefours where the meaner sorts of criminals dangled unconscious from the whipping-posts, and they would come into St. Germain des Pres, outside the walls: a large quadrangle of monks' residences surrounded by open land, where huge fairs of rare goods would sometimes convene. Following the Seine downstream, they'd pass by a few noble families' hotels, but in general the buildings got lower and simpler and gave way to vegetable- and flower-patches tended by upscale peasants. The river was mostly blocked from view by the piles of timber and baled goods that lined the Left Bank. But after a while, it would bend around to the south, and they would cross the green before Les Invalides—surrounded by its own wall and moat— and arrive at the Champs de Mars where King Looie would be, with all of his pomp, having ridden up from Versailles to inspect his troops—which, in those pre-Martinet days, basically meant counting them. So the *passe-volantes* (as people like Jack were called) would stand up (or if unable to stand, prop themselves up on someone who could) and be counted. The aristocrats would get paid off, and the *passe-volantes* would fan out into innumerable Left Bank taverns and bordellos and spend their money. Jack had become aware of this particular line of work during a ride from Dunkirk to Waterloo with Bob, who had spent some time campaigning under John Churchill, alongside the French, in Germany, laying waste to various regions that had the temerity to lie adjacent to *La France*. Bob had complained bitterly that many French regiments had practically zero effective strength because of this practice. To Jack it had sounded like an opportunity only a half-wit would pass up.

In any case, this procedure was the central tent-pole holding up Jack's understanding of how Paris worked. Applied to the problem of selling Turk, it told him that somewhere in the southern part of the Marais, near the river, there lived rich men who had no choice to be in the market for war-horses—or, if they had any brains in their heads at all, for stud-horses capable of siring new ones. Jack talked to the man who managed the livery stable, and he followed hay-wains coming in from the countryside, and he tailed aristo-crats riding back from the military parades at the Champs de Mars, and learned that there was a horse-market *par excellence* at the Place Royale.

Now this was one of those places that Jack's kind of per-son knew only as a void in the middle of the city, sealed off by gates through which an attentive loiterer could some-times get a flash of sunlit green. By trying to penetrate it from all sides, Jack learnt that it was square, with great barn-doors at the four cardinal compass-points, and high grand buildings rising above each of these gates. Around its fringes were a number of *hôtels*, which in Paris meant pri-vate compounds of rich nobles. Twice a week, the gates were jammed solid with carts bringing hay and oats in, and ma-nure out, and an astounding number of fine horses being burnished by grooms. Some horse-trading went on in sur-rounding streets, but Jack could plainly see that this was lit-tle more than a flea-market compared to whatever was going on in the Place Royale.

He bribed a farmer to smuggle him into the place in a hay-wain. When it was safe to get out, the farmer poked him in the ribs with the handle of a pitchfork, and Jack wriggled and slid out onto the ground—the first time he had stood on growing grass since he'd reached Paris.

The Place Royale was found to be a park shaded by chestnut trees (in theory, that is; when Jack saw it the leaves had fallen, and been raked off). In the center was a statue of King Looie's dear old pop, Looie the Thirteenth—on horseback, naturally. The whole square was surrounded by vaulted colonnades, like the trading-courts at Leipzig and the Stock Exchange at Amsterdam, but these were very wide and high, with barn-doors giving way to private courtyards beyond. All of the gates, and all of the arcades, were large enough, not merely for a single rider, but for a coach drawn by four or six horses. It was, then, like a city within the city, built entirely for people so rich and important that they *lived* on horseback, or in private coaches.

Only that could explain the size of the horse-market that was raging all around him when Jack climbed out of the haywain. It was as crowded with horses as the streets of Paris were with people—the only exceptions being a few ropedoff areas where the merchandise could prance around and be judged and graded by the buyers. Every horse that Jack saw, he would've remembered as the finest horse he'd ever seen, if he'd encountered it on a road in England or Germany. Here, not only were such horses common, but they were meticulously groomed and brushed almost to the point of being polished, their manes and tails coiffed, and they'd been taught to do tricks. There were horses meant to be saddled, horses in matched sets of two and four and even six, for drawing coaches, and—in one corner—chargers: warhorses for parading beneath the eyes of the King on the Champ de Mars. Jack went thataway and had a look. He did not see a single mount there that he would've traded Turk for, if he were about to ride into battle. But these were in excellent condition and well shod and groomed compared to Turk, who had been languishing in a livery stable for weeks, with only the occasional walk round the stable-yard for exercise.

Jack knew how to fix that. But before he left the Place Royale, he raised his sights for a few minutes, and spent a while looking at the buildings that rose over the park—trying to learn something about his customers-to-be.

Unlike most of Paris, these were brick, which warmed Jack's heart strangely, reminding him of Merry England. The four great buildings rising over the gates at the cardinal points of the compass had enormous steep rooves, two and three stories high, with balconies and lace-curtained dormers, currently all shut up against the cold—but Jack could well imagine how a wealthy horse-fancier would have his Paris pied-à-terre here, so that he could keep an eye on the market by gazing out his windows.

In one of the great squares hereabouts—Jack had lost track of all of them—he'd seen a statue of King Looie riding off to war, with blank spaces on the pedestal to chisel the names of victories he hadn't won yet, and of countries he hadn't captured. Some buildings, likewise, had empty niches: waiting (as everyone in Paris must understand) to receive the statues of the generals who would win those victories for him. Jack needed to find a man whose ambition was to stand forever in one of those niches, and he needed to convince him that he was more likely to win battles with Turk, or Turk's offspring, between his legs. But first he needed to get Turk in some kind of decent physical condition, and that meant riding him.

He was on his way out of the Place Royale, walking under the gate on its south side, when behind him a commotion broke out. The hiss of iron wheel-rims grinding over pavingstones, the crisp footfalls of horses moving in unnatural unison, the shouts of footmen and of bystanders, warning all to make way. Jack was still getting about with the crutch (he daren't let the sword out of his sight, and couldn't bear it openly). So when he didn't move fast enough, a burly servant in powder-blue livery crushed him out of the way and sent him tumbling across the pavement so that his "good" leg plunged knee-deep in a gutter filled with stagnating shit.

Jack looked up and saw the Four Horses of the Apocalypse bearing down on him—or so he imagined for a moment, because it seemed that they all had glowing red eyes. But as they went past, this vision cleared from his mind, and he decided that their eyes, actually, had been pink. Four horses, all white as clouds, save for pink eyes and mottled hooves, harnessed in white leather, pulling a rare coach, sculpted and painted to look like a white sea-shell riding a frothy wave over the blue ocean, all encrusted with garlands and laurels, cherubs and mermaids, in gold.

Those horses put him in mind of Eliza's story; for she had been swapped for one such, back in Algiers.

Jack proceeded crosstown to Les Halles where the fish-wives—pretending to be dismayed by the shit on his leg—flung fish-heads at him while shouting some sort of pun on *par fume*.

Jack inquired whether it ever happened that some rich man's servant would come around specifically to purchase *rotten* fish for his master.

It was clear, from the looks on their faces, that he had struck deep with this question—but then, looking him up and down, one of them made a certain guttural jeering noise, and then the fishwives all sneered and told him to hobble back to *Les Invalides* with his ridiculous questions. "I am not a veteran—what idiot goes out and fights battles for rich men?" Jack answered.

They liked that, but were in a cautious mood. "What are you then?" *"Passe-volante!"* "Vagabond!"

Jack decided to try what the Doctor would call an experiment: "Not *any* Vagabond," Jack said, "here stands Half-Cocked Jack."

"L'Emmerdeur!" gasped a younger, and not quite so gorgon-like, fishwife, almost before he'd gotten it out of his mouth.

There was a moment of radical silence. But then the guttural noise again. "You are the fourth Vagabond to make that claim in the last month—"

"And the least convincing—"

"L'Emmerdeur is a King among Vagabonds. Seven feet tall."

"Goes armed all the time, like a Gentleman."

"Carries a jeweled scimitar he tore from the hands of the Grand Turk himself—"

"Has magic spells to burn witches and confound Bishops."

"He's not a broken-down cripple with one leg withered and the other dipped in *merde*!"

Jack kicked off his fouled pants, and then his drawers, revealing his Credential. Then, to prove he wasn't really a cripple, he flung the crutch down, and began to dance a bare-assed jig. The fishwives could not decide between swooning and rioting. When they recovered their self-possession, they began to fling handfuls of blackened copper *deniers* at him. This attracted beggars and street-musicians, and one of the latter began to play accompanying music on a *cornemuse* whilst shuffling around racking the worthless coins into a little pile with his feet, and kicking the beggars in the head as necessary.

Having now verified his identity by personal inspection, each of the fishwives had to prance out, shedding glitt'ry showers of fish-scales from their flouncing, gut-stained skirts, and dance with Jack—who had no patience for this, but did take advantage of it to whisper into any ear that came close enough, that if he ever had any money, he'd give some of it to whomever could tell him the name of the noble personage who liked to eat rotten fish. But before he could say it more than two or three times, he had to grab his drawers and run away, because a commotion at the other end of Les Halles told him that the Lieutenant of Police was on his way to make a show of force, and to extract whatever bribes, sexual favors, and/or free oysters he could get from the fishwives in exchange for turning a blind eye to this unforgivable brouhaha.

From there Jack proceeded to the livery stable, got Turk, and also rented two other horses. He rode to the House of the Golden Frigate on Rue Vivienne, and let it be known that he was on his way down to Lyons—any messages?

· This made Signor Cozzi very pleased. His place was crowded today with tense Italians scribbling down messages and bills of exchange, and porters hauling what looked like money-boxes down from the attic and up from the cellar, and there was a sparse crowd of street-messengers and competing bankers in the street outside, exchanging speculations as to what was going on in there—what did Cozzi know that no one else did? Or was it just a bluff?

Signor Cozzi scrawled something on a scrap of paper and did not bother to seal it. He came up and lunged for Jack's hand, because Jack was not reaching out fast enough, and shoved the message into his palm, saying, "To Lyons! I don't care how many horses you kill getting there. What are you waiting for?"

Actually Jack was waiting to say he didn't particularly *want* to kill his horse, but Signor Cozzi was not in a mood for sentiment. So Jack whirled, ran out of the building, and mounted Turk. "Watch your back!" someone called after him, "word on the street is that *L'Emmerdeur* is in town!"

"I heard he was *on his way,*" Jack said, "at the head of a Vagabond-Army."

It would have been amusing to stay around and continue this, but Cozzi was standing in the doorway glaring at him, and so, riding Turk and leading the rented horses behind him, Jack galloped down Rue Vivienne in what he hoped was dramatic style, and hung the first available left. This ended up taking him right back through Les Halles—so he made a point of galloping through the fish-market, where the police were turning things upside-down searching for a one-legged, short-penised pedestrian. Jack winked at that one young fishwife who'd caught his eye, touching off a thrill that spread like fire through gunpowder, and then he was gone, off into the Marais—right past the Place Royale. He maneuvered round the trundling manure-carts all the way to the Bastille: just one great sweaty rock pocked with a few tiny windows, with grenadiers roaming around on top—the highest and thickest in a city of walls. It sat in a moat fed by a short canal leading up from the Seine. The bridge over the canal was crowded, so Jack rode down to the river and then turned to follow the right bank out of town, and thereby left

Paris behind him. He was afraid that Turk would be exhausted already. But when the war-horse saw open fields ahead, he surged forward, yanking on the lead and eliciting angry whinnies from the spare horses following behind.

To Lyons was a long journey, almost all the way to Italy (which was, he reckoned, why the Italian banks were situated there), or, if you wanted to look at it that way, almost all the way to Marseille. The countryside was divided up into innumerable separate *pays* with their own tolls, which were commonly exacted at inns controlling the important crossroads. Jack, changing horses from time to time, seemed to be racing the whole way against a slippery narrow black coach that scuttled down the road like a scorpion, drawn by four horses. It was a good race, meaning that the lead changed hands many times. But in the end, those inns, and the need to change horse-teams frequently, were too much of an impediment for the coach, and Jack was the first to ride down into Lyons with the news—whatever it was.

Another Genoese banker in vivid clothing received Signor Cozzi's note. Jack had to track him down in a marketplace unlike any in Paris, where things like charcoal, bales of old clothing, and rolls of undyed fabric were for sale in large quantities. The banker paid Jack out of his pocket, and read the note.

"You are English?"

"Aye, what of it?"

"Your King is dead." With that the banker went briskly to his office, whence other messengers galloped away within the hour, headed for Genoa and Marseilles. Jack stabled his horses and wandered round Lyons amazed, munching some dried figs he bought at a retail market. The only King he'd ever known was dead, and England was, somehow, a different country now—ruled by a Papist!

✧

The Hague
FEBRUARY 1685

❦

WEE DRIFTS OF wind-skimming snow had already parenthe-
sized the cherry-red platform soles of the French delegation's boots, and inch-long snotcicles had grown from the
moustaches of the English delegation. Eliza glided up on her
skates, and swirled to a halt on the canal to admire what she
took (at first) to be some sort of colossal sculpture group. Of
course sculptures did not normally wear clothing, but these
Ambassadors and their entourages (a total of eight Englishmen facing off against seven French) had been standing
long enough that snow had permeated every pore of their
hats, wigs, and coats, giving them the appearance (from a
distance) of having been butcherously carved out of a large
block of some very low-grade, grayish sculptural medium.
Much more lively (and more warmly dressed) was the crowd
of Dutchmen who had gathered round to watch, and to stake
small wagers on which delegation would first succumb to the
cold. A rabble of porters and wood-carriers seemed to have
taken the English side, and better-dressed men had gathered
round the French, and strode to and fro stamping their feet
and blowing into their hands and dispatching swift-skating
message-boys towards the States-General and the Binnenhof.

But Eliza was the only girl on skates. So as she came to a
stop there on the canal's edge, only a few yards away from,
and a foot or two lower than, the two groups of men on the
adjoining street, the entire sculpture came to life. Rimes of

ice cracked and tinkled as fifteen French and English heads rotated towards her. 'Twas now a standoff of a *different* nature.

The best-dressed man in the French delegation shuddered. They were *all* shivering, but this gentleman *shuddered.* "Mademoiselle," he said, "do you speak French?"

Eliza regarded him. His hat was the size of a washtub, filled with exotic plumes, now crushed under drifts. His boots had the enormous tongues just coming into fashion, erupting from his instep and spreading and curling up and away from the shin—these had filled with snow, which was melting and trickling down inside the boots and darkening the leather from the inside.

"Only when there is some *reason* to, monsieur," she returned.

"What is a reason?"

"How French of you to ask . . . I suppose that when a gentleman, who has been correctly introduced to me, flatters me with a compliment, or amuses me with a witticism . . ."

"I humbly beg Mademoiselle's forgiveness," the Frenchman said, through gray and stiff lips that ruined his pronunciation. "But as you did not arrive with an escort, there was no one to beg for the favor of a decent introduction."

"He is yonder," said Eliza, gesturing half a league down the canal.

"*Mon Dieu*, he flails his limbs like a lost soul tumbling backwards into the Pit," the Frenchman exclaimed. "Tell me, mademoiselle, why does a *swan* venture out on the canals with an *orang-utan*?"

"He claimed he knew how to skate."

"But a lass of your *beauty*, must have heard many brave claims from young men's lips—and one of your *intelligence* must have perceived that all of them were rank nonsense."

"Whereas you, monsieur, are honest and pure of heart?"

"Alas, mademoiselle, I am merely old."

"Not so old."

"And yet I may have perished from *age* or *pneumonia* before your beau struggles close enough to make introductions, so . . . Jean Antoine de Mesmes, comte d'Avaux, your most humble servant."

"Charmed. My name is Eliza . . ."

"Duchess of Qwghlm?"

Eliza laughed at this absurdity. "But how did you know I was Qwghlmian?"

"Your native tongue is English—but you skate like one who was born on ice, *sans* the staggering drunken gait of the Anglo-Saxons who so cruelly oppress your islands," d'Avaux answered, raising his voice so that the English delegation could hear.

"Very clever—but you know perfectly well that I am no Duchess."

"And yet blue blood flows in your veins, I cannot but believe . . ."

"Not half so blue as *yours,* Monsieur, as I cannot but *see.* Why don't you go inside and sit by a warm fire?"

"Now you tempt me cruelly in a *second* way," d'Avaux said. "I must stand here, to uphold the honor and glory of *La France.* But you are bound by no such obligations—why do you go out here, where only harp-seals and polar-bears should be—and in such a skirt?"

"The skirt *must* be short, lest it get caught in the blades of my skates—you see?" Eliza said, and did a little pirouette. Before she'd gotten entirely turned around, a groaning and cracking noise came from the center of the French delegation as a spindly middle-aged diplomat collapsed dizzily to the ground. The men to either side of him crouched down as if to render assistance, but were straightened up by a brisk idiom from d'Avaux. "Once we begin to make exceptions for those who fall—or who *pretend* to—the whole delegation will go down like ninepins," d'Avaux explained, addressing the remark to Eliza, but *intending* it for his entourage. The fallen man contracted to a fœtal position on the pavement; a couple of sword-wearing Dutchmen scurried in with a blanket. Meanwhile a wench came down out of a side-street bearing a large tray, and walked past the French delegation, letting them smell the flip-aroma, and feel the steam, from eight tankards—which she took direct to the Englishmen.

"Exceptions to *what*?" Eliza asked.

"To the rules of diplomatic protocol," d'Avaux answered. "Which state—for example—that when one Ambassador meets another in a narrow way, the junior Ambassador must give way for the senior."

"Ah, so that's it. You're having a dispute as to whether you, or the English Ambassador, has seniority?"

"I represent the Most Christian King,* *that* lot represent King James II of England . . . or so we can only assume, as we have received word that King Charles II has died, but not that his brother has been properly crowned."

"Then it's clear *you* have seniority."

"Clear to you and me, mademoiselle. But *that* fellow has asserted that, since he cannot represent an uncrowned king, he must still be representing the late Charles II, who was crowned in 1651 after the Puritans chopped off the head of his father and predecessor. My King was crowned in 1654."

"But with all due respect to the Most Christian King, monsieur, doesn't that mean that Charles II, if he still lived, would have three years' seniority over him?"

"A rabble of Scots at Scone tossed a crown at Charles's head," d'Avaux said, "and then he came and lived *here*, begging for handouts from Dutchmen, until 1660 when the cheese-mongers *paid* him to leave. *Practically* speaking, his reign began when he sailed to Dover."

"If we are going to be *practical,* sir," shouted an Englishman, "let us consider that *your* King did not *practically* begin his reign until the death of Cardinal Mazarin on the ninth of March, 1661." He raised a tankard to his lips and

---

*Louis XIV of France.

quaffed deeply, pausing between gulps to emit little moans of satisfaction.

"At least *my* King is alive," d'Avaux muttered. "You see? And they love to accuse *Jesuits* of sophistry! I say, is your beau wanted by the Guild of St. George?"

Civic order in the Hague was maintained by two Guilds of civic guards. The part of the city around the market and the town hall, where normal Dutchmen lived, was looked after by the St. Sebastian Guild. The St. George Guild was responsible for the Hofgebied, which was the part of the city containing the royal palace, foreign embassies, houses of rich families, and so on. Both Guilds were represented among the crowd of spectators who had gathered round to partake of the spectacle of d'Avaux and his English counterparts freezing to death. So d'Avaux's question was partly intended to flatter and amuse the genteel and aristocratic St. George men—perhaps at the expense of the more plebeian St. Sebastian guards, who seemed to be favoring the English delegation.

"Don't be absurd, monsieur! If he *were,* those brave and diligent men would have apprehended him long ago. Why do you ask such a question?"

"He has covered up his face like some sort of a *volunteer.*" Which meant, a soldier-turned-highwayman.

Eliza turned round to see Gomer Bolstrood lurking (there was no other word for it) around a corner of the canal a stone's throw away with a long strip of tartan wrapped over his face.

"Those who live in northerly climes often do this."

"It seems extremely disreputable and in the poorest taste. If your beau cannot tolerate a bit of a sea-breeze—"

"He is not my beau—merely a business associate."

"Then, mademoiselle, you will be free to meet with me here, at this hour, tomorrow, and give me a skating-lesson."

"But, monsieur! From the way you shuddered when you beheld me, I thought you considered such sports beneath your dignity."

"Indeed—but I am an Ambassador, and must submit to any number of degradations . . ."

"For the honor and glory of *la France*?"

"Pourquoi non?"

"I hope that they widen the street soon, comte d'Avaux."

"Spring is just around the corner—and when I gaze upon your face, mademoiselle, I feel it is already here."

"'Twas perfectly innocent, Mr. Bolstrood—I thought they were sculpture until eyes turned my way."

They were seated before a fire in a stately hunting-lodge. The place was warm enough, but smoky, and bleak, and entirely too filled with heads of dead animals, who seemed *also* to be turning their eyes Eliza's way.

"You imagine I'm angry, but I'm not."

"What's troubling you, then? I daresay you are the brooding-est fellow I have ever seen."

"These chairs."

"Did I hear you correctly, sir?"

"Look at them," Gomer Bolstrood said, in a voice hollow with despair. "Those who built this estate had no shortage of money, of that you can be sure—but the furniture! It is either stupid and primitive, like this ogre's throne I'm seated on, or else—like yours—raked together out of kindling, with about as much structural integrity as a *faggot*. I could make better chairs in an *afternoon, drunk,* given a *shrub* and a *jackknife*."

"Then I must apologize for having misread you, as I supposed you were angry about that chance encounter, there—"

"My faith teaches me it was inevitable—predestined— that you would enter into a flirtation with the French Ambassador just now. If I'm brooding over *that*, it's not because I'm angry, but because I must understand what it means."

"It means he's a horny old goat."

Gomer Bolstrood shook his colossal head hopelessly, and gazed toward a window. The pane shouted as it was hit by a burst of wind-driven slush. "I pray it did not develop into a riot," he said.

"How much of a riot can eight frozen Englishmen and seven half-dead Frenchmen accomplish?"

"It's the Dutchmen I'm worried about. The commoners and country folk, as always, side with the Stadholder.* The merchants are all Frenchified—and because the States-General are meeting here at the moment, the town's crowded with the latter—all of 'em wearing swords and carrying pistols."

"Speaking of Frenchified merchants," Eliza said, "I have some good news for the Client—whoever he is—from the commodities market. It seems that during the run-up to the 1672 war, an Amsterdam banker committed treason against the Republic—"

"Actually any number of 'em did—but pray continue."

"Acting as a cat's-paw for the Marquis de Louvois, this traitor—Mr. Sluys by name—bought up nearly all of the lead in the country to ensure that William's army would be short of ammunition. No doubt Sluys thought the war would be over in a few days, and that King Louis, after planting the French flag on the Damrak, would reward him personally. But of course that is not how it happened. Ever since, Sluys has had a warehouse full of lead, which he's been afraid to sell openly, lest word get out, and an Orangist mob burn his warehouses, and tear him apart, as they did so memorably to the de Witt brothers. But now Sluys *has* to sell it."

"Why?"

"It's been thirteen years. His warehouse has been sinking into the Amsterdam-mud twice as fast as the ones to either side of it, because of the weight of all that lead. The neighbors are beginning to complain. He is taking the whole neighborhood down!"

"So Mr. Sluys should offer an excellent price," Gomer Bolstrood said. "Praise God! The Client will be most pleased. Did this same traitor buy up gunpowder? Matches?"

---

*William of Orange.

"All ruined by humidity. But a fleet of Indiamen are expected at Texel any day—they'll be heavy laden with saltpeter, most likely—powder prices are already dropping."

"Probably not dropping *enough* for our purposes," Bolstrood muttered. "Can we buy up saltpeter, and make our own?"

"Sulfur prices are also agreeable, owing to some fortuitous volcanic eruptions in Java," Eliza said, "but proper charcoal is very dear—the Duke of Braunschweig-Lüneburg controls his Faulbaum inventory like a miser counting his coins."

"We may have to capture an arsenal very early in the campaign," Bolstrood said, "God willing."

Talk of campaigns and arsenal-captures made Eliza nervous, so she attempted a change of subject: "When may I have the pleasure of meeting the Client?"

"As soon as we can find him clothed and sober," Bolstrood answered immediately.

"That should be easy, in a Barker."

"The Client is nothing of the sort!" Gomer Bolstrood scoffed.

"How very strange."

"What is strange about it?"

"How came he to oppose Slavery if not through religion?"

"You oppose it, and you're no Calvinist," Bolstrood parried.

"I have personal reasons for feeling as I do. But I phant'sied that the Client was one of your co-religionists. He *does* oppose slavery, does he not?"

"Let us set aside phant'sies, and speak of facts."

"Can't help noticing, sir, that my question is unanswered."

"You appeared at the door of our church in Amsterdam—some felt, like an Angelic visitation—with a most generous donation, and offered to make yourself useful in any way that would further our work 'gainst Slavery. And that is just what you are doing."

"But if the Client is *not* opposed to slavery, how does it further the cause to buy him powder and musket-balls?"

"You may not know that my father—God rest his soul—

served as the late King's Secretary of State before he was
hounded to exile and death by the Papists who do France's
work in England. He submitted to that degradation because
he knew that upright men must sometimes treat with the
likes of King Charles II for the greater good. In the same
way, we who oppose slavery, and Established religion, and
in particular all of the abominations and fopperies of the
Romish faith, must give our support to any man who might
prevent James, Duke of York, from long remaining on the
throne."

"James *is* the rightful heir, is he not?"

"As those diplomats just proved, cavilling over the seniority of their Kings," Bolstrood said, "there is no question
that cannot be muddled—and powder-smoke muddles
things 'specially well. King Louis stamps *Ultima Ratio
Regum* on all of his cannon—"

"The last argument of kings."

"You know Latin, too—?"

"I had a Classical education."

"In Qwghlm!?"

"In Constantinople."

THE COMTE D'AVAUX MOVED THROUGH the Hague's canal-
network in the gait of a man walking across red-hot coals,
but some innate aplomb kept him from falling down even
once.

"Would you like to go home now, monsieur?"

"Oh no, mademoiselle—I am enjoying myself," he returned, biting off the syllables one by one, like a crocodile
working its way up an oar.

"You dressed more warmly today—is that Russian sable?"

"Yes, but of an inferior grade—a much finer one awaits
you—if you get me back alive."

"That is quite unnecessary, monsieur—"

"The entire point of gifts is to be unnecessary." D'Avaux
reached into a pocket and pulled out a square of neatly
folded black velvet. *"Voilà,"* he said, handing it over to her.

"What is it?" Eliza asked, taking it from his hand, and using the opportunity to grab his upper arm for a moment and steady him.

"A little nothing. I should like you to wear it."

The velvet unfolded into a long ribbon about the width of Eliza's hand, its two ends joined together with a rather nice gold brooch made in the shape of a butterfly. Eliza guessed it was meant to be a sash, and put one arm and her head through it, letting it hang diagonally across her body. "Thank you, monsieur," she said, "how does it look?"

The comte d'Avaux, for once, failed to offer her a compliment. He merely shrugged, as if how it looked was not the point. Which confirmed Eliza's suspicion that a black velvet sash over skating-clothes was rather odd-looking.

"How did you escape your predicament yesterday?" she asked him.

"Made arrangements for the Stadholder to summon the English Ambassador back to the Binnenhof. This compelled him to make a *volte-face:* a maneuver in which the diplomats of perfidious Albion are well practiced. We followed him down the street and made the first available turn. How did you escape *yours?*"

"What—you mean, being out for a skate with a lug?"

"Naturally."

"Tormented him for another half an hour—then returned to his place in the country to transact business. You think I'm a whore, don't you, monsieur? I saw it in your face when I mentioned *business.* Though you would probably say *courtesan.*"

"Mademoiselle, in my circles, anyone who transacts business of any sort, on any level, is a whore. Among French nobility, no distinctions are recognized between the finest commerçants of Amsterdam and common prostitutes."

"Is that why Louis hates the Dutch so?"

"Oh no, mademoiselle, unlike these dour Calvinists, we *love* whores—Versailles is aswarm with them. No, we have any number of *intelligent* reasons to hate the Dutch."

"What *sort* of whore do you suppose I am, then, monsieur?"

"That is what I am trying to establish."

Eliza laughed. "Then you should be eager to turn back."

"Non!" The comte d'Avaux made a doddering, flailing turn onto another canal. Something bulky and grim shouldered its way into a gap ahead of them. Eliza mistook it, at first, for an especially gloomy old brick church. But then she noticed up on the parapet light shining like barred teeth through crenellations, and many narrow embrasures, and realized it had been made for another purpose besides saving souls. The building had tall poky conical spires at the corners, and Gothic decorations along the fronts of the gables that thrust out into the cold air like clenched stone fists. "The Ridderzaal," she said, getting her bearings; for she had gotten quite lost following d'Avaux along the labyrinth of canals that were laced through the Hofgebied like capillaries through flesh. "So we are on the Spij now, going north." A short distance ahead of them, the Spij forked in twain, bracketing the Ridderzaal and other ancient buildings of the Counts of Holland between its branches.

D'Avaux careered into the right fork. "Let us go through yonder water-gate, into the Hofvijver!" Meaning a rectangular pond that lay before the Binnenhof, or palace of the Dutch court. "The view of the Binnenhof rising above the ice will be—er—"

"Magical?"

"Non."

"Magnificent?"

"Don't be absurd."

"Less bleak than anything else we have seen?"

"Now truly you are speaking French," the ambassador said approvingly. "The princeling* is off on another of his insufferable hunting expeditions, but *some* persons of quality are there." He had put on a surprising—almost alarming—burst of speed and was several paces ahead of Eliza

---

*William of Orange.

now. "They will open the gate for me," he said confidently, tossing the words back over his shoulder like a scarf. "When they do, you put on one of those magnificent *accélérations* and sail past me into the Hofvijver."

"Very devious . . . but why don't you simply ask them to let me through?"

"This will make for a gayer spectacle."

The gate was so close to the Binnenhof that they would nearly pass underneath the palace as they went through. It was guarded by musketeers and archers dressed in blue outfits with lace cravats and orange sashes. When they recognized Jean Antoine de Mesmes, comte d'Avaux, they ventured out onto the ice, skidding on their hard-soled boots, pulled one side of the gate open for him, and bowed—doffing their hats and sweeping the ice with the tips of their orange plumes. The gate was wide enough to admit pleasure-boats during the warmer months, and so Eliza had plenty of room to whoosh past the French Ambassador and into the rectangle of ice that was spread out before William of Orange's palace. It was a maneuver that would have earned her a broad-headed arrow between the shoulder blades if she were a man. But she was a girl in a short skirt and so the guards took her entrance in the spirit intended— as an amusing courtly *plaisanterie* of the comte's devising.

She was going very fast—faster than she needed to, for this had given her an excuse to stretch cold stiff leg-muscles. She'd entered the southeast corner of the Hofvijver, which extended perhaps a hundred yards north–south and thrice that east–west. Slicing up along its eastern bank, she was distracted by musket-fire from open ground off to her right, and had a wild moment of fear that she was about to be cut down by snipers. But not to worry, it was a party of gentlemen honing their markmanship on a target-range spread out between the bank of the pond and an ornate building set farther back. She recognized this, now, as the headquarters of the St. George Guild. Beyond it, wooded land stretched away to the east as far as she could see: the Haagsche Bos, a game-park for the Counts of Holland, where people of all classes went to ride and stroll when the weather was better.

Directly ahead of her was a cobblestone ramp: a street that plunged directly into the water of the pond, when it wasn't frozen, and where horses and cattle could be taken down and watered. She had to lean hard and make a searing turn to avoid it. Swaying her hips from side to side, she picked up a bit of speed as she glided down the long northern shore of the Hofvijver. The south shore, spreading off to her left, was a hodgepodge of brown brick buildings with black slate rooves, many having windows just above the level of the pond, so that she could have skated right up and conversed with people on the inside. But she wouldn't have dared, for this was the Binnenhof, the palace of the Stadholder, William of Orange. Her view of it was obscured, for a time, by a tiny round island planted in the center of the Hofvijver like a half-cherry on a slice of cake. Trees and shrubs grew on it, and moss grew on them, though all was brown and leafless now. But above and behind the Binnenhof she could see the many narrow towers of the Ridderzaal jabbing at the sky like a squadron of knights with lances upright.

That was the end of sightseeing. For as she shot clear of the little island, and curled round to swing back towards d'Avaux, she discovered that she was sharing the ice with a slow-moving clique of skaters. She glimpsed both men and women, finely dressed. To knock them down would have been bad form. To stop and introduce herself would have been infinitely worse. She spun round to face towards d'Avaux, skating backwards now, letting her momentum carry her past the group. She carved a long sweeping U round the west end of the Hofvijver, spun round to face forward again, built more speed without lifting her skates from the ice, by means of sashaying hip-movements that took her down the long front of the Binnenhof, in a serpentine path, and finally stopped just before running into d'Avaux by planting the blades sideways and shaving up a glittering wall of ice. Nothing very acrobatic really—but it was enough to draw applause from Blue Guards, St. George Guildsmen, and noble skaters alike.

"I learnt defencing at the Academy of Monsieur du Plessis in Paris, where the finest swordsmen of the world gather to flaunt their prowess—but none of them can match *your* grace with a pair of steel blades, mademoiselle," said the prettiest man Eliza had ever seen, as he was raising her gloved hand to smooch it.

D'Avaux had been making introductions. The gorgeous man was the Duke of Monmouth. He was escorting a tall, lanky, yet jowly woman in her early twenties. This was Mary—the daughter of the new King of England, and William of Orange's wife.

As d'Avaux had announced these names and titles, Eliza had come close to losing her nerve for the first time in memory. She was remembering Hanover, where the Doctor had planted her in a steeple near the Herrenhausen Palace, so that she could gaze upon Sophie through a field-glass. Yet this d'Avaux—who didn't know Eliza nearly as well as the Doctor did—had taken her straight into the Dutch court's inner sanctum. How could d'Avaux introduce her to persons of royal degree—when he didn't have the first idea who she was in the first place?

In the end it couldn't have been simpler. He had leaned in towards Monmouth and Mary and said, discreetly: "This is—*Eliza*." This had elicited knowing nods and winks from the others, and a little buzz of excitement from Mary's entourage of English servants and hangers-on. These were apparently not even worth introducing—and that went double for the Negro page-boy and the shivering Javanese dwarf.

"No compliments for *me*, your Grace?" d'Avaux asked, as Monmouth was planting multiple kisses on the back of Eliza's glove.

"On the contrary, monsieur—you are the finest skater of all France," Monmouth returned with a smile. He still had most of his teeth. He had forgotten to let go of Eliza's hand.

Mary nearly fell off her skates, partly because she was laughing at Monmouth's jest a little harder than was really warranted, and partly because she was a miserable skater (in the corner of Eliza's eye, earlier, she'd looked like a wind-mill—flailing without moving). It had been obvious from the first moment Eliza had seen her that she was infatuated with the Duke of Monmouth. Which to some degree was embarrassing. But Eliza had to admit that she'd chosen a likely young man to fall in love with.

Mary of Orange started to say something, but d'Avaux ran her off the road. "Mademoiselle Eliza has been trying valiantly to teach me how to skate," he said commandingly, giving Eliza a wet look. "But I am like a peasant listening to one of the lectures of Monsieur Huygens." He glanced over toward the water-gate through which he and Eliza had just passed, for the house of the Huygens family lay very nearby that corner of the palace.

"I should've fallen ever so many times without the Duke to hold me up," Mary put in.

"Would an Ambassador do as well?" d'Avaux said, and before Mary could answer, he sidled up to her and nearly knocked her over. She flailed for the Ambassador's arm and just got a grip on it in time. Her entourage closed in to get her back on her blades, the Javanese dwarf getting one hand on each buttock and pushing up with all his might.

The Duke of Monmouth saw none of this drama, engaged as he was in a minute inspection of Eliza. He began with her hair, worked his way down to her ankles, then back up, until he was startled to discover a pair of blue eyes staring back at him. *That* led to a spell of disorientation just long enough for d'Avaux (who had pinned Mary's hand between his elbow and ribcage) to say, "By all means, your Grace, go for a skate, stretch your legs—we novices will just totter around the Vijver for a few minutes."

"Mademoiselle?" said the Duke, proffering a hand.

"Your grace," said Eliza, taking it.

Ten heartbeats later they were out on the Spij. Eliza let go Monmouth's hand and spun round backwards to see the water-gate being closed behind them, and, through the bars, Mary of Orange, looking as if she'd been punched in the stomach, and Jean Antoine de Mesmes, comte d'Avaux, looking as if he did this kind of thing several times a day. Once, in Constantinople, Eliza had helped hold one of the other slave-girls down while an Arab surgeon took out her appendix. It had taken all of two minutes. She'd been astonished that a man with a sharp knife and no hesitation about using it could effect such changes so rapidly. Thus d'Avaux and Mary's heart.

Once they got clear of the Spij the canal broadened and Monmouth executed a dramatic spin—lots of flesh and bone moving fast—not really graceful, but she couldn't not look. If anything, he was a more accomplished skater than Eliza. He saw Eliza *watching,* and assumed she was *admiring,* him. "During the Interregnum I divided my time between here and Paris," he explained, "and spent many hours on these canals—where did you learn, mademoiselle?"

Struggling across heaving floes to chip gull shit off rocks struck Eliza as a tasteless way to answer the question. She might have come up with some clever story, given enough time—but her mind was too busy trying to fathom what was going on.

"Ah, forgive me for prying—I forget that you are *incognito,*" said the Duke of Monmouth, his eyes straying momentarily to the black sash that d'Avaux had given her. "That, and your coy silence, speak volumes."

"Really? What's in those volumes?"

"The tale of a lovely innocent cruelly misused by some Germanic or Scandinavian noble—was it at the court of Poland-Lithuania? Or was it that infamous woman-beater, Prince Adolph of Sweden? Say nothing, mademoiselle, except that you forgive me my curiosity."

"Done. Now, are you that same Duke of Monmouth who distinguished himself at the Siege of Maestricht? I know a man who fought in that battle—or who was *there,* anyway—and who spoke at length of your doings."

"Is it the Marquis de—? Or the comte d'—?"

"You forget yourself, Monsieur," said Eliza, stroking the velvet sash.

"Once again—please accept my apology," said the Duke, looking wickedly amused.

"You *might* be able to redeem yourself by explaining something to me: the Siege of Maestricht was part of a campaign to wipe the Dutch Republic off the map. William sacrificed half his country to win that war. You fought against him. And yet here you are enjoying the hospitality of that same William, in the innermost court of Holland, only a few years later."

"That's nothing," Monmouth said agreeably, "for only a few years after Maestricht I was fighting by William's side, *against* the French, at Mons, *and* William was *married* to that Mary—who as you must know is the daughter of King James II, formerly the Duke of York, and Admiral of the English Navy until William's admirals blew it out of the water. I could go on in this vein for hours."

"If I had such an enemy I would not rest until he was dead," Eliza said. "As a matter of fact, I *do* have an enemy, and it has been a long time since I have rested . . ."

"Who is it?" Monmouth asked eagerly, "the one who taught you to skate and then—"

"It is *another*," Eliza said, "but I know not his name—our encounter was in a dark cabin on a ship—"

"What ship?"

"I know not."

"What flag did it fly?"

"A black one."

"Stab me!"

"Oh, 'twas the typical sort of heathen pirate-galleon—nothing remarkable."

"You were captured by heathen pirates!?"

"Only once. Happens more often than you might appreciate. But we are digressing. I will not rest until my enemy's identity is known, and I've put him in the grave."

"But suppose that when you learn his identity, he turns out to be your great-uncle, *and* your cousin's brother-in-law, *and* your best friend's godfather?"

"I'm only speaking of one enemy—"

"I know. But royal families of Europe are so tangled together that your enemy might bear all of those relations to you *at once*."

"Eeyuh, what a mess."

"On the contrary—'tis the height of civilization," Monmouth said. "It is not—mind you—that we *forget* our grievances. That would be unthinkable. But if our only redress were to put one another into graves, all Europe would be a battleground!"

"All Europe *is* a battleground! Haven't you been paying attention?"

"Fighting at Maestricht and Mons and other places has left me little time for it," Monmouth said drily. "I say to you it could be much worse—like the Thirty Years' War, or the Civil War in England."

"I suppose that is true," Eliza said, remembering all of those ruined castles in Bohemia.

"In the *modern* age we pursue revenge at Court. Sometimes we might go so far as to fight a duel—but in general we wage battles with *wit,* not *muskets*. It does not kill as many people, and it gives ladies a chance to enter the lists— as it were."

"I beg your pardon?"

"Have you ever fired a musket, mademoiselle?"

"No."

"And yet in our conversation you have already discharged any number of *verbal* broadsides. So you see, on the *courtly* battle-ground, women stand on an equal footing with men."

Eliza coasted to a stop, hearing the bells of the town hall chiming four o'clock. Monmouth overshot her, then swooped through a gallant turn and skated back, wearing a silly grin.

"I must go and meet someone," Eliza said.

"May I escort you back to the Binnenhof?"

"No—d'Avaux is there."

"You no longer take pleasure in the Ambassador's company?"

"I am afraid he will try to give me a fur coat."

"That would be terrible!"

"I don't want to give him the satisfaction . . . he has used me, somehow."

"The King of France has given him orders to be as offensive as possible to Mary. As Mary's in love with *me* today . . ."

"Why?"

"Why is she in love with me? Mademoiselle, I am offended."

"I know perfectly well why she is in love with you. I meant, why would the King of France send a Count up to the Hague simply to behave offensively?"

"Oh, the comte d'Avaux does many other things besides. But the answer is that King Louis hopes to break up the marriage between William and Mary—destroying William's power in England—and making Mary available for marriage to one of his French bastards."

"I knew it had to be a family squabble of some sort—it's so mean, so petty, so vicious."

"*Now* you begin to understand!"

"Doesn't Mary love her husband?"

"William and Mary are a well-matched couple."

"You *say* little but *mean* much . . . what *do* you mean?"

"Now it is my turn to be mysterious," Monmouth said, "as it's the only way I can be sure of seeing you again."

He went on in that vein, and Eliza dodged him elaborately, and they parted ways.

But two hours later they were together again. This time Gomer Bolstrood was with them.

A COUPLE OF MILES NORTH of the Hague, the flat polder-land of the Dutch Republic was sliced off by the sea-coast. A line of dunes provided a meager weather-wall. Sheltering behind it, running parallel to the coast, was a strip of land, frequently wooded, but not wilderness, for it had been improved with roads and canals. In that belt of green had grown up diverse estates: the country retreats of nobles and merchants. Each had a proper house with a formal garden. The bigger ones also had wooded game-parks, and hunting-lodges where men could seek refuge from their women.

Eliza still knew little about Gomer Bolstrood and his scheme; but it was obvious enough that he was in league with some merchant or other, who was the owner of one such estate, and that he had gotten permission to use the hunting-lodge as a pied-à-terre. A canal ran along one side of the game-park and connected it—if you knew which turns to take—to the Haagsche Bos, that large park next to the Binnenhof. The distance was several miles, and so it might have been a morning's or an afternoon's journey in the summer. But when ice was on the canals, and skates were on the traveler's feet, it could be accomplished in very little time.

Thus Monmouth had arrived, by himself, incognito. He was seated on the chair that Bolstrood had likened to an ogre's throne, and Eliza and Bolstrood were on the creaking faggot-chairs. Bolstrood tried to make a formal introduction of the Client, but—

"So," Eliza said, "as you were saying a short time ago: fighting battles with muskets and powder is an out-moded practice and . . ."

"It suits my purposes for people to think that I actually *believe* such nonsense," Monmouth said, "and women are ever eager to believe it."

"Why—because in battle, women become swag, and we don't like being swag?"

"I suppose so."

"I've been swag. It didn't suit me. So, for me, your little lecture about modernity was inspiring in a way."

"As I said—women are eager to believe it."

"The two of you are acquainted—?—!" Bolstrood finally forced out.

"As my late Dad so aptly demonstrated, those of us who are predestined to burn in Hell must try to have a *bit* of fun while we are alive," Monmouth said. "Men and women— ones who are not Puritans, anyway—know each other in all sorts of ways!" Regarding Eliza warmly. Eliza gave him a look that was intended to be like a giant icicle thrust through his abdomen—but Monmouth responded with a small erotic quiver.

Eliza said, "If you play into the comte d'Avaux's hands so easily, by diverting your affections from Mary—what use will you be when you sit on the throne of England?"

Monmouth drooped and looked at Bolstrood.

"I didn't tell her, exactly," Gomer Bolstrood protested, "I only told her what commodities we wish to purchase."

"Which was enough to make your plan quite obvious," Eliza said.

"Doesn't matter, I suppose," Monmouth said. "As we cannot make the purchases anyway without putting up some collateral—and in our case the collateral *is* the throne."

"That's not what I was told," Eliza said. "I've been assuming the account would be settled with gold."

"And so it will be—*after.*"

"After what?"

"After we've conquered England."

"Oh."

"But most of England is on our side, so—a few months at most."

"Does most-of-England have *guns*?"

"It's true what he says," put in Gomer Bolstrood. "Everywhere this man goes in England, people turn out into the streets and light bonfires for him, and burn the Pope in effigy."

"So *in addition* to purchasing the required *commodities,* you require a bridge loan, for which your collateral will be—"

"The Tower of London," Monmouth said reassuringly.

"I am a trader, not a shareholder," Eliza said. "I cannot be your financier."

"How can you trade, without being a shareholder?"

"I trade ducat shares, which have one-tenth the value of proper V.O.C. shares and are far more liquid. I hold them—or options—only long enough to eke out a small profit. You will need to skate about forty miles that way, your grace," Eliza said, pointing northeast, "and make connections with

Amsterdam moneylenders. There are great men there, princes of the market, who've accumulated stacks of V.O.C. stock, and who will lend money out against it. But as you cannot put the Tower of London in your pocket and set it on the table as security for the loan, you'll need something else."

"We know that," Bolstrood said. "We are merely letting you know that when time comes to effect the transaction, the payment will come, not from us, but—"

"From some credulous lender."

"Not *so* credulous. Important men are with us."

"May I know who those men are?"

A look between Bolstrood and Monmouth. "Not now. Later, in Amsterdam," Bolstrood said.

"This is never going to work—those Amsterdammers have more *good* investments than they know what to do with," Eliza said. "But there might be another way to get the money."

"Where do you propose to get it from, if not the money-lenders of Amsterdam?" Monmouth asked. "My mistress has already pawned all of her jewels—*that* resource is exhausted."

"We can get it from Mr. Sluys," Eliza said, after a long few minutes of staring into the fire. She turned to face the others. The air of the lodge was suddenly cool on her brow.

"The one who betrayed his country thirteen years ago?" Bolstrood asked warily.

"The same. He has many connections with French investors and is very rich."

"You mean to blackmail him, then—?" Monmouth asked.

"Not precisely. First we'll find some *other* investor and tell him of your plan to invade England."

"But the plan is a secret!"

"He'll have every incentive to *keep* it secret—for as soon as he knows, he will begin selling V.O.C. stock short."

"That, 'selling short,' is a bit of zargon I have heard Dutchmen and Jews bandy about, but I know not what it means," Monmouth said.

"There are two factions who war with each other in the market: *liefhebberen* or bulls who want the stock to rise, and *contremines* or bears who want it to fall. Frequently a group of bears will come together and form a secret cabal—they will spread false news of pirates off the coast, or go into the market loudly selling shares at very low prices, trying to create a panic and make the price drop."

"But how do they make money from this?"

"Never mind the details—there are ways of using options so that you will make money if the price falls. It is called short selling. Our investor—once we tell him about your invasion plans—will begin betting that V.O.C. stock will drop soon. And rest assured, it will. Only a few years ago, mere *rumors* about the state of Anglo/Dutch relations were sufficient to depress the price by ten or twenty percent. News of an invasion will plunge it through the *floor.*"

"Why?" Monmouth asked.

"England has a powerful navy—if they are hostile to Holland, they can choke off shipping, and the V.O.C. drops like a stone."

"But *my* policies will be far more congenial to the Hollanders than King James's!" Monmouth protested.

Bolstrood meanwhile had a look on his face as if he were being garrotted by an invisible cord.

Eliza composed herself, breathed deeply, and smiled at Monmouth—then leaned forward and put her hand on his forearm. "Naturally, when it becomes generally understood that your rebellion is going to succeed, V.O.C. stock will soar like a lark in the morning. But *at first* the market will be dominated by ignorant ninehammers who'll foolishly assume that King James will prevail—and that he will be ever so annoyed at the Dutch for having allowed their territory to serve as spring-board for an invasion of his country."

Bolstrood relaxed a bit.

"So at first the market will drop," Monmouth said distractedly.

"Until the *true* situation becomes generally known," Eliza said, patted his arm firmly, and drew back. Gomer Bolstrood seemed to relax further. "During that interval," Eliza continued, "our investor will have the opportunity to reap a colossal profit, by selling the market short. And in exchange for that opportunity he'll gladly buy you all the lead and powder you need to mount the invasion."

"But that investor is *not* Mr. Sluys—?"

"In any short-selling transaction there is a *loser* as well as a *winner*," Eliza said. "Mr. Sluys is to be the loser."

"Why him specifically?" Bolstrood asked. "It could be *any* liefhebber."

"Selling short has been illegal for three-quarters of a century! Numerous edicts have been issued to prevent it—one of them written in the time of the Stadholder Frederick Henry. Now, if a trader is caught short—that is, if he has signed a contract that will cause him to lose money—he can 'appeal to Frederick.'"

"But Frederick Henry died *ages* ago," Monmouth protested.

"It is an expression—a term of art. It simply means to repudiate the contract, and refuse to pay. According to Frederick Henry's edict, that repudiation will be upheld in a court of law."

"But if it's true that there must always be a loser when selling short, then Frederick Henry's decree must've stamped out the practice altogether!"

"Oh, no, your grace—short selling thrives in Amsterdam! Many traders make their living from it!"

"But why don't all of the losers simply 'appeal to Frederick'?"

"It all has to do with how the contracts are structured. If you're clever enough you can put the loser in a position where he dare not appeal to Frederick."

"So it *is* a sort of blackmail after all," Bolstrood said, gazing out the window across a snowy field—but hot on Eliza's trail. "We set Sluys up to be the loser—then if he appeals to Frederick, the entire story comes out in a court of law—including the warehouse full of lead—and he's exposed as a traitor. So he'll eat the loss without complaint."

"But—if I'm following all of this—it relies on Sluys *not knowing* that there is a plan to invade England," Monmouth said. "Otherwise he'd be a fool to enter into the short contract."

"That is certainly true," Eliza said. "We want him to believe that V.O.C. stock will rise."

"But if he's selling us the lead, he'll know we're planning *something*."

"Yes—but he needn't know *what* is being planned, or *when*. We need only manipulate his mental state, so that he has reason to believe that V.O.C. shares are soon to rise."

"And—as I'm now beginning to understand—you are something of a virtuoso when it comes to manipulating men's mental states," Monmouth said.

"You make it sound ever so much more difficult than it really is," Eliza answered. "Mostly I just sit quietly and let the men manipulate themselves."

"Well, if that's all for now," Monmouth said, "I feel a powerful urge to go and practice some self-manipulation in private—unless—?"

"Not today, your grace," Eliza said, "I must pack my things. Perhaps I'll see you in Amsterdam?"

"Nothing could give me greater pleasure."

France

But know that in the Soule
Are many lesser Faculties that serve
Reason as chief; among these Fansie next
Her office holds; of all external things,
Which the five watchful Senses represent,
She forms Imaginations, Aerie shapes,
Which Reason joyning or disjoyning, frames
All what we affirm or what deny, and call
Our knowledge or opinion; then retires
Into her private Cell when Nature rests.
Oft in her absence mimic Fansie wakes
To imitate her; but misjoyning shapes,
Wilde work produces oft, and most in dreams,
Ill matching words and deeds long past or
    late.

—MILTON, *Paradise Lost*

JACK RODE BETWEEN PARIS and Lyons several times in the early part of 1685, ferrying news. Paris: the King of England is dead! Lyons: some Spanish governorships in America are up for sale. Paris: King Looie has secretly married Mademoiselle de Maintenon, and the Jesuits have his ear

now. Lyons: yellow fever is slaying mine-slaves by the thousands in Brazil—the price of gold ought to rise.

It was disconcertingly like working for someone—just the
sort of arrangement he'd given up, long ago, as being beneath his dignity. It was, to put it more simply, too much like
what Bob did. So Jack had to keep reminding himself that he
was not *actually* doing it, but *pretending* to do it, so that he
could get his horse ready to sell—then he would tell these
bankers to fuck themselves.

He was riding back toward Paris from Lyons one day—an
unseasonably cold day in March—when he encountered a
column of three score men shuffling toward him. Their
heads were shaved and they were dressed in dirty rags—
though most had elected to tear up whatever clothes they
had, and wrap them around their bleeding feet. Their arms
were bound behind their backs and so it was easy to see their
protruding ribs, mottled with sores and whip-marks. They
were accompanied by some half-dozen mounted archers
who could easily pick off stragglers or runaways.

In other words, just another group of galley slaves on their
way down to Marseille. But these were more miserable than
most. Your typical galley slave was a deserter, smuggler, or
criminal, hence young and tough. A column of such men setting out from Paris in the winter might expect to lose no
more than half its number to cold, disease, starvation, and
beatings along the way. But this group—like several others
Jack had seen recently—seemed to consist entirely of old
men who had no chance whatever of making it to Marseille—or (for that matter) to whatever inn their guards expected to sleep in tonight. They were painting the road with
blood as they trudged along, and they moved so slowly that
the trip would take them weeks. But this was a journey you
wanted to finish in as few days as possible.

Jack rode off to the side and waited for the column to pass
him by. The stragglers were tailed by a horseman who, as
Jack watched, patiently uncoiled his *nerf du boeuf,* whirled
it round his head a time or two (to make a scary noise and
build up speed), and then snapped it through the air to bite a

chunk out of a slave's ear. Extremely pleased with his own prowess, he then said something not very pleasant about the R.P.R. Which made everything clear to Jack, for R.P.R. stood for *Religion Pretendue Réformée*, which was a contemptuous way of referring to Huguenots. Huguenots tended to be prosperous merchants and artisans, and so naturally if you gave them the galley slave treatment they would suffer much worse than a Vagabond.

Only a few hours later, watching another such column go by, he stared right into the face of Monsieur Arlanc—who stared right back at him. He had no hair, his cheeks were grizzly and sucked-in from hunger, but Monsieur Arlanc it was.

There was nothing for Jack to do at the time. Even if he'd been armed with a musket, one of the archers would've put an arrow through him before he could reload and fire a second ball. But that evening he circled back to an inn that lay several miles south of where he'd seen Monsieur Arlanc, and bided his time in the shadows and the indigo night for a few hours, freezing in clouds of vapor from the nostrils of his angry and uncomfortable horses, until he was certain that the guards would be in bed. Then he rode up to that inn and paid a guard to open the gate for him, and rode, with his little string of horses, into the stable-yard.

Several Huguenots were just standing there, stark naked, chained together in the open. Some jostled about in a feeble effort to stay warm, others looked dead. But Monsieur Arlanc was not in this group. A groom shot back a bolt on a stable door and allowed Jack to go inside, and (once Jack put more silver in his pocket) lent him a lantern. There Jack found the rest of the galley slaves. Weaker ones had burrowed into piles of straw, stronger ones had buried themselves in the great steaming piles of manure that filled the corners. Monsieur Arlanc was among these. He was actually snoring when the light from Jack's lantern splashed on his face.

Now the next morning, Monsieur Arlanc set out with his column of fellow-slaves, not very well-rested, but with a belly full of cheese and bread, and a pair of good boots on his feet. Jack meanwhile rode north with his feet housed in some wooden shoes he'd bought from a peasant.

He'd been ready and willing to gallop out of there with Arlanc on one of the spare horses, but the Huguenot had calmly and with the most admirable French logic explained why this would not work: "The other slaves will be punished if I am found missing in the morning. Most of them are my co-religionists and might accept this, but others are common criminals. In order to prevent it, these would raise the alarm."

"I could just kill 'em," Jack pointed out.

Monsieur Arlanc—a disembodied, candlelit head resting on a great misty dung-pile—got a pained look. "You would have to do so one at a time. The others would raise the alarm. It is most gallant of you to make such an offer, considering that we hardly know each other. Is this the effect of the English Pox?"

"Must be," Jack allowed.

"Most unfortunate," Arlanc said.

Jack was irritated to be pitied by a galley slave. "Your sons—?"

"Thank you for asking. When *le Roi* began to oppress us—"

"Who the hell is Leroy?"

"The King, the King!"

"Oh, yeah. Sorry."

"I smuggled them to England. And what of your boys, Jack?"

"Still waiting for their legacy," Jack said.

"Did you manage to sell your ostrich plumes?"

"I've got some Armenians on it."

"I gather you have not parted with the horse yet—"

"Getting him in shape."

"To impress the brokers?"

"Brokers! What do I want with a broker? It's to impress the *customers.*"

Arlanc's head moved in the lantern-light as if he were burrowing into the manure—Jack realized he was shaking his head in that annoying way that he did when Jack had blurted out something foolish. "It is not possible," Arlanc said. "The horse trade in Paris is absolutely controlled by the brokers—a Vagabond can no more ride in and sell a horse at the Place Royale than he could go to Versailles and get command of a regiment—it is simply *not done*."

If Jack had just arrived in France recently he'd have said, *But that's crazy—why not?* but as it was he knew Arlanc spoke the truth. Arlanc recommended such-and-such a broker, to be found at the House of the Red Cat in the Rue du Temple, but then recollected that this fellow was himself a Huguenot, hence probably dead and certainly out of business.

They ended up talking through the night, Jack feeding him bits of bread and cheese from time to time, and tossing a few morsels to the others to shut them up. By the time dawn broke, Jack had given up his boots as well as his food, which was stupid in a way. But he was riding, and Monsieur Arlanc was walking.

He rode north cold, hungry, exhausted, and essentially barefoot. The horses had not been rested or tended to properly and were in a foul mood, which they found various ways to inflict on Jack. He groggily took a wrong turn and ended up approaching Paris by an unfamiliar route. This got him into some scrapes that did nothing to improve his state of mind. One of these misadventures led to Jack's staying awake through *another* night, hiding from some nobleman's game-keepers in a wood. The rented horses kept whinnying and so he had no choice but to leave them staked out as decoys, to draw his pursuers while he slipped away with stalwart Turk.

So by the time the sun rose on the next day he was just one step away from being a miserable Vagabond again. He had lost two good horses for which he was responsible, and so all the livery stables and horse-brokers in Paris would be up in arms against him, which meant that selling Turk would be even more thoroughly impossible. So Jack would not get his money, and Turk would not get the life he deserved: eating good fodder and being fastidiously groomed in a spacious nobleman's stable, his only responsibility being to roger an endless procession of magnificent mares. Jack would not get his money, which meant he'd probably never even see his boys, as he couldn't bring himself to show up on their Aunt Maeve's doorstep empty-handed . . . all of Mary Dolores's brothers and cousins erupting to their feet to pursue him through East London with their shillelaghs . . .

It would've made him mad even if he hadn't been afflicted with degeneration of the brain, and awake for the third consecutive day. Madness, he decided, was easier.

As he approached Paris, riding through those vegetable-fields where steam rose from the still-hot shit of the city, he came upon a vast mud-yard, within sight of the city walls, streaked with white quick-lime and speckled with human skulls and bones sitting right out on the surface. Rude crosses had been stuffed into the muck here and there, and jutted out at diverse angles, spattered with the shit of the crows and vultures that waited on them. When Jack rode through it, those birds had, however, all flown up the road to greet a procession that had just emerged from the city-gates: a priest in a long cloak, so ponderous with mud that it hung from his shoulders like chain-mail, using a great crucifix as walking-stick, and occasionally hauling off a dolorous clang on a pot-like bell in the opposite hand. Behind him, a small crowd of paupers employing busted shovels in the same manner as the priest did the crucifix, and then a cart, driven by a couple of starveling mules, laden with a number of long bundles wrapped and sewn up in old grain-sacks.

Jack watched them tilt the wagon back at the blurred brink of an open pit so that the bundles—looked like three adults, half a dozen children, and a couple of babies—slid and tumbled into the ground. While the priest rattled on in rote Latin, his helpers zigzagged showers of quick-lime over the bodies and kicked dirt back into the hole.

Jack began to hear muffled voices: coming from under the ground, naturally. The skulls all around him began to jaw themselves loose from the muck and to rise up, tottering, on incomplete skeletons, droning a monkish sort of chant. But meanwhile those grave-diggers, now pivoting on their shovels, had begun to hum a tune of their own: a jaunty, Irish-inflected hornpipe.

Cantering briskly out onto the road (Turk now positively sashaying), he found himself at the head of a merry procession: he'd become the point man of a flying wedge of Vagabond grave-diggers, whose random shufflings had resolved into dazzling group choreography, and who were performing a sort of close-order drill with their shovels.

Behind them went the priest, walloping his bell and walking ahead of the corpse-wain, where the dead people—who had hopped up out of the pit and back into the wagon—but who were still wrapped up in their shrouds—made throaty moaning noises, like organ-pipes to complement the grim churchly droning of the skeletons. Once all were properly arranged on the road, the skeletons finally broke into a thudding, four-square type of church-hymn:

> *O wha-at the Hell was on God's mind,*
> *That sixteen-sixty day,*
> *When he daubed a Vag-a-bond's crude form*
> *From a lump of Thames-side clay?*

> *Since God would ne'er set out to make*
> *A loser of this kind*
> *Jack's life, if planned in Heaven, doth prove*
> *Jehovah's lost His mind.*

Switching to Gregorian chant for the chorus:

> *Quod, erat demonstrandum. Quod, erat*
> *demonstrandum . . .*

But at this point, as they were all nearing the city gates, they encountered a southbound column of *galériens*, obviously Huguenots, who were shuffling along in a syncopated gait that made their chains jingle like sleigh-bells; the guards

riding behind them cracked their whips in time with a
sprightly tune that the Huguenots were singing:

> *Chained by the necks,*
> *Slaves of Louis the Rex,*
> *You might think that we've lost our freedom,*
> *But the Cosmos,*
> *Like clock-work,*
> *No more than a rock's worth*
> *Of choices, to people, provides!*

But now at this point the grave-diggers were greeted by an
equal number of fishwives, issuing from the city-gates, who
paired up with them, kicked in with trilling soprano and
lusty alto voices, and drowned out both the Huguenots and
the Skeletons with some sort of merry Celtic reel:

> *There once was a jolly Vagabond*
> *To the Indies he did sail,*
> *When back to London he did come*
> *He wanted a fe-male.*
>
> *He found a few in Drury-Lane*
> *In Hounsditch found some more*
> *But cash flow troubles made him long*
> *For a girlfriend, not a whore.*
>
> *Now Jack he loved the theatre*
> *But didn't like to pay*
> *He met an Irish actress there*
> *While sneaking in one day.*

Now the Priest, far from objecting to this interruption,
worked it into his solemn hymnody, albeit with a jarring
change of rhythm:

> *He could have gone to make his peace*
> *With Jesus and the Church*

Instead he screwed a showgirl
Then he left her in the lurch.

Now God in Heaven ne'er could wish
That Irish lass so ill
Jack's life's proves irrefutably
Th'existence of Free Will

Quod, erat demonstrandum. Quod, erat
    demonstrandum . . .

And the irrepressible *galériens* seemed to pop their heads
into the middle of this scene and take it over with the continuation of their song:

Will he, or nill he,
It's all kinda silly
When predestination prevails!

He can't make decisions
His will just ain't his, and
His destiny runs on fix'd rails!

Now the Priest again:

The Pope would say, that he who blames
The Good Lord for his deeds
Is either cursed with shit for brains
Or is lost 'mong Satan's Weeds.

The former group should take good care
To do as they are told
The latter'd best clean up their act
And come back to the fold.

Quod, erat demonstrandum. Quod, erat
    demonstrandum . . .

And then the *galériens*, obviously wanting to stay and continue the debate, but driven southward, ever southward, by the guards:

> *We're off to row boats*
> *Off the Rhone's sunny côtes*
> *Because God, long ago, said we must*
>
> *If it makes you feel better*
> *You too, Jack, are fettered*
> *By your bodily humours and lusts.*

They were now pulled "offstage," as it were, in the following comical way: a guard rode to the front of the column, hitched the end of their chain to the pommel of his saddle, and spurred his horse forward. The tightening chain ran free through the neck-loops of the *galériens* until it jerked the last man in the queue violently forward so that he crashed into the back of the slave in front of him, who likewise was driven forward into the next, *et cetera* in a *chain reaction* as it were, until the whole column had accordioned together and was dragged off toward the Mediterranean Sea.

Now at the same time the rest of the procession burst through the city-gates into lovely Paris. The skeletons, who'd been exceptionally gloomy until this point, suddenly began disassembling themselves and bonking themselves and their neighbors with thigh-bones to produce melodious xylophony. The priest jumped up on the corpse-wain and began to belt out a new melody in a comely, glass-shattering counter-tenor.

> *Oh, Jaaaack—*
> *Can't say I blame you for feeling like shit*
> *Oh, Jaaaack—*
> *Never seen any one step into it*
> *Like Jaaack—*
> *Corporal punishment wouldn't suffice*
> *The raaack—*

Would be too good for you,
Would simply be
Too slaaack—
Even if all of the skin were whipped off of
Your baaack—
Not only evil,
But stupid to boot,
Not charismatic
And not even cute,
The brains that God granted
You now indisput-
ably gone down the tubes
And you don't give a hoot,
You stink!
No getting round it,
It's true, Jack, confound it,
You stink!

And so on; but then here there was a little pause in the music, occasioned by a small and perfectly adorable French girl in a white dress, which Jack recognized as the sort of get-up that young Papists wore to their first communion. Radiant—but gloomy. The priest reined in the mules and vaulted down off the corpse-wain and squatted down next to her.

"Bless me, Father, for I have sinned!" said the little girl.

Awww, gushed all of the skeletons, corpses, gravediggers, fishwives, *et cetera,* gathered round in vast circle as if to watch an Irish brawl.

"Believe me, girl, you ain't alone!" hollered a fishwife through cupped hands; the others grinned and nodded supportively.

The priest hitched up his muddy cassock and scooted even closer to the girl, then turned his ear toward her lips; she whispered something into it; he shook his head in sincere, but extremely short-lived dismay; then stood, drawing himself up to his full height, and said something back to her. She put her hands together, and closed her eyes. All of Paris went silent, and every ear strained to listen as she in her high piping voice said a little Papist prayer in Latin. Then she opened her baby blues and looked up in trepidation at the priest—whose stony face suddenly opened up in a big grin as he made the sign of the cross over her. With a great big squeal of delight, the girl jumped up and turned a cartwheel in the street, petticoats a-flyin', and suddenly the whole procession came alive again: the priest walking along behind the handspringing girl and the dancers, the wrapped corpses up in the cart swinging their hips in time to the music and uttering pre-verbal *woo! woo!* noises to fill in the chinks in the tune. The grave-diggers and fishwives, plus a number of flower-girls and rat-catchers who joined in along the way, were now dancing to the priest's song in a medley of different dance steps, viz. high-stepping whorehouse moves, Irish stomping, and Mediterranean tarantellas.

> *When you have been bad*
> *A naughty young lad*
> *Or lass who has had*
> *A man or two sans—marriage,*
>
> *When painting the town*
> *Carousing around*
> *You run a child down*
> *While driving your big—carriage,*

And so on at considerable length, as they had the whole University to parade through, and then the Roman baths at Cluny. As they came over the Petit Pont, about a thousand wretches emerged from the gates of the Hôtel-Dieu—that colossal poorhouse just by Notre Dame, which was where the priest, grave-diggers, and dead persons had all originated—and, accompanied by Notre Dame's organ, boomed out a mighty chorus to ring down the curtain on this entire pageant.

> *Everyone does it—everyone sins*
> *Everyone at the party has egg on their chins*

Everyone likes to get, time to time, skin to skin
With a lad or a lass, drink a tumbler of gin.

So confess all your sins and admit you were bad,
It isn't a fashion, nor is it a fad,
It's what the Pope says we should do when we've had
Just a bit too much fun, and we need to be pad-
dled or spanked on the buttocks (unless we enjoy it)
If there's sin in our hearts then it's time to destroy it,
From the poorest of poor all the way to Le Roi, lit-
tle sins or mass murder, if you made the wrong choice it

Is fine if you say so, and change your bad ways
You can do it in private, only God sees your face
In a church or cathedral, your time and your place
What's the payoff? UNDESERVED GRACE!

This song developed into a sort of round, meant (Jack supposed) to emphasize the cyclical nature of the procedure: some of the wretches, fishwives, *et cetera*, engaging in carnal acts right there in the middle of the street, others rushing, in organized infantry-squares, toward the priest to confess, then turning away to genuflect in the direction of the Cathedral, then charging pall-mall back into fornication. In any case, every skeleton, corpse, wretch, grave-digger, fishwife, street-vendor, and priest now had a specific role to play, and part to sing, except for Jack; and so, one by one, all of Jack's harbingers and outriders peeled away from him, or evaporated into thin air, so that he rode alone (albeit, watched and cheered on by the thousands) into the great Place before the Cathedral of Notre Dame, which was as fine and gorgeous a vision as had ever been seen. For all of King Looie's Regiments were having their colors blessed by some sort of extremely resplendent mitre-wearing Papist authority figure, one or two notches shy of the Pope himself, who stood beneath a canopy of brilliant fleur-de-lis-embroidered cloth that burnt in the sun. The regiments *themselves* were not present—there wouldn't've been room—but their noble commanders were, and their heralds and color-bearers, carrying giant banners of silk and satin and cloth-of-gold: banners meant to be seen from a mile away through squalls of gun-powder-smoke, designed to look resplendent when planted atop the walls of Dutch or German or English cities and to overawe the populace with the glory, might, and, above all, good taste of Leroy. Each one had its own kind of magickal power over the troops of its regiment, and so to see them drawn up here in rows, all together, was like seeing all Twelve of the Apostles sitting round the same table, or some-thing.

As much as Jack hated Leroy, he had to admit it was a hell of a thing to look at—so much so, that he regretted he hadn't arrived sooner, for he only caught the terminal quarter-hour of the ceremony. Then it all broke up. The color-bearers rode off toward their regimental headquarters in the territory outside of the city walls, and the nobility generally rode north over the Pont d'Arcole to the Right Bank where some went down in the direction of the Louvre and others went round back of the Hôtel de Ville toward the Place Royale and the Marais. One of the latter group was wearing an Admiral's hat and riding a white horse with pink eyes—a big one—apparently meant to be some sort of a war-horse.

Jack was not set on what he should do next, but as he (for lack of any other purpose in life) followed this admiral into the narrow streets he began to hear fidgety noises from the walls all around him, like the gnawing of mice, and noticed a lot of radiant dust in the air: on a closer look, he formed the impression that all of the tiny animals trapped in the stones of the city were coming alive and squirming about in their prisons, kicking up dust, as if some invisible tide of quicksilver had seeped up through the walls and brought them back to life; and construing this as an omen, Jack spurred Turk forward with the heels of his wooden *sabots* and, by taking certain back-streets, ducking beneath those jutting balconies, overtook the Admiral on the pink-eyed horse, and rode out into the street in front of him, just short of the entrance to the Place Royale—in the very street where he'd once been knocked into the shit by (he guessed) the same fellow's servants.

Those servants were now clearing the way for the Admiral and the large contingent of friends and hangers-on riding with him, and so when Jack rode out into the middle of the street, it was empty. A footman in blue livery came toward him, eyeing Jack's wooden shoes and his crutch, and probably sizing him up as a peasant who'd stolen a plowhorse— but Jack gave Turk a little twitch of the reins that meant *I give you leave* and Turk surged toward this man and crushed him straight into the gutter where he ended up stopping turd-rafts. Then Jack drew up to face the Admiral from perhaps half a dozen lengths. Several other footmen were situated in the space between them, but having seen what Turk knew how to do, they were now shrinking back against walls.

The Admiral looked nonplussed. He couldn't stop looking at Jack's shoes. Jack kicked off the *sabots* and they tumbled on the stones with pocking footstep-noises. He wanted to make some kind of insightful point, here, about how the shoe thing was just another example of Frogs' obsession with form over substance—a point worth making here and now, because it related to their (presumed) inability to appreciate what a fine mount Turk was. But in his present state of mind, he couldn't even get that out in *English.*

Someone, anyway, had decided that he was dangerous—a younger man costumed as a Captain of Horse, who now rode out in front of the Admiral and drew his sword, and waited for Jack to do something.

"What'd you pay for that nag?" Jack snarled, and, since he didn't have time to disassemble his crutch, raised it up like a knight's lance, bracing the padded cross-piece against his ribs, and spurred Turk forward with his heels. The cold air felt good rushing over his bare feet. The Captain got a look of dignified befuddlement on his face that Jack would always remember, and the others, behind him, got out of the way in a sudden awkward clocking and scraping of hooves—and then at the last moment this Captain realized he was in an impossible situation, and tried to lean out of the way. The crutch-tip caught him in the upper arm and probably gave him a serious bruise. Jack rode through the middle of the Admiral's entourage and then got Turk turned around to face them again, which took longer than he was comfortable with—but all of those Admirals and Colonels and Captains had to get turned around, *too,* and their horses were not as good as Jack's.

One in particular, a pretty black charger with a bewigged and beribboned aristocrat on top of it, was declining to follow orders, and stood broadside to Jack, a couple of lengths away. "And what do I hear for this magnificent Turkish charger?" Jack demanded, spurring Turk forward again, so that after building up some speed he T-boned the black horse just in the ribcage and actually knocked it over sideways—the horse went down in a fusillade of hooves, and the rider, who hadn't seen it coming, flew halfway to the next *arrondissement.*

"I'll buy it right *now,* Jack," said an English voice, somehow familiar, "if you stop being such a fucking *tosser,* that is."

Jack looked up into a face. His first thought was that this was the handsomest face he had ever seen; his second, that it belonged to John Churchill. Seated astride a decent enough horse of his own, right alongside of Jack.

Someone was maneuvering towards them, shouting in French—Jack was too flabbergasted to consider *why* until Churchill, without taking his eyes off Jack's, whipped out his rapier, and spun it (seemingly over his knuckles) so as to deflect a sword-thrust that had been aimed directly at Jack's heart. Instead it penetrated several inches into Jack's thigh. This hurt, and had the effect of waking Jack up and forcing him to understand that all of this was *really happening.*

"Bob sends greetings from sunny Dunkirk," said Churchill.

"If you shut up, there is an infinitesimal chance of my being able to save you from being tortured to death before sundown."

Jack said nothing.

Amsterdam

APRIL 1685

⚕

> The Art of War is so well study'd, and so equally
> known in all Places, that 'tis the longest Purse
> that conquers now, not the longest Sword. If
> there is any Country whose people are less
> martial, less enterprising, and less able for the
> Field; yet if they have but more Money than
> their Neighbors, they shall soon be superior to
> them in Strength, for Money is Power . . .
>
> —DANIEL DEFOE, *A Plan of the English Commerce*

"IT WAS PHANTASTICKAL in the extreme—Mademoiselle, it
was *beyond French*—"

Like a still pond into which a boy has flung a handful of
gravel, the Duke of Monmouth's beauty—aglow in the
golden light of an Amsterdam afternoon—was now marred
by a thought. The eyebrows steepled, the lips puckered, and
the eyes might've crossed slightly—it was very difficult to
tell, given his and Eliza's current positions: straight out of a
Hindoo frieze.

"What is it?"

"Did we actually achieve sexual, er, *congress,* at any point
during those, er, proceedings?"

"Poh! What're you, then, some Papist who must draw up a
schedule of his sins?"

"You know that I am not, mademoiselle, but—"

"You're the sort who keeps a tally, aren't you? Like a tavern-goer who prides himself on the Ps and Qs chalked up on the wall next his name—save in your case it's wenches."

Monmouth tried to look indignant. But at the moment his body contained, of the yellow bile, less than at any time since infancy, and so even his indignation was flaccid. "I don't think there's anything untoward in wanting to know whom I have, and haven't, rogered! My father—God rest his soul—rogered simply *everyone*. I'm merely the first and foremost of a *legion* of royal bastards! Wouldn't be proper to lose track."

". . . of *your* royal bastards?"

"Yes."

"Then know that no royal bastards can possibly result from what we just did."

Monmouth got himself worked round to a less outlandish position, viz. sitting up and gazing soulfully into Eliza's nipples. "I say, would you like to be a Duchess or something?"

Eliza arched her back and laughed. Monmouth shifted his attention to her oscillating navel, and looked wounded.

"What would I have to do? Marry some syphilitic Duke?"

"Of course not. Be my mistress—when I am King of England. My father made *all* his mistresses into Duchesses."

"Why?"

Monmouth, scandalized: "Elsewise, 'tweren't proper!"

"You already have a mistress."

"It's *common* to have one . . ."

"And *noble* to have *several*?"

"What's the point of being a king if you can't fuck a lot of Duchesses?"

"Just so, sir!"

"Though I don't know if 'fuck' is *le mot juste* for what *we* did."

"What *I* did. You just fidgeted and shuddered."

"Well it's like some modish dance, isn't it, where only

one knows the steps. You just have to teach me the other part of it."

"I am honored, Your Grace—does that mean we'll be seeing each other again?"

Monmouth, miffed and slightly buffaloed: "I was *sincere* about making you a Duchess."

"First you have to make yourself a King."

The Duke of Monmouth sighed and slammed back into the mattress, driving out an evoluting cloud of dust, straw-ends, bedbugs, and mite fœces. All of it hung beautifully in the lambent air, as if daubed on canvas by one of those Brueghels.

"I know it is ever so tiresome," Eliza said, stroking the Duke's hair back from his brow and tucking it neatly behind his ear. "*Later* you'll be slogging round dreadful battlefields. *Tonight* we go to the Opera!"

Monmouth made a vile face. "Give me a battlefield any time."

"William's going to be there."

"Eeeyuh, he's not going to do any tedious *acting,* is he?"

"What, the Prince of Orange—?"

"After the Peace of Breda he put on a ballet, and appeared as Mercury, bringing news of Anglo-Dutch *rapprochement. Embarrassing* to see a rather good warrior prancing about with a couple of bloody goose-wings lashed to his ankles."

"That was a long time ago—he is a grown man, and it is beneath his dignity now. He'll just peer down from his box. Pretend to whisper *bons mots* to Mary, who'll pretend to get them."

"If *he* is coming, we can go late," Monmouth said. "They'll have to search the place for bombs."

"Then we must go early," Eliza countered, "as there'll be that much more time for plots and intrigues."

LIKE ONE WHO HAS ONLY read books and heard tales of a foreign land, and finally goes there and sees the real thing—thus Eliza at the Opera. Not so much for the *place* (which was only a building) as for the *people,* and not so much for the ones with titles and formal ranks (viz. the Raadspension-ary, and diverse Regents and Magistrates with their fat jew-elled wives) as for the ones who had the power to move the market.

Eliza, like most of that caterwauling, hand-slapping crowd who migrated between the Dam and the Exchange, did not have enough money to trade in actual V.O.C. shares. When she was flush, she bought and sold *ducat* shares, and when she wasn't, she bought and sold options and contracts to buy or sell them. Strictly speaking, ducat shares didn't even exist. They were splinters, fragments, of actual V.O.C. shares. They were a fiction that had been invented so that people who weren't enormously wealthy could participate in the market.

Yet even above the level of those who traded full V.O.C. shares were the princes of the market, who had accumulated large numbers of those shares, and borrowed money against them, which they lent out to diverse ventures: mines, sailing-voyages, slave-forts on the Guinea coast, colonies, wars, and (if conditions were right) the occasional violent overthrow of a king. Such a man could move the market simply by showing his face at the Exchange, and trigger a crash, or a boom, simply by strolling across it with a particular expres-sion on his face, leaving a trail of buying and selling in his wake, like a spreading cloud of smoke from a bishop's censer.

All of those men seemed to be here at the Opera with their wives or mistresses. The crowd was something like the in-nards of a harpsichord, each person tensed to thrum or keen when plucked. Mostly it was a cacophony, as if cats were lovemaking on the keyboard. But the arrival of certain Per-sonages was a palpable striking of certain chords.

"The French have a word for this: they name it a *frisson*," muttered the Duke of Monmouth behind a kid-gloved hand as they made their way toward their box.

"Like Orpheus, I struggle with a desire to turn around and look behind me—"

"Stay, your turban would fall off."

Eliza reached up to pat the cyclone of cerulean Turkish silk. It was anchored to her hair by diverse heathen brooches, clips, and pins. "Impossible."

"Anyway, why would you want to look behind you?"

"To see what has caused this *frisson.*"

"It is *we,* you silly." And for once, the Duke of Monmouth had said something that was demonstrably true. Countless sets of jewelled and gilded opera-glasses had been trained on them, making the owners look like so many goggle-eyed amphibians crowded together on a bank.

"Never before has the Duke's woman been more gloriously attired than *he,*" Eliza ventured.

"And never *again,*" Monmouth snarled. "I only hope that *your* magnificence does not distract them from what we *want* them to see."

They stood at the railing of their box as they talked, presenting themselves for inspection. For the proscenium where the actors cavorted was only the most obvious of the Opera House's stages, and the story that they acted out was only one of several dramas all going on at once. For example, the Stadholder's box, only a few yards away, was being ransacked by Blue Guards looking for French bombs. *That* had grown tedious, and so now the Duke of Monmouth and his latest mistress had the attention of most everyone. The gaze of so many major V.O.C. shareholders, through so many custom-ground lenses, made Eliza feel like an insect 'neath a Natural Philosopher's burning-glass. She was glad that this Turkish courtesan's get-up included a veil, which hid everything but her eyes.

Even through the veil's narrow aperture, some of the observers might've detected a few moments' panic, or at least anxiety, in Eliza's eyes, as the *frisson* drew out into a general murmur of confusion: opera-goers all nudging one another down below, pointing upwards with flicks of the eyeballs or discreet waftings of gloved and ringed fingers, getting their wigs entangled as they whispered speculations to each other.

It took a few moments for the crowd to even figure out who Eliza's escort *was*. Monmouth's attire was numblingly practical, as if he were going to jump on a war-horse immediately following the Opera and gallop through fen, forest, and brush until he encountered some foe who wanted slaying. Even his sword was a cavalry saber—not a rapier. To that point, at least, the message was clear enough. The question was, in what *direction* would Monmouth ride, and what sorts of heads, specifically, did he intend to be lopping off with that saber?

"I knew it—to expose your navel was a mistake!" the Duke hissed.

"On the contrary—'tis the *keyhole* through which the entire riddle will be *unlocked*," Eliza returned, the t's and k's making her veil ripple gorgeously. But she was not as confident as she sounded, and so, at the risk of being obvious, she allowed her gaze to wander, in what she hoped would be an innocent-seeming way, around the crescent of opera-boxes until she found the one where the comte d'Avaux was seated along with (among other Amsterdammers who had recently gone on shopping sprees in Paris) Mr. Sluys the traitorous lead-hoarder.

D'Avaux removed a pair of golden opera-glasses from his eyes and stared Eliza in the face for a ten-count.

His eyes shifted to William's box, where the Blue Guards were making an *endless* thrash.

He looked at Eliza again. Her veil hid her smile, but the invitation in her eyes was clear enough.

"It's . . . not . . . working," Monmouth grunted.

"It is working *flawlessly,*" Eliza said. D'Avaux was on his feet, excusing himself from the crowd in that box: Sluys, and an Amsterdam Regent, and some sort of young French nobleman, who must have been of high rank, for d'Avaux gave him a deep bow.

A few moments later he was giving the same sort of bow to the Duke of Monmouth, and kissing Eliza's hand.

"The *next* time you grace the Opera, mademoiselle, the Blue Guards will have to search *your* box, too—for you may be sure that every Lady in this building is shamed by your radiance. None of them will ever forgive you." But as he was saying these words to Eliza, his gaze was traveling curiously up and down Monmouth, searching for clues.

The Duke was wearing several pins and badges that had to be viewed from close range in order to be properly interpreted: one bearing the simple red cross of a Crusader, and another with the arms of the Holy League—the alliance of Poland, Austria, and Venice that was nudging the wreckage of the Turkish Army back across Hungary.

"Your Grace," d'Avaux said, "the way East is dangerous."

"The way West is barred forever, to me anyway," Monmouth replied, "and my presence in Holland is giving rise to all manner of ugly rumors."

"There is always a place for you in France."

"The only thing I've ever been any good for is fighting—" Monmouth began.

"Not the *only* thing . . . my lord," Eliza said lasciviously. D'Avaux flinched and licked his lips. Monmouth flushed slightly and continued: "as my uncle* has brought peace to Christendom, I must seek glory in *heathen* lands."

Something was happening in the corner of Eliza's eye: William and Mary entering their box. Everyone rose and applauded. It was dry, sparse applause, and it didn't last. The comte d'Avaux stepped forward and kissed the Duke of Monmouth on both cheeks. Many of the opera-goers did not see the gesture, but some did. Enough, anyway, to strike a new chord in the audience: a baritone commotion that was soon covered up by the opening strains of the overture.

The ladies and gentlemen of Amsterdam were settling into their seats, but their servants and lackeys still stood in the shadows under the boxes and loges, and some of them were now moving as their masters beckoned to them: stepping forward and cocking their heads to hear whispered con-

---

*King Louis XIV of France—not really Monmouth's uncle, but the brother of the widower of the sister of his illegitimate father, as well as the son of the brother of his grandmother, and many other connexions besides.

fidences, or holding out their hands to accept scribbled notes.

The market was moving. Eliza had moved it with her turban and her navel, and d'Avaux had moved it by showing slightly greater than normal affection for the Duke of Monmouth. Together, these clues could only mean that Monmouth had given up his claim to the English throne and was bound for Constantinople.

The market was moving, and Eliza desperately wanted to be out on the Dam, moving with it—but her place was here for now. She saw d'Avaux return to his box and sit down. Actors had begun to sing down on the stage, but d'Avaux's guests were leaning towards him to whisper and listen. The young French nobleman nodded his head, turned towards Monmouth, crossed himself, then opened his hand as if throwing a prayer to the Duke. Eliza half expected to see a dove fly out of his sleeve. Monmouth pretended to snatch it from the air, and kissed it.

But Mr. Sluys was not in a praying mood. He was thinking. Even in semi-darkness, through a miasma of candle and tobacco smoke, Eliza could read his face: *Monmouth slaying Turks in Hungary means he won't use Holland as a platform to invade England—so there won't be a catastrophe in Anglo-Dutch relations—so the English Navy won't be firing any broadsides at the Dutch merchant fleet—so V.O.C. stock will rise.* Sluys held his right hand up slightly and caressed the air with two fingers. A servant was suddenly draped over his epaulet, memorizing something, counting on his fingers. He nodded sharply, like a pecking gull, and was gone.

Eliza reached up behind her head, untied her veil, and let it fall down onto her bosom. Then she enjoyed the opera.

A hundred feet away, Abraham de la Vega was hiding in the wings with a spyglass, made of lenses ground, to tolerances of a few thousandths of an inch, by his late second cousin, Baruch de Spinoza. Through those lenses, he saw the veil descend. He was nine years old. He moved through the backstage and out of the opera-house like the moon-shadow of a nightingale. Aaron de la Vega, his uncle, was waiting there astride a swift horse.

"HAS HE OFFERED to make you a Duchess yet?" d'Avaux asked during the intermission.

"He said that he *would have*—had he not renounced his claim to the throne," Eliza said.

D'Avaux was amused by her carefulness. "As your gallant is renewing his Platonic friendship with the Princess, may I escort you to Mr. Sluys's box? I cannot stand to see you neglected."

Eliza looked at the Stadholder's box. Mary was there but William had already sneaked out, leaving the field clear for Monmouth, whose brave resolve to go East and fight the Turk had Mary almost in tears.

"I never even *saw* the Prince," Eliza said, "just glimpsed him scurrying in at the last minute."

"Rest assured, mademoiselle, he is nothing to look at." And he offered Eliza his arm. "If it's *true* that your beau is leaving soon for the East, you'll need new young men to amuse you. Frankly, you are overdue for a change. *La France* did her best to civilize Monmouth, but the Anglo-Saxon taint had penetrated too deeply. He never developed the innate discretion of a Frenchman."

"I'm *mortified* to learn that Monmouth has been indiscreet," Eliza said gaily.

"All of Amsterdam, and approximately half of London and Paris, have learned of your charms. But, although the Duke's descriptions were unspeakably vulgar—when they were not completely incoherent—*cultivated* gentlemen can look beyond ribaldry, and infer that you possess qualities, mademoiselle, beyond the merely gynæcological."

"When you say 'cultivated' you mean 'French'?"

"I know you are teasing me, mademoiselle. You expect me to say 'Why yes, all French gentlemen are cultivated.' But it is not so."

"Monsieur d'Avaux, I'm shocked to hear you say such a thing."

They were almost at the door to Sluys's box. D'Avaux drew back. "Typically only the *worst* sort of French nobility would be in the box that you and I are about to enter, associating with the likes of Sluys—but tonight is an exception."

"Louis le Grand—as he's now dubbed himself—built himself a new château outside of Paris, at a place called Versailles," Aaron de la Vega had told her, during one of their meetings in Amsterdam's narrow and crowded Jewish quarter—which, by coincidence, happened to be built up against the Opera House. "He has moved his entire court to the new place."

"I'd heard as much, but I didn't believe it," Gomer Bolstrood had said, looking more at home among Jews than he ever had among Englishmen. "To move so many people out of Paris—it seems insane."

"On the contrary—it is a master-stroke," de la Vega had said. "You know the Greek myth of Antaeus? For the French nobility, Paris is like the Mother Earth—as long as they are ensconced there, they have power, information, money. But Louis, by forcing them to move to Versailles, is like Hercules, who mastered Antaeus by raising him off the ground and slowly strangling him into submission."

"A pretty similitude," Eliza had said, "but what does it have to do with our putting a short squeeze on Mr. Sluys?"

De la Vega had permitted himself a smile, and looked over at Bolstrood. But Gomer had not been in a grinning mood. "Sluys is one of those rich Dutchmen who craves the approval of Frenchmen. He has been cultivating them since before the 1672 war—mostly without success, for they find him stupid and vulgar. But now it's different. The French nobles used to be able to live off their land, but now Louis forces them to keep a household in Versailles, as well as one in Paris, and to go about in coaches, finely dressed and wigged—"

"The wretches are desperate for lucre," Gomer Bolstrood had said.

* * *

AT THE OPERA, before the door to Sluys's box, Eliza said, "You mean, monsieur, the sort of French nobleman who's not content with the old ways, and likes to play the markets in Amsterdam, so he can afford a coach and a mistress?"

"You will spoil me, mademoiselle," d'Avaux said, "for how can I return to the common sort of female—stupid and ignorant—after I have conversed with you? Yes, normally Sluys's box would be *stuffed* with *that* sort of French nobleman. But *tonight* he is entertaining a young man who came by his endowment *properly*."

"Meaning—?"

"Inherited it—or is going to—from his father, the Duc d'Arcachon."

"Would it be vulgar for me to ask how the Duc d'Arcachon got it?"

"Colbert built our Navy from twenty vessels to three hundred. The Duc d'Arcachon is Admiral of that Navy—and was responsible for much of the building."

The floor around Mr. Sluys's chair was strewn with wadded scraps. Eliza would have loved to smooth some out and read them, but his hard jollity, and the way he was pouring champagne, told her that the evening's trading was going well for him, or so he imagined. "Jews don't go to the Opera—it is against their religion! What a show de la Vega has missed tonight!"

"'Thou shalt not attend the Opera . . . ' Is that in Exodus, or Deuteronomy?" Eliza inquired.

D'Avaux—who seemed uncharacteristically nervous, all of a sudden—took Eliza's remark as a witticism, and produced a smile as thin and dry as parchment. Mr. Sluys took it as stupidity, and got sexually aroused. "De la Vega is still selling V.O.C. stock short! He'll be doing it all night long—until he hears the news tomorrow morning, and gets word to his brokers to stop!" Sluys seemed almost outraged to be making money so easily.

Now Mr. Sluys looked as if he would've been content to drink champagne and gaze 'pon Eliza's navel until any number of fat ladies sang (which actually would not have been long in coming), but some sort of very rude commotion, originating from this very box, forced him to glance aside. Eliza turned to see that young French nobleman—the son of the Duc d'Arcachon—at the railing of the box, where he was being hugged, passionately and perhaps even a little violently, by a bald man with a bloody nose.

Eliza's dear Mum had always taught her that it wasn't polite to stare, but she couldn't help herself. Thus, she took in that the young Arcachon had actually flung one of his legs over the railing, as if he were trying to vault out into empty space. A large and rather good wig balanced precariously on the same rail. Eliza stepped forward and snatched it. It was unmistakably the periwig of Jean Antoine de Mesmes, comte d'Avaux, who must, therefore, be the bald fellow wrestling young Arcachon back from the brink of suicide.

D'Avaux—demonstrating a weird strength for such a refined man—finally slammed the other back into a chair, and had the good grace to so choreograph it that he ended up down on both knees. He pulled a lace hanky from a pocket and stuffed it up under his nose to stanch the blood, then spoke through it, heatedly but respectfully, to the young nobleman, who had covered his face with his hands. From time to time he darted a look at Eliza.

"Has the young Arcachon been selling V.O.C. stock short?" she inquired of Mr. Sluys.

"On the contrary, mademoiselle—"

"Oh, I forgot. He's not the sort who dabbles in markets. But why else would a French duke's son visit Amsterdam?"

Sluys got a look as if something were lodged in his throat.

"Never mind," Eliza said airily, "I'm sure it is *frightfully* complicated—and I'm no good at such things."

Sluys relaxed.

"I was only wondering why he tried to kill himself— assuming that's what he was doing?"

"Étienne d'Arcachon is the politest man in France," Sluys said ominously.

"Hmmph. You'd never know!"

"Sssh!" Sluys made frantic tiny motions with the flesh shovels of his hands.

"Mr. Sluys! Do you mean to imply that this spectacle has something to do with *my* presence in your box?"

Finally Sluys was on his feet. He was rather drunk and very heavy, and stood bent over with one hand gripping the box's railing. "It would help if you'd confide in me that, if Étienne d'Arcachon slays himself in your presence, you'll take offense."

"Mr. Sluys, watching him commit suicide would ruin my evening!"

"Very well. Thank you, mademoiselle. I am in your debt *enormously.*"

"Mr. Sluys—you have no idea."

IT LED TO HUSHED INTRIGUES in dim corners, palmed messages, raised eyebrows, and subtle gestures by candle-light, continuing all through the final acts of the opera—which was fortunate, because the opera was very dull.

Then, somehow, d'Avaux arranged to share a coach with Eliza and Monmouth. As they jounced, heaved, and clattered down various dark canal-edges and over diverse drawbridges, he explained: "It was Sluys's box. Therefore, he was the host. Therefore, it was his responsibility to make a formal introduction of Étienne d'Arcachon to you, mademoiselle. But he was too Dutch, drunk, and distracted to perform his proper rôle. I never cleared my throat so many times—but to no avail. Monsieur d'Arcachon was placed in an *impossible* situation!"

"So he tried to take his own life?"

"It was the only honourable course," d'Avaux said simply.

"He is the politest man in France," Monmouth added.

"You saved the day," d'Avaux said.

"Oh, that—'twas Mr. Sluys's suggestion."

D'Avaux looked vaguely nauseated at the mere mention of Sluys. "He has much to answer for. This *soirée* had better be *charmante.*"

* * *

AARON DE LA VEGA, who was assuredly *not* going to a party tonight, treated balance-sheets and V.O.C. shares as a scholar would old books and parchments—which is to say that Eliza found him sober and serious to a fault. But he could be merry about a few things, and one of them was Mr. Sluys's house—or rather his widening collection of them. For as the first one had pulled its neighbors downwards, skewing them into parallelograms, popping window-panes out of their frames, and imprisoning doors in their jambs, Mr. Sluys had been forced to buy them out. He owned five houses in a row now, and could afford to, as long as he was managing the assets of half the population of Versailles. The one in the middle, where Mr. Sluys kept his secret hoard of lead and guilt, was at least a foot lower than it had been in 1672, and Aaron de la Vega liked to pun about it in his native language, saying it was "*embarazada*," which meant "pregnant."

As the Duke of Monmouth handed Eliza down from the carriage in front of that house, she thought it was apt. For— especially when Mr. Sluys was burning thousands of candles at once, as he was tonight, and the light was blazing from all those conspicuously skewed window-frames—hiding the secret was like a woman seven months pregnant trying to conceal her condition with clever tailoring.

Men and women in Parisian fashions were entering the pregnant house in what almost amounted to a continuous queue. Mr. Sluys—belatedly warming to his rôle as host— was stationed just inside the door, mopping sweat from his brow every few seconds, as if secretly terrified that the added weight of so many guests would finally drive his house straight down into the mud, like a stake struck with a maul.

But when Eliza got into the place, and suffered Mr. Sluys to kiss her hand, and made a turn round the floor, gaily ig- noring the venomous stares of pudgy Dutch churchwives and overdressed Frenchwomen—she could see clear signs that Mr. Sluys had brought in mining-engineers, or something, to shore the house up. For the beams that crisscrossed the ceiling, though hidden under festoons and garlands of Barock plasterwork, were uncommonly huge, and the pillars that rose up to support the ends of those beams, though fluted and capitalled like those of a Roman temple, were the size of mainmasts. Still she thought she could detect a pregnant convexity about the ceiling . . .

"Don't come out and say you want to buy lead—tell him only that you want to lighten his burdens—better yet, that you wish to transfer them, forcefully, onto the shoulders of the Turks. Or something along those lines," she said, distractedly, into Monmouth's ear as the first galliard was drawing to a close. He stalked away in a bit of a huff—but he was moving towards Sluys, anyway. Eliza regretted—briefly—that she'd insulted his intelligence, or at least his breeding. But she was too beset by sudden worries to consider his feelings. The house, for all its plaster and candles, reminded her of nothing so much as the Doctor's mine, deep beneath the Harz: a hole in the earth, full of metal, prevented from collapsing in on itself solely by cleverness and continual shoring-up.

Weight could be transferred from lead to floor-boards, and thence into joists, and thence into beams, and from beams into pillars, then down into footings, and thence into log piles whose strength derived from the "stick" (as Dutchmen called it) between them and the mud they'd been hammered into. The final settling of accounts was there: if the "stick" sufficed, the structure above it was a building, and if it didn't, it was a gradual avalanche . . .

"It is very curious, mademoiselle, that the chilly winds of the Hague were balmy breezes to you—yet in this warm room, you alone clutch your arms, and have goosebumps."

"Chilly thoughts, Monsieur d'Avaux."

"And no wonder—your beau is about to leave for Hungary. You need to make some new friends—ones who live in warmer climes, perhaps?"

No. Madness. I belong here. Even Jack, who loves me, said so.

From a corner of the room, clouded with men and pipe-smoke, a trumpeting laugh from Mr. Sluys. Eliza glanced over that way and saw Monmouth plying him—probably reciting the very sentences she'd composed for him. Sluys was giddy with hope that he could get rid of his burden, frantic with anxiety that it might not happen. Meanwhile the market was in violent motion all over Amsterdam as Aaron de la Vega sold the V.O.C. short. It would all lead to an invasion of England. Everything had gone fluid tonight. This was no time to stand still.

A man danced by with an ostrich-plume in his hat, and she thought of Jack. Riding across Germany with him, she'd had nought but her plumes, and his sword, and their wits—yet she'd felt safer then than she did now. What would it take to feel safe again?

"Friends in warm places are lovely to have," Eliza said distractedly, "but there is no one here who would have me, monsieur. You know very well that I am not of noble, or even gentle, birth—I'm too exotic for the Dutch, too common for the French."

"The King's mistress was born a *slave*," d'Avaux said. "Now she is a Marquise. You see, nothing matters *there* save wit and beauty."

"But wit fails and beauty fades, and I don't wish to be a house on piles, sinking into the bog a little each day," Eliza said. "Somewhere I must *stick*. I must have a foundation that does not always move."

"Where on this earth can such a miracle be found?"

"Money," Eliza said. "Here, I can make money."

"And yet this money you speak of is but a chimæra—a figment of the collective imagination of a few thousand Jews and rabble bellowing at one another out on the Dam."

"But in the end I may convert it—bit by bit—into gold."

"Is *that* all you want? Remember, mademoiselle, that gold only has value because some people say it does. Let me tell you a bit of recent history: My King went to a place called Orange—you've heard of it?"

"A principality in the south of France, near Avignon—William's fiefdom, as I understand it."

"My King went to this Orange, this little family heirloom of Prince William, three years ago. Despite William's pretensions of martial glory, my King was able to walk in without a battle. He went for a stroll atop the fortifications. *Le Roi* paused, there along a stone battlement, and plucked out a tiny fragment of loose masonry—no larger than your little finger, mademoiselle—and tossed it onto the ground. Then he walked away. Within a few days, all the walls and fortifications of Orange had been pulled down by *le Roi*'s regiments, and Orange had been absorbed into France, as easily as Mr. Sluys over there might swallow a bit of ripe fruit."

"What is the point of the story, Monsieur, other than to explain why Amsterdam is crowded with Orangish refugees, and why William hates your King so much?"

"Tomorrow, *le Roi* might pick up a bit of Gouda cheese and throw it to his dogs."

"Amsterdam would fall, you are saying, and my hard-earned gold would be loot for some drunken regiment."

"Your gold—and you, mademoiselle."

"I understand such matters far better than you imagine, monsieur. What I do *not* understand is why you pretend to be interested in what happens to me. In the Hague, you saw me as a pretty girl who could skate, and who would therefore catch Monmouth's eye, and make Mary unhappy, and create strife in William's house. And it all came to pass just as you intended. But what can I do for you *now*?"

"Live a beautiful and interesting life—and, from time to time, talk to me."

Eliza laughed out loud, lustily, drawing glares from women who never laughed that way, or at all. "You want me to be your spy."

"No, mademoiselle. I want you to be my friend." D'Avaux said this simply and almost sadly, and it caught Eliza up short. In that moment, d'Avaux spun smartly on the balls of his feet and trapped Eliza's arm. She had little choice but to walk with him—and soon it became obvious that they were walking directly towards Étienne d'Arcachon. In the dimmest and smokiest corner of the room, meanwhile, Mr. Sluys kept laughing and laughing.

Paris

SPRING 1685

✣

Thou hast met with something (as I perceive) already; for I see the dirt of the Slough of Despond is upon thee; but that Slough is the beginning of the sorrows that do attend those that go on in that way; hear me, I am older than thou!

—JOHN BUNYAN, *The Pilgrim's Progress*

JACK WAS BURIED up to his neck in the steaming manure of the white, pink-eyed horses of the duc d'Arcachon, trying not to squirm as a contingent of perhaps half a dozen maggots cleaned away the dead skin and flesh surrounding the wound in his thigh. This itched, but did not hurt, beyond the normal wholesome throbbing. Jack had no idea how many days he'd been in here, but from listening to the bells of Paris, and watching small disks of sunlight prowl around the stable, he guessed it might be five in the afternoon. He heard boots approaching, and a pad-lock negotiating with its key. If that lock were the only thing holding him in this stable, he would've escaped long ago; but as it was, Jack was chained by the neck to a pillar of white stone, with a few yards of slack so that he could, for example, bury himself in manure.

The bolt shot and John Churchill stepped in on a tongue

of light. In contrast to Jack, he was *not* covered in shit—far from it! He was wearing a jeweled turban of shimmering gold cloth, and robes, with lots of costume jewelry; old scuffed boots, and a large number of weapons, viz. scimitar, pistols, and several granadoes. His first words were: "Shut up, Jack, I'm going to a fancy-dress ball."

"Where's Turk?"

"I stabled him," Churchill said, pointing with his eyes toward an adjacent stable. The duc had several stables, of which this was the smallest and meanest, and used only for shoeing horses.

"So the ball you mean to attend is *here*."

"At the Hotel d'Arcachon, yes."

"What're you supposed to be—a Turk? Or a Barbary Corsair?"

"Do I look like a Turk?" Churchill asked hopefully. "I understand you have personal knowledge of them—"

"No. Better say you're a Pirate."

"A breed of which *I* have personal knowledge."

"Well, if you hadn't fucked the King's mistress, he wouldn't have sent you to Africa."

"Well, I *did,* and *he* did—send me there, I mean—and I came back."

"And now he's dead. And you and the duc d'Arcachon have something to talk about."

"What is that supposed to mean?" Churchill asked darkly.

"Both of you have been in contact with the Barbary Pirates—that's all I meant."

Churchill was taken aback—a small pleasure and an insignificant victory for Jack. "You are well-informed," he said. "I should like to know whether *everyone in the world* knows of the duc d'Arcachon's intercourse with Barbary, or is it just that you are special?"

"Am I, then?"

"They say *l'Emmerdeur* is King of the Vagabonds."

"Then why didn't the duc put me up in his finest apartment?"

"Because I have gone to such extravagant lengths to prevent him from knowing who you are."

"So *that's* why I'm still alive. I was wondering."

"If they knew, they would tear you apart with iron tongs, over the course of several days, at the Place Dauphine."

"No better place for it—lovely view from there."

"Is that all you have for me, in the way of thanks?"

Silence. Gates were creaking open all round the Hotel d'Arcachon as it mobilized for the ball. Jack heard the hollow grumbling of barrels being rolled across stone courtyards, and (since his nose had stopped being able to smell shit) he could smell birds roasting, and buttery pastries baking in ovens. There were less agreeable odors, too, but Jack's nose sought out the good ones.

"You could at least answer my question," Churchill said. "Does everyone know that the duc has frequent dealings with Barbary?"

"Some small favor would be appropriate at this point," Jack said.

"I can't let you go."

"I was thinking of a pipe."

"Funny, so was I." Churchill went to the stable door and flagged down a boy and demanded *des pipes en terre* and *du tabac blond* and *du feu.*

"Is King Looie coming to the duc's fancy-dress ball, too?"

"So it is rumored—he has been preparing a costume in great secrecy, out at Versailles. Said to be of a radically shocking nature. *Impossibly* daring. All the French ladies are aflutter."

"Aren't they *always?*"

"I wouldn't know—I've taken a sound, some would say stern, English bride: Sarah."

"What's *she* coming as? A nun?"

"Oh, she's back in London. This is a diplomatic mission. Secret."

"You stand before me, dressed as you are, and say that?"

Churchill laughed.

"You take me for an imbecile?" Jack continued. The pain in his leg was most annoying, and shaking away flies had given his neck a cramp, as well as raw sores from the abrasion of his iron collar.

"You are only *alive* because of your recent imbecility, Jack. *L'Emmerdeur* is known to be clever as a fox. What you did was so stupid that it has not occurred to anyone, yet, that you could be he."

"So, then . . . in France, what's considered suitable punishment for an imbecile who does something stupid?"

"Well, naturally they were going to kill you. But I seem to have convinced them that, as you are not only a rural half-wit, but an *English* rural half-wit, the whole matter is actually *funny*."

"Funny? Not likely."

"The duc de Bourbon hosted a dinner party. Invited a certain eminent writer. Became annoyed with him. Emptied his snuff-box into the poor scribbler's wine when he wasn't looking, as a joke. The writer drank the wine and died of it—hilarious!"

"What fool would drink wine mixed with snuff?"

"That's not the point of the story—it's about what French nobility do, and don't, consider to be funny—and how I saved your life. Pay attention!"

"Let's set aside *how,* and ask: *why* did you save my life, guv'nor?"

"When a man is being torn apart with pliers, there's no telling what he'll blurt out."

"Aha."

"The last time I saw you, you were ordinary Vagabond scum. If there happened to be an old connexion between the two of us, it scarcely mattered. *Now* you are *legendary* Vagabond scum, a picaroon, much talked of in salons. *Now* if the old link between us came to be widely known, it would be inconvenient for me."

"But you *could* have let that other fellow run me through with his rapier."

"And probably *should* have," Churchill said ruefully, "but

I wasn't thinking. It is very odd. I saw him lunging for you. If I had only stood clear and allowed matters to take their natural course, you'd be dead. But some impulse took me—"

"The Imp of the Perverse, like?"

"Your old companion? Yes, perhaps he leapt from your shoulder to mine. Like a perfect imbecile, I saved your life."

"Well, you make a most splendid and gallant perfect imbecile. Are you going to kill me now?"

"Not directly. You are now a *galérien*. Your group departs for Marseille tomorrow morning. It's a bit of a walk."

"I know it."

Churchill sat on a bench and worried off one boot, then the other, then reached into them and pulled out the fancy Turkish slippers that had become lodged inside, and drew the slippers on. Then he threw the boots at Jack and they lodged in the manure, temporarily scaring away the flies. At about the same time, a stable-boy came in carrying two pipes stuffed with tobacco, and a taper, and soon both men were puffing away contentedly.

"I learned of the duc's Barbary connexions through an escaped slave, who seems to consider the information part of a closely guarded personal secret," Jack said finally.

"Thank you," said Churchill. "How's the leg, then?"

"Someone seems to've poked it with a sword . . . otherwise fine."

"Might need something to lean on." Churchill stepped outside the door for a moment, then returned carrying Jack's crutch. He held it crosswise between his two hands for a moment, weighing it. "Seems a bit *heavy* on this end—a *foreign* sort of crutch, is it?"

"Exceedingly foreign."

"Turkish?"

"Don't toy with me, Churchill."

Churchill spun the crutch around and chucked it like a spear so that it stuck in the manure-pile. "Whatever you're going to do, do it *soon* and then get the hell out of France. The road to Marseille will take you, in a day or two, through the *pays* of the Count of Joigny."

"Who's that?"

"That's the fellow you knocked off his horse. Notwithstanding my earlier reassuring statements, he *does not* find you amusing—if you enter his territory . . ."

"Pliers."

"Just so. Now, as insurance, I have a good friend lodging at an inn just to the north of Joigny. He is to keep an eye on the road to Marseille, and if he sees you marching down it, he is to make sure that you never get past that inn alive."

"How's he going to recognize me?"

"By that point, you'll be starkers—exposing your most distinctive feature."

"You really *are* worried I'll make trouble for you."

"I told you I'm here on a diplomatic mission. It is important."

"Trying to work out how England is to be divvied up between Leroy and the Pope of Rome?"

Churchill puffed on his pipe a few times in a fine, but not altogether convincing, display of calmness, and then said, "I *knew* we'd reach this point in the conversation, Jack—the point where you accused me of being a traitor to my country and my religion—and so I'm ready for it, and I'm actually *not* going to cut your head off."

Jack laughed. His leg hurt a great deal, and it itched, too.

"Through no volition of my own, I have for many years been a member of His Majesty's household," Churchill began. Jack was confused by this until he recollected that "His Majesty" no longer meant Charles II, but James II, the whilom Duke of York. Churchill continued: "I suppose I could reveal to you my innermost thoughts about what it's like to be a Protestant patriot in thrall to a Catholic King who loves France, but life is short, and I intend to spend as little of it as possible standing in dark stables apologizing to shit-covered Vagabonds. Suffice it to say that it's better for England if *I* do this mission."

"Suppose I do get away, before Joigny . . . what's to prevent me from telling everyone about the longstanding connexions between the Shaftoes and the Churchills?"

"No one of Quality will ever believe a word you say, Jack, unless you say it while you are being expertly tortured . . . it's only when you are stretched out on some important person's rack that you are dangerous. Besides, there is the Shaftoe legacy to think of." Churchill pulled out a little purse and jiggled it to make the coins ring.

"I *did* notice that you'd taken possession of my charger, without *paying* for it. Very bad form."

"The price in here is a fair one—a handsome sum, even," Churchill said. Then he pocketed the purse.

"Oh, come on—!"

"A naked *galérien* can't carry a purse, and these French coins are too big to stuff up even *your* asshole, Jack. I'll make sure your spawn get the benefit of this, when I'm back in England."

"Get *it,* or get *the benefit of* it? Because there is a slipperiness in those words that troubles me."

Churchill laughed again, this time with a cheerfulness that really made Jack want to kill him. He got up and plucked the empty pipe from Jack's mouth, and—as stables were notoriously inflammable, and he did not wish to be guilty of having set fire to the duc's—went over to the little horseshoe-forge, now cold and dark, and whacked the ashes out of the pipes. "Try to concentrate. You're a galley slave chained to a post in a stable in Paris. Be troubled by *that.* Bon voyage, Jack."

Exit Churchill. Jack had been meaning to advise him not to sleep with any of those French ladies, and to tell him about the Turkish innovation involving sheep-intestines, but there hadn't been time—and besides, who was he to give John Churchill advice on fucking?

Equipped now with boots, a sword, and (if he could just reach it, and slay a few stable-boys) a horse, Jack began considering how to get the damned chain off his neck. It was a conventional slave-collar: two iron semicircles hinged together on one side and with a sort of hasp on the other, consisting of two loops that would align with each other when the collar was closed. If a chain was then threaded through the loops, it would prevent the collar from opening. This made it possible for a single length of chain to secure as many collars, and hence slaves, as could be threaded onto it, without the need for expensive and unreliable padlocks. It kept the ironmongery budget to a minimum and worked so handily that no French Château or German Schloss was without a few, hanging on a wall-peg just in case some persons needed enslaving.

The particular chain that went through Jack's collar-hasp had a circular loop—a single oversized link—welded to one end. The chain had been passed around the stone pillar and its narrow end threaded through this loop, then through Jack's collar, and finally one of the duc's smiths had heated up the chain-end in the stable's built-in forge, and hammered an old worn-out horseshoe onto it, so it could not be withdrawn. Typical French extravagance! But the duc had an infinite fund of slaves and servants, so it cost him nothing, and there was no way for Jack to get it off.

The tobacco-embers from the pipes had formed a little mound on the blackened hearth of the forge and were still glowing, just barely. Jack squirmed free of the manure-pile and limped over to the forge and blew on them to keep them alive.

Normally this whole place was swarming with stable-boys, but now, and for the next hour or two, they'd be busy with ball duty: taking the horses of the arriving guests and leading them to stalls in the duc's better stables. So a fire in this hearth would be detectable only as a bit of smoke coming out of a chimney, which was not an unusual sight on a cool March evening in seventeenth-century Paris.

But he was getting ahead of himself. This was a long way from being a fire. Jack began looking about for some tinder. Straw would be perfect. But the stable-boys had been careful not to leave anything so tinderlike anywhere near the forge. It was all piled at the opposite end of the stable, and Jack's chain wouldn't let him go that far. He tried lying flat on the floor, with the chain stretched out taut behind him, and reaching out with the crutch to rake some straw towards him.

But the end of the crutch came a full yard short of the goal. He scurried back and blew on the tobacco some more. It would not last much longer.

His attention had been drawn to the crutch, which was bound together with a lot of the cheapest sort of dry, fuzzy twine. Perfect tinder. But he'd have to burn most of it, and then he'd have no way to hold the crutch together, and therefore to conceal the existence of the sword—so, if the attempt failed tonight, he was doomed. In that sense 'twere safer to wait until tomorrow, when they'd take the chain off of him. But only to chain him up, he supposed, to a whole file of other *galériens*—doddering Huguenots, most likely. And he wasn't about to wait for *that*. He must do it now.

So he unwound the crutch and frizzed the ends of the twine and put it to the last mote of red fire in the pipe-ashes, and blew. The flame almost died, but then one fiber of twine warped back, withered, flung off a little shroud of steam or smoke, then became a pulse of orange light: a tiny thing, but as big in Jack's vision as whole trees bursting into flames in the Harz.

After some more blowing and fidgeting he had a morsel of yellow flame on the hearth. While supplying it more twine with one hand, he rummaged blindly for kindling, which ought to be piled up somewhere. Finding only a few twigs, he was forced to draw the sword and shave splints off the crutch-pole. This didn't last long, and soon he was planing splinters off pillars and beams, and chopping up benches and stools. But finally it was big and hot enough to ignite coal, of which there was plenty. Jack began tossing handfuls of it into his little fire while pumping the bellows with the other hand. At first it just lay in the fire like black stones, but then the sharp, brimstony smell of it came into the stable, and the fire became white, and the heat of the coal annihilated the remaining wood-scraps, and the fire became a meteor imprisoned in a chain—for Jack had looped the middle part of his chain around it. The cold iron poisoned the fire, sucked life from it, but Jack heaped on more coal and worked the bellows, and soon the metal had taken on a chestnut color which gave way to various shades of red. The heat of the blaze first dried the moist shit that was all over Jack's skin and then made him sweat, so that crusts of dung were flaking off of him.

The door opened. *"Où est le maréchal-ferrant?"* someone asked.

The door opened *wider*—wide enough to admit a horse—then did just that. The horse was led by a Scot in a tall wig—or maybe *not*. He was wearing a kiltlike number, but it was made of red *satin* and he had some sort of ridiculous contrivance slung over one shoulder: a whole pigskin, sewn up and packed with straw to make it look as if it had been inflated, with trumpet-horns, flutes, and pennywhistles dangling from it: a caricature of a bagpipe. His face was painted with blue woad. Pinned to the top of his wig was a tam-o'-shanter with an approximate diameter of three feet, and thrust into his belt, where a gentleman would sheathe his sword, was a sledgehammer. Next to that, several whiskey-jugs holstered.

The horse was a prancing beauty, but it seemed to be favoring one leg—it had thrown a shoe on the ride over.

"Maréchal-ferrant?" the man repeated, squinting in his direction. Jack reckoned that he, Jack, was visible only as a silhouette against the bright fire, and so the collar might not be obvious. He cupped a hand to his ear—smiths were notorious for deafness. That seemed to answer the question—the "Scot" led his horse toward the forge, nattering on about a *fer à cheval* and going so far as to check his pocket-watch. Jack was irritated. *Fer* meant "iron," *fer à cheval* as he knew perfectly well meant "horseshoe." But he had just understood that the English word "farrier" must be derived somehow from this—even though "horseshoe" was completely different. He was aware, vaguely—from watching certain historical dramas, and then from roaming round *la France* listening to people talk—that French people had conquered England at least one time, and thereby confused the English language with all sorts of words such as "farrier," and "mutton," which common folk now used all the time without

knowing that they were speaking the tongue of the conquerors. Meanwhile, the damned French had a tidy and proper tongue in which, for example, the name of the fellow who put shoes on horses was clearly related to the word for horseshoe. Made his blood boil—and now that James was King, Katie bar the door!

"Quelle heure est-il?" Jack finally inquired. The "Scot" without pausing to wonder why a *maréchal-ferrant* would need to know the time went once again into the ceremony of withdrawing his pocket-watch, getting the lid open, and reading it. In order to do this he had to turn its face towards the fire, and then he had to twist himself around so that he could see it. Jack waited patiently for this to occur, and then just as the "Scot" was lisping out something involving *sept* Jack whipped the chain out of the fire and got it round his neck.

It was stranglin' time in gay Paree. Most awkwardly, the red-hot part of the chain ended up around the throat of the "Scot," so Jack could not get a grip on it without first rummaging in the tool-box for some tongs. But it had already done enough damage, evidently, that the "Scot" could not make any noise.

His horse was another matter: it whinnied, and backed away, and showed signs of wanting to buck. That was a problem, but Jack had to take things one at a time here. He solved the tong problem and murdered the "Scot" in a great sizzling cloud of grilled neck-flesh—which, he felt sure, must be a delicacy in some part of France. Then he peeled the hot chain off, taking some neck parts with it, and tossed it back into the fire. Having settled these matters, he turned his attention—somewhat reluctantly—to the horse. He was dreading that it might have run out through the open stable doors and drawn attention to itself in the stable-yard beyond. But—oddly—the stable-doors were now *closed,* and were being bolted shut, by a slender young man in an assortment of not very good clothes. He had evidently seized the horse's reins and tied them to a post, and had the presence of mind to toss a grain-sack over its head so that it could not see any more of the disturbing sights that were now so abundant in this place.

Having seen to these matters, the gypsy boy—it was certainly a gypsy—turned to face Jack, and made a somber, formal little bow. He was barefoot—had probably gotten here by clambering over rooftops.

"You must be Half-Cocked Jack," he said, as if this weren't funny. Speaking in the zargon.

"Who are you?"

"It does not matter. St.-George sent me." The boy came over, stepping carefully around the glowing coals that had been scattered on the floor when Jack had whipped out the chain, and began to work the bellows.

"What did St.-George tell you to do?" asked Jack, throwing on more coal.

"To see what kind of help you would need, during the entertainment."

"What entertainment would that be?"

"He did not tell me *everything*."

"Why should St.-George care so much?"

"St.-George is angry with you. He says you have shown poor form."

"What are you going to tell him?"

"I will tell him," the gypsy boy said, and here he smiled for the first time, "that *l'Emmerdeur* does not need his help."

"That's just it," Jack said, and grabbed the bellows-handle. The boy turned and ran across the stable and vanished through an opening up in the eaves that Jack hadn't known was there.

While the chain heated, Jack amused himself by going through his victim's clothing and trying to guess how many gold coins were in his purse. After a couple of minutes (by the pocket-watch, which lay open on the floor) Jack reached into the fire with the tongs and drew out a length of yellow-hot chain. Before it could cool he draped it across an anvil, then smashed it with a heavy chisel-pointed hammer, and then he was free. Except that a yard of hot chain still dangled from his neck, and he could not pull it through his neck-loop without burning himself. So he quenched it in a trough of water. But then he found that in breaking it he'd smashed the last link, and broadened it, so it would no longer pass through the neck-loop. He did not want to spend the time to heat the chain back up, so he was stuck with the collar, and an arm's length of chain, for now. No matter, really. It was dark outside, he would be seen only as a silhouette, and he needed only that it be a respectable type of silhouette—a shape that people would not discharge weapons at without thinking twice. So he yanked the wig (now wrecked and burnt, but still a wig) off the dead "Scot" and put it on—discarding, however, the unwieldy tam-o'-shanter. He pulled on the boots that John Churchill had donated, and took the long cape that the "Scot" had been wearing. Also his gloves—an old habit to cover the V branded on his thumb. Finally he pilfered the saddle from the horse—it was a magnificent saddle—and carried it out into the stable-yard.

The sight of a supposed Person of Quality toting his own saddle was anomalous, and even if it weren't, Jack's dragging one leg, brandishing a scimitar, and muttering out loud in vulgar English also cast uncertainty on his status as a French nobleman. But, as he'd hoped, most of the stable-boys were busy in the main courtyard. The guests were now arriving in force. He barged into the next stable, which was dimly lit by a couple of lanterns, and came face-to-face with a stable-boy who, in an instant, became the most profoundly confused person Jack had ever seen.

"Turk!" Jack called, and was answered by a whinny from several stalls down the line. Jack sidled closer to the stable-boy and allowed the saddle to slide off his shoulders. The boy caught it out of habit, and seemed relieved to have been given a specific job. Then Jack, using his sword as a pointing-device, got him moving in the direction of Turk.

The boy now understood that he was being asked to help steal a horse, and stiffened up in a way that was almost penile. It took no end of prodding to get him to heave the saddle onto Turk's back. Then Jack socked him in the chin with the guard of the sword, but failed to knock him out. In the end, he had to drag the fool over to a convenient place by the

entrance and push him down and practically draw him a picture of how to go about pretending he'd been surprised and
knocked unconscious by the English villain.

Then back to Turk, who seemed pleased to see him. As
Jack tightened the girth, and made other adjustments, the
war-horse's sinews became taut and vibrant, like the strings
of a lute being tuned up. Jack checked his hooves and noted
that Churchill had gotten some expert *maréchal-ferrant* to
shoe him. "You and me both," Jack said, slapping his new
boots so that the horse could admire them.

Then he put one of those boots into a stirrup, threw his leg
over the saddle, and was hurtling across the duc's stable-
yard before he could even get himself situated properly.
Turk wanted out of here as badly as *he* did. Jack had intended to look for a back exit, but Turk was having none of
that, and took him *out* the way Churchill had ridden him *in:*
straight through a gate into what Jack reckoned must be the
main courtyard of the Hôtel d'Arcachon.

Jack sensed quite a few people, but couldn't really see
them because he was dazzled by all of the light: giant
torchières like bonfires on pikes, and lanterns strung on colored ropes, and the light of thousands of lanterns and tapers
blasting out through the twenty-foot-high windows that con-
stituted most of the front wall of a large noble House directly in front of him. A hundred sperm whales must have
given up their bodily fluids to light the lanterns. And as for
the tapers in those chandeliers, why, even over the smells of
cuisine, fashionable perfume, wood-smoke, and horse-
manure, Jack's nose could detect the fragrance of honey-
scented Mauritanian beeswax. All of this sweet-smelling
radiance glanced wetly off a large fountain planted in the
middle of the court: various Neptunes and Naiads and sea
monsters and dolphins cleverly enwrithed to form a support
for a naval frigate all speckled with fleurs-de-lis. Wreckage
of Dutch and English ships washed up on shores all around,
forming benches for French people to put their buttocks on.

The force of the light, and Jack's hauling back on the
reins, had taken the edge off of Turk's impetuous charge for

the exit, but not quite soon enough: the fact remained that
Turk, and thus Jack, had effectively burst into the courtyard
at a near-gallop and then stood agape for several seconds, almost as if *demanding* to be noticed. And they *had* been: little knots of Puritans, Færy-Queens, Persians, and Red
Indians were looking at them. Jack gave the war-horse an encouraging nudge, while holding fast to the reins so he
wouldn't bolt.

Turk began following a groomed gravel path among
flower-beds, which Jack hoped would take them round the
fountain eventually and to a place where they could at least
see the way out. But they were moving directly toward the
light rushing from those banks of windows. Through them
Jack saw an immense ballroom, with white walls garlanded
with gold, and white polished marble floors where the nobility, in their fancy-dress, were dancing to music from a consort stuffed into a corner.

Then—like anyone else coming towards a grand party—
Jack glanced down at his own person. He had been counting
on darkness, but had blundered into light, and was shocked
at how clearly his shit-covered rags and neck-iron stood out.

He saw a man inside who'd been in the duc's entourage
the other day. Not wanting to be recognized, Jack turned up
the collar of the stolen cape, and drew it round to conceal the
bottom half of his face.

A few small clusters of party-goers had formed in the
lawn between the front of the house and the fountain, and *all*
conversation had been suspended so that all faces could turn
to stare at Jack. But they did not raise a hue and cry. They
stared for a remarkably long time, as if Jack were a new and
extremely expensive sculpture that had just been unveiled.
Then Jack sensed a contagious thrill, a *frisson* like the one
that had run through the fishmarket at Les Halles when he'd
galloped through it. There was a strange pattering noise. He
realized they were *applauding* him. A serving-girl flashed
away into the ballroom, hitching up her skirts as she ran, to
spread some news. The musicians stopped playing, all faces
turned to the windows. The people on the lawn had con-

verged toward Jack, while maintaining a certain respectful distance, and were bowing and curtseying, very low. A pair of footmen practically sprawled out onto the grass in their anxiety to hurl the front doors open. Framed in the arch was a porky gentleman armed with a long Trident, which naturally made Jack flinch when he saw it—this fellow, Jack suspected, was the duc d'Arcachon, dressed up as Neptune. But then the duc held the weapon out towards him, resting crossways on his outstretched hands—*offering* it to Jack. Neptune then backed out of the way, still doubled over in a deep bow, and beckoned him into the ballroom. Inside, the party-goers had formed up in what he instinctively recognized as a gauntlet to whip all the skin off his back—but then understood must actually be a pair of lines to *receive* him!

Everything seemed to point to that he was expected to ride into the ballroom on horseback, which was unthinkable. But Jack had become adept (or so he believed) at distinguishing things that were really happening from the waking dreams or phant'sies that came into his head more and more frequently of late, and, reckoning that this was one of the latter, he decided to enjoy it. Accordingly, he now rode Turk (who was extremely reluctant) right past the duc and into the ballroom. Now *everyone* bowed low, giving Jack the opportunity to look down a large number of white-powdered cleavages. A trumpeter played some sort of fanfare. One cleavage in particular Jack was afraid he might fall into and have to be winched out on a rope. The lady in question, noticing Jack's fixed stare, seemed to think that he was staring at least partly at the string of pearls around her neck. Something of a complicated nature occurred inside her head, and then she blushed and clasped both hands to her black-spotted face and squealed and said something to the effect of "No, no, please, not my jewels . . . Emmerdeur," and then she unclasped the pearls from behind her neck; clasped them back together into a loop; *threw* it over the point of Jack's sword, like a farm girl playing ring-toss at the fair; and then expertly swooned back into the waiting arms of her escort: a satyr with a two-foot-long red leather penis.

Another woman shrieked, and Jack raised his weapon in case he was going to have to kill her—but all he saw was another mademoiselle going into the same act—she ran up and pinned a jeweled brooch to the hem of his cloak, muttering *"pour les Invalides,"* then backed away curtseying before Jack could say what was on his mind, which was: *If you want to give this away to charity, lady, you came to the wrong bloke.*

Then they were *all* doing it, the thing was a sensation, the ladies were practically elbowing each other to get near and decorate Jack's clothes and his sword, and Turk's bridle, with jewelry. The only person *not* having a good time was a certain handsome young Barbary Pirate who stood at the back of the crowd, red-faced, staring at Jack with eyes that, had they been pliers . . .

A stillness now spread across the ballroom like a blast of frigid air from a door blown open by a storm. Everyone seemed to be looking toward the entrance. The ladies were backing away from Jack in hopes of getting a better view. Jack sat up straight in the saddle and got Turk turned around, partly to see what everyone else was staring at and partly because he had the sense it would soon be time to leave.

A *second* man had ridden into the ballroom on horseback. Jack identified him, at first, as a Vagabond recently escaped from captivity—no doubt well-deserved captivity. But of course it was really some nobleman *pretending* to be a Vagabond, and his costume was *much better* than Jack's—the chain around his neck, and the broken fetters on his wrists and ankles, appeared to've been forged out of *solid gold,* and he was brandishing a gaudy jeweled scimitar, and wearing a conspicuous, diamond-studded, but comically tiny codpiece. Behind him, out in the courtyard, was a whole entourage: Gypsies, jeweled and attired according to some extremely romantic conception of what it was to be a gypsy; ostrich-plume-wearing Moors; and fine ladies dressed up as bawdy Vagabond-wenches.

Jack allowed the cape to fall clear of his face.

There followed the longest period of silence that he had

ever known. It was so long that he could have tied Turk's reins to a candelabra and curled up under the harpsichord for a little nap. He could have run a message down to Lyons during this silence (and, in retrospect, probably *should* have). But instead he just sat there on his horse and waited for something to happen, and took in the scene.

Silence made him aware that the house was a hive of life and activity, even when all of the Persons of Quality were frozen up like statues. There was the normal dim clattering of the kitchen, for example. But his attention was drawn to the ceiling, which was (a) a hell of a thing to look at, and (b) making a great deal of noise—he thought perhaps a heavy rain had begun to thrash the roof, partly because of this scrabbling, rushing noise that was coming from it, and partly because it was leaking rather badly in a number of places. It had been decorated both with plaster relief-work and with paint, so that if you could lie on your back and stare at it you would see a vast naval Tableau: the gods of the four winds at the edges of the room, cheeks all puffed as they blew out billowy plaster clouds, and the Enemies of France angling in from various corners, viz. English and Dutch frigates riding the north wind, Spanish and Portuguese galleons the south, as well as pirates of Barbary and Malta and the Turk, and the occasional writhing sea-monster. Needless to say, the center was dominated by the French Navy in massive three-dimensional plasterwork, guns pointing every which way, and on the poop-deck of the mightiest ship, surrounded by spyglass-toting Admirals, stood a laurel-wreath-crowned Leroy, one hand fingering an astrolabe and the other resting on a cannon. And as if to add even greater realism, the entire scene was now running and drizzling, as if there really were an ocean up above it trying to break through and pay homage to the living King who had just rode in. From this alarming leakage, and from the rustling noise, Jack naturally suspected a sudden violent storm coming through a leaky roof. But when he looked out the windows into the courtyard he saw no rain. Besides (he remembered with some embarrassment), the Hôtel d'Arcachon was not some farmhouse, where the ceiling was merely the underside of the roof. Jack well knew, from having broken into a few places like this, that the ceiling was a thin shell of plaster troweled over horizontal lath-work, and that there would be a crawl space above it, sandwiched between ceiling and roof, with room for dull, dirty things like chandelier-hoists and perhaps cisterns.

That was it—there must be a cistern full of collected rainwater up there, which must have sprung a leak—in fact, had probably been encouraged to do so by St.-George or one of his friends, just to create a distraction that might be useful to Jack. The water must be gushing out across the top of the plaster-work, percolating down between the laths, saturating the plaster, which was darkening in several large irregular patches—gathering storm-clouds besetting the French Navy and darkening the sea from robin's-egg blue to a more realistic iron-gray. Gray, and heavy, and no longer flat and smooth—the ceiling was swelling and bulging downwards. In several places around the room, dirty water had begun to spatter down onto the floor. Servants were fetching mops and buckets, but dared not interrupt the Silence.

Turk complained of something, and Jack looked down to discover that the satyr with the very long, barbed, red leather penis had sidled up and grabbed Turk's bridle.

"That's an *incredibly* bad idea," Jack said in English (there was no point in even *trying* his French among *this* crowd). He said it *sotto voce,* not wanting to officially break the Silence, and indeed most people could not hear him over the odd scrabbling noises and muffled squeaks emanating from above. The squeaks might be the sound of lath-nails being wrenched out of old dry joists by the growing weight of the ceiling. Anyway, it was good that Jack glanced down, because he also noticed John Churchill striding round the back of the crowd, examining the flintlock mechanism on a pistol, very much in the manner of an experienced slayer of men who was looking forward to a moment soon when he'd fire the weapon. Jack didn't have a firearm, only a sword, freighted with jewelry at the moment. He shoved its tip through the satin lining of the riding-cloak, cutting a small gash, and then allowed all of the goods to avalanche into it.

The satyr responded in better English than Jack would ever speak: "It is a *dreadful* thing for me to have done—life is not long enough for me to make sufficient apologies. Please know that I have simply tried to make the best of an awkward—"

But then he was interrupted by King Louis XIV of France, who, in a mild yet room-filling voice, delivered some kind of witticism. It was only a sentence, or phrase, but it said more than any bishop's three-hour Easter homily. Jack could scarcely hear a word, and wouldn't've understood it anyway, but he caught the word Vagabond, and the word *noblesse,* and inferred that something profoundly philosophical was being said. But not in a dry, fussy way—there was worldly wisdom here, there was irony, a genuine spark of wit, droll but never vulgar. Leroy was amused, but would never be so common as to laugh aloud. *That* was reserved for the courtiers who leaned in, on tiptoe, to hear the witticism. Jack believed, just for a moment, that if John Churchill—who had no sense of humor at all—had not been homing in on him with that loaded pistol, all might have been forgiven, and Jack might have stayed and drunk some wine and danced with some ladies.

He could not move away from Churchill when the satyr was gripping Turk's bridle. "Are you going to make me cut that off?" he inquired.

"I freely confess that I deserve no better," said the satyr. "In fact—I am so humiliated that I must do it myself, to restore my, and my father's, honor." Whereupon he pulled a dagger from his belt and began to saw through the red leather glove on the hand that was gripping the bridle— attempting to cut off his left hand with his right. In doing so he probably saved Jack's life, for this spectacle—the man sawing at his own arm, blood welling out of the glove and dribbling onto the white floor—stopped Churchill in his curly-toed tracks, no more than a fathom away. It was the only time Jack had ever seen Churchill hesitate.

There was a ripping and whooshing noise from one end of the room. The East Wind had been split open by a sagging crevice that unloaded a sheet of dirty, lumpy water onto the floor. A whole strip of ceiling, a couple of yards wide, peeled away now, like a plank being ripped away from the side of a boat. It led straight to the French Navy—half a ton of plaster, bone dry—which came off in a single unified fleet action and seemed to hang in space for a moment before it started accelerating toward the floor. Everyone got out of the way. The plaster exploded and splayed snowballs of damp crud across the floor. But stuff continued to rain down from above, small dark lumps that, when they struck the floor, shook themselves and took off running.

Jack looked at Churchill just in time to see the flint whipping round on the end of its curved arm, a spray of sparks, a preliminary bloom of smoke from the pan. Then a lady blundered in from one side, not paying attention to where she was going because she had realized that there were rats in her wig—but she didn't know how many· (Jack, at a quick glance, numbered them at three, but more were raining down all the time and so he would've been loath to commit himself to a specific number). She hit Churchill's arm. A jet of fire as long as a man's arm darted from the muzzle of Churchill's pistol and caught Turk in the side of the face, though the ball apparently missed. The polite satyr was lucky to be alive—it had gone off inches from his head.

Turk was stunned and frozen, if only for a moment. Then a Barbary pirate-galley, driven downwards by a gout of water/rat slurry, exploded on the floor nearby. Some of the water, and some of the rats, poured down on Turk's neck—and then he detonated. He tried to rear up and was held down by the satyr's bloody but steadfast clutch, so he bucked—fortunately Jack saw this coming—and then kicked out with both hind-legs. Anyone behind him would've been decapitated, but the center of the ballroom had been mostly given over to rats now. A few more of those bucks and Jack would be flung off. He needed to let Turk run. But Churchill was now trying to get round the satyr to lay a second hand on Turk's bridle.

"This is the worst fucking party I've ever been to!" Jack said, whirling his sword-arm around like a windmill.

"Sir, I am sorry, but—"

The polite satyr did not finish the apology, because Jack delivered a cut to the middle of his forearm. The blade passed through sweetly. The dangling hand balled itself into a fist and maintained its grip on the bridle, even as the now one-armed satyr was falling back on top of Churchill. Turk sensed freedom and reared up. Jack looked down at Churchill and said, "Next time you want one of my horses— pay in *advance,* you rogue!"

Turk tried to bolt for the front door, but his hard *fers de cheval* slipped and scrabbled on the marble, and he could not build up speed. A sea-monster came down across his path, shedding a hundred rats from its crushed entrails. Turk wheeled and scrambled off toward a crowd of ladies who were doing a sort of tarantella, inspired by the belief that rats were scaling their petticoats. Then, just as Jack was convinced that the charger was going to crush the women under his hooves, Turk seemed to catch sight of a way out, and veered sideways, his hooves nearly sliding out from under him, and made for a doorway set into the back corner of the ballroom. It was a low doorway. Jack had little time to react—seeing the lintel headed for his face, decorated in the middle with a plaster d'Arcachon coat of arms,* and not wanting to have it stamped on his face forever, he flung himself backwards and fell off the horse.

He managed to get his right foot, but not his left, out of the stirrup, and so Turk simply dragged him down the ensuing corridor (which had a smooth floor, but not smooth enough for Jack). Nearly upside-down, Jack pawed desperately against that floor with the hand that wasn't gripping the sword, trying to pull himself sideways so that Turk's hooves wouldn't come down on him. Time and again his hand slammed down onto the backs of rats, who all seemed to be

---

*A quartering of elements old (fleurs-de-lis, denoting their ancient connections to the royal family) and new (Negro-heads in iron neck-collars).

fleeing down this particular corridor—drawn by some scent, perhaps, that struck them as promising. Turk outpaced the rats, of course, and was making his own decisions. Jack knew that they were passing into diverse rooms because the thresholds barked his hips and ribs and he got fleeting views of servants' breeches and skirts.

But then, suddenly, they were in a dimly lit room, alone, and Turk wasn't running anymore. Nervous and irritable to be sure, though. Jack cautiously wiggled his left foot. Turk startled, then looked at him.

"Surprised to see me? I've been with you the whole way—loyal friend that I am," Jack announced. He got his boot out of that stirrup and stood. But there was no time for additional banter. They were in a pantry. Squealing noises heralded the approach of the rats. Pounding of boots was not far behind, and where there were boots, there'd be swords. There was a locked door set into the wall, opposite to where they had come in, and Turk had gone over to sniff at it curiously.

If this was not a way out, Jack was dead—so he went over and pounded on it with the pommel of his sword, while looking significantly at Turk. It was a stout door. Curiously, the crevices between planks had been sealed with oakum, just like a ship's planking, and rags had been stuffed into the gaps round the edges.

Turk wheeled around to face away from it. Jack hopped out of the way. The war-horse's hindquarters heaved up as he put all weight on his forelegs, and then both of his rear hooves smashed into the door with the force of cannonballs. The door was half caved in, and torn most of the way loose from its upper hinge. Turk gave it a few more, and it disappeared.

Jack had sunk to his knees by that point, though, and wrapped a manure-plastered sleeve up against his nose and mouth, and was trying not to throw up. The stench that had begun to leak from the room beyond, after the first blow, had nearly felled him. It nearly drove Turk away, too. Jack just had the presence of mind to slam the other door and prevent the horse's fleeing into the hallway.

Jack grabbed the candle that was the pantry's only illumination, and stepped through, expecting to find a sepulchre filled with ripe corpses. But instead it was just another small kitchen, as tidy a place as Jack had ever seen.

There was a butcher's block in the center of the room with a fish stretched out on it. The fish was so rotten it was bubbling.

At the other end of this room was a small door. Jack opened it and discovered a typical Parisian back-alley. But what he *saw* in his mind's eye was the moment, just a few minutes ago, when he had ridden right past the duc d'Arcachon while carrying an unsheathed sword. One twitch of the wrist, and the man who (as he now knew) had taken Eliza and her mother off into slavery would be dead. He could run back into the house now, and have a go at it. But he knew he'd lost the moment.

Turk planted his head in Jack's back and shoved him out the door, desperate to reach the comparative freshness of a Paris alley choked with rotting kitchen-waste and human excrement. Back inside, Jack could hear men battering at the pantry door.

Turk was eyeing him as if to say, *Shall we?* Jack mounted him and Turk began to gallop down the alley without being told to. The alarm had gone up. So as Jack thundered out into the Place Royale, sparks flying from his mount's new shoes, the wind blowing his cape out behind him—in other words, cutting just the silhouette he'd intended—he turned round and pointed back into the alley with his sword and shouted: *"Les Vagabonds! Les Vagabonds anglaises!"* And then, catching sight of the bulwark of the Bastille rising above some rooftops, under a half-moon, and reckoning that this would be a good place to pretend to summon reinforcements—not to mention a way out of town—he got Turk pointed in that direction, and gave him free rein.

Amsterdam
1685

Must businesse thee from hence remove?
Oh, that's the worst disease of love,
The poore, the foule, the false, love can
Admit, but not the busied man.
He which hath businesse, and makes love,
   doth doe
Such wrong, as when a maryed man doth
   wooe.

—JOHN DONNE, "Breake of Day"

"WHO IS YOUR GREAT BIG tall, bearded, ill-dressed, unmannerly, harpoon-brandishing, er—?" asked Eliza; and ran out of adjectives. She was peering out the windows of the *Maiden* coffee-house at a loitering Nimrod who was blotting out the sun with an immense, motley fur coat. The management had been reluctant to let even *Jack* come into the place, but they had drawn the line at the glaring wild man with the harping-iron.

"Oh, him?" Jack asked, innocently—as if there were more than one such person who owned that description. "That's Yevgeny the Raskolnik."

"What's a Raskolnik?"

"Beats me—all I know is they're all getting out of Russia as fast as they can."

"Well, then . . . how did you *meet* him?"

"I've no idea. Woke up in the Bomb & Grapnel—there he was, snuggled up against me—his beard thrown over my neck like a muffler."

Eliza shuddered exquisitely. "But the Bomb & Grapnel's in Dunkirk . . ."

"Yes?"

"How'd you get there from Paris? Weren't there adventures, chases, duels—?"

"Presumably. I've no idea."

"What of the leg wound?"

"I was fortunate to engage the services of a fine, lusty crew of maggots along the way—they kept it clean. It healed without incident."

"But how can you simply forget about a whole week's journey?"

"It's how my mind works now. As in a play, where only the most dramatic parts of the story are shown to the audience, and the tedious bits assumed to happen offstage. So: I gallop out of the Place Royale; the curtain falls, there is a sort of intermission; the curtain rises again, and I'm in Dunkirk, in Mr. Foot's finest bedchamber, upstairs of the Bomb & Grapnel, and I'm with Yevgeny, and stacked around us on the floor are all of his furs and skins and amber."

"He's some sort of commodities trader, then?" Eliza asked.

"No need to be waspish, lass."

"I'm simply trying to work out how he found his way into the drama."

"I've no idea—he doesn't speak a word of *anything*. I went down stairs and asked the same question of Mr. Foot, the proprietor, a man of parts, former privateer—"

"You've told me, and told me, and told me, about Mr. Foot."

"He said that just a week or two earlier, Yevgeny had rowed a longboat into the little cove where the Bomb & Grapnel sits."

"You mean—rowed ashore from some ship that had dropped anchor off Dunkirk."

"No—that's just it—he came from *over the horizon.* Rode a swell up onto the beach—dragged the longboat up as far as it would go—collapsed on the threshold of the nearest dwelling, which happened to be the old Bomb. Now, Mr. Foot has been lacking for customers these last few years— so, instead of throwing him back like a fish, as he might've done in the B & G's heyday, and discovering, furthermore, that the longboat was filled to the gunwales with Arctic valuables, he toted it all upstairs. Finally he rolled Yevgeny himself onto a cargo net, and hoisted him up through the window with a block and tackle—thinking that when he woke up, he might know how to obtain more of the same goods."

"Yes, I can see his business strategy very clearly."

"There you go again. If you'd let me finish, you wouldn't judge of Mr. Foot so harshly. At the cost of many hours' backbreaking labor, he gave a more or less Christian burial to the remains—"

"*Which?* There has been no discussion of *remains.*"

"I may've forgotten to mention that Yevgeny was sharing the longboat with several comrades who'd all succumbed to the elements—"

"—or possibly Yevgeny."

"The same occurred to me. But then, as the Good Lord endowed me with more *brains,* and less *bile,* than *some,* I reckoned that if this had been the case, the Raskolnik would've thrown the victims overboard—especially after they waxed gruesome. Mr. Foot—and I only tell you this, lass, in order to clear Yevgeny's name—said that the meatier parts of these corpses had been picked clean to the bone by seagulls."

"Or by a peckish Yevgeny," Eliza said, lifting a teacup to her lips to conceal a certain triumphal smile, and looking out the window toward the furry Russian, who was whiling away the time by puffing on a rude pipe and honing the flukes of his harping-iron with a pocket-whetstone.

"Making a good character for my Raskolnik friend—though he truly has a heart of gold—will be impossible when, tidy and stylish girl that you are, you are gaping at his rude exterior form. So let us move on," Jack said. "Next thing Mr. Foot knows, I show up, all decorated with baubles from France, nearly as spent as Yevgeny. So he took me in, in the same way. And finally, a French gentleman approached him and let it be known that he'd like to purchase the Bomb & Grapnel—proving the rule that things tend to happen in threes."

"Now you've amazed me," Eliza said. "What do those events have in common with each other, that you should conceive of them as a group of three?"

"Why, just as Yevgeny and I were wandering lost—yet, in possession of things of great value—Mr. Foot was cast out into the wilderness—I am making a similitude, here—"

"Yes, you have the daft look you always get, when you are."

"Dunkirk's not the same since Leroy bought it from King Chuck. It is a great *base navale* now. All the English, and other, privateers who used to lodge, drink, gamble, and whore at the Bomb & Grapnel have signed on with Monsieur Jean Bart, or else sailed away to Port Royal, in Jamaica. And despite these troubles, Mr. Foot had something of value: the Bomb & Grapnel itself. An opportunity began to take shape in Mr. Foot's mind, like a stage-ghost appearing from a cloud of smoke."

"Much as a profound sense of foreboding is beginning to take shape in my bosom."

"I had a vision in Paris, Eliza—rather of a complex nature—there was considerable singing and dancing in it, and ghastly and bawdy portions in equal measure."

"Knowing you as I do, Jack, I'd expect nothing less from one of your visions."

"I'll spare you the details, most of which are indelicate for a lady of your upbringing. Suffice it to say that on the strength of this heavenly apparition, and other signs and omens, such as the Three Similar Events at the Bomb &

Grapnel, I have decided to give up Vagabonding, and, along with Yevgeny and Mr. Foot, to go into Business."

Eliza faltered and shrank, as if a large timber, or something, had snapped inside of her.

"Now why is it," Jack said, "then when I suggest you reach in and grab me by the *chakra,* it's nothing to you, and yet, when the word *business* comes out of my mouth, you get a wary and prim look about you, like a virtuous maiden who has just had lewd proposals directed her way by a bawdy Lord?"

"It's nothing. Pray continue," Eliza said, in a colorless voice.

But Jack's nerve had faltered. He began to digress. "I'd hoped brother Bob might be in town, as he commonly traveled in John Churchill's retinue. And indeed Mr. Foot said he had been there very recently, inquiring after me. But then the Duke of Monmouth had surprised them all by coming to Dunkirk incognito, to meet with certain disaffected Englishmen, and proceeding inland toward Brussels in haste. Bob, who knows that terrain so well, had been dispatched by one of Churchill's lieutenants to follow him and report on his doings."

At the mention of the Duke of Monmouth, Eliza began to look Jack in the face again—from which he gathered that one of two things might be the case: either she was looking for a romantic fling with a claim (highly disputable) to the English throne, or else she numbered political intrigues among her interests now. Indeed, when he had surprised her by coming into the Maiden, she'd been writing a letter with her right hand while doing that binary arithmetic on her left, according to the Doctor's practice.

At any rate—as long as he had her attention—he decided to strike. "And that is when I was made aware, by Mr. Foot, of the Opportunity."

Eliza's face became a death mask, as when a physician says, *Please sit down . . .*

"Mr. Foot has many contacts in the shipping industry—"

"Smugglers."

"Most shipping is smuggling to some degree," Jack said learnedly. "He had received a personal visit from one Mr. Vliet, a Dutch fellow who was in the market for a seaworthy vessel of moderate size, capable of crossing the Atlantic with a cargo of such-and-such number of tons. Mr. Foot was not slow in securing the *God's Wounds,* a well-broken-in double-topsail brig."

"Do you even know what that *means*?"

"It is both square, and fore-and-aft rigged, hence well-suited for running before the trade winds, or plying the fickle breezes of coastlines. She has a somewhat lopsided but sea-soned crew—"

"And only needed to be victualled and refitted—?"

"Some capital was, of course, wanted."

"So Mr. Vliet went to Amsterdam and—?"

"To *Dunkirk* went Mr. Vliet, and explained to Mr. Foot, who then explained to me and, as best he could, Yevgeny, the nature of the proposed trading voyage: of lapidary sim-plicity, yet guaranteed to be lucrative. We agreed to cast in our lots together. Fortunately, it is not difficult to sell goods quickly in Dunkirk. I liquidated the jewelry, Yevgeny sold his furs, whale-oil, and some fine amber, and Mr. Foot has sold the Bomb & Grapnel to a French con-cern."

"It seems a farfetched way for this Mr. Vliet to raise money," Eliza said, "when there is a large and extremely vigorous capital market right here in Amsterdam."

This was (as Jack figured out later, when he had much time to consider it) Eliza's way of saying that she thought Mr. Vliet was a knave, and the voyage not fit for persons in their right minds to invest in. But having been in Amsterdam for so long, she said it in the zargon of bankers.

"Why not just sell the jewels and give the money to your boys?" she continued.

"Why not invest it—as they have no immediate need for money—and, in a few years, give them quadruple the amount?"

"Quadruple?"

"We expect no less."

Eliza made a face as if she were being forced to swallow a whole English walnut. "Speaking of money," she murmured, "what of the horse, and the ostrich plumes?"

"That noble steed is in Dunkirk, awaiting the return of John Churchill, who has voiced an intention of buying him from me. The plumes are safe in the hands of my commission-agents in Paris," Jack said, and gripped the table-edge with both hands, expecting a thorough interrogation. But Eliza let the matter drop, as if she couldn't stand to come any nearer to the truth. Jack realized she'd *never* expected to see him, or the money, again—that she'd withdrawn, long ago, from the partnership they'd formed beneath the Emperor's palace in Vienna.

She would not look him in the eye, nor laugh at his jokes, nor blush when he provoked her, and he thought that chill Amsterdam had frozen her soul—sucked the humour of passion from her veins. But in time he persuaded her to come outside with him. When she stood up, and the Maiden's proprietor helped her on with a cape, she looked finer than ever. Jack was about to compliment her on her needle-work when he noticed rings of gold on her fingers, and jewels round her neck, and knew she probably had not touched needle and thread since reaching Amsterdam.

"*Windhandel,* or gifts from suitors?"

"I did not escape slavery to be a whore," she answered. "*You* might wake up next to a Yevgeny and jest about it—I would be of a different mind."

Yevgeny, unaware that he was being abused in this way, followed them through the scrubbed streets of the town, thumping at the pavement with the butt of his harping-iron. Presently they came to a southwestern district *not* so well scrubbed, and began to hear a lot of French and Ladino, as Huguenots and Sephardim had come to live here—even a few Raskolniks, who stopped Yevgeny to exchange rumors and stories. The houses became cracked and uneven, settling into the muck so fast you could practically see them moving, and the canals became narrow and scummed-over, as if rarely troubled by commerce.

They walked up such a street to a warehouse where heavy sacks were being lowered into the hold of a sloop. "There it is—our Commodity," Jack said. "Good as—and in some parts of the world, preferable to—gold."

"What is it—hazelnuts?" Eliza asked. "Coffee beans?" Jack had no particular reason to keep the secret from her, but this was the first time she'd shown any interest at all in his venture, and he wanted to make it last.

The sloop's hold was full. So even as Jack, Eliza, and Yevgeny were approaching, the lines were cast off and sails raised, and she began to drift down the canal ahead of a faint breeze, headed for the inner harbor, a few minutes' walk away.

They followed on foot. "You have insurance?" she asked.

"Funny you should ask," Jack said, and at this Eliza rolled her eyes, and then slumped like one of those sinking houses. "Mr. Foot says that this is a great adventure, but—"

"He means that you have made Mr. Vliet a loan *à la grosse aventure,* which is a typical way of financing trading-voyages," Eliza said. "But those who make such loans always buy insurance—*if they can find anyone to sell it to them.* I can point you to coffee-houses that specialize in just that. But—"

"How much does it cost?"

"It depends on *everything,* Jack, there is no one fixed price. Are you trying to tell me you don't have enough money left to buy insurance?"

Jack said nothing.

"If so, you should withdraw now."

"Too late—the victuals are paid for and stowed in the hold of *God's Wounds.* But perhaps there is room for one more investor."

Eliza snorted. "What's come over you? Vagabonding you do very well, and you cut a fine figure doing it. But investing—it's not your *métier.*"

"I wish you had mentioned that before," Jack said. "From the first moment Mr. Foot mentioned it to me, I saw this trading-voyage as a way I might become worthy in your eyes." Then Jack nearly toppled into a canal, as recklessly telling the truth had given him an attack of giddiness. Eliza, for her part, looked as if she'd been butt-stroked by Yevgeny's harpoon—she stopped walking, planted her feet wide, and crossed her arms over her bodice as if nursing a stomach-ache; looked up the canal with watery eyes for a moment; and sniffled once or twice.

Jack ought to've been delighted. But all he felt, finally, was a dull sense of doom. He hadn't told Eliza about the rotten fish or the pink-eyed horses. He *certainly* had not mentioned that he could have killed, but had idiotically spared, the villain who had once made her a slave. But he knew that someday she would find out, and when that happened, he did not want to be on the European continent.

"Let me see the ship," she said finally.

They came round a bend and were greeted by one of those sudden surprising Amsterdam-vistas, down the canal to the ship-carpeted Ijsselmeer. Planted on the Ij-bank was the Herring-Packers' Tower, a roundish brick silo rising above a sloppy, fragrant quay where three vessels were tied up: a couple of hulks that were shuttling victuals out to bigger ships in the outer harbor, and *God's Wounds,* which looked as if she were being disassembled. All her hatches were removed for loading, and what remained had a structurally dubious look—especially when great sweating barrels of herring, and these mysterious sacks from the warehouse, were being dropped into it.

But before Jack could really dwell on the topic of seaworthiness, Eliza—moving with a decisiveness he could no longer muster—had gone out onto the quay, her skirts sweeping up all manner of stuff that she would later regret having brought home. A sack had split open and spilled its contents, which snapped, crackled, and popped beneath the soles of her shoes as she drew up close. She bent over and thrust her hand into the hole, somewhat like doubting Thomas, and raised up a handful of the cargo, and let it spill in a colorful clinking shower.

"Cowrie shells," she said distractedly.

Jack thought, at first, that she was dumbfounded—probably by the brilliance and magnificence of the plan—but on a closer look he saw that she was showing all the symptoms of thinking.

"Cowrie shells to you," Jack said. "In Africa, this is money!"

"Not for long."

"What do you mean? Money's money. Mr. Vliet has been sitting on this hoard for twenty years, waiting for prices to drop."

"A few weeks ago," said Eliza, "news arrived that the Dutch had acquired certain isles, near India, called the Maldives and Laccadives, and that vast numbers of cowrie shells had been found there. Since that news arrived, these have been considered worthless."

It took Jack some time to recover from this.

He had a sword, and Mr. Vliet, a pudgy flaxen-haired man, was just a stone's throw away, going over some paperwork with a ship's victualer, and it was natural to imagine simply running over and inserting the tip of the sword between any two of Mr. Vliet's chins and giving it a hard shove. But this, he supposed, would simply have proved Eliza's point (viz. that he was not cut out to be a businessman), and he did not want to give her such satisfaction. Jack wasn't going to get the kind of satisfaction *he* had been craving for the last six months, and so why should *she* get any? As a way of keeping his body occupied while the mind worked, he helped roll some barrels over the plank to the deck of the ship.

"Now I understand the word *Windhandel* in a new way," was all that he could come up with. "This is real," he said, slapping a barrel-head, "and this" (stomping the deck of *God's Wounds*) "is real, and these" (lofting a double handful of cowrie shells) "are real, and all of them every bit as real, *now,* as they were, ten minutes ago, or before this rumor arrived from the Maldives and the Laccadives . . ."

"The news came over land—faster than ships normally travel, when they have to round the Cape of Good Hope. So it is possible that you will reach Africa in advance of the great cargo-ships of cowrie-shells that, one can only presume, are headed that way now from the Maldives."

"Just as Mr. Vliet had it planned, I'm sure."

"But when you get to Africa, what will you buy with your cowrie-shells, Jack?"

"Cloth."

"Cloth!?"

"Then we sail west—there is said to be a great market for African cloth in the West Indies."

"Africans do not export cloth, Jack. They import it."

"You must be mistaken—Mr. Vliet is very clear on this— we will sail to Africa and exchange our cowrie-shells for *pieces of India,* which as I'm sure you know means India cloth, and then carry it across the Atlantic . . ."

"A *piece of India* is an expression meaning a male African slave between fifteen and forty years of age," Eliza said. "India cloth—just like cowrie shells—is money in Africa, Jack, and Africans will sell other Africans for one piece of it."

Now a silence nearly as long as the one at the duc d'Arcachon's party. Jack standing on the slowly moving deck of the *God's Wounds,* Eliza on the quay.

"You are going into the slave trade," she said, in a dead voice.

"Well . . . I had no idea, until *now.*"

"I believe you. But now you have to get off that boat and walk away."

This was a superb idea, and part of Jack was thrilled by it. But the Imp of the Perverse prevailed, and Jack decided to take Eliza's suggestion in a negative and resentful spirit.

"And simply *throw away* my investment?"

"Better than throwing away your immortal soul. You threw away the ostrich plumes and the horse, Jack, I know you did—so why not do the same now?"

"This is more valuable *by far.*"

"What about the other item you looted from the Grand Vizier's camp, Jack?"

"What, the sword?"

Eliza shook her head no, looked him in the eye, and waited.

"I remember that item," Jack allowed.

"Will you throw her away, too?"

"She is far more valuable, true . . ."

"*And* worth more money," Eliza put in slyly.

"You're not proposing to sell yourself—?"

Eliza went into a strange amalgam of laughing and crying. "I mean to say that I have already made more money than the plumes, sword, and horse were *worth,* and stand to make far more, soon—and so if it is money that concerns you, walk away from the *God's Wounds* and stay with me, here in Amsterdam—soon you'll forget this ship ever existed."

"It does not seem respectable—being supported by a woman."

"When in your life have *you* ever cared about *respect?*"

"Since people began to respect me."

"I am offering you safety, happiness, wealth—and *my* respect," Eliza said.

"You would not respect me for *long.* Let me take this one voyage, and get my money back, then—"

"One voyage for *you.* Eternal wretchedness for the Africans you'll buy, and their descendants."

"Either way I've lost my Eliza," Jack said with a shrug. "So that makes me something of an authority when it comes to eternal wretchedness."

"Do you want your life?"

"*This* life? Not especially."

"Get off the boat, if you want to have a life at all."

Eliza had noticed what Jack hadn't, which was that *God's Wounds* had finished being loaded. The hatch-covers were back in place, the herring was paid for (in silver coins, not cowrie-shells), and the sailors were casting off lines. Only Mr. Vliet, and Yevgeny, remained on the quay—the former haggling with an apothecary over a medicine-chest, and the latter being blessed by an outlandish Raskolnik priest in a towering hat. This scene was so curious that it diverted Jack's attention completely, until all of the sailors began to holler. Then he looked at *them*. But *they* were all looking at some apparently horrid spectacle on the quay, putting Jack suddenly in fear that ruffians, or something, were assaulting Eliza.

Jack turned around just in time to discover that Eliza had seized the harpoon, which Yevgeny had left leaning against a stack of crates, and was just in the act of launching it toward Jack. She was not, of course, a professional harpooneer, but she had the womanly knack of aiming for the heart, and so the weapon came at him straight as Truth. Jack, recalling a dim bit of sword-fighting lore from his Regimental days, twisted sideways to present a narrower target, but lost his balance and fell toward the mainmast and threw out his left arm to break his fall. The broad flukes of the harpoon made a slashing attack across the breadth of his chest and glanced off a rib, or something, so that its point struck his forearm and passed sideways through the narrow space between the two bones and buried itself in the mast—pinning him. He felt all of this before he saw it because he was looking for Eliza. But she'd already turned her back on him and was walking away, not even caring whether she had hit him or not.

Amsterdam

JUNE 1685

❦

D'AVAUX AND A PAIR OF tall, uncommonly hard-bitten "valets" saw her to the brink of a canal, not far from the Dam, that ran westwards toward Haarlem. A vessel was tied up there, accepting passengers, and from a distance Eliza thought it a tiny one, because it had an amusing toylike look, with the stem and the stern both curved sharply upwards—giving it the profile of a fat boy doing a bold belly-flop. But as they drew closer she saw it was a large (albeit lightly built) ship, at least twenty yards long, and narrower of beam than she'd expected—a crescent moon.

"I do not mean to belabor you with tedious details—that sort of thing is the responsibility of Jacques, here, and Jean-Baptiste . . ."

"*These* are coming with me!?"

"The way to Paris is not devoid of perils, mademoiselle," d'Avaux said drily, "even for the *weak* and the *innocent.*" Then he turned his head in the direction of the still lightly smoking wrack of Mr. Sluys's string of houses, only a musket-shot away along this very canal.

"Evidently you think I am *neither,*" Eliza sniffed.

"Your practice of harpooning sailors along the waterfront would make it difficult for even the most *lubrique* to harbor illusions as to your true nature—"

"You've heard about that?"

"Miracle you weren't arrested—here, in a city where *kissing* someone is a misdemeanour."

"Have you had me followed, monsieur?" Eliza looked indignantly at Jacques and Jean-Baptiste, who pretended, for the time being, to be deaf and blind, and busied themselves with a cartload of rather good luggage. She'd never seen most of these bags before, but d'Avaux had implied, more than once, that they and their contents all belonged to her.

"Men will ever follow you, mademoiselle, you'd best *adapt.* In any event—setting aside the odd harpooning—in this town are certain busybodies, scolds, and *cancaniers* who insist that you were involved in the financial implosion of Mr. Sluys; the invasion fleet that sailed for England, from Texel, the other day, flying the Duke of Monmouth's colors; and the feral mob of Orangist patriots who, some say, set Mr. Sluys's dwelling afire. I, of course, do not believe in any of these nonsenses—and yet I worry about you—"

"Like a fretful uncle. Oh, how dear!"

"So. This *kaag* will take you, and your escorts—"

"Over the Haarlemmermeer to Leiden, and thence to Den Briel via the Hague."

"How did you guess?"

"The coat of arms of the City of Den Briel is carved on the taffrail, there, opposite that of Amsterdam," Eliza said, pointing up at the stern. D'Avaux turned to look, and so did Jacques and Jean-Baptiste; and in the same moment Eliza heard behind her a weird sighing, whistling noise, like a bagpipe running out of wind, and was jostled by a passing boer headed for the gangplank. As this rustic clambered up onto the *kaag* she saw his oddly familiar hump-backed profile, and caught her breath for a moment. D'Avaux turned to peer at her. Something told Eliza that this would be an awkward time to make a fuss, and so she let her mouth run: "She carries more sail than the usual canal-barge— presumably for crossing the Haarlemmermeer. She is a slender vessel, made to pass through that narrow lock between Leiden and the Hague. And yet she's too flimsy to traverse Zeeland's currents and tides—she could never afford the insurance."

"Yes," d'Avaux said, "at Den Briel you must transfer to a *more insurable* ship that will take you to Brussels." He was looking at Eliza queerly—so suspicious! The boer, meanwhile, had disappeared into the clutter of passengers and cargo on the *kaag*'s deck. "From Brussels you will travel over land to Paris," d'Avaux continued. "The inland route is less comfortable during summer—but much *safer* during an armed rebellion against the King of England."

Eliza sighed deeply, trying to hold in her mind the phant'sy of a million slaves being released from bondage. But it was a frail gauzy construction ripped apart by the strong summer-light of Amsterdam, the hard clear shapes of black buildings and white windows. "My lovely Dukie," she said, "so impetuous."

"Étienne d'Arcachon—who asks about you, by the way, in every one of his letters—suffers from a similar fault. In *his* case it is tempered by breeding and intelligence; yet he has lost a hand to a Vagabond because of it!"

"Oh, nasty Vagabonds!"

"They say he is recovering as well as can be expected."

"When I get to Paris, I'll send you news of him."

"Send me news of *everything,* especially what does not *appear* to be news," d'Avaux insisted. "If you can learn to read the comings and goings at Versailles as well as you do the taffrails and insurance-policies of Dutch boats, you'll be running France in a trice."

She kissed the cheeks of the comte d'Avaux and he kissed hers. Jacques and Jean-Baptiste escorted her up the plank and then, as the *kaag* began to drift down the canal, busied themselves storing her luggage away in the small cabin d'Avaux had procured for her. Eliza meanwhile stood at the *kaag*'s railing, along with many other passengers, and enjoyed the view of Amsterdam's canal-front. When you were on dry land in that city you could never slow down, never stop moving, and so it was strange and relaxing to be so close to it, yet so still and placid—like a low-flying angel spying on the doings of men.

Too, that she was escaping cleanly from Amsterdam, after all that had happened of late, was something akin to a miracle. D'Avaux was right to wonder why she had not been arrested for the matter of the harpoon. She had stumbled away from the scene—the Herring Packers' Tower—weeping with anger at Jack. But soon anger had been shouldered aside by fear as she'd realized she was being followed, rather obviously, by several parties at once. Looking back wouldn't've done her any good and so she'd kept walking, all the way across the Dam and then through the Exchange, which was as good a place as any to lose pursuers—or at least to remind them that they could be doing more profitable things with their time. Finally she'd gone to the Maiden and sat by a window for several hours, watching—and had seen very little. A couple of tall loiterers, whom she now knew to've been Jacques and Jean-Baptiste, and one lolling Vagabond-beggar, identifiable by his humpbacked posture and insistent hacking cough.

The *kaag* was being towed in the direction of Haarlem by a team of horses on the canal-bank, but on deck the crew were making preparations to swing her side-boards down into the water and deploy her clever folding mast, so that they could hoist a sail or two. The horses faltered as they came to a section of pavement that was broken and blackened, and ridged with trails of lead that had flowed molten from Mr. Sluys's house, and spread across the paving-stones in glowing rivers that had divided and combined as they crept toward the bank. Finally the streams of molten lead had plunged gorgeously over the stone quay and dropped into the canal, where they'd flung up a column of steam that dwarfed and enveloped the pillar of smoke from Mr. Sluys's burning houses. By that time, of course, those who'd set the fire had long since disappeared. It was up to the *drost* to interrogate the very few witnesses and to figure out whether it had really been done by infuriated Orangers, taking revenge on Sluys for backing the French, or by arsonists in the pay of Mr. Sluys. Sluys had lost so much, so fast, in the recent crash of V.O.C. stock* that his only way of getting any liquidity would have been to set fire to everything he still owned and then make claims against those who'd been rash enough to sell him insurance. This morning—three days since the fire—salvagers in the pay of those insurers were busy with pry-bars and hoists, pulling congealed rivulets and puddles of lead from the canal.

She heard that whining sound next to her again, but it suddenly crescendoed, as if a cart-wheel were rolling over that leaky bagpipe and forcing the last bit of air through its drones. Then it broke open into a croaking, hacking laugh. That humpbacked boer had taken up a spot on the *kaag*'s rail not far from Eliza, and was watching the salvagers. "The Duke of Monmouth's rebellion has made lead a valuable commodity again," he said (Eliza could understand that much Dutch, anyway). "It's as valuable as gold."

"I beg your pardon, *meinheer,* but—though it's true the price of lead has risen—it is nowhere near as valuable as gold, or even silver." Eliza said this in stumbling Dutch.

The wheezing boer startled her by coming back in passable English. "That depends on *where you are.* An army, surrounded by the enemy, running low on balls, will happily exchange coins of gold for an equal weight of lead balls."

Eliza didn't doubt the truth of this, but it struck her as an oddly bleak point of view, and so she broke off the conversation, and spoke no more to that boer as the *kaag* passed through a water-gate in Amsterdam's western wall and entered flat Dutch countryside, diced by drainage ditches into pea-green bricks that were arrayed by the canal-side as if on a table in the market. The other passengers likewise gave the fellow a wide berth, partly because they didn't want to catch whatever was afflicting his lungs, and mostly because they tended to be prosperous mercers and farmers coming back

---

*It dropped from 572 to 250 when word of Monmouth's rebellion spread.

from Amsterdam with bags of gold and silver coins; they did not want to come anywhere near a man who would contemplate using florins as projectiles. The boer seemed to understand this all too well, and spent the first couple of hours of the voyage regarding his fellow-passengers with a glum knowingness that verged on contempt, and that would have earned him a challenge to a duel in France.

Aside from that, he did nothing noteworthy until much later in the day, when, all of a sudden, he murdered Jacques and Jean-Baptiste.

It came about like this: the *kaag* sailed down the canal to Haarlem, where it stopped to pick up a few more passengers, and then it raised more sails and set out across the Haarlemmermeer, a fairly sizable lake ventilated by a stiff maritime breeze. The fresh air had an obvious effect on the boer. The pitiable wheezing and hacking stopped with miraculous speed. His ribcage no longer labored with each breath. He stood up straighter, bringing him to average height, and seemed to shed a decade or two. He now appeared to be in his mid-thirties. He lost his dour expression and, instead of lurking at the stern glowering at the other passengers, began striding round the deck almost cheerfully. By the time he'd made several laps around the deck, all the other passengers had gotten used to this, and paid him no mind—which is how he was able to walk up behind Jacques, grab both of his ankles, and pitch him overboard.

This happened so quickly, and with so little ado, that it might have been easy to believe it had never happened at all. But Jean-Baptiste believed it, and rushed at the boer with sword drawn. The boer had no sword, but the Antwerp merchant standing nearby had a perfectly serviceable one, and so the boer simply yanked it out of the owner's scabbard and then dropped neatly into a defencing stance.

Jean-Baptiste stopped to think, which probably did him no good, and much harm. Then he charged anyway. The pitching of the *kaag* ruined his attack. When he actually stumbled close enough to cross swords with the boer, it was obvious that Jean-Baptiste was the inferior swordsman—

miserably so. But even setting aside these differences, the boer would have prevailed anyway, because to him, killing other men in close combat was as kneading dough was to a baker. Jean-Baptiste considered it to be an important matter, requiring certain formalities. A ring of dark windmills, ranged around the shore of the Haarlemmermeer, looked on like grim Dutch eminences, chopping the air. Rather soon, Jean-Baptiste had a couple of feet of bloody steel protruding from his back, and a jeweled hilt fixed to his chest like an awkward piece of jewelry.

That was all that Eliza was allowed to take in before the gunny sack descended over her head, and was made snug—but not tight—around her neck. Someone hugged her around the knees and lifted her feet off the deck while another caught her by the armpits. She feared, only for a moment, that she was about to be thrown overboard like Jacques (and—to judge from a booming splash audible through the gunny sack—Jean-Baptiste). As she was being carried be-lowdecks she heard a terse utterance in Dutch, then, all around the *kaag*, a storm of thudding and rustling: passengers' knees hitting the deck, and hats being whipped off their heads.

When the sack came off her head, she was in her little cabin with two men: a brute and an angel. The brute was a thick-set boer, who had managed the gunny sack and borne most of her weight. He was immediately dismissed and sent out by the angel: a blond Dutch gentleman, so beautiful that Eliza was more inclined to be jealous of, than attracted to, him. "Arnold Joost van Keppel," he explained curtly, "page to the Prince of Orange." He was looking at Eliza with the same coolness as she was showing him—obviously he had little interest in women. And yet rumor had it that William kept an English mistress—so perhaps he was the sort who could love *anything*.

William, Prince of Orange, Stadholder, Admiral-General, and Captain-General of the United Provinces, Burgrave of Besançon, and Duke or Count or Baron of diverse other tiny fragments of Europe,* entered the cabin a few minutes later, ruddy and unshaven, slightly blood-flecked, and, in general, looking anything but Dutch. As d'Avaux never got tired of pointing out, he was a sort of European mongrel, with ancestors from all corners of the Continent. He looked as comfortable in that rough boer's get-up as Monmouth had in Turkish silk. He was too excited and pleased with himself to sit down—which anyway would have led to a tedious welter of protocol, since there was only one place to sit in this cabin, and Eliza had no intention of vacating it. So William shooed Arnold Joost van Keppel out of the place, then braced his shoulder against a curving overhead knee-brace and remained on his feet. "My god, you're but a child—not even twenty yet? That's in your favor—it excuses your foolishness, while giving hope that you may improve."

Eliza was still too angry about the gunny sack to speak, or even to give any sign that she'd heard him.

"Don't delay writing a thank-you note to the Doctor," said William, "if it weren't for him, you'd be on a slow boat to Nagasaki."

"You are acquainted with Doctor Leibniz?"

"We met at Hanover about five years ago. I traveled there, and to Berlin—"

"Berlin?"

"A town in Brandenburg, of little significance, save that the Elector has a palace there. I have various relations among the Electors and Dukes of that part of the world—I was making the rounds, you see, trying to bring them into an alliance against France."

"Evidently, without success—?"

"*They* were willing. Most *Dutchmen* were, too—but *Amsterdam* was not. In fact, the Regents of Amsterdam were plotting with your friend d'Avaux to go over to the French so that Louis could wield their fleet against England."

---

*E.g., Nassau, Katsenellenbogen, Dietz, Vianden, Meurs.

"*Also* without success, or someone would've heard about it."

"I like to flatter myself that *my* efforts in northern Germany—aided to no small degree by your friend Doctor Leibniz—and d'Avaux's exertions here, produced a stalemate," William announced. "I was pleased to have fared so well, and Louis was furious to have made out so poorly."

"Is that the reason he raped Orange?"

This made William of Orange very angry, which Eliza considered to be fair exchange for the gunny sack. But he mastered his rage, and answered in a tight voice: "Understand: Louis is not like us—he does not trifle with *reasons*. He *is* a reason. Which is why he must be destroyed."

"And it's *your* ambition to do the destroying?"

"Humor me, girl, by using the word 'destiny' instead of 'ambition.'"

"But you don't even have control over your own territory! Louis has Orange, and here in Holland you skulk about in disguise, for fear of French dragoons—"

"I am not here to rehearse these facts with you," William said, now much calmer. "You are right. Furthermore, I cannot dance or write poetry or entertain a company at dinner. I'm not even a particularly good general, never mind what my supporters will tell you. All I know is that nothing that opposes me endures."

"France seems to be enduring."

"But I will see to it that France's ambitions fail, and in some small way, you will help me."

"Why?"

"You should be asking *how.*"

"Unlike *le Roi*, I need reasons."

William of Orange thought it was amusing that she thought she needed reasons, but killing a couple of French dragoons had put him into a playful mood. "The Doctor says you hate slavery," he offered. "Louis wants to enslave all of Christendom."

"Yet, all of Africa's great slave-forts belong to the Dutch or the English."

"Only because the duc d'Arcachon's navy is still too in-competent to take them away from us," William returned. "Sometimes in life it is necessary to do things *incrementally,* and that goes double for a Vagabond girl-child who is trying to do away with a universal institution such as slavery."

Eliza said, "How remarkable that a Prince would dress up like a farmer and go on a boat-trip only to edify a Vagabond girl-child."

"You glorify yourself. First: as you have already pointed out, I always go incognito in Amsterdam, for d'Avaux has assassins all over the city. Second: I was going back to the Hague any-way, since your lover's invasion of England has imposed cer-tain obligations on me. Third: I have got rid of your escorts, and brought you to this cabin, not to edify you or anyone else, but to intercept the messages d'Avaux hid in your baggage."

Eliza now felt her face getting hot. William eyed her be-musedly for a few moments, and decided, perhaps, not to press his advantage. "Arnold!" he shouted. The cabin door opened. Through it, Eliza could see her things spread out all over the deck, stained with tar and bilge-water, some of the more complicated garments ripped into pieces. The luggage given to her by d'Avaux had been broken up into fragments, now being peeled apart layer by layer. "Two letters so far," Arnold said, stepping into the cabin and, with a little bow, handing over sheets covered with writing.

"Both encyphered," William observed. "No doubt he's had the wit to change over to a new code since last year."

Like a rock that had been struck by a cannon-ball, Eliza's mind split into a few large independent pieces about now. One piece understood that the existence of these letters made her a French spy in the eyes of Dutch law, and pre-sumably gave William the right to inflict any imaginable punishment on her. Another part was busily trying to figure out what d'Avaux's plan had been (this seemed an over-elaborate way of mailing some letters!—or perhaps not?), and yet a third part seemed to be carrying on polite conver-sation without really thinking (maybe not such a good idea, but—). "What happened last year?"

"I had d'Avaux's *previous* dupe arrested. The messages *he* was carrying to Versailles were deciphered by my cryptologist. They had to do with all the fine things Sluys and certain Amsterdam Regents were doing on behalf of Louis."

This remark, at least, gave Eliza something to think about other than Doom and Rage. "Étienne d'Arcachon was visiting Sluys several weeks ago—but apparently *not* to discuss investments . . ."

"She stirs—the eyelids flutter—I do believe she is about to Wake Up, sire," said Arnold Joost van Keppel.

"Would you get that man out of my cabin now, please?" said Eliza to William, with evenness that surprised everyone. William made some subliminal gesture and van Keppel was gone, the door closed—though the shredding and seam-popping noises now redoubled.

"Is he going to leave me with *any* clothing *at all*?"

William considered it. "No—except for one garment— the one you are wearing now. You will sew this letter into the corset, after Arnold has made a copy. When you arrive in Paris—exhausted, dishevelled, sans escort or luggage— you'll have a magnificent tale to tell, of how the cheesemongers molested you, slew your traveling-companions, rifled your bags—and yet you'll be able to produce one letter that you cleverly secreted in your undergarments."

"It is a beautiful romance."

"It will create a sensation at Versailles—much better, for you, than if you'd showed up fresh and well-dressed. Duchesses and Countesses will pity you, instead of fearing you, and take you under their wings. It is such an excellent plan that I wonder why d'Avaux didn't come up with it himself."

"Perhaps d'Avaux never *intended* for me to find a place in the French court. Perhaps I was to deliver these messages, and then be discarded."

This remark was meant to be a self-pitying trifle. William was supposed to object vehemently. Instead he seemed to weigh it seriously—which did nothing to steady Eliza's nerves.

"Did d'Avaux introduce you to anyone?" he asked thoughtfully.

"That same Étienne d'Arcachon."

"Then d'Avaux has plans for you—and I know what they are."

"You have a smug look about you, O Prince, and I don't doubt that you have read Monsieur d'Avaux's mind, just as you'll read those letters. But since you have me at such a disadvantage, I would fain know of *your* plans for me."

"Doctor Leibniz has taught you cyphers that put these French ones quite to shame," said William, rattling d'Avaux's letter. "Use them."

"You want me to spy for you, at Versailles."

"Not only for *me* but for Sophie and all of the others who oppose Louis. For now, that's how you can be useful. Later, perhaps, I will require something else."

"*Now* I am in your power—but when I reach France, and those Duchesses begin fawning over me, I'll have all of *le Roi*'s armies and navies to protect me . . ."

"So how can I trust you, girl-child, not to tell the *entire* tale to the French, and become a double-agent?"

"Just so."

"Isn't it sufficient that Louis is repellent, and I stand for freedom?"

"Perhaps . . . but you'd be foolish if you trusted me to act accordingly . . . and I won't spy for a fool."

"Oh? You did for Monmouth."

Eliza gasped. "Sir!"

"You should not *joust* if you are afraid to be punched out of the saddle, girl-child."

"Monmouth is no scholar, admitted—but he's a fine warrior."

"He is *adequate*—but he's no John Churchill. You don't really believe he'll overthrow King James, do you?"

"I wouldn't have abetted him if I didn't think so."

William laughed very grimly. "Did he offer to make you a Duchess?"

"Why does everyone ask me that?"

"He addled your brain when he did that. Monmouth is doomed. I have six English and Scottish regiments garrisoned in the Hague, as part of a treaty with England . . . as soon as I get there, I'll send them back across the narrow seas to help put down Monmouth's rebellion."

"But why!? James is almost a *vassal* to Louis! You should be supporting Monmouth!"

"Eliza, did Monmouth skulk about Amsterdam incognito?"

"No, he cut a brave swath."

"Did he continually watch his back for French assassins?"

"No, he was carefree as a jay-bird."

"Were bombs with sputtering fuses found in his carriage?"

"No bombs—only bon-bons."

"Is d'Avaux an intelligent man?"

"Of course!"

"Then—since he must have known what Monmouth was planning—as you made it so obvious—why did he make no effort to assassinate *Monmouth*?"

Nothing from poor Eliza.

"Monmouth has landed, of all places, in Dorset—John Churchill's home ground! Churchill is riding out from London to engage him, and when that happens the rebellion will be crushed. My regiments will arrive much too late . . . I despatch them only for the sake of appearances."

"Don't you want a Protestant King of England?"

"Of course! In order to defeat Louis, I'll need Britain."

"You say it ever so casually."

"It is a simple truth." William shrugged. Then, an idea. "I rather like simple truths. Arnold!"

Once again, Arnold was in the cabin—he'd found another two letters. "Sire?"

"I need a witness."

"A witness to what, sire?"

"This girl fears that I'd be a fool to trust her, as matters stand. She is a Qwghlmian girl . . . so I'm going to make her Duchess of Qwghlm."

"But . . . Qwghlm is part of the King of England's do-
mains, sire."

"That's just the point," William said. "This girl will be a
duchess, *secretly,* and in name only, until such time as I sit
upon the Throne of England . . . at which time she'll become
a duchess *in fact.* So I can trust her to take my side—and she
won't think I'm a fool for doing so."

"It's either this, or the slow boat to Nagasaki?" Eliza
asked.

"It's not *so very* slow," Arnold said. "By the time you arrive, you should still have one or two teeth remaining."

Eliza ignored this, and kept her gaze on William's eyes.
"On your knees!" he commanded.

Eliza gathered her skirts—the only intact clothes she had
left—rose from her chair, and fell to her knees in front of the
Prince of Orange, who said: "You cannot be ennobled without
a ceremony that demonstrates your submission to your new
liege-lord. This has been the tradition since ancient times."

Arnold drew a small-sword from its sheath and held it out
in both hands, making it available to the Prince; but not
without striking several braces, bulkheads, and items of furniture with elbows, hilt, sword-tip, *et cetera,* for the cabin
was tiny and crowded. The Prince watched with sour amusement. "Sometimes the lord taps the vassal on the shoulder
with his sword," he allowed, "but there is no room in here to
wield such a weapon safely; besides, I am trying to make a
Duchess here, not a Knight."

"Would you prefer a dagger, my lord?" Arnold asked.

"Yes," said the Prince, "but don't concern yourself with it, I
have one handy." Whereupon he peeled his belt open with a
quick movement of the hand, and dropped his breeches. A
hitherto concealed weapon popped up into view, so close to
Eliza's face that she could feel its heat. It was neither the
longest nor the shortest such blade she had ever seen. She was
pleased to note that it was clean—a Dutch virtue—and well-
maintained. It oscillated with the beating of the Prince's heart.

"If you are going to tap me on the shoulder with that, you

are going to have to step a bit closer, my lord," Eliza said, "for, as splendid as it is, it does not compete with the other for length."

"On the contrary, you shall have to approach closer to me," said the Prince. "And as you know perfectly well, it is not your shoulder that I am aiming for: neither the left one, nor the right, but a softer and more welcoming berth in between. Do not feign ignorance, I know your history, and that you learned this and many other practices in the *Harim* of the Sultan."

"There, I was a slave. Here, it is how I become a Duchess?"

"As it was with Monmouth, and as it shall be in France, so it is here and now," William said agreeably. His hand came down on the top of her head, and grabbed a handful of hair. "Perhaps you can teach Arnold a trick or two. Arnold, witness carefully." William pulled Eliza forward. Eliza's eyes clenched shut. What was about to happen wasn't so very bad, in and of itself; but she couldn't stand to have that other man watching.

"There now," the Prince said, "ignore *him*. Open your eyes, and stare into mine, boldly, as befits a Duchess."

Coast of Europe and of Northern Africa
1685

And Midas joyes our Spanish journeys give,
We touch all gold, but find no food to live.
And I should be in the hott parching clyme,
To dust and ashes turn'd before my time.
To mew me in a Ship, is to inthrall
Mee in a prison, that weare like to fall;
Or in a Cloyster; save that there men dwell
In a calme heaven, here in a swaggering hell.
Long voyages are long consumptions,
And ships are carts for executions.
Yea they are Deaths; Is't not all one to flye
Into an other World, as t'is to dye?
—JOHN DONNE, "Elegie XX: Loves Warre"

JACK SOBBED FOR THE FIRST time since he'd been a boy, and brother Dick had been pulled up, all stiff and white, from the Thames.

The crew was not especially surprised. The moment of a ship's departure was commonly a time for the colorful venting of emotions, and that went double or triple for young women being left behind at dockside. Mr. Vliet was obviously worried that it would lead to some kind of legal en-

snarements, and fled over the plank onto the ship, followed
shortly by the duly blessed and sacramentalized Yevgeny.
God's Wounds cast off without any ceremonies and skulked
out of the harbor into the Ijsselmeer, where the sails were
raised to drive her through ragged, swelling seas. Yevgeny
came and planted a giant mukluk against the mast and
pulled his harpoon out of it, and of Jack's arm, muttering in
what sounded like embarrassment. One of the crew, who
was said to have some experience as a barber-surgeon,
stoked up the galley-fire to heat some irons. As Jack had
been slashed deeply across the chest, as well as pierced
through the forearm, there was much cauterizing to be
done. Half the ship's crew, it seemed, sat on Jack to make
him be still while the irons were applied, reheated, applied,
reheated, seemingly all the way across the Ijsselmeer. At
the beginning of this interminable cattle-branding, Jack
screamed for mercy. Some of the men who were sitting on
him looked disgusted and some looked amused, but none
looked merciful—which made sense when Jack recalled he
was on a slaver-ship. So after that he just screamed until he
lost his voice and could hear only the wet sizzle of his own
flesh.

When it was done, Jack sat, wrapped in blankets, out on
the bowsprit, as sort of a Vagabond-wretch-figurehead, and
smoked a pipe that Yevgeny had brought him. Queerly, he
felt nothing at all. Big merchant ships, locked into huge air-
filled boxes to lift them higher in the water, were being
towed over the sand-banks, which were all cluttered with old
spidery wrecks. Beyond that, the rhythm of the ocean subtly
changed, as before a play, when a frilly overture gives way
to the booming music of a Tragedy or History. It got darker
and palpably colder, and those ships were set free from their
boxes, and began to spread cloth before the wind, like
canvas-merchants displaying their wares to an important
buyer. The offerings were grudgingly accepted—the sails
filled with air, became taut and smooth, and the ships accel-
erated toward the sea. Later, they came to Texel, and all the
sailors paused in their chores to view the immense Ships of

the Line of the Dutch Navy riding on the huge waves of the North Sea, their flags and banners swirling like colored smoke-clouds and their triple gun-decks frowning at England.

Then finally they were at sea, bringing a certain kind of solace to Jack, who felt that he must be a condemned man, now, on every scrap of dry land in the world. They put in briefly at Dunkirk to recruit a few more hands. His brother Bob came out to visit Jack, who was in no condition to leave the ship, and they exchanged a few stories, which Jack forgot immediately. This last encounter with his brother was like a dream, a sweeping-together of fragments, and he heard someone telling Bob that Jack was not in his right mind.

Then south. Off St.-Malo they were overhauled and boarded by French privateers, who only laughed when they learned of the worthless cargo, and let them go with only token pilfering. But one of these Frenchmen, as he left the deck of *God's Wounds,* walked up to Mr. Vliet, who cringed. And in response to that cringing, more than anything else, the privateer slapped the Dutchman on the side of the head so hard that he fell down.

Even with his mind impaired in several ways, Jack understood that this action was more damaging to his investment than if the French had fired a broadside of cannonballs through their hull. The sailors became more surly after that, and Mr. Vliet began to spend most of his time closeted in his wardroom. The only thing that kept *God's Wounds* from becoming an ongoing mutiny was Mr. Foot, who (with Yevgeny as his muscle) became the real captain of the ship after that, stepping easily into the role, as if his twenty-year hiatus tending bar at the Bomb & Grapnel had never happened.

Following the coast, they rounded the various capes of Brittany and then steered a southwesterly rhumb-line across the Bay of Biscay, coming in view of the Galician coast after a number of anxious days. Jack did not really share in the anxiety because his wounds had become infected. Between the fevers, and the relentless bleedings meted out by the ship's barber to cure them, he lacked the faintest idea of where they were, and sometimes even forgot he was aboard ship. Mr. Vliet refused to move from the best wardroom, which was probably a savvy position for him to take, as there was sentiment among the crew for tossing him overboard. But he was the only man on the ship who knew how to navigate. So Jack was tucked into a hammock belowdecks, peering up day after day at blue needles of light between the deck-planks, hearing little but the merry clink of cowrie-shells being sifted to and fro by the ship's pitching and rolling.

When he finally got well enough to come abovedecks again, it was hot, and the sun was higher in the sky than he'd ever seen it. He was informed that they had, for a time, dropped anchor in the harbor of Lisbon, and since moved on. Jack regretted missing that, for there was said to be a very great Vagabond-camp outside that city, and if he'd managed to slip away, he might be on dry land again, reigning as Vagabond-king. But that was only the crack-pated phant'sy of a condemned man chained by the neck to a wall, and he soon made himself forget it.

According to Mr. Vliet, who spent hours taking measurements with a backstaff and making laborious calculations with numbers and tables, they had passed through the latitude of Gibraltar, and so the land they glimpsed off to port from time to time was Africa. But the Slave Coast was yet far, far to the south, and many weeks of sailing lay ahead of them.

But he was wrong about that. Later on the same day there was a commotion from the lookouts, and coming abovedecks Jack and the others saw two strange vessels approaching from abaft, seeming to crawl across the water on countless spindly legs. These were galleys, the typical warships of the Barbary Corsairs. Mr. Vliet watched them through his spyglass for a time, making certain geometrickal calculations on a slate. Then he commenced vomiting, and retreated to his cabin. Mr. Foot broke open some chests and began to pass out rusty cutlasses and blunderbusses.

"But why fight for cowrie-shells?" one of the English sailors asked. "It'll be just like the Frenchies at St.-Malo."

"They are not hunting us for what is in our hold," Mr. Foot explained. "Do you think *free* men would pull oars like that?"

Now Jack was not the first or last man aboard *God's Wounds* to question the wisdom of nailing their colors to the mast, but when he understood that those Barbary Corsairs intended to make galley-slaves out of them, his view changed. As when powder-smoke is driven away from a battle by a sea-breeze, he saw with clarity that he would die that day. He saw also that the arrival of the corsairs was fortunate for him, since his death was not long in coming *anyway,* and better to die in fighting for his liberty, than in scheming to take away some other man's.

So he went down belowdecks and opened up his sea-chest and took out his Janissary-sword in its gaudy sheath, and brought it up abovedecks. The crew had formed up into a few distinct clusters, obviously the beginnings of mutinous conspiracies. Jack climbed up onto the prow of a longboat that was lashed to the deck, and from there vaulted up onto the roof of a pilot-house that stood just aft of the foremast. From this height, he had a view up and down the length of *God's Wounds* and was struck (as usual) by what a narrow sliver of a thing she was. And yet she, or any other European cargo-vessel, was a wallowing pig compared to those galleys, which slid over the top of the water like Dutch ice-skates hissing over the top of a frozen canal. They had enormous saffron-colored triangular sails to drive them forward as well as the oars, and they were approaching in single file from directly astern, so that *God's Wounds*'s few paltry cannon could not fire a broadside. There was a single swivel-gun astern that might have pelted the lead galley with a tangerine-sized cannonball or two, but the men near it were arguing, instead of loading the weapon.

"What a world!" Jack hollered.

Most everyone looked at him.

"Year after year at home, chopping wood and drawing water and going to church, nothing to divert us save the odd hailstorm or famine—and yet all a man need do is board ship and ride the wind for a few days, and what've you got? Barbary Corsairs and pirate-galleys off the coast of Morocco! Now, Mr. Vliet, he has no taste for adventure. But as for myself, I would rather cross swords with corsairs than pull oars for them—so I'm for fighting!" Jack pulled out the Janissary-sword, which, compared to Mr. Foot's pitted relics, burnt and glittered beneath the African sun. Then he flung the scabbard away. It *fup-fup-fupped* off to port and then stopped in midair and dove vertically into the waves. "*This* is the only thing they're going to get from Half-Cocked Jack!"

This actually wrung a cheer from the approximately half of the crew who'd made up their minds to fight anyway. The other half only looked embarrassed on Jack's behalf. "Easy for you to say—everyone knows you're dying," said one of the latter group, one Henry Flatt, who until this moment had been on easy terms with Jack.

"And yet I'll live longer'n *you*," Jack said, then jumped down from the pilot-house and began to approach Flatt—who stood and watched dumbly at first, perhaps not aware that all of his fellows had fled to other parts of the ship. When Jack drew closer, and turned sideways, and bent his knees, and showed Flatt the edge of his blade, Flatt went *en garde* for just a moment, then seemed to come to his senses, backpedaled several yards, then simply turned and ran. Jack could hear men laughing—satisfying in a way, but, on second thought, vexing. This was serious work, not play-acting. The only way to make these half-wits understand that weighty matters were at stake was probably to kill someone. So Jack cornered Flatt up at the bow, and pursued him, actually, out onto the very bowsprit, weaving and dodging around the points of the inner jib, the outer jib, and the flying jib, all of which were quivering and snapping in the wind as no one was paying attention to keeping them trimmed. Finally the wretch Flatt was perched on the tip of the bowsprit, gripping the last available line* to keep from being tossed away by the routine pitching of the ship. With the other hand he raised a cutlass in a feeble threat. "Be killed now by a Christian or in ten minutes by a heathen— it's all one to me—but if you choose to be a slave, your life is worthless, and I'll flick you into the ocean like a turd," Jack said.

"I'll fight," Flatt said. Jack could see plainly that he was lying. But everyone was watching now—not just the crew of *God's Wounds,* but a startlingly large crowd of armed men who had emerged onto the decks of the galleys. Jack had to observe proper form. So he made a great show of turning his back on Henry Flatt, and began to work his way back down the bowsprit, with the intent of whirling around and striking Flatt down when Flatt inevitably came after him. In fact, he was just about to do so when he saw Mr. Foot swinging his cutlass at a taut line that had been made fast to a pinrail at the bow: the sheet that held the obtuse corner of the flying jib, and transferred all of its power into the frame of the ship. The jib went slack above him. Jack dove, and grabbed at a line. He heard a sort of immense metallic fart as the shivering canvas wrapped around Flatt like a shroud, held him for a moment, and then dropped him into the sea, where he was immediately driven under by the onrushing hull.

Jack nearly fell overboard himself, as he ended up dangling by a rope with one hand, maintaining a grip on the sword with the other—but Yevgeny's big hand seized his forearm and hauled him up to safety.

That is, if *this* could be considered safety: the two galleys, which until now had been idling along in single file, had, during the dispute with Flatt, forked apart so that they could come up on both flanks of *God's Wounds* at the same time.

---

*The flying jib downhaul.

For some minutes it had been possible to hear, from those galleys, a faint musick: an eerie chaunt sung by many voices, in a strange keening melody, that, somewhat like an Irish tune, struck Jack's English ears as being Not from Around Here. Though, come to think of it, it probably *was* from around here. Anyway, it was a strange alien melody sung in some barbarous tongue. And until very recently, it had been sung slowly, as the crashing of the galleys' many oar-blades into the brine had served as the drum-beat marking the time.

But now that the galleys had got themselves sorted out into parallel courses, they emitted a sudden fusillade of snapping noises—Jack thought, some sort of outlandish gunfire. Immediately the singing grew louder. Jack could just make out the heathen syllables:

Havah nagilah, Havah nagilah, Havah nagilah,
  v'nism'chah!
Havah nagilah, Havah nagilah, Havah nagilah,
  v'nism'chah.

"It is like the bagpipes of the Scots," he announced, "a sort of shrill noise that they make before battle, to cover the sound of their knees knocking together."

One or two men laughed. But even these were shushed by others, who were now listening intently to the song of the corsairs. Rather than proceeding to a steady beat, as good Christian music always did, it seemed to be getting faster.

Uru, uru achim
Uru achim b'lev sa me ach!
Uru achim b'lev sa me ach!
Uru achim b'lev sa me ach!
Uru achim b'lev sa me ach!
Havah nagilah . . .

It was most certainly getting faster; and as the oars bit into the water on each beat of the song, this meant that they were

now *rowing* as well as *singing* faster. And indeed the gap between the bow of the foremost galley, and the stern of *God's
Wounds,* was getting rapidly narrower.

Uru, uru achim
Uru achim b'lev sa me ach!
Uru achim b'lev sa me ach!
Uru achim b'lev sa me ach!
Uru achim b'lev sa me ach!
Havah nagilah.
Havah nagilah, Havah nagilah, Havah nagilah,
  v'nism'chah!
Havah nagilah, Havah nagilah, Havah nagilah,
  v'nism'chah.

The corsairs were singing and rowing with abandon now,
easily coming up along both flanks, maintaining just enough
distance to give their oars the freedom to claw at the waves.
Even not counting the unseen oar-slaves, the number of men
aboard was insane, reckless, as if a whole pirate-city had
crowded into each galley.

The one to port came alongside soonest, its sails and rigging struck and furled for the attack, its rail, and the poop
deck, crowded with corsairs, many of them swinging
grappling-hooks on the ends of ropes, others brandishing
boarding-ladders with vicious curved spikes on the ends.
Jack—and all of the others aboard *God's Wounds*—saw, and
understood, the same thing at the same time. They *saw* that
almost none of the fighting men were Arabs except for the
agha shouting the orders. They were, instead, white men,
black Africans, even a few Indians. They *understood* that all
of them were Janissaries, which is to say non-Turks who did
the Turks' fighting for them.

Having understood *that,* they would not be slow to grasp
that becoming a Barbary Corsair might, for men such as
them, constitute a fine opportunity.

Jack, being half a step quicker than the average sea-scum,
understood this a moment sooner than anyone else, and de-

cided that he would blurt it out, so that everyone would think it had been his idea. He picked up a grappling-hook and coil of rope that had been rattling around in the bottom of the weapons-chest, and returned to his former podium atop the pi-lot-house, and hollered, "All right! Who's for turning Turk?"

A lusty cheer came up from the crew. It seemed to be unanimous, with the single exception of Yevgeny, who as usual had no idea what was being said. While the others were all shaking hands and congratulating one another, Jack clenched his sword in his teeth, tossed the rope-coil over his shoulder, and began ascending the ladderlike web of rig-ging—the fore shrouds, so called—that converged on the fore-top: a platform about halfway up the mast. Reaching it, he jammed the point of the sword into the planking, and regarded the galleys from above. The singing had sped up into a frenzy now, and the movements of the oars were be-ginning to get into disarray, as not all of the slaves could move their implements fast enough!

Uru, uru achim
Uru achim b'lev sa me ach!
Uru achim b'lev sa me ach!
Uru achim b'lev sa me ach!
Uru achim b'lev sa me ach!
Havah nagilah . . .

Uru achim b'lev sa me ach
Uru achim b'lev sa me ach
Uru achim b'lev sa me ach
Uru achim b'lev sa me ach

Both of the galleys had moved half a length ahead of *God's Wounds* now. Upon a signal from one of the *aghas,* both suddenly folded their oars and steered inwards, falling back and converging on *God's Wounds.* The oar-slaves col-lapsed onto their benches, and the only thing that kept all of them from landing flat on their backs was that they were packed into the hull too tightly to lie down.

"You men are only seeing the turbans and jewels and polished weapons of the Janissaries!" Jack hollered. "I can see
the slaves pulling the oars now—she's a coffin packed with
half-dead wretches. Did you hear those snapping noises before? 'Twas not gunfire—'twas the long bullwhips of the
slave-drivers! I see a hundred men with fresh stripes torn
from their backs, slumped over their oars. We'll all be slaves
in half an hour's time—unless we show the *agha* that we
know how to fight, and deserve to be Janissaries instead!"

As Jack was delivering this oration, he was laying his
rope-coil out on the planking of the fore-top, so it would un-
furl cleanly. A grappling-hook flung from the rail of the port
galley nearly struck him in the face. Jack ducked and
shrugged. It bit into the planking at his feet, which popped
and groaned as some Janissary put his weight on the attached
line. Jack jerked his sword loose and chopped through it,
sending a corsair down to be crushed between the converging hulls of the two ships.

The engagement, which had been miraculously quiet—
almost serene—until now, became a cacophony of booms as
the Barbary pirates fired all of their guns. Then it became
silent again, as no one would have time to reload before it
was all over. Jack's view below was temporarily clouded by
smoke. He was looking almost level across to the port galley's tall mainmast, which had a narrow crow's nest near the
top. It was an obvious target for a grappling-hook and indeed Jack snagged it on the first throw—then, pulling the
slack out of the line, was almost torn off the fore-top as the
ships rocked in opposite directions and their masts suddenly
spread apart. Jack decided to construe this as an opportunity,
and quickly wrapped the rope round his left forearm several
times. The next movement of the ships ripped him off the
fore-top, putting a few thousand splinters into his abdomen,
and sent him plunging into space. The rope broke his fall, by
nearly pulling his arm off. He whizzed across the middle of
the galley in an instant, seeing just a blur of crimson and saffron, and a moment later found himself hanging out over the
blue ocean, ponderously changing direction. Looking back

the way he'd just come, and was shortly to go again, he saw a few non-combatants staring back at him curiously—including one of those slave-drivers. When Jack's next pendulum-swing took him back over the galley's deck, he reached out with the sword and cut that man's head in two. But the impact of sword on skull sent him spinning round, out of control. Flailing, he swung back over the deck of *God's Wounds* and slammed into the base of the foremast hard enough to knock the wind out of his lungs and make him let go of the rope. He slid to the deck and looked around at a number of men's legs—but not legs he recognized. The whole ship was covered with Janissaries, and Jack was the only one who'd done any fighting at all.

The one exception to that rule was Yevgeny, who had got the gist of Jack's stirring first speech, but not understood the more pragmatic second one. Accordingly, he had harpooned the *rais*, or captain of the starboard galley, right through the throrax.

This and other statistics of the battle (such as it was) were conveyed to Jack by Mr. Foot later, after they had been stripped of all clothes and possessions and moved onto a galley, where a blacksmith was stoking up his forge and making ready to weld fetters around narrow parts of their bodies.

The corsairs rifled the holds of *God's Wounds* in all of about fifteen minutes, and obviously lacked enthusiasm for the cowrie shells. The only captive who wasn't transferred to a galley was Mr. Vliet, who had been ferreted out of the bilge, where he had concealed himself. The Dutchman was brought up abovedecks, stripped naked, and tied over a barrel. An African was roundly fucking him now.

"What was all that nonsense you were raving from the fore-top?" Mr. Foot asked. "No one could understand a word you were saying. We were all just looking at each other—" Mr. Foot pantomimed a bewildered shrug.

"That you'd all better show what magnificent fighters you were," Jack summarized, "or else they'd have you chained up straight off."

"Hmph," Mr. Foot said, too diplomatic to point out that it hadn't worked in Jack's case. Though a few discreet winks from some of the bleeding sunburned wretches told Jack that his partial decapitation of that one slave-driver might make him as popular among galley-slaves as he'd formerly been among Vagabonds.

"Why should you care?" Mr. Foot asked a few minutes later, as the anal violation of his erstwhile business partner showed no sign of coming to a climax any time soon. The barrel supporting Mr. Vliet had slowly worked its way across the deck of *God's Wounds* until it lodged against a rail, and was now booming like a drum. "You're not long for this world anyway."

"If you ever visit Paris, you can take this question up with St.-George, *mort-aux-rats*," Jack said. "He taught me a few things about correct form. I have a reputation, you know—"

"So they say."

"I hoped that you, or one of the *younger* men, might show some valor, and become a Janissary, and one day make his way back to Christendom, and tell the tale of my deeds 'gainst the Barbary Corsairs. So that all would know how my story came out, and that it came out well. That's all."

"Well, next time enunciate," Mr. Foot said, "because we literally could not make out a word you were saying."

"Yes, yes," Jack snapped—hoping he would not be chained to the same oar as Mr. Foot, who was already becoming a bore. He sighed. "That is one prodigious butt-fucking!" he marveled. "Like something out of the Bible!"

"There's no butt-fucking in the Good Book!" said the scandalized Mr. Foot.

"Well, how should I know?" Jack said. "Back off! Soon, I'll be in a place where everyone reads the Bible all the time."

"Heaven?"

"Does it sound like heaven to you?"

"Well, it appears they are leading me off to a different oar, Jack," Mr. Foot said. Indeed, a dead man was being cut loose from an oar at the stern, and Mr. Foot was being signalled for. "So if we never speak again—as seems likely—God-speed!"

"Godspeed? *Godspeed!* What kind of a thing is that to say to a fucking *galley slave*?" were Jack's last words, or so he supposed, to Mr. Foot.

Mr. Vliet was being pushed overboard by a couple of Janissaries. Jack heard the splash just as he was sitting down on the shit-stained bench where he would row until he died.

$\clubsuit$

Dramatis Personae

$\maltese$

MEMBERS OF THE NOBILITY went by more than one name: their family surnames and Christian names, but also their titles. For example, the younger brother of King Charles II had the family name Stuart and was baptized James, and so might be called James Stuart; but for most of his life he was the Duke of York, and so might also be referred to, in the third person anyway, as "York" (but in the second person as "Your Royal Highness"). Titles frequently changed during a person's lifetime, as it was common during this period for commoners to be ennobled, and nobles of lower rank to be promoted. And so not only might a person have several names at any one moment, but certain of those names might change as he acquired new titles through ennoblement, promotion, conquest, or (what might be considered a combination of all three) marriage.

This multiplicity of names will be familiar to many readers who dwell on the east side of the Atlantic, or who read a lot of books like this. To others it may be confusing or even maddening. The following Dramatis Personae may be of help in resolving ambiguities.

If consulted too early and often, it may let cats out of bags by letting the reader know who is about to die, and who isn't.

The compiler of such a table faces a problem similar to the one that bedeviled Leibniz when trying to organize his patron's library. The entries (books in Leibniz's case, personages here) must be arranged in a linear fashion according

to some predictable scheme. Below, they are alphabetized by
name. But since more than one name applies to many of the
characters, it is not always obvious where the entry should
be situated. Here I have sacrificed consistency for ease of
use by placing each entry under the name that is most commonly used in the book. So, for example, Louis-François de
Lavardac, duc d'Arcachon, is under "A" rather than "L" because he is almost always called simply the duc d'Arcachon
in the story. But Knott Bolstrood, Count Penistone, is under
"B" because he is usually called Bolstrood. Cross-references
to the main entries are spotted under "L" and "P," respectively.

Entries that are relatively reliable, according to scholarly
sources, are in Roman type. Entries in italics contain information that is more likely to produce confusion, misunder-
standing, severe injury, and death if relied upon by time
travelers visiting the time and place in question.

ↄ⊰

ANGLESEY, LOUIS: 1648–. *Earl of Upnor. Son of Thomas
More Anglesey. Courtier and friend of the Duke of Monmouth during the Interregnum and, after the Restoration,
at Trinity College, Cambridge.*

ANGLESEY, PHILLIP: 1645–. *Count Sheerness. Son of
Thomas More Anglesey.*

ANGLESEY, THOMAS MORE: 1618–1679. *Duke of Gunfleet.
A leading Cavalier and a member of Charles II's court in
exile during the Interregnum. After the Restoration, one
of the A's in Charles II's CABAL (which see). Relocated
to France during the Popish Plot troubles, died there.*

ANNE I OF ENGLAND: 1665–1714. Daughter of James II by
his first wife, Anne Hyde.

APTHORP, RICHARD: 1631–. *Businessman and banker. One
of the A's in Charles II's CABAL (which see). A founder
of the Bank of England.*

D'ARCACHON, DUC: 1634–. *Louis-François de Lavardac. A cousin to Louis XIV. Builder, and subsequently Admiral, of the French Navy.*

D'ARCACHON, ÉTIENNE: 1662–. *Étienne de Lavardac. Son and heir of Louis-François de Lavardac, duc d'Arcachon.*

D'ARTAGNAN, CHARLES DE BATZ-CASTELMORE: c. 1620–1673. French musketeer and memoirist.

ASHMOLE, SIR ELIAS: 1617–1692. Astrologer, alchemist, autodidact, Comptroller and Auditor of the Excise, collector of curiosities, and founder of Oxford's Ashmolean Museum.

D'AVAUX, JEAN-ANTOINE DE MESMES, COMTE: French ambassador to the Dutch Republic, later an advisor to James II during his campaign in Ireland.

BOLSTROOD, GOMER: 1645–. *Son of Knott. Dissident agitator, later an immigrant to New England and a furniture maker there.*

BOLSTROOD, GREGORY: 1600–1652. *Dissident preacher. Founder of the Puritan sect known as the Barkers.*

BOLSTROOD, KNOTT: 1628–1682. *Son of Gregory. Ennobled as Count Penistone and made Secretary of State by Charles II. The B in Charles II's CABAL (which see).*

BOYLE, ROBERT: 1627–1691. Chemist, member of the Experimental Philosophical Club at Oxford, Fellow of the Royal Society.

VON BOYNEBURG, JOHANN CHRISTIAN: 1622–1672. An early patron of Leibniz in Mainz.

CABAL, THE: unofficial name of Charles II's post-Restoration cabinet, loosely modeled after Louis XIV's Conseil d'en-Haut, which is to say that each member had a general area of responsibility, but the boundaries were vague and overlapping (see table, p. 352).

CAROLINE, PRINCESS OF BRANDENBURG-ANSBACH: 1683–1737. Daughter of Eleanor, Princess of Saxe-Eisenach.

CASTLEMAINE, LADY: see Villiers, Barbara.

CATHERINE OF BRAGANZA: 1638–1705. Portuguese wife of Charles II of England.

The CABAL

Responsible party	General area[s] of responsibility	Corresponding roughly to formal position of*
C COMSTOCK, JOHN (EARL OF EPSOM)	(Early in the reign) domestic affairs and justice. Later retired	Lord High Chancellor
A ANGLESEY, LOUIS (DUKE OF GUNFLEET)	(Early) the Exchequer and (covertly) foreign affairs, especially vis-a-vis France. Later Apthorp came to dominate the former. After Comstock's retirement, but before the Popish Plot, domestic affairs, and the Navy.	Various, including Lord High Admiral
B BOLSTROOD, KNOTT (COUNT PENISTONE)	Foreign affairs (ostensibly)	Secretary of State
A APTHORP, SIR RICHARD	Finance	Chancellor of the Exchequer
L LEWIS, HUGH (DUKE OF TWEED)	Army	Marshal, or (though no such position existed at the time) Defense Minister

*But sometimes they formally held these positions and sometimes they didn't.

CHARLES I OF ENGLAND: 1600–1649. Stuart king of England, decapitated at the Banqueting House after the victory of Parliamentary forces under Oliver Cromwell.
CHARLES II OF ENGLAND: 1630–1685. Son of Charles I. Exiled to France and later the Netherlands during the Inter-

regnum. Returned to England 1660 and re-established monarchy (the Restoration).

CHARLES LOUIS, ELECTOR PALATINATE: 1617–1680. Eldest surviving son of the Winter King and Queen, brother of Sophie, father of Liselotte. Re-established his family in the Palatinate following the Thirty Years' War.

CHARLES, ELECTOR PALATINATE: 1651–1685. Son and heir to Charles Louis. War-gaming enthusiast. Died young of disease contracted during a mock siege.

CHESTER, LORD BISHOP OF: see Wilkins, John.

CHURCHILL, JOHN: 1650–1722. Courtier, warrior, duellist, cocksman, hero, later Duke of Marlborough.

CHURCHILL, WINSTON: Royalist, Squire, courtier, early Fellow of the Royal Society, father of John Churchill.

CLEVELAND, DUCHESS OF: see Villiers, Barbara.

COMENIUS, JOHN AMOS (JAN AMOS KOMENSKY): 1592–1670. Moravian Pansophist, an inspiration to Wilkins and Leibniz among many others.

COMSTOCK, CHARLES: 1650–1708. *Son of John. Student of Natural Philosophy. After the retirement of John and the death of his elder brother, Richard, an immigrant to Connecticut.*

COMSTOCK, JOHN: 1607–1685. *Leading Cavalier, and member of Charles II's court in exile in France. Scion of the so-called Silver branch of the Comstock family. Armaments maker. Early patron of the Royal Society. After the Restoration, the C in Charles II's CABAL (which see). Father of Richard and Charles Comstock.*

COMSTOCK, RICHARD: 1638–1673. *Eldest son and heir of John Comstock. Died at naval battle of Sole Bay.*

COMSTOCK, ROGER: 1646–. *Scion of the so-called Golden branch of the Comstock family. Classmate of Newton, Daniel Waterhouse, the Duke of Monmouth, the Earl of Upnor, and George Jeffreys at Trinity College, Cambridge, during the early 1660s. Later, a successful developer of real estate, and Marquis of Ravenscar.*

DE CRÉPY: *French family of gentlemen and petty nobles until the Wars of Religion in France, during which time they began to pursue a strategy of aggressive upward mobility. They intermarried in two different ways with the older but declining de Gex family. One of them (Anne Marie de Crépy, 1653–) married the much older duc d'Oyonnax and survived him by many years. Her sister (Charlotte Adélaide de Crépy 1656–) married the Marquis d'Ozoir.*

CROMWELL, OLIVER: 1599–1658. Parliamentary leader, general of the anti-Royalist forces during the English Civil War, scourge of Ireland, and leading man of England during the Commonwealth, or Interregnum.

CROMWELL, ROGER: 1626–1712. Son and (until the Restoration) successor of his much more formidable father, Oliver.

EAUZE, CLAUDE: see *d'Ozoir, Marquis.*

ELEANOR, PRINCESS OF SAXE-EISENACH: D. 1696. Mother (by her first husband, the Margrave of Ansbach) of Caroline, Princess of Brandenburg-Ansbach. Late in life, married to the Elector of Saxony.

ELISABETH CHARLOTTE: 1652–1722. Liselotte, La Palatine. Known as Madame in the French court. Daughter of Charles Louis, Elector Palatinate, and niece of Sophie. Married Philippe, duc d'Orléans, the younger brother of Louis XIV. Spawned the House of Orléans.

EPSOM, EARL OF: see *Comstock, John.*

FREDERICK V, ELECTOR PALATINATE: 1596–1632. King of Bohemia ("Winter King") briefly in 1618, lived and died in exile during the Thirty Years' War. Father of many princes, electors, duchesses, etc., including Sophie.

FREDERICK WILLIAM, ELECTOR OF BRANDENBURG: 1620–1688. Known as the Great Elector. After the Thirty Years' War created a standing professional army, small but effective. By playing the great powers of the day (Sweden, France, and the Hapsburgs) against each other, consolidated the scattered Hohenzollern fiefdoms into a coherent state, Brandenburg-Prussia.

DE GEX: *A petty-noble family of Jura, which dwindled until the early seventeenth century, when the two surviving children of Henry, Sieur de Gex (1595–1660), Francis and Louise-Anne, each married a member of the more sanguine family de Crépy. The children of Francis carried on the de Gex name. Their youngest was Édouard de Gex. The children of Louise-Anne included Anne Marie de Crépy (later duchesse d'Oyonnax) and Charlotte Adélaide de Crépy (later marquise d'Ozoir).*

DE GEX, FATHER ÉDOUARD: 1663–. *Youngest offspring of Marguerite Diane de Crépy (who died giving birth to him) and Francis de Gex, who was thirty-eight years old and in declining health. Raised at a school and orphanage in Lyons by Jesuits, who found in him an exceptionally gifted pupil. Became a Jesuit himself at the the age of twenty. Was posted to Versailles, where he became a favorite of Mademoiselle. de Maintenon.*

GREAT ELECTOR: see Frederick William.

GUNFLEET, DUKE OF: see *Anglesey, Thomas More.*

GWYN, NELL: 1650–1687. Fruit retailer and comedienne, one of the mistresses of Charles II.

HAM, THOMAS: 1603–. *Money-goldsmith, husband of Mayflower Waterhouse, leading man of Ham Bros. Goldsmiths. Created Earl of Walbrook by Charles II.*

HAM, WILLIAM: 1662–. *Son of Thomas and Mayflower.*

HENRIETTA ANNE: 1644–1670. Sister of Charles II and James II of England, first wife of Philippe, duc d'Orléans, Louis XIV's brother.

HENRIETTA MARIA: 1609–1669. Sister of King Louis XIII of France, wife of King Charles I of England, mother of Charles II and James II of England.

HOOKE, ROBERT: 1635–1703. Artist, linguist, astronomer, geometer, microscopist, mechanic, horologist, chemist, optician, inventor, philosopher, botanist, anatomist, etc. Curator of Experiments for the Royal Society, Surveyor of London after the fire. Friend and collaborator of Christopher Wren.

HUYGENS, CHRISTIAAN: 1629–1695. Great Dutch astronomer, horologist, mathematician, and physicist.

HYDE, ANNE: 1637–1671. First wife of James, Duke of York (later James II). Mother of two English queens: Mary (of William and Mary) and Anne.

JAMES I OF ENGLAND: 1566–1625. First Stuart king of England.

JAMES II OF ENGLAND: 1633–1701. Duke of York for much of his early life. Became King of England upon the death of his brother in 1685. Deposed in the Glorious Revolution, late 1688–early 1689.

JAMES VI OF SCOTLAND: see James I of England.

JEFFREYS, GEORGE: 1645–1689. Welsh gentleman, lawyer, solicitor general to the Duke of York, lord chief justice, and later lord chancellor under James II. Created Baron Jeffreys of Wem in 1685.

JOHANN FRIEDRICH: 1620–1679. Duke of Braunschweig-Lüneburg, book collector, a patron of Leibniz.

JOHN FREDERICK: see Johann Friedrich.

KÉROUALLE, LOUISE DE: 1649–1734. Duchess of Portsmouth. One of the mistresses of Charles II.

KETCH, JACK: Name given to executioners.

LAVARDAC: *A branch of the Bourbon family producing various hereditary dukes and peers of France, including the duc d'Arcachon (see).*

LEFEBURE: French alchemist/apothecary who moved to London at the time of the Restoration to provide services to the Court.

LEIBNIZ, GOTTFRIED WILHELM: 1646–1716. Refer to novel.

LESTRANGE, SIR ROGER: 1616–1704. Royalist pamphleteer and (after the Restoration) Surveyor of the Imprimery, hence chief censor for Charles II. Nemesis of Milton. Translator.

LEWIS, HUGH: 1625–. *General. Created Duke of Tweed by Charles II after the Restoration, in recognition of his crossing the River Tweed with his regiment (thenceforth called the Coldstream Guards) in support of the resurgent monarchy. The L in Charles II's CABAL (which see).*

LISELOTTE: *see* Elisabeth Charlotte.

LOCKE, JOHN: 1632–1704. Natural Philosopher, physician, political advisor, philosopher.

DE MAINTENON, MME.: 1635–1719. Mistress, then second and last wife of Louis XIV.

MARY: 1662–1694. Daughter of James II and Anne Hyde. After the Glorious Revolution (1689), Queen of England with her husband, William of Orange.

MARY OF MODENA: 1658–1718. Second and last wife of James II of England. Mother of James Stuart, aka "the Old Pretender."

MAURICE: 1621–1652. One of the numerous princely offspring of the Winter Queen. Active as a Cavalier in the English Civil War.

DE MESMES, JEAN-ANTOINE: see d'Avaux.

MINETTE: see Henrietta Anne.

MONMOUTH, DUKE OF (JAMES SCOTT): 1649–1685. Bastard of Charles II by one Lucy Walter.

MORAY, ROBERT: c. 1608–1673. Scottish soldier, official, and courtier, a favorite of Charles II. Early Royal Society figure, probably instrumental in securing the organization's charter.

NEWTON, ISAAC: 1642–1727. Refer to novel.

OLDENBURG, HENRY: 1615–1677. Emigrant from Bremen. Secretary of the Royal Society, publisher of the *Philosophical Transactions,* prolific correspondent.

D'OYONNAX, ANNE MARIE DE CRÉPY, DUCHESSE: 1653–. *Lady in Waiting to the Dauphine, Satanist, poisoner.*

D'OZOIR, CHARLOTTE ADÉLAIDE DE CRÉPY, MARQUISE: 1656–. *Wife of Claude Eauze, Marquis d'Ozoir.*

D'OZOIR, CLAUDE EAUZE, MARQUIS: 1650–. *Illegitimate son of Louis-François de Lavardac, duc d'Arcachon, by a domestic servant, Luce Eauze. Traveled to India in late 1660s as part of ill-fated French East India Company expedition. In 1674, when noble titles went on sale to raise funds for the Dutch war, he purchased the title Marquis d'Ozoir using a loan from his father secured by revenues from his slaving operations in Africa.*

PENISTONE, COUNT: see *Bolstrood, Knott.*

PEPYS, SAMUEL: 1633–1703. Clerk, Administrator to the Royal Navy, Member of Parliament, Fellow of the Royal Society, diarist, man about town.

PETERS, HUGH: 1598–1660. Fulminant Puritan preacher. Spent time in Holland and Massachusetts, returned to England, became Cromwell's chaplain. Poorly thought of by Irish for his involvement with massacres at Drogheda and Wexford. For his role in the regicide of Charles I, executed by Jack Ketch, using a knife, in 1660.

PHILIPPE, DUC D'ORLÉANS: 1640–1701. Younger brother of King Louis XIV of France. Known as Monsieur to the French Court. Husband first of Henrietta Anne of England, later of Liselotte. Progenitor of the House of Orléans.

PORTSMOUTH, DUCHESS OF: see Kéroualle, Louise de.

QWGHLM: *Title bestowed on Eliza by William of Orange.*

RAVENSCAR, MARQUIS OF: see *Comstock, Roger.*

ROSSIGNOL, ANTOINE: 1600–1682. "France's first full-time cryptologist" (David Kahn, *The Codebreakers,* which buy and read). A favorite of Richelieu, Louis XIII, Mazarin, and Louis XIV.

ROSSIGNOL, BONAVENTURE: D. 1705. Cryptanalyst to Louis XIV following the death of his father, teacher, and collaborator Antoine.

RUPERT: 1619–1682. One of the numerous princely offspring of the Winter Queen. Active as a Cavalier in the English Civil War.

DE RUYTER, MICHIEL ADRIAANSZOON: 1607–1676. Exceptionally gifted Dutch admiral. Particularly effective against the English.

VON SCHÖNBORN, JOHANN PHILIPP: 1605–1673. Elector and Archbishop of Mainz, statesman, diplomat, and early patron of Leibniz.

SHEERNESS, COUNT: see *Anglesey, Phillip.*

SOPHIE: 1630–1714. Youngest daughter of the Winter Queen. Married Ernst August, who later became duke of Braunschweig-Lüneburg. Later the name of this principality was changed to Hanover, and Ernst August and Sophie elevated to the status of Elector and Electress. From 1707 onwards, she was first in line to the English throne.

SOPHIE CHARLOTTE: 1668–1705. Eldest daughter of Sophie. Married Frederick III, elector of Brandenburg and son of the Great Elector. In 1701, when Brandenburg-Prussia was elevated to the status of a kingdom by the Holy Roman Emperor, she became the first Queen of Prussia and spawned the House of Prussia.

STUART, ELIZABETH: 1596–1662. Daughter of King James I of England, sister of Charles I. Married Frederick, Elector Palatinate. Proclaimed Queen of Bohemia briefly in 1618, hence her sobriquet "the Winter Queen." Lived in exile during the Thirty Years' War, mostly in the Dutch Republic. Outlived her husband by three decades. Mother of many children, including Sophie.

STUART, JAMES: 1688–1766. Controversial but probably legitimate son of James II by his second wife, Mary of Modena. Raised in exile in France. Following the death of his father, styled James III by the Jacobite faction in England and "the Old Pretender" by supporters of the Hanoverian succession.

UPNOR, EARL OF: see *Anglesey, Louis.*

VILLIERS, BARBARA (LADY CASTLEMAINE, DUCHESS OF CLEVELAND): 1641–1709. Indefatigable mistress of many satisfied Englishmen of high rank, including Charles II and John Churchill.

WALBROOK, EARL OF: see *Ham, Thomas.*

WATERHOUSE, ANNE: 1649–. *Née Anne Robertson. English colonist in Massachusetts. Wife of Praise-God Waterhouse.*

WATERHOUSE, BEATRICE: 1642–. *Née Beatrice Durand. Huguenot wife of Sterling.*

WATERHOUSE, CALVIN: 1563–1605. *Son of John, father of Drake.*

WATERHOUSE, DANIEL: 1646–. *Youngest (by far) child of Drake by his second wife, Hortense.*

WATERHOUSE, DRAKE: 1590–1666. *Son of Calvin, father of Raleigh, Sterling, Mayflower, Oliver, and Daniel. Inde-*

pendent trader, political agitator, leader of Pilgrims and Dissidents.

WATERHOUSE, ELIZABETH: 1621–. *Née Elizabeth Flint. Wife of Raleigh Waterhouse.*

WATERHOUSE, EMMA: 1656–. *Daughter of Raleigh and Elizabeth.*

WATERHOUSE, FAITH: 1689–. *Née Faith Page. English colonist in Massachusetts. (Much younger) wife of Daniel, mother of Godfrey.*

WATERHOUSE, GODFREY WILLIAM: 1708–. *Son of Daniel and Faith in Boston.*

WATERHOUSE, HORTENSE: 1625–1658. *Née Hortense Bowden. Second wife (m. 1645) of Drake Waterhouse, and mother of Daniel.*

WATERHOUSE, JANE: 1599–1643. *Née Jane Wheelwright. A pilgrim in Leiden. First wife (m. 1617) of Drake, mother of Raleigh, Sterling, Oliver, and Mayflower.*

WATERHOUSE, JOHN: 1542–1597. *Devout early English Protestant. Decamped to Geneva during reign of Bloody Mary. Father of Calvin Waterhouse.*

WATERHOUSE, MAYFLOWER: 1621–. *Daughter of Drake and Jane, wife of Thomas Ham, mother of William Ham.*

WATERHOUSE, OLIVER I: 1625–1646. *Son of Drake and Jane. Died in Battle of Newark during English Civil War.*

WATERHOUSE, OLIVER II: 1653–. *Son of Raleigh and Elizabeth.*

WATERHOUSE, PRAISE-GOD: 1649–. *Eldest son of Raleigh and Elizabeth. Immigrated to Massachusetts Bay Colony. Father of Wait Still Waterhouse.*

WATERHOUSE, RALEIGH: 1618–. *Eldest son of Drake, father of Praise-God, Oliver II, and Emma.*

WATERHOUSE, STERLING: 1630–. *Son of Drake. Real estate developer. Later ennobled as Earl of Willesden.*

WATERHOUSE, WAIT STILL: 1675–. *Son of Praise-God in Boston. Graduate of Harvard College. Congregational preacher.*

WEEM, WALTER: 1652–. *Husband of Emma Waterhouse.*

WHEELWRIGHT, JANE: see *Waterhouse, Jane.*

WILHELMINA CAROLINE: see Caroline, Princess of Brandenburg-Ansbach.

WILKINS, JOHN (BISHOP OF CHESTER): 1614–1672. Cryptographer. Science fiction author. Founder, first chairman, and first secretary of the Royal Society. Private chaplain to Charles Louis, Elector Palatinate. Warden of Wadham (Oxford) and Master of Trinity (Cambridge). Prebendary of York, Dean of Ripon, holder of many other ecclesiastical appointments. Friend of Nonconformists, Supporter of Freedom of Conscience.

WILLESDEN, EARL OF: see *Waterhouse, Sterling.*

WILLIAM II OF ORANGE: 1626–1650. Father of the better-known William III of Orange. Died young (of smallpox).

WILLIAM III OF ORANGE: 1650–1702. With Mary, daugher of James II, co-sovereign of England from 1689.

WINTER KING: see Frederick V.

WINTER QUEEN: see Stuart, Elizabeth.

WREN, CHRISTOPHER: 1632–1723. Prodigy, Natural Philosopher, and Architect, a member of the Experimental Philosophical Club and later Fellow of the Royal Society.

YORK, DUKE OF: The traditional title of whomever is next in line to the English throne. During much of this book, James, brother to Charles II.

DE LA ZEUR: *Eliza was created Countess de la Zeur by Louis XIV.*

ODALISQUE continues The Baroque Cycle, with the beautiful and ambitious Eliza playing a most dangerous game as double agent and confidante of enemy kings—as the trials of Dr. Daniel Waterhouse and the Natural Philosophers increase one hundredfold in an England plagued by the impending war and royal insecurities.

Read on for the continuation of Neal Stephenson's extraordinary saga of a remarkable age and its momentous events . . . Coming soon from HarperTorch!

"The sort of book that lays waste to your social life . . . It might also play merry havoc with whatever late seventeenth-century and early eighteenth-century history you have, so skillfully does Stephenson mash together facts and flights of lurid fancy . . . Stephenson covers a terrific amount of theoretical, social, and geographical ground to persuade us that the period shaped the modern world. Bawdy, learned, hilarious, and utterly compelling, [it] is sprawling to the point of insanity and resoundlingly, joyously good."

Times of London

Versailles

> For the market is against our sex just now; and
> if a young woman has beauty, birth, breeding,
> wit, sense, manners, modesty, and all to an ex-
> treme, yet if she has not money she's nobody,
> she had as good want them all; nothing but
> money now recommends a woman; the men
> play the game all into their own hands.
>
> —DANIEL DEFOE, *Moll Flanders*

To M. le comte d'Avaux
12 July 1685
Monseigneur,

As you see I have encyphered this letter according
to your instructions, though only you know whether
this is to protect it from the eyes of Dutch spies, or
your rivals at Court. Yes, I have discovered that you
have rivals.

On my journey I was waylaid and ill-used by some
typically coarse, thick Dutchmen. Though you would
never have guessed it from their looks and manners,
these had something in common with the King of
France's brother: namely, a fascination with women's
undergarments. For they went through my baggage
thoroughly, and left it a few pounds lighter.

Shame, shame on you, monseigneur, for placing those letters among my things! For a while I was afraid that I would be thrown into some horrid Dutch work-house, and spend the rest of my days scrubbing sidewalks and knitting hose. But from the questions they asked me, it soon became obvious that they were perfectly baffled by this French cypher of yours. To test this, I replied that I could read those letters as well as *they* could; and the dour looks on the faces of my interrogators demonstrated that their incompetence had been laid bare, and my innocence proved, in the same moment.

I will forgive you, monseigneur, for putting me through those anxious moments if you will forgive me for believing, until quite recently, that you were utterly mad to send me to Versailles. For how could a common girl such as I find a place in the most noble and glorious palace in the world?

But now I know things and I understand.

There is a story making the rounds here, which you must have heard. The heroine is a girl, scarcely better than a slave—the daughter of a ruined petty noble fallen to the condition of a Vagabond. Out of desperation this waif married a stunted and crippled writer in Paris. But the writer had a *salon* that attracted certain Persons of Quality who had grown bored with the insipid discourse of Court. His young wife made the acquaintance of a few of these noble visitors. After he died, and left this girl a penniless widow, a certain Duchess took pity on her, brought her out to Versailles, and made her a governess to some of her illegitimate children. This Duchess was none other than the *maîtresse déclarée* to the King himself, and her children were royal bastards. The story goes that King Louis XIV, contrary to the long-established customs of Christian royalty, considers his bastards to be only one small step beneath the Dauphin and the other *En-*

fants de France. Protocol dictates that the governess of *les Enfants de France* must be a duchess; accordingly, the King made the governess of his bastards into a marquise. In the years since then, the King's *maîtresse déclarée* has gradually fallen from favor, as she has grown fat and histrionic, and it has been the case for some time that when the King went every day to call upon her at one o'clock in the afternoon, just after Mass, he would simply walk through her apartment without stopping, and go instead to visit this widow—the Marquise de Maintenon, as she was now called. Finally, Monseigneur, I have learned what is common knowledge at Versailles, namely that the King secretly married the Marquise de Maintenon recently and that she is the Queen of France in all but name.

It is plain to see that Louis keeps the powerful of France on a short leash here, and that they have nothing to do but gamble when the King is absent and ape his words and actions when he is present. Consequently every Duke, Count, and Marquis at Versailles is prowling through nurseries and grammar-schools, disrupting the noble children's upbringing in the hunt for nubile governesses. No doubt you knew this when you made arrangements for me to work as a governess to the children of M. le comte de Béziers. I cringe to think what awful debt this poor widower must have owed you for him to consent to such an arrangement! You might as well have deposited me in a bordello, Monseigneur, for all the young blades who prowl around the entrance of the count's apartment and pursue me through the gardens as I try to carry out my nominal duties—and not because of any native attractiveness I may possess but simply because it is what the King did.

Fortunately the King has not seen fit to grace me with a noble title yet or I should never be left alone long enough to write you letters. I have reminded some of these loiterers that Madame de Maintenon is a famously pious woman and that the King (who could have any woman in the world, and who ruts with disposable damsels two or three times a week) fell in love with her because of her intelligence. This keeps most of them at bay.

I hope that my story has provided you with a few moments' diversion from your tedious duties in the Hague, and that you will, in consequence, forgive me for not saying anything of substance.

Your obedient servant,
Eliza

P.S. M. le comte de Béziers' finances are in comic disarray—he spent fourteen percent of his income last year on wigs, and thirty-seven percent on interest, mostly on gambling debts. Is this typical? I will try to help him. Is this what you wanted me to do? Or did you want him to remain helpless? That is easier.

> My dark and cloudy words they do but hold
> The truth, as cabinets enclose the gold.
> —JOHN BUNYAN, *The Pilgrim's Progress*

To Gottfried Wilhelm Leibniz
4 August 1685
Dear Doctor Leibniz,

Difficulty at the beginning* is to be expected in any new venture, and my move to Versailles has been no exception. I thank God that I lived for several years in the *harim* of the Topkapi Palace in Constantinople, be-

---

*▤ The name of Hexagram 3 of the *I Ching*, or 010001, that being the encryption key for the subliminal message embedded in the script of this letter.

ing trained to serve as a consort to the Sultan, for only
this could have prepared me for Versailles. Unlike Versailles, the Sultan's palace grew according to no coherent plan, and from the outside looks like a jumble
of domes and minarets. But seen from the inside both
palaces are warrens of stuffy windowless rooms created by subdividing other rooms. This is a mouse's-
eye view, of course; just as I was never introduced to
the domed pavilion where the Grand Turk deflowers
his slave-girls, so I have not yet been allowed to enter
the Salon of Apollo and view the Sun King in his radiance. In both Palaces I have seen mostly the wretched
closets, garrets, and cellars where courtiers dwell.

Certain parts of this Palace, and most of the gardens, are open to anyone who is decently dressed. At
first this meant they were closed to me, for William's
men ripped up all of my clothes. But after I arrived,
and word of my adventures began to circulate, I received cast-offs from noblewomen who either sympa-
thized with my plight or needed to make room in their
tiny closets for next year's fashions. With some
needle-work I have been able to make these garments
over into ones that, while not quite fashionable, will at
least not expose me to ridicule as I lead the son and
daughter of M. le comte de Béziers through the gardens.

To describe this place in words is hopeless. Indeed
I believe it was meant to be so, for then anyone who
wants to know it must come here in person, and that is
how the King wants it. Suffice it to say that here,
every dram of water, every leaf and petal, every
square inch of wall, floor, and ceiling bear the signa-
ture of Man; all have been thought about by superior
intellects, nothing is accidental. The place is pregnant
with Intention and wherever you look you see the
gaze of the architects—and by extension, Louis—
staring back at you. I am contrasting this to blocks of
stone and beams of wood that occur in Nature and, in

most places, are merely harvested and shaped a bit by artisans. Nothing of that sort is to be found at Versailles.

At Topkapi there were magnificent carpets everywhere, Doctor, carpets such as no one in Christendom has ever seen, and all of them were fabricated thread by thread, knot by knot, by human hands. That is what Versailles is like. Buildings made of plain stone or wood are to this place what a sack of flour is to a diamond necklace. Fully to describe a routine event, such as a conversation or a meal, would require devoting fifty pages to a description of the room and its furnishings, another fifty to the clothing, jewelry, and wigs worn by the participants, another fifty to their family trees, yet another to explaining their current positions in the diverse intrigues of the Court, and finally a single page to setting down the words actually spoken.

Needless to say this will be impractical; yet I hope you will bear with me if I occasionally go on at some length with florid descriptions. I know, Doctor, that even if you have not seen Versailles and the costumes of its occupants, you have seen crude copies of them in German courts and can use your incomparable mind to imagine the things I see. So I will try to restrain myself from describing every little detail. And I know that you are making a study of family trees for Sophie, and have the resources in your library to investigate the genealogy of any petty nobleman I might mention. So I will try to show restraint there as well. I will try to explain the current state of Court intrigue, since you have no way of knowing about such things. For example, one evening two months ago, my master M. le comte de Béziers was given the honor of holding a candle during the King's going-to-bed ceremony, and consequently was invited to all the best parties for a fortnight. But lately his star has been in eclipse, and his life has been very quiet.

If you are reading this it means you detected the key from the I Ching. *It appears that French cryptography is not up to the same standard as French interior decoration; their diplomatic cypher has been broken by the Dutch, but as it was invented by a courtier highly thought of by the King, no one dares say anything against it. If what they say about Colbert is true, he never would have allowed such a situation to arise, but as you know he died two years ago and cyphers have not been upgraded since. I am writing in that broken cypher to d'Avaux in Holland on the assumption that everything I write will be decyphered and read by the Dutch. But as is probably obvious already, I write to you on the assumption that your cypher affords us a secure channel.*

Since you employ the Wilkins cypher, which uses five plaintext letters to encrypt one letter of the actual message, I must write five words of drivel to encypher one word of pith, and so you may count on seeing lengthy descriptions of clothing, etiquette, and other tedious detail in future letters.

I hope I do not seem self-important by presuming that you may harbor some curiosity concerning *my* position at Court. Of course I am a nothing, invisible, not even an ink-speck in the margin of the Register of Ceremonies. But it has not escaped the notice of the nobles that Louis XIV chose most of his most important ministers (such as Colbert, who bought one of your digital computers!) from the middle class, and that he has (secretly) married a woman of low degree, and so it is fashionable in a way to be seen speaking to a commoner if she is clever or useful.

Of course hordes of young men want to have sex with me, but to relate details would be repetitious and in poor taste.

Because M. le comte de Béziers' bolt-hole in the south wing is so uncomfortable, and the weather has been so fine, I have spent several hours each day going on walks with my two charges, Beatrice and Louis, who have 9 and 6 years of age, respectively. Versailles has vast gardens and parks, most of which are deserted except when the King goes to hunt or promenade, and then they are crowded with courtiers. Until very recently they were also filled with common people who would come all the way from Paris to see the sights, but these pressed around the King so hotly, and made such a shambles of the statues and waterworks, that recently the King banned the *mobile* from all of his gardens.

As you know, it is the habit of all well-born ladies to cover their faces with masks whenever they venture out of doors, so that they will not be darkened by the sun. Many of the more refined men do likewise—the King's brother Philippe, who is generally addressed as Monsieur, wears such a mask, though he frets that it smears his makeup. On such warm days as we have had recently, this is so uncomfortable that the ladies of Versailles, and by extension their attendants, households, and gallants, prefer simply to remain indoors. I can wander for hours through the park with Beatrice and Louis in train and encounter only a few other people: mostly gardeners, occasionally lovers on their way to trysts in secluded woods or grottoes.

The gardens are shot through with long straight paths and avenues that, as one steps into certain intersections, provide sudden unexpected vistas of fountains, sculpture groups, or the château itself. I am teaching Beatrice and Louis geometry by having them draw maps of the place.

If these children are any clue as to the future of the nobility, then France as we know it is doomed.

Yesterday I was walking along the canal, which is a cross-shaped body of water to the west of the château; the long axis runs east–west and the crossbar north–south, and since it is a single body of water its surface is, of course, level, that being a known property of water. I put a needle in one end of a cork and weighted the other end (with a corkscrew, in case you are wondering!) and set it afloat in the circular pool where these canals intersect, hoping that the needle would point vertically upwards—trying (as you have no doubt already perceived) to acquaint Beatrice and Louis with the idea of a third spatial dimension perpendicular to the other two. Alas, the cork did not float upright. It drifted away and I had to lie flat on my belly and reach out over the water to rake it in, and the sleeves of my hand-me-down dress became soaked with water. The whole time I was preoccupied with the whining of the bored children, and with my own passions as well—for I must tell you that tears were running down my sunburned cheeks as I remembered the many lessons I was taught, as a young girl in Algiers, by Mummy and by the Ladies' Volunteer Sodality of the Society of Britannic Abductees.

At some point I became aware of voices—a man's and a woman's—and I knew that they had been conversing nearby for quite some time. With all of these other concerns and distractions I had taken no note of them. I lifted my head to gaze directly across the canal at two figures on horseback: a tall magnificent well-built man in a vast wig like a lion's mane, and a woman, built something like a Turkish wrestler, dressed in hunting clothes and carrying a riding crop. The woman's face was exposed to the sun, and had been for a long time, for she was tanned like a saddlebag. She and her companion had been talking about something else, but when I looked up I somehow drew the notice of the man; instantly he reached up and doffed his hat to me, from across the canal! When he did, the sun fell directly on his face and I recognized him as King Louis XIV.

I simply could not imagine any way to recover from this indignity, and so I pretended I had not seen him. As the crow flies we were not far apart, but by land we were far away—to reach me, the King and his Diana-

like hunting-companion would have had to ride west
for some distance along the bank of the canal; circum-
navigate the large pool at that end; and then go the
same distance eastwards along the opposite bank. So I
convinced myself that they were far away and I pretended not to see them; God have mercy on me if I
chose wrong. I tried to cover my embarrassment by
ranting to the children about Descartes and Euclid.

The King put his hat back on and said, "Who is she?"

I closed my eyes and sighed in relief; the King had
decided to play along, and act as if we had not seen
each other. Finally I had coaxed the floating cork back
into my hands. I drew myself up and sat on the brink
of the canal with my skirts spread out around me, in
profile to the King, and quietly lectured the children.

Meanwhile I was praying that the woman would not
know my name. But as you will have guessed, Doctor,
she was none other than his majesty's sister-in-law,
Elisabeth Charlotte, known to Versailles as Madame,
and known to Sophie—her beloved aunt—as Liselotte.

*Why didn't you tell me that the Knight of the
Rustling Leaves was a* clitoriste? *I suppose this should
come as no surprise given that her husband Philippe is
a homosexual, but it caught me somewhat off guard.
Does she have lovers? Hold, I presume too much; does
she even know what she is?*

She gazed at me for a languid moment; at Versailles, no one of importance speaks quickly and
spontaneously, every utterance is planned like a move
in a chess game. I knew what she was about to say: "I
do not know her." I prayed for her to say it, for then the
King would know that I was not a person, did not exist, was no more worthy of his attention than a fleeting
ripple in the surface of the canal. Then finally I heard
Madame's voice across the water: "It looks like that
girl who was duped by d'Avaux and molested by the
Dutchmen, and showed up dishevelled and expecting
sympathy."

It strikes me as unlikely that Liselotte could have recognized me in this way without another channel of information; did you write a letter to her, Doctor? It is never clear to me how much you are acting on your own and how much as a pawn—or perhaps I should say "knight" or "rook"—of Sophie.

These cruel words would have brought me to tears if I'd been one of those rustic countesses who flock to Versailles to be deflowered by men of rank. But I had already seen enough of this place to know that the only truly cruel words here are "She is nobody." And Madame had not said that. Consequently, the King had to look at me for a few moments longer.

Louis and Beatrice had noticed the King, and were frozen with a mixture of awe and terror—like statues of children.

Another one of those pauses had gone by. I heard the King saying, "That story was told in my presence." Then he said, "If d'Avaux would only put his letters into the bodice of some poxy old hag he could be assured of absolute secrecy, but what Dutchman would not want to break the seal on *that* envelope?"

"But, Sire," said Liselotte, "d'Avaux is a Frenchman—and what Frenchman *would*?"

"He is not as refined in his tastes as he would have you think," the King returned, "and *she* is not as coarse as *you* would have *me* think."

At this point little Louis stepped forward so suddenly that I was alarmed he would topple into the Canal and oblige me to swim; but he stopped on the brink, thrust out one leg, and bowed to the King just like a courtier. I pretended now to notice the King for the first time, and scrambled to my feet. Beatrice and I made curtseys across the canal. Once more the King acknowledged us by doffing his hat, perhaps with a certain humorous exaggeration.

"I see that look in your eye, *vôtre majesté*," said Liselotte.

"I see it in yours, Artemis."

"You have been listening to gossip. I tell you that these girls of low birth who come here to seduce noblemen are like mouse droppings in the pepper."

"Is *that* what she wants us to believe? How banal."

"The best disguises are the most banal, Sire."

This seemed to be the end of their strange conversation; they rode slowly away.

The King is said to be a great huntsman, but he was riding in an extremely stiff posture—I suspect he is suffering from hemorrhoids or possibly a bad back.

I took the children back straightaway and sat down to write you this letter. For a nothing like me, today's events are the pinnacle of honor and glory, and I wanted to memorialize them before any detail slipped from my memory.

To M. le comte d'Avaux
1 September 1685
Monseigneur,

I have as many visitors as ever (much to the annoyance of M. le comte de Béziers), but since I got a deep tan and took to wearing sackcloth and quoting from the Bible a lot, they are not as interested in romance. Now they come asking me about my Spanish uncle. "I am sorry that your Spanish uncle had to move to Amsterdam, mademoiselle," they say, "but it is rumored that hardship has made him a wise man." The first time some son of a marquis came up to me spouting such nonsense I told him he must have me mixed up with some other wench, and sent him packing! But the next one dropped your name and I understood that he had in some sense been dispatched by you—or, to be more precise, that his coming to me under the delusion of my having a wise Spanish uncle was a consequence or ramification of some chain of events that had been set in motion by you. On that assumption, I began to play along, quite cautiously, as I did not know what sort of game might be afoot. From the way this fellow talked I soon understood that he believes me to be a sort of crypto-Jew, the bastard offspring of a swarthy Spanish Kohan and a butter-haired Dutch-woman, which might actually seem plausible as the sun has bleached my hair and darkened my skin.

These conversations are all the same, and their particulars are too tedious to relate here. Obviously you have been spreading tales about me, Monseigneur, and half the petty nobles of Versailles now believe that I (or, at any rate, my fictitious uncle) can help them get out from under their gambling debts, pay for the re-modeling of their châteaux, or buy them splendid new carriages. I can only roll my eyes at their avarice. But if the stories are to be believed, their fathers and grandfathers used what money they had to raise private armies and fortify their cities against the father and grandfather of the present King. I suppose it's better for the money to go to dressmakers, sculptors, painters, and *chefs de cuisine* than to mercenaries and musket-makers.

Of course it is true that their gold would fetch a higher rate of return wisely invested in Amsterdam than sitting in a strong-box under their beds. The only difficulty lies in the fact that I cannot manage such investments from a closet in Versailles while at the same time teaching two motherless children how to read and write. My Spanish uncle is a fiction of yours, presumably invented because you feared that these French nobles would never entrust their assets to a woman. This means that I must do the work personally, and this is impossible unless I have the freedom to travel to Amsterdam several times a year . . .